the elm stone saga

FRACTURED

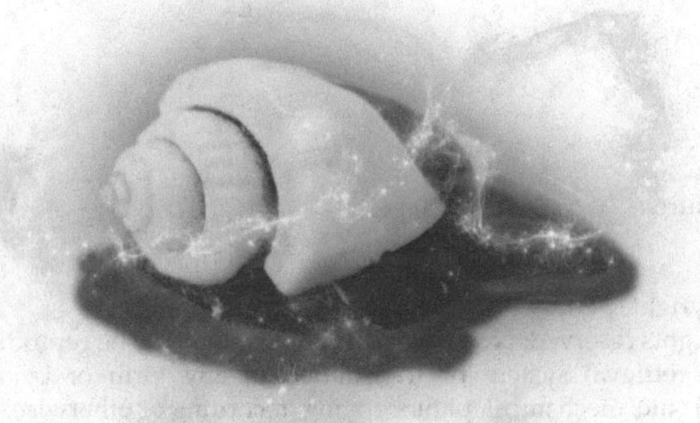

shayla MORGANSEN

Fractured

Published by Ouroborus Book Services
www.ouroborusbooks.com

Cover design by Sabrina RG Raven
www.sabrinargraven.com

For Leonard Taplin and Graham Olsen, grandfathers without compare. If all I ever do is make you proud, I've done enough.

Also by Shayla Morgansen

The Elm Stone Saga
Chosen (2014)
Scarred (2015)
Unbidden (2016)
Haunted (2019)
Burned: A Prequel Novella (2020)

prologue

1994

The growl of thunder through a grey sky only added to the grim ambience of the graveside scene, and Lisandro hoped no one noticed him flinch. It was just a storm. A little natural light show, some rumbles, a bit of rain. Nothing to worry about.

It wasn't like it could hurt him. Others, though…

Still troubled, he tried to refocus on the steady words of the minister. All around him, blinking away tears under black umbrellas, those who knew the deceased were gathered in shared shock and grief. 'Such a terrible loss,' he kept hearing before the minister and the rain started. 'Too young' and 'Not fair' and 'How could something like this happen?' They were the normal things to say – the things he'd come here to hear. Miserable eyes cast uneasy looks at the storm clouds that had rolled in overhead, but nobody had made the impossible connection. Nobody had spun with a pointed finger to accuse Lisandro of what he kept waiting for someone to realise. Instead, moment after painstaking moment, this crowd of Kenneth and Stella Hawke's friends and family remained too preoccupied with their own mortality to imagine that anyone might break their own heart and do what he had.

Orphan a girl to save another. Create a future in which she grows into her power. Get away with it.

Lisandro forced his gaze from the glossy black caskets to the small girl watching on, surrounded by family, and swallowed the acid climbing his throat. Every night for the past week, after

1

vomiting anything he ate straight down the toilet, he'd laid awake expecting the doors to be beaten down by some figure of justice. Maybe the police. Ghosts of the victims. Most likely the White Elm, magical peacekeepers and lawmakers, of which Lisandro happened to be a member. They existed to prevent exactly this sort of thing.

Possibly the most mortifying element of all this was that if they ever caught someone who'd done what he had, *he* would be the one to make the arrest. *He* would be responsible for the interrogation. So as he'd shamefully shaped the magic and regretfully directed it after his childhood friend, he'd had the thrilling thought: who would make the arrest and conduct the interrogation when *he* was the perpetrator?

No one will, he'd been promised, and so far, that promise had held fast. No one suspected a thing. At last night's monthly council circle, the death of Kenneth Hawke and his wife in a vicious storm hadn't even come up. And why would it? There was no evidence to suggest anything other than a natural tragedy. Weather control had been outlawed since 1958 and there was no reason to think anyone could still perform it. Kenneth was no person of interest and had no concerning connections, having burned the few bridges he had in the magical community when he married Stella – a perfectly nice lady, but not a witch, a slight their other friend Aindréas Morrissey and his ilk had not tolerated.

Lisandro extended his awareness through the crowd of black-clad mourners. Life signatures, most of them non-magical, except for three – Kenneth's stern-looking aunt, who had a hand each on the other two. The Hawke orphan Shelly was a witch, though less powerful than the teenaged boy at her side. Unsurprisingly, Aindréas wasn't here. With Kenneth, they had grown up close, their mothers and fathers joined at the hip and up to their necks in illegal business more or less to spite the White Elm Lisandro now served. The eldest of them, Aindréas was the most set in his ways, and whatever their history, however deeply the three brothers had loved one another, the concession of pride required to attend this farewell after their falling out was simply too much to bear.

The rain increased its assault on the umbrellas as the minister finished up. Even being responsible for their deaths couldn't have kept Lisandro away from paying his respects. Nor from meeting his friend's little girl. Again, he looked across to the child with a deep mixture of guilt and disappointment. She didn't look like someone who would change the outcome of the future, but that sort rarely did. Red-haired like Kenneth and button-nosed like Stella, Asheleigh – Shelly – was a barely magical pre-schooler with the faint markers of a budding Seer in her aura, along with the same black sinkholes Lisandro himself carried.

Like Kenneth. Like Aindréas. Like his two children, and like the missing elder generation of their families had borne, too. Shelly Hawke, who might have grown up to be a chemist or a deli worker or a hairdresser but for Lisandro's intervention, was heir to an immense fate, and would be part of saving all of them from it.

The crowd dispersed to escape the downpour. The elderly aunt prompted Shelly to drop the flowers she clutched into the open grave, and the girl tentatively stepped forward, but dropped them too short and they landed in the mud at the graveside. The child's mouth went tight to see her offering ruined, the first sign of her enormous grief, and the boy cousin hastened to hand over his umbrella to someone else so he could rescue the flowers.

Flowers she had clearly picked herself, for this, because Lisandro had orchestrated the deaths of her parents. His friend. That acid taste wouldn't go away.

'Shelly,' he said, stepping forward and closing his umbrella. The magic it cost was so minor he didn't even think about it. The little girl looked up and watched as a full-bloom white rose took the place of the black umbrella. She took it, wonder briefly distracting from her misery. The sweetness of the moment made him uncomfortable. He glanced up at her family, the silent great-aunt and cousin, and wondered from their expressionless faces whether they knew. Seers. Hard to know with their kind.

He shouldn't have come. Briefcase swinging from his other hand, rain pounding on his shoulders, he spun and strode away, and with a final glance back – *goodbye, Kenneth* – he opened a wormhole through space.

In Northern Ireland, there was no storm, just morning sunshine melting snow on rolling green hills and, over them, the stone-walled expanse of the most beautiful place in it.

Morrissey Estate, otherwise known as *home*.

Lisandro withdrew his key from his pocket as he savoured the walk across the sprawling moors. It had been more than a month since he was last here – much too long, but guilt and self-doubt had kept him away. He wasn't a killer the last time he was here. Now that distinction seemed silly. He had travelled every continent and seen hundreds of beautiful landscapes and cityscapes, but nothing compared with the place he'd come to a million times as a child, the only place he could think to go when his mother had ceased to come home. Morrissey Estate was not the home he'd been born to but it was where Aindréas and his mother Áine had made him feel loved and safe. They'd become his family, and there wasn't a thing he wouldn't do for them.

Including what he'd just done to the Hawkes.

He shook off some of the Scottish rain as he reached the iron gate. It was rare to see any of his family out in the lovely grounds but as soon as he turned the key, he could sense the familiar aura of young Ana near the orchard. After a moment's hesitation, Lisandro set off in her direction. Aindréas would have already noticed his arrival and wouldn't be offended by the delay. Lisandro was always welcome here.

He Skipped the distance and approached his favourite Morrissey from behind. Despite the cold she was sitting on the lawn with her back to the house, glaring into the trees. Glaring was this girl's resting expression. Her arms were locked around her knees and her old-fashioned dress flared around her in sharp folds that reflected the spikiness of her energy field.

Her *intense* energy field, it should be said. Like their father, the Morrissey children were unreasonably powerful, certainly surpassing any standard measure of magical capacity. It was why the White Elm continued its surveillance of this household, much to Lisandro's discomfort in his dual roles of council Dark Keeper and a member of this family. Magic could be as dangerous as it was miraculous, and typically, unless they employed more time-consuming styles of magic like blood magic or spell craft – like, say, the creation and control of a storm cell in the lower atmosphere over a small rural town in Scotland – a sorcerer's personal power limitations helped minimise the trouble they could cause. Not so with the Morrisseys. Ticking time bombs, all three of them, though Anastasia out of control was a particularly confronting, and worryingly regular, spectacle.

The concern that she might one day prove the White Elm right was one Lisandro hated to consider and endeavoured to avoid. Taking out Kenneth and his wife was an unfortunate but easy price to pay to bypass one such future.

'Hi,' she said shortly, obviously trying to keep emotion out of her voice but failing. Her brother was the expert at this. Ana was the open book.

'Hi, treasure,' Lisandro responded, sitting beside her. Ugh, the grass was damp. A little magic could improve that. 'What's your dad done this time?'

Because it was always Aindréas versus Anastasia, and always would be. Luella and Ana were amicable if not warm, and the siblings were very tight, so the tensions in Morrissey House always erupted between the two hotheads.

'Nothing. It's snowy and I hate it.'

Hmm. Doubtful to be the only factor. But Lisandro could pretend if that's what she wanted.

'Alright. I have something for you.'

The fifteen-year-old kept her face trained forward, feigning disinterest, but her dark eyes angled towards him as Lisandro opened his briefcase and extracted an oddly shaped gift, wrapped roughly in brown paper. He held it out to her. She didn't respond.

'Obtained by slightly dishonest means,' Lisandro warned. That got her attention. She accepted the gift and turned it over, feeling its weight.

'You *stole* this for me?'

'Well, *stole* is a strong word,' Lisandro reasoned as Ana began to unwrap her present, anticipation building in her delicately beautiful features. 'I paid for it. He just needed convincing that it was for sale.'

The brown paper fell away and Ana unravelled layers of tissue to get to the prize within. Her excited intake of breath when she saw it made him smile, the pleasure of bringing her out of her misery enough to send haunting thoughts of storms and funerals and orphaned daughters flying from his mind. She admired the semi-polished crystal, about the size of her fist.

'Where did you get it?' she asked, not noticing the snow melting around them, the air warming to comfort her.

'Salem, Massachusetts.' Lisandro watched as she ran long white fingers across the Burmese ruby's surface and didn't have to tell her that that was where he went to reflect on his lost mother. She cast understanding eyes his way. 'The guy I got it from had a beautiful old shop, you would have loved it. This one was just a display,' he added, indicating the stone she held. She listened wistfully as he described this meaningless shopping event in minute detail, one of any number of stories she craved from the world beyond her stone walls. 'There were heaps of other stones, bigger and smaller, and I already had a big rhodonite picked out. Really clear and a dark pink, like the one we saw in that book I got you, and as big as, I don't know… Maybe a remote control.' He'd made the approximate size with his hands and at her confused tilt of the head, he quickly corrected himself to something she'd have seen before. 'A hotdog.' Her expression cleared; he'd sneaked in plenty of street food her fancy kitchen staff would never dream of exposing her to. 'Anyway, I spotted this in a cabinet. He said it was his favourite piece, smuggled out of Myanmar, so I said I had to have it for my favourite kid.'

Ana smiled discreetly, unable to hold it in.

'Thanks,' she said, rewarding him with eye contact. Her irises were dark chocolate, like her mother's. 'But I'm not a kid.'

With some degree of shock, Lisandro realised that she was

right. A month apart and now he was a killer and she was someone new, too. It had probably happened a long time ago, without him noticing, but Ana Morrissey was not a child anymore. She still had a lean frame but now it had curves that weren't there before, and her cheeks were brushed with make-up. Did she have that when he was here last? Lisandro had to quash his immediate disappointment. He didn't want little Ana to grow up. He didn't want to lose his fun, playful sidekick to the bores of adulthood. Soon that curiosity would be gone, along with her childish adoration for Lisandro. She wouldn't want to listen to his stories anymore; she wouldn't want his hard-earned, thoughtful presents.

'Oh,' Lisandro answered smoothly, 'I suppose I'm in need of a new favourite kid, then.'

Ana screwed her nose up at him and went back to admiring her stone, but with a slight shuffle closer to his side. The frayed edges of her aura were clearer now, everything a matter of degree.

Ana was the most erratic and unstable person Lisandro knew, but he couldn't love her any less for it. With the crankiness came a spirited, independent and indomitable soul unlike any other, a fascinating little person full of questions and wild dreams and a passionate counterargument to anything she didn't want to do. He could while away endless hours in conversation with her, inspired by her wonderful imagination, enchanted by her oddly dark humour, challenged by her staunchly black and white view of the world. He'd fallen in love with her as a newborn baby with a shock of dark hair. He'd thought she was the most precious thing he'd ever been entrusted to hold in his thirteen years. Aindréas had been unable to see it – still couldn't. Lisandro couldn't count the number of times he'd wanted to tell his brother that he was missing out.

Kenneth, too. Kenneth had missed out on this amazing girl he'd promised to guide and protect as her godfather. No longer a problem, Lisandro supposed, but someone else who'd let Ana down, and would have lived to do worse.

Lisandro couldn't fathom it. Though always rigid and

stubborn, Aindréas had been fun to grow up with. Now he challenged and squashed his daughter's incredible spirit at every turn, seeming to have love only for Renatus, the son and heir he'd waited so long for. Even that was a cold, expectant sort of love. Neither parenting style was conducive to a healthy child. Ana, starved of affection by her parents, was moody and insecure, while her ten-year-old brother was distant, unemotional and introspective.

No doubt the boy knew Lisandro was here, but the likelihood of him getting his nose out of a book long enough to come greet him was so slim as to be negligible. As his godfather, Lisandro had *tried* to love the boy as much as he loved the girl. It was an honour to be pledged to watch over and protect his best friend's son, but the Morrissey heir lacked the indignant sparkle of his older sister. Instead he had a cool intelligence in his pale eyes, one that made him intimidating, hard to warm to, like he was measuring your worth under his gaze. Though Mánus Morrissey hadn't been seen since before Lisandro's mother disappeared, Lisandro recognised the discerning coolness of the boy's grandfather in those eyes. When his godson looked at him, as much as he hated to admit it, he knew the child knew he wasn't loved as thoroughly as his sister.

'If I'm not a kid anymore, my da is going to find someone to marry me,' Ana said eventually. 'I scried him discussing it with Cian. He's planning my debut for three months' time.'

Three months?! That was nowhere near enough time for Lisandro to get used to the idea of Ana as a grown woman. She was a *girl*. He resisted the urge to fire an irritable glare back at the four-storey manor where her father was undoubtedly licking his wounds after this morning's row with his eldest. What was Aindréas thinking, matchmaking his sheltered *fifteen-year-old child* like the calendar hadn't changed in a century or so?

'I see,' Lisandro said carefully, watching for her inevitable reaction but trying to give her an avenue to discuss her feelings. Nobody in these walls wanted to see or hear those feelings, and they burned her up inside. 'You're not happy about it?'

'Of course not!' Ana burst out, her aura fraying again. 'I don't need a husband. I need to run away to France and kiss a boy who doesn't speak English and not even ask his name, and get drunk with a bunch of mortal kids, like Aleanbh Mac Carthaigh did in the summer. I need...' She struggled to think of something else. She had nothing, her life experience almost entirely limited to this one place, so she changed tack. 'Everybody else my age is living their lives and I'm just sitting here, nothing ever changing, waiting to see what happens with me.'

Pityingly, Lisandro extended his arm to her. With a frustrated huff, Ana leaned stiffly into his embrace, but soon she softened against his shoulder, comforted by his familiarity. He went to work on the air around her, changing her atmosphere to a quiet, calm one. He would do it to the whole world if he had the power, if it meant she could be happy all the time, wherever she went.

'I just hate my life,' Ana finished finally, very quietly. Lisandro's heart ached for her. Renatus, at least, knew himself and what he wanted – poor Ana lived her life in an eternal unsecured downward spiral, barely aware of her own desires, with an uneventful past and a stark future as a socio-political pawn of her father's, married off into some rich and powerful family. She was thinking the same. 'I never thought he really meant it. The marriage thing. I never thought Mother–' she'd stopped saying Mama some years ago now, that relationship long cooled '–would let him just... send me off with some man. But she's not going to do anything.' Ana distractedly played with the ruby in her hands, nestling her head into his shoulder to get comfortable. 'I overheard them declining an offer for Ren once, and I thought that meant... but that girl just wasn't good enough a match, or maybe it means there's one rule for my brother, and another for me. Because I dared be born a girl.'

It was unfair. It was archaic. But he knew that last part was true. She'd hit the nail on the head in her song-like Irish accent. He stroked her hair back from her dear face and chanced a look back at the house. As expected, the narrow silhouette of Aindréas could be seen in the arched top window of the grand home. Even from this distance, Lisandro could see that when he raised a hand in a helplessly annoyed "what gives?" shrug, his friend rolled his eyes and turned away. They'd argue about this later. He'd say Aindréas was being unreasonable; Aindréas would say Lisandro didn't have to live with a teenager and shouldn't believe everything she said.

It wouldn't change Lisandro's mind. He settled his hand back on the girl's shoulder and she glanced up at him, perceiving his shift.

'Are you here to see my da?' she asked, looking at him properly now, up close. Her brows drew together and her eyes warmed, the way they did whenever she started worrying about someone other than herself. 'You look tired. And… wet.'

'That's because it's four in the morning at home, and I haven't been sleeping,' he told her. He gestured at his briefcase, lying nearby. 'The council had their circle last night. I have a list of intended raids for your father to, ahem, take care of.'

Warning old magical families ahead of White Elm raids, as well as letting them know what Qasim and Jackson expected to find, had won Lisandro considerable popularity among the less politically tolerant citizens of the blood magic community. It couldn't come from him, of course, and luckily the Morrissey family was connected enough to ensure this information was discreetly and efficiently distributed. Though most of the contraband was hidden ahead of time, enough relevant material was made available for the raid that the council enjoyed diminishing returns, assuming that their efforts over the years had almost eliminated the illegal magic trade. When Lisandro himself showed up at the specified time to conduct the promised raid, treating powerful underworld citizens with respect as he collected up materials of minor infringement, trust in him and in the White Elm as a government seemed to grow. The White Elm ordered fewer raids every year; the least obliging citizens resisted law and order less with every passing quarter; and the result was a happy, cohesive society.

The White Elm, for all its flaws, could be great for the world, eventually. Lisandro had to believe it. He had to try and *make* it great.

His life might depend on it.

Ana ignored the briefcase, caring only for what interested her.

'Why haven't you been sleeping?' she asked, concerned and intrigued. He forced a smile, not wanting to go there but realising he'd known it would come up here. His family knew him well, and he was clearly exhausted and underfed. He gave her shoulder a reassuring squeeze.

'Guilty conscience,' he admitted, and she questioningly looked down at the dishonestly obtained Burmese ruby. 'Not that. I...' *murdered your godfather*. But he didn't think that. He'd always been careful with his thoughts around her, mindful not to think things inappropriate for delicate ears. Like her father and brother, Anastasia Morrissey was more than a common scrier. It was one of the reasons Aindréas went to such lengths to keep his children safely under wraps here at the estate, lest anyone outside the family find out their extraordinary secret strengths... and their tragic weakness. Lisandro cleared his throat. 'I did something I didn't think myself capable of. Something I knew was wrong, and I did it anyway. I haven't forgiven myself yet.'

She had developed tact in her recent years, and she thought on that for a moment rather than openly asking what he'd done. She knew well how hard it was for him to deny her anything, and knew just as well how best to avoid putting him in situations where he'd have to.

'This thing you did,' she said slowly, gazing off into the orchard with a calculating look in her eyes, 'do you wish you hadn't done it?'

It wasn't that Lisandro didn't already know his favourite girl modelled her morality on the answers he gave; it was that he couldn't imagine a scenario in which that was a problem.

His imagination was severely limited then.

'No,' he confessed after a moment's glance up at the cloudless country sky. No storms here, and no one coming to make him atone for what he did to the Hawkes. 'I only wish I felt worse about it.'

Renatus, he thought, would have shot him a disgusted look and gotten up to leave. Oddly altruistic, he'd make a solid White

Elm scrier if his parents could bear the shame of breaking bread with *two* councillors in the family. Ana, though, was too self-serving. She pushed away from him to flop down on the warmed grass at his side, frowning.

'Sometimes I think about running away,' she admitted. She'd not told him this before but it came as no surprise. 'I know Da would be furious and Mother would worry. I know Renatus would be beside himself and if I never came home, he'd be stuck with them. That upsets me,' she realised, 'but the rest... I think I'm supposed to care more. But I don't.'

Lisandro sighed and lay back beside her.

'I'd worry, too,' he reminded her. She scoffed, clutching her new ruby to her chest.

'Well, I'd tell *you* where I went,' she said as though this were a given. He smiled indulgently at her childish plans. He was literally the first person Aindréas would ask if she disappeared, the most obvious connection she had outside the walls of this estate. Ana smiled at the sky, dreaming up impossible futures. 'Maybe France, like Aleanbh.'

Lisandro tilted his head back to look again at the house. It sounded like Aleanbh was a society friend the Morrisseys should have screened more carefully, if they were going to continue this business of choosing their daughter's associates. He was sure they regretted that match already. He cleared his throat.

'What made Aleanbh Mac Carthaigh happy might not work the same for you,' Lisandro cautioned, 'so don't do anything stupid. I hear she's holidaying in the States with a cousin... for nine months... as a result of her escapade. I expect the cousin will announce a new baby at about that time.'

Ana's eyes widened as she realised the implication, and she looked across at him with an awed and growing grin at the unexpected gossip.

'I wondered why she hadn't replied to my last letter,' she mused, going back to sky-gazing. Her expression darkened. 'I stopped writing to Caitlin. Uncle Thomas arranged a match for her with *Reilly Murphy*, and she can't shut up about it.'

All these little girls, not so little anymore, being married off like bartering chips to broker alliances between these old families. No wonder Ana was fixated on this. Everyone in her small social circle was either accepting or rejecting this expectation. However they were handling it, they were all facing it, and their choices were uncomfortably thin.

'How long are you staying?' Ana asked him. He shrugged against the grass. He hadn't thought about it, only that he would feel better when he came here, and though he was frustrated with his friend, he definitely wasn't worrying about Kenneth or storms or little orphaned Shelly Hawke any longer.

'A few days, if you'll all have me.'

Ana rolled onto her side to look at him more intently. 'And you'll talk to my da about this?'

'You know I will.'

She hesitated. 'He's been in a bad mood. Did you hear…? About… Mr Hawke?'

She might have been about to say Uncle Ken or some other epithet from her fond childhood memories of the other kind man who used to visit here and lather her with attention, but she had learned from her father's reactions to be more careful.

He, too, was careful in his reply, checking the emotional atmosphere he'd built over her.

'I just came from the funeral. Their little girl's an orphan. She's maybe five, six.'

'Hmm,' Ana expressed in mild agreement, then added, 'At least her father won't be able to pick her out a husband now.'

A dark way of looking at things, but that was very Ana. Lisandro nodded, conceding the point. She was still watching him, thinking her Ana thoughts.

'You could marry me,' she suggested sweetly, and Lisandro choked on his responding laughter, sitting up to clear his airway.

'That,' he said with a grin, 'sounds like the fastest way to your father's inevitable, stress-induced heart attack. I think I'm about ten years and precisely one surname to give you away from being his ideal match.'

'Ten years isn't that much,' Ana mused. He smiled easily back at her, unconfronted by her anything-goes manner of conversation.

'Neither is three minutes,' he replied, eliciting the expected look of confusion. 'That's how long ago you upgraded from "favourite kid" to "favourite young lady". I'm sure we can come up with a solution that doesn't involve my brutal death and subsequent banishment from this family.'

Ana was amused, but she pouted playfully to hide the seriousness of what she said next.

'But then I'd belong to you instead of Da,' she pointed out, a knife to Lisandro's heart, 'and he couldn't make decisions…'

'Listen to me.' Lisandro took her hand possessively and she sat up. 'You already don't belong to your father. This is your life, whatever it looks like from inside these walls. Do you understand?' He sighed when she dropped her gaze, revealing how little faith she had in that concept. 'I'll talk to your father about the debut. I don't think I'll be able to change his mind about the party, and let's be real, you can probably compromise on that much, but,' he paused, lifting Ana's chin to look her in the eyes, 'I promise you, nothing is going to happen to you that you don't want. No one is going to marry you or even court you if you don't want it, not until you're ready.' *Until you're old enough to know what you want.* 'Even if I have to bribe, threaten and memory-wipe every society creep your father introduces you to. Okay?'

She looked uncertain.

'That could be dangerous if someone found out,' she worried. 'The White Elm…'

'Are not my real family,' he finished for her, getting half a smile. He had a lot of respect for his council brothers and sisters, but they were not Ana Morrissey. 'Besides, I do plenty of bribing, threatening and memory-wiping on their behalf, and they happily look the other way. It would look like another day on the job.'

She turned his hand distractedly in hers.

'I don't want you to do anything for me that would get you into trouble.'

Maturity looked good on her. But unlike some, he'd always known this big heart was in there, considering others, weighing up their interests against her own.

'Look at this stone,' Lisandro said, taking the ruby from her and holding it up so the sunlight made it sparkle with a warm pinkish red. 'You think I was worrying about getting into trouble when I procured this?' He waited for her worried mouth to soften, the beginnings of a smile, and to shake her head. 'I'd only be in trouble if they *caught* me.'

Ana smiled her most adoring smile, the most genuine expression in her repertoire. It made her into the most beautiful thing on the planet, every time, without exception.

'Okay,' she agreed contentedly, settling back against his shoulder. Happy, because of him, and nothing made him happier than this. 'Just promise you won't get caught.'

'Treasure,' Lisandro laughed, 'that's an easy promise to make. I never get caught.'

chapter one

The black of the void clung at me like a cold wet sheet, and I held my breath. I couldn't remember whether there was air here, in this space between spaces, though it was probably in a lesson I'd missed. There was nothing conscious about my closed mouth or my seized lungs whenever I was pulled through a controlled tear in the Fabric of the world from one place to another, but I knew I had nothing to worry about.

In that regard, at least. I was in safe hands, even if nothing else about our situation was safe.

Hiroko never let me go as she jumped us from the gates of Morrissey House to some faraway field. The noise and terror of the scene we'd just left were noticeably absent but my heart still thudded in my chest and she still radiated worry. As soon as our feet were on solid ground she was running, with me in tow.

'Quickly,' she urged, and I matched her pace, not sure where we'd run to or even where we'd landed. The sun was sitting in a similar position in the sky so I gathered it was a small Skip. I cast out my senses, trying to determine whether she was rushing us toward some sign of civilisation, but then she opened another wormhole and barrelled us through to somewhere else.

The void slid over me, slick and clingy and dark. Again, and again, as Hiroko kept us running, kept jumping.

An alley in a noisy city.

A library.

A construction site.

A shallow tributary of salty tide, frigid water splashing up our legs.

A wooded area smelling of smoke. My eyes burned.

And then my shoes were pounding on hard-packed dirt and there was *noise* and movement, and we had to veer violently to avoid crashing into some sort of bicycle cart. Someone yelled at us in a language I didn't recognise. I grabbed for Hiroko's arm, disorientated and unnerved, and we backed up quickly to get out of the busy street she'd landed us in. But there was no out.

Was it a street? The area was *packed*, some combination of two-lane multi-vehicle highway and marketplace. People milled about under lanterns, talking, laughing, bartering, arguing, picking over crates of food and tables of clothes that lined what really *had* to be a street, with its bustling chaotic streams of people, bicycles, animal-drawn carts, motorcycles and unsafe-looking hybrids of the above. Crowds jostled us without paying us any notice, body heat and humidity adding fuel to the uncomfortable embers of anxiety inside me; I looked up and saw a black starless sky. It was midday at home.

'Where are we?!' I asked loudly to be heard over the muddled sounds. Behind me, I bumped into the edge of an unsteady stall table and quickly apologised to the woman behind it. She barely glanced at me, busy haggling with someone else.

'South-east Asia,' Hiroko called back, breathless, looking around, getting her bearings. 'Thailand, perhaps. I'm not certain.' She tugged on my arm and pushed into the crowd. I kept as close as I could. 'I cannot jump with so many people watching.'

'No one seemed to notice us land,' I countered, but I knew she was right. Sorcery had been persecuted throughout history, and part of the responsibility of being a practitioner was keeping the secret. Extending my senses, I brushed the auras of the hundreds, *thousands* of people bustling about this colourful marketplace. Unlike where we'd started, no one here seemed upset or stressed. I couldn't detect anyone whose energy I recognised, either. I leaned closer to my friend as we squeezed between groups of people and stopped abruptly for a donkey. 'How do we know if we've been followed?'

She looked uncomfortable. 'We cannot. I left each Displacement open.'

'So if they have a Displacer, they could follow your paths.' I swiped the donkey's tail away when it swung at my face and tried not to feel overwhelmed by how far from home we'd come. And what we were running from. 'Elijah could be following us.'

'Is that a problem?' Hiroko asked, chancing another step forward when the crowd gave us that opportunity. Elijah was one of our teachers, and someone we both trusted implicitly, and yet, yes, for him to catch up to us right now could be very problematic, at least for me. I was failing at that not-getting-overwhelmed thing.

'It's a long story, but yes. Do you know how to block your wormholes?'

'In theory.'

She raised her hand in the warm air between us, and I realised she'd walked us back to our landing spot. I couldn't see the magic she wove, but even in the scattered light of the night markets I could see the focus of her eyes change to look at the fine details of the Fabric she saw behind the physical world.

Amazing to think that when I met her six months ago, she was only confident with small Skips, and I helped her scour the library for books on Displacement. Now she was a superhero, teleporting the both of us safely all over the *planet*, opening wormholes in space and closing them like a pro.

Tourists and locals alike meandered the market and ignored us equally, and I likewise ignored them, my attention back in Northern Ireland. The situation there had spiralled so far out of control, and we'd left the magic school we attended in a terrified rush on the order of our headmaster, Renatus. The last thing I'd seen was the Academy under siege from a dozen enemy sorcerers, my scrying teacher carrying my maybe-dead wards teacher through the gate and yelling for Renatus to hurry.

Hiroko seemed to be thinking along the same lines.

'When we left,' she said nervously, raising her voice to be

heard, 'was Emmanuelle…?'

'I don't know.'

'And everyone else at the house?'

'I don't know.'

I swallowed a frightened lump in my throat. Emmanuelle could be dead. Renatus… I could know in an instant how he was, whether he was okay, but that would involve opening the door at the back of my mind where we were bonded as master and apprentice. I could walk straight into his head and know his every thought, feel what he felt, even see through his eyes and hear what he was hearing right now.

And he'd be able to do the same. He'd know where I was, which would make this escape futile.

Hiroko got moving again, the energetic pit of her wormhole filled in. 'We cannot stay here. Aristea!' she called suddenly when we were cut off from each other. I felt her hand slip from mine and felt the flutter of her panic. Outwardly she appeared to have it together but after our recent experiences she was thoroughly shaken. I let a couple of tourists pass, and then pushed to return to my friend's side. My arms felt pinned down by the hot crush of people but I felt her clutch at my wrist when it was close enough. Her palm was sweaty, like mine.

'I'm here. Where are we supposed to go?' I asked, mostly rhetorically, as we squeezed through the dense mass of humanity sticking to each other like glue. We were operating well outside the bounds of *supposed to* by now, having run away from both the bad guys and good guys – or the people I'd once have allocated those simplistic labels to. I really had no plan and no idea of what we were doing. An hour ago, I was grounded but safe at Renatus's house. An hour before that, I was covered in blood, clutching stolen property and worried I'd gotten Renatus killed. An hour before *that*… well, I didn't know, because there were two hours or so of missing time, but since the girl I was with was now in hospital, her dad was demanding my head and the guy who was meant to have Renatus's back had disappeared, I'd inferred it hadn't gone well.

Needless to say, this wasn't my best day. I still had the stolen property in the satchel I was keeping close at my side, my future with the council was in shreds, and I still couldn't remember what had happened in those missing two hours.

Okay, today wasn't a total loss. I had something now that I didn't have earlier today.

Hiroko and I were almost separated again by a family group pushing past, but she stopped and stepped back, resolutely digging in her heels. I did the same, trying to see a potential escape over the heads of the people pressing in around us. Her anxiety with our predicament fed mine, and I could feel myself descending into panic – we were, after all, lost in a foreign place we'd never visited before, half a world away from anyone who could help us, with no plan, surrounded, utterly surrounded by strangers.

But we had each other. I tightened my grip on her hand and made myself inhale one deep breath. I needed to calm down. My best friend was here with me, and she was so super talented. I had talents, too.

I let my vision slide out of focus as I concentrated instead on what this scene would look like from above. I imagined the tops of our heads, two dark spheres lit by lanterns and surrounded by a moving sea of other heads… And on my next inhalation, I wasn't imagining anymore. I could see the lanterns, the stalls, the tents, the tides of people going to-and-fro, and us, two dark heads standing still, not far from a north-western edge to the crowd.

Hiroko was a Displacer, innately attuned to the structures of magic that held the world together. I was a scrier. Remote viewing of events past and present were my chief skill, and I had been getting steadily better at it since we met. I blinked my attention back to my real vision.

'That way,' I directed, pointing, and Hiroko took my word for it. We waded our way through the people, a slideshow of unfamiliar faces and a garbled audio track of voices I didn't know. I found myself hyperaware of every person I saw, expecting to recognise someone. Lisandro, or one of his followers. Nastassja, maybe, Renatus's psycho sister who'd already tried to kill me once today. One of the White Elm councillors, who'd been my teachers for the past half year. Perhaps Renatus himself, whose penchant for swooping in when I most needed him was one of many great qualities I had come to count on. I didn't see a single face I knew, but that didn't inspire much confidence. That theatre we'd escaped with Renatus and Qasim was full of at least a hundred strangers eager to get their hands on me and what I had in my satchel.

At least this crowd wasn't violent. My friend and I kept pushing westward until we broke free of the crush, and slipped under the awning of a blue market tent. Apologising to the irate vendor whose table of trinkets and bangles we knocked, we hurried through the small gap between his tent and the next and burst into the blessed fresh air of the space behind it.

Onto a train track.

I wanted to take a moment to get my breath back but Hiroko wasted no time. I saw her glancing around, looking for trains, and I knew she was right. I ran my attention over my wards, a series of energetic shields layered around my body to prevent magical attack or scrying. We didn't bail all the way to Thailand just to be spied from afar.

'Where next?' Hiroko finally asked over the continuing noise on the other side of this wonky line of tents, and I realised I was in charge of making the decision. This was my escape, not hers. She wouldn't have been in any danger had she not stepped up to help me when I found myself powerless in that theatre. Had she not teleported me there against both our better judgement. Had she not come back to the school she'd left weeks ago to avoid ultimately getting caught up in something exactly like this, which I'll admit happened to me more frequently than I enjoyed.

I was the criminal and she was my getaway driver; she was never a target before now. I'd dragged her into my world. Feeling guilty, I opened my mouth to apologise, but felt a distant pressure at the edge of my awareness and snapped my lips shut.

Someone was trying to scry me. My wards were deflecting their attention, and I was usually very good with wards, but a few minutes ago in that theatre, I'd found myself totally powerless, unable to access any of my magic. My wards were dismantled. Hiroko had discovered the spell was cast only on the location, and everything came back online, so to speak, as soon as we left – but after that experience I didn't want to test the assumption that my shields were infallible, and I didn't know how good my spy was.

'Somewhere else,' I suggested, starting to follow the tracks in the direction of fewer lights, assuming that was the way out of town. I was thinking through our path to get here. A talented Displacer like Hiroko, or our teacher Elijah, could feel and even follow the wells in space left behind by a teleportation. Theoretically, someone could already have followed our footsteps to that field, to that alley, to the library, to the construction site, to the beach, and as far as that smoky woodland by now. From there, they'd know we'd jumped again, and may even be able to glean an idea of world region. Thanks to Hiroko's block, *theoretically*, they shouldn't be able to follow any further, but like I wasn't going to put a hundred percent stock in my anti-scrying wards, I wasn't sure how solid her first attempt at wormhole blocking was.

Perhaps now's a good time to remind everyone at home we're not *real* sorcerers, just students.

'I can take you to your sister's house?' Hiroko suggested, walking slightly ahead of me. Her shiny sheet of black hair swung against the tops of her shoulders, a fresh haircut I wasn't used to after being apart for weeks. I shook my head, my still-wet locks sticking uncomfortably to my sweaty neck.

'That's where they'll expect me to go.' More to the point, if I did go back to my sister's, she'd be dragged into this as surely as Hiroko was, and Angela was considerably less prepared for this sort of misadventure than Hiroko had proven to be. Feeling faintly sick, I watched the gravel my boots sent scattering with each reluctant step. Was someone there at Angela's even now?

It wasn't hard to check. My scrying gift gave me insights into things near and far, and in the front of my mind, a picture formed on request. I saw an overcast village street, gently sloped, small homes with neat little gardens either side of narrow paths leading up the doors. Though each house looked much like the next, my attention was with the one in the centre of the vision.

I used to call it home, and perhaps part of me still did, because a wave of homesickness washed through me. I swallowed. From what I could see, no one was around my sister's house right now, but it could still be under watch. I wasn't worried about the White Elm – they'd kind of kicked me out earlier today but they were the devil I knew, and I could count on them to keep Angela out of their issues with me, even defend her if it came to it. It was the others I was looking for. Lisandro, Shanahan, Nastassja, Jackson, any number of strangers working in their names.

'How far can we go?' I asked as we picked our way along the old wooden sleepers. The market stalls were backed right up against the tracks – I imagined that when the trains came through, they almost brushed the flimsy rear walls of those tents. Hiroko half-shrugged.

'Anywhere, it seems,' she said flatly, and I took her point. We were testing her limits today in an uncontrolled experiment and she'd just zapped us halfway around the planet. There was no further to go without aiming quite literally for the moon and dying in the vacuum of space. She'd told me in the past that Displacement was the kind of skill in which accuracy got tougher with distance, but I also knew she was one of the best of her age, Elijah's favourite student. The distance wasn't an issue for someone of her power, provided I appreciated that there was a margin for error which could throw us off by as much as a small nation.

'Okay.' Time to get it together, Aristea. 'Let's steer clear of home, but try to get somewhere we can stop and regroup. But take little jumps to get there,' I warned, recalling something I heard a long time ago. 'Elijah keeps tabs on the bigger Displacements.'

Crazy, to be hiding from him for the second time today. He was one of the nicest people on the White Elm council. In the space of hours, I'd gone from prize apprentice to fugitive. Keeping track of my deteriorating circumstances made me feel dizzy.

'Alright.' Hiroko nodded like she had somewhere in mind.

An alley came up in the solid wall of buildings lining the other side of track, and she crossed toward it. We could use its cover to Displace out of here to prevent anyone seeing us through the fluttery gaps in the tents. 'In here?'

I edged ahead of her to put myself in any line of fire, extending my wary senses into the dark lane. Behind me, beyond the tents, there was a mass of human energy, but ahead there was nothing much. A handful of presences, all inside the brick buildings pressing in on this empty little alley. Clear.

'Hey!'

Startled, we both whipped around to the sharp voice and saw a huddle of angry-looking people poking out from the back of one of the tents. One man looked like a police officer, and another was the stallholder whose tent we'd passed through to reach this train track. He was pointing to us with one hand and shaking a fistful of his beaded threads in the other. Instinctively I glanced over myself, trying to identify his problem with us, and spotted a tangle of similar trinkets dangling from the corner of my satchel, caught on the pommel of my sai blades.

Hurriedly I pulled Hiroko into the alley out of sight, and she was ready. I felt the slippery cool of the empty place between places as she manipulated the Fabric to allow us to pass between here and somewhere else, and she held onto me as we stepped out of the Thai market. I took a quick and desperate breath – I had never mastered this feeling – and took the usual leap of faith in lifting my foot clear of solid ground for the promise of more somewhere else. It was always quick, but never quick enough, the black clutching at my chest, my arms, dragging on my hair, my clothes, the entire universe passive-aggressively suggesting I stay in the natural world and not try to break its rules.

Then, just as I was about to give myself over to the inevitable panic this sensation deserved, my shoe struck a new floor, and the split second we'd stretched out closed at the same instant my second foot arrived. Normally at this point, the blackness of the void gave way to the new location, but that didn't happen this time.

'I can't see,' Hiroko whispered, afraid, though I sensed her already working to block her exit point from any followers. I squeezed her hand as I quickly cast out my awareness and concentrated on my eyes. My time as Renatus's apprentice had been short but not without exposure to a range of magic someone of my level normally wouldn't access. I blinked hard, activating the weresight he'd taught me, and our surroundings came into sharp focus.

'This way,' I instructed, gently pressing the top of her head down to make her stoop as I led her to a clearer area free of equipment. She'd brought us to a dark factory garage and we'd landed squarely between the prongs of a half-raised forklift. One thing we did not need right now was a concussion from walking blindly into that.

From there, it took us another four small jumps, which I'd heard Displacers like Hiroko and our other friends Addison and Garrett refer to as 'Skips', to get ourselves across China. A rainy forest, a classroom, a darkened restaurant, then a well-lit boardwalk overlooking choppy water reflecting the heavy sky above it. A big city loomed behind a line of decorative trees and I stepped up to the safety fence separating me from the sea. Or was it a lake? I couldn't see its edges from here, only smell the salt of the nearby ocean, strong enough to determine through the dirtier scents of smoke and city smog.

I inhaled deep while Hiroko finished blocking her Displacement. Sea air had a grounding effect on me, reminding me of simpler times when I was a little girl. When my biggest problems were keeping my bedroom clean and getting good enough at catching or goalkeeping to be allowed to join my brother and sister's street games with the other local big kids. When all other problems were solved for me.

At the back of my mind I felt that familiar door, currently shut tight, and wanted so badly to open it and make contact with Renatus. I wanted to know he was okay, after almost burning out in some mysterious accident during our missing two hours of time at Shanahan's penthouse and coming under attack with no power to defend himself at that theatre. I wanted to hear his voice in my head demanding to know *I* was okay, commandeering the use of my eyes to see where I was so he could be here in a single world-hopping jump to come to my aid.

You have to go. Somewhere I wouldn't guess.

I wound my hand around the stupid beaded necklaces I'd accidentally lifted in Thailand and disentangled them from the clutches of my sai. More stolen property. I let my beaded fist fall against the satchel, feeling the sacred weight and shape of the book hidden inside. All this trouble for something so basic. I remembered Nastassja's green eyes narrowing when she saw it in the office. Fifteen minutes ago, was it? Before I'd realised how she knew where to look for it. Before I'd realised I wasn't the only one with access to Renatus's mind.

'Where are we?'

'Near Shanghai. I have landed here in the past.'

China's coast, and we were facing out over an eastern sea.

'If we're going where I think we're going, he'll guess it,' I mentioned as Hiroko joined me at the railing. And if Renatus could guess, his back-from-the-dead telepathic sister could read that guess right out of his thoughts, but I wasn't sure Hiroko understood this. She was running entirely on faith at this point, and I loved her for it.

'We are going where you think,' she confirmed. 'We do need to regroup and we cannot hide in places we do not know – anyone following us may know the places better than we do.'

I hadn't considered that. I wasn't that well-travelled and I didn't think Hiroko was either, which meant that of the million places available for us to Displace, chances were higher that we'd land in any one of our international enemies' stomping grounds than anywhere we had home advantage.

Hiroko took my wrist and jumped us once more, across that sea, and it wasn't a big jump but when the void slid off me and my feet found purchase again, it was like she'd sent us to a whole new world. A flash went off, briefly blinding me and reminding me to switch back to normal vision, and I followed when Hiroko swept aside a curtain and stepped out of the cramped space.

We'd landed in an instant photo booth outside a convenience store, and the drizzly sidewalk was busy and happening despite the hour. The temperature was lower, closer to what I was used to. The same dark sky that had looked heavy at the edge of Shanghai seemed here to lift above the sudden light pollution of colourful neon signs that hung over us. After the crushing chaos of the Thai market, the purposeful currents of legs under black umbrellas felt orderly and unimposing as they strode straight past us.

I clutched my satchel and my wards close, looking around for potential danger, but now that she'd blocked her Displacement, Hiroko's levels of tension had dropped almost totally away, which naturally influenced me, too. She collected the photo from our booth's printer and waved it like an old polaroid.

'Renatus and others may guess we would hide at my home,' she conceded as she looped an arm through mine and guided me into the crowd, 'but my home is only one of thousands for them to check, and I suspect I know this city better than he or anyone inside that theatre. Aristea, welcome to Sapporo.'

chapter two

Ten uneventful minutes of wandering the city with Hiroko did a lot to set me at ease after our blurry getaway. She Displaced an umbrella into her hand, presumably from her house but I wasn't judging if it came from somewhere else, and guided me with the absolute confidence of a girl who'd spent her life walking these streets.

'Best breakfasts in Sapporo,' she advised, nodding at a window display of text-heavy menus I couldn't read. There were dozens of photos of meals, some recognisable, others more exotic to my very western and limited palate, all surrounded by bubbly advertising script boasting various qualities I couldn't guess. Good value? Great flavours? The English I spotted seemed mostly decorative and didn't add much, though 'Tasty days!' and 'Wow, fresh and happy, great!' at least gave a good impression. The prices I could discern, but I couldn't guess at the exchange rate or what those prices equated to.

The language barrier was disorientating, the lights overwhelming, the disregard for the late hour disarming… I felt like I had been dropped down a rabbit hole. And I loved it.

'I think this is the coolest place I have ever been,' I admitted as we passed an electronics store, its window thoroughly eclectic with blinking devices and noisy toys. With Renatus and the White Elm, I'd been to a woodland safehouse in Germany, the middle of Prague during a riot, the Mojave Desert and a secret archive hidden underground near Stonehenge, but none had felt as otherworldly as I felt here, disconnected from my master, hidden from the council, wandering free and aimless with my best friend. Hiroko shot me a warm smile.

'I think so, too.'

She led the way to her favourite coffee shop and we took a snug little booth with a clear view of the exits. Hiroko ordered for us while I stood mute, and as soon as we were settled in with our drinks warming our hands and I had established a silencing ward that would keep our words firmly between just us, I knew to expect her question.

'What is going on?'

I barely understood that myself, but since we had the time now, I appreciated the chance to talk it through with her.

'I have so missed having you around,' I confessed as I began to empty the satchel out onto the table between us. Before she'd left the Academy where we met as hopefuls aiming for apprenticeships we didn't fully comprehend, I'd told her everything – all the crazy and scary stuff I was exposed to as a teenage apprentice for the world's magical peacekeepers. Using her as a sounding board had done little for her except confirm that she wasn't on a track she wanted, but for me it had kept me sane and grounded. Without someone to share my worries and experiences with, well... My recent choices were a testament to the value of Hiroko's level-headed input.

The all-important leather-strapped journal landed amidst the other detritus of the satchel that wasn't even really mine, and Hiroko extended a hand as though to touch it, her fingers hovering in curiosity.

'Go ahead,' I invited, still unpacking. The brassy bowl from the orchard where I apparently spelled both myself and Renatus into forgetting whatever we did at Thomas Shanahan's penthouse lair to get the book. The knife I'd found beside me, apparently used to cut a lock of my own hair for the spell. Not that I remembered. 'You can even try to read it. There's nothing written in it.'

Tentatively, Hiroko opened the fabled Shanahan ledger. As I'd predicted, the pages were blank, just as Qasim and Renatus had noted after confiscating it from me. But moments earlier, I'd opened it in my lap, there in the ballroom at Morrissey House, and each page had been painstakingly ruled up, with dates, names, figures, notes all meticulously kept and ordered. Renatus and I only meant to get a look at it, not take it, and certainly not hurt anyone – it wasn't worth all that, not to us, especially if it couldn't even confirm the shady dealings we'd been hoping to reveal.

'And this is what Sterling was looking for in the headmaster's office?' Hiroko asked, flipping old blank pages back and forth as though they might change their mind. They didn't.

'Nastassja,' I corrected. Sterling was a classmate at the Academy, once a friend, and it was her face and body rummaging through Renatus's desk, but the person I'd really been looking at was Renatus's sister, long presumed dead until about half an hour ago. A scrier like him and me, Nastassja was older and more aware of her talents, capable not just of *viewing* remote events, but attending them in spirit form, and of possessing actual people. What looked like a schoolgirl breaking into an office was actually an undead psychopath wearing a schoolgirl. We call the practice "Haunting" and as you can imagine, it's hugely frowned upon and entirely illegal.

I flattened out some documents I'd grabbed from Renatus's desk, to protect them in case Nastassja came back. Lists, and a stapled legal document confirming me as his heir and next of kin, should anything happen. I swallowed a lump threatening in my throat. I didn't want to be separated from Renatus, by distance or by the closed door at the back of my head. He was the last person I wanted to be hiding from – he was my protector, my mentor, my friend. In a short space of time, he'd become family.

But even the people who love you most can still hurt you without meaning to. And though he'd *never* mean to, he couldn't control what Nastassja could do with the things he knew.

'*Anastasia*?' Hiroko checked. 'Renatus's...? But you said she was dead.'

'I couldn't work out how she knew we had the ledger,' I explained, laying my sai down the centre of the small table so I could reach the smaller items at the bottom of the satchel. A blood-stained puzzle box. A pen. 'Then in the theatre, Lisandro said things he shouldn't have known – that I lost my guaranteed position on the council, that I memory-spelled Renatus, that I Haunted before.' No, I didn't possess anyone, and I did my time in detention for the underage crime. It was my first experience with scrying, a breakthrough, and I hadn't done it again and didn't intend to. But the point was, Renatus kept that quiet. He and Qasim knew what I'd done, and he buried it so I wouldn't be kicked out of the school before he got the chance to train me. Unless my most trusted teachers had been casually speaking with their number one enemy lately, Lisandro should not have known that. 'I realised when Nastassja was trying to talk to Renatus, they've still got some weird bond. She can see through his eyes. Hear his thoughts, maybe, if she wants to. That's how they knew those things.'

Hiroko closed the ledger and sipped her coffee. 'But I thought only you and Renatus could do that, because you were bonded at your initiation?'

I played with the handle of my coffee mug. Apparently not. I tried not to feel envious or possessive, and mostly I think I succeeded, though it still sat uncomfortably in my chest. Renatus was the most powerful sorcerer on the White Elm council, a prodigy the others weren't sure whether to harness or point and shoot. That his mind could be invaded without his knowing was very concerning, both professionally speaking and personally. I could imagine his shaken confidence in this moment, half a world away, not trusting his own mind, his own thoughts. I wished I was there to reassure him, to help if I could, but right now I knew I was doing the most helpful thing I could.

Staying safe. Staying out of their hands by staying out of his, and giving him one less thing to worry about.

'If she can access his thoughts,' I told Hiroko, pulling the ledger through the junk on the table to open it in front of me, 'then she and Lisandro can know where I am as soon as he does. If they get this ledger before I can work out how to get the words to come back, they'll destroy it and any evidence it holds that proves they were responsible for all those deaths in Prague.' Including that of Anouk, a White Elm councillor who'd been killed right in front of me, just outside the bounds of my protective ward.

'So we're hiding you from Renatus, in order to hide you from Nastassja, and Lisandro by extension,' Hiroko clarified. I flipped the pages, willing the inky black words to return, wondering what helpful spells I might find in Renatus's head if I just opened that door.

'Yes, but also from the entire White Elm, who will put me back on house arrest if they find me,' I reminded her. 'I was meant to have a trial scheduled when they got back from their meeting in Germany.'

I tried not to think about the blood on my hands when I'd suddenly found myself half a breath, a whole country and two hours out of sync with my last memory. Teagan, the sheltered but very sweet daughter of magical underworld king Thomas Shanahan, was in hospital being treated by White Elm Healers for a curse, and Renatus had come back from that mysterious altercation almost dead. Wiping both our memories of the event was an obvious obstruction of justice, but the method of the spell – illegal blood magic – hadn't helped my case. I'd dug the hole deeper still when I'd neglected to mention spelling myself, so currently they also believed I was withholding information. And I mean, I was, but not information that I had any memory of.

I didn't know what I'd done, but I could guess that Renatus had done worse, and taking this fall for him was hardly a choice, even if the consequences were grave.

Whatever it takes. That was the extent of the oh-so-helpful message I left myself before spelling away my memory, and that's what I was doing now.

'If I'm found guilty, they'll separate me from Renatus, and that can't happen. If I'm found innocent, it'll be because they've gotten my memory back and discovered Renatus is guilty, and I'll be in the same situation.'

'Maybe neither of you is guilty,' Hiroko suggested. I wished I had her optimism. 'You were not alone there, on your mission.'

She was right, and I had a sizeable capacity for disliking Declan O'Malley, so I had no problem assuming he was largely at fault for whatever had gone down. Half-buried memories of an ill-advised impromptu visit to his decrepit mansion – several minutes of which I'd thought lost, when *he* had performed a memory spell on *me* under the guise of teaching it to me – had returned to me throughout today, revealing that Declan had in fact wanted this ledger for himself. He'd disappeared without a trace, though, too slippery to put himself in the path of taking blame. And ultimately, the inescapable fact was that the ledger was with me, not him. If he'd stolen it, if he'd coerced me, if he'd really been in control of that whole situation like I'd prefer to believe, then he would have this prize.

No. Something went terribly wrong. Declan was Renatus's friend (a loosely employed word in this instance, but I didn't have a better one) more than he was mine, but I felt I knew him well enough to discern his more predictable behaviours. Running away when we needed him? Not surprising. Leaving me with a valuable treasure he had been seeking? Not likely, unless circumstances prevented him from getting it back.

I didn't want to be so charitable, but when I considered that he might have been killed, I immediately and unwillingly hoped he hadn't.

'Perhaps,' I relented finally, laying out the last of the items I'd brought with me from the house. My ruby, a fist-sized stone that had once belonged to Renatus's sister before she'd faked her death and run off with her father's best friend – yep, eww – and a handful of small cloth bags filled with herbs and salts. Declan had ominously prepared this satchel with the exact contents required to forge a memory spell. I didn't know why he'd thought he'd need this stuff when he came to meet us at Shanahan's house for what was supposed to be a reconnaissance mission, but apparently I'd made good use of most of the ingredients. 'Either way, I can't risk going to any of the council right now. Their minds are loosely connected to each other in this big thirteen-way network–'

'And Renatus is part of that network,' Hiroko finished, seeing the problem. We sipped our coffees in silence. I enjoyed the unusual taste of my drink, prepared so differently from those at home. I wondered what Hiroko had thought of foods and drinks served to her at Morrissey House, Renatus's home-turned-boarding-school in Northern Ireland not far from where I'd lived my whole sheltered life. 'So… we must think of a place to hide you from Renatus, Lisandro, all of Magnus Moira *and* the White Elm.'

'And everyone else,' I added casually, though I knew it was anything but. 'It turns out Declan and I weren't the only ones to theorise the existence of this stupid ledger, and with half the magical community of the United Kingdom indebted to Thomas Shanahan or doing business with him, I marked myself with a target when I showed my hand in that theatre.' I gazed at the odd arrangement of mismatched items on the tabletop and realised it was a pitiful kit for going on the run. I blinked, startled. 'I'm on the *run*.'

From the government, which the White Elm continued to be, even as Lisandro's growing free-magic movement Magnus Moira tried to destabilise them. From the rebels and the anarchists, from the community at large, and the most difficult pill to swallow, from Renatus. I felt suddenly very small and vulnerable. If he were here, if he'd jumped with us, I knew I'd feel ten times more confident about everything right now.

'It's not forever,' Hiroko tried to reassure me, though neither of us knew how long "not forever" was likely to be. Was this a mess that would resolve itself with time, or had I just leapt off a cliff into a new life I never asked for? Was this the beginning of a new normal? I felt panic building in my chest, and Hiroko must have seen it in my face, because she clasped my hand across the table. 'It is *not* forever. Do you think, in ten years, in even one week, you will still be running all over this world in hiding, and Renatus will just allow this?'

'No,' I admitted, reminding myself to be calm and rational. No, Renatus would not abandon me to this. He was angry enough that I'd taken the fall today; he wasn't about to leave me out here in the world alone any longer than circumstances demanded. *We're not done*, he said when I left. He'd be back for me as soon as he could, trying to problem-solve a way out of the punishments I'd lined myself up for. But when? I couldn't guess.

'Let's start with one night,' my friend suggested, going back to her drink. I resumed sipping on mine, warming myself up and trying to apply that warmth to my confidence. 'What do we need for one night off the magical grid?'

'What do *I* need,' I corrected. 'You should go home to your dad before he starts to worry. It was unfair of me to involve you at all, and you've already done so much.'

'You want me to leave you?' Hiroko looked around the coffee shop doubtfully. 'In Sapporo? For how long?'

I shrugged. I really did not want her to leave, but even more so, I really, really did not want her to suffer any further consequences of helping me. The White Elm knew I'd gone with her, and they knew where she lived, though whenever I strayed my attention to Morrissey House, I saw that front gate still locked tight, the enemies we'd escaped still milling about, a reminder of the dangers. They didn't know Hiroko, by name or reputation, but would likely now recognise her on sight after that confrontation. I wanted her well out of harm's way.

'Let's start with one night,' I echoed. 'You go home, and find me in the morning. And I'll have a think tonight about what to do next.' I sat back in my seat, surveying my table's worth of random objects and beyond it, the little coffee shop. 'How late is this place open?'

'No.' Hiroko's voice was firm, and she downed the last of her drink in one determined mouthful. 'You will not spend the night sleeping in a coffee shop.'

'I won't be sleeping,' I countered, but I started packing up my things anyway. 'It's the middle of the day for me.'

'And you look like you missed two nights of sleep,' Hiroko replied, showing me the polaroid from the photo booth. She wasn't wrong. She helped me put everything away. 'I will take you somewhere you can rest.'

Within a minute we were back out on the street under her umbrella, winding through people and crossing busy streets. Everything seemed vibrantly alive, every shopfront open for business, every window alight behind the raindrops streaming down the glass. Passing a clock, I saw that it wasn't as late as I'd thought, but still later than I'd expect anything other than pubs to be open back at home.

'You will need money,' Hiroko, the daughter of a banker, counselled wisely. 'If you do not stay with me or with your own family, and you cannot return to Renatus...'

'I know.' I hadn't ever had a real job, just a casual shop assistant role for a few months before I'd started with the White Elm, so I didn't have my own money, not really. I used to have a bank card to access Angela's account – she never wanted me to be caught short – but that was still buried at the bottom of my possessions at Morrissey House, half-forgotten in an enclosed magical environment where money wasn't necessary.

I hadn't expected to find myself outside of that cushy, safe environment. I certainly hadn't expected to find myself caught short on such a grand scale.

'You need a change of clothes,' my friend went on, still focused. 'Toothbrush. A plan.'

'The plan is to stay one step ahead of everyone trying to catch up with me.'

'Until?'

'Until...' I sighed and skirted wide around a puddle. 'Until I work out a better plan.'

She was right, my plan wasn't very solid. But so much remained unknown. Renatus could show up in an hour, say everything with the council had been sorted out and he had come to bring me home where we could map out our next step, together. Or, almost as unlikely and not something I wanted to consider, I could still be wandering the streets of Sapporo at Christmas, exhausted and alone.

I hoped not.

This walk was a bit longer, but Hiroko still led the way with utter confidence, never once pausing to determine the correct turn or to check a street name. I was glad for her natural pace; it helped to deflect the occasional glance my way. There were other foreigners around, most of them snapping photos as they went.

I hoped I blended in better, though with my well-known appearance and my distinctive scar running down the left side of my face, I didn't suppose any level of "blending" would help if someone who recognised me showed up.

Hiroko didn't stop until we arrived outside a noisy, colourful arcade.

'It looks loud,' she admitted, 'but upstairs there is a quiet level for games. Often people fall asleep while they are waiting for their turn. The chairs are very comfortable.'

Entering on the ground level, it was hard to believe that anywhere inside this building could be quiet, but the lift doors immediately cut a decent proportion of the sound, and two floors up, we exited to a library-like sereneness. The softly lit level was open plan, with different couches, hammocks and armchairs arranged in little cosy nooks around tables and bars covered in decks of cards and board games. About two dozen people, mostly teens and young adults, were sitting quietly and playing games together. A handful were relaxed in hammocks or along sofas, reading game guides or listening to music in their headphones.

Given that no one leapt to their feet on sight of me, it was a perfect spot to wait for tomorrow.

'You're sure?' she murmured, even that softest volume sounding too loud in this near-silent space. Amazing that pinballs were pinging and toy guns were making obnoxious pew-pew noises just two floors down. My senses, running on high alert now for hours, were finally settling, even as another tingle at my energetic edges warned that again, someone was trying to scry me. Good luck to them. This was the perfect place to lie low for a few hours and take stock.

Hiroko was awaiting my answer. She was the picture of controlled calm, but at a deeper layer I recognised her uncertain tension. Our hasty escape today had shaken her. This, exactly this, was why she'd left the Academy.

'You go,' I insisted, as quietly as I could. I dropped the satchel on an unoccupied couch and hugged Hiroko tightly. 'Please. I'll be here in the morning. Just… be safe, and take care of your dad, okay? Be wary tonight, in case…'

In case anyone worked out who she was and came after her.

It shouldn't happen, I reminded myself as she stepped reluctantly back into the elevator and its doors closed between us. She was a complete unknown to Lisandro, Shanahan and any of their followers. She'd tipped the balance of power in that theatre today simply by being unexpected but despite the chaos she'd inspired, they had no means of divining her name without breaching the White Elm, and if they could do that, Hiroko Sasaki would not be the top of their list of priorities. Neither would I.

The light above the elevator went out, and I collapsed onto the sofa. Hiroko was right, I was exhausted. Today, what I remembered and what I didn't, had taken a lot out of me, and I hadn't slept properly in days. Still, I doubted I'd get my mind still enough to fall asleep before Hiroko returned for me.

How did everything get so screwed up so quickly? I stared at the ceiling and did a quick check of my energy levels – low, not surprising; I was powering almost every kind of ward that I knew of – and then turned my attention to Morrissey House. I couldn't scry inside, where Renatus would be. The magic layered over the estate deflected my attempts to view past the front gate, much the way my magic was deflecting other scriers from finding me now. But I centred my focus on the dirt road that led up to the gate from the country road beyond the moors. The picture took shape in my head, a top-down view: sprawling Irish landscape, curving dirt trail, and people who weren't meant to be there. No fighting, thankfully. Renatus and Qasim should have been safely inside long ago. But what I saw didn't make me feel any better.

From this steep viewpoint, I could count at least ten people, and recognised the big man in the middle with the high-top afro as Jackson. My hands tightened beside me, tension from some mixture of hatred and fear. Lisandro's righthand man and another former council member, the big American Crafter had fired on Hiroko, eating through her ward and almost killing her, but before that, he'd been chasing Emmanuelle through that theatre when he'd smugly snapped his fingers... and from a distance, without touching her, snapped her neck. The moment she fell, the sick lurch of Renatus's horror mixing with mine, ran on repeat like an ugly gif at the edge of all my thoughts.

Wherever Jackson pointed and yelled, someone went, and I could see that the positions they took up established a deliberate formation. One of them sat down behind a hillock, getting comfortable where she could see the gate, and my concern grew into something closer to certainty. They were settling in. They were going to wait.

Nearby me, one of the chess players sniggered as they cornered their opponent's queen and put their king in check. I let my eyes drift closed, unnerved by the parallel as I watched the scene outside the White Elm's base of operations with my mind's eye. The White Elm was a centuries-old council of elite sorcerers who governed most of our magical world, but though they had an immense range of powers and had been formed originally from a band of warriors, few on the modern council had what I'd call warrior skillsets. Morrissey House, Renatus's ancestral home, had only one heavily fortified gate, and locked behind that gate were all the council's toughest assets. Tian, who'd taught me sword fighting. Qasim, who could view and process fifty or more scenes at once. Elijah, who could move through space like a ghost. Emmanuelle, who may or may not have just died right in front of me. Renatus himself, reckless magical prodigy, knower of many darkly effective spells he shouldn't, who never hesitated to take a shot. Not to mention the twenty-ish students the White Elm had been fostering and shaping into potential apprentices, several of them my friends, all of them amazing talents. I suppressed a shiver despite the warmth in the games room.

After decades in the shadows as an underground free-magic movement, Magnus Moira were making a bold stand. Locking down or eliminating their biggest threats was a solid chess move, preventing further progress or retaliation and allowing them time to move their own forward steps, whatever those might be.

Jackson and his band of merry madmen continued to settle in and wait, so I let my awareness stray further. I let images come to me at random. You get some irrelevant stuff this way, visions of past and present that don't seem connected to me at all, but amidst it is always the information Fate thinks you need. Recent events, as recent as my dreams last night, had helped solidify my faith in this concept of my scrying ability as some sort of conduit of a networked, borderline-conscious universe. I wouldn't have believed in anything so shonky six months ago – I couldn't even scry six months ago – but I was repeatedly learning that very little in my magical life happened in isolation. My whole family died in a freak accident; four years later I met Renatus, whose family died the *exact* same way and whose actual job was to track down Lisandro, the man responsible for those deaths. Last night, after eight years of stubbornly avoiding his own dreams, Renatus finally took down the spells over his estate that prevent dreaming; within half an hour, my sleeping brain was putting together realisations from different sources and we had a plan for getting our hands on Shanahan's ledger – evidence against Magnus Moira's claims that the White Elm had killed two dozen people in Prague last month.

Disconnected scenes drifted across my awareness. A young girl with bright eyes and skin the colour of rich caramel lay on her bedroom floor, journaling. Elsewhere, a frowning nurse approached a closed door but stopped when she reached it, changing her mind and continuing on her round. Somewhere else again, a stranger was scouring a familiar field, parting tufts of long grass with a muscular arm that ended in an amputated stump at the wrist.

This is how I differ a little from other scriers. This is why Renatus picked me to be his apprentice. Like Renatus and Qasim, I can see and hear the events happening in other places just as if I were watching it on a screen. Unlike them, I'm also an Empath, so I *feel* what the people in those scenes feel just as if I were feeling it myself. I could feel the one-handed stranger's frustration as he searched for Hiroko's Displacement well. I felt his patience wearing thin, and guessed he'd been there a while.

They were looking for me – case in point, another scrying tingle brushed over my aura and was dispersed, unseen – but they were a long way back. I had time.

In fact, I had hours. Hours to lie there, conflicted and worried. I shifted my attention intermittently between Hiroko's home and Renatus's, as well as both Angela's empty house and her workplace. I watched Jackson hold his ground for hours. I watched Nastassja eventually return to his side to confer quietly, though I didn't get to hear what was discussed. I watched Angela fitting someone's new glasses, oblivious. I watched Hiroko sleep and saw nobody approach her building. Good.

I tried a few times to scry Declan O'Malley and Teagan Shanahan, but I couldn't find either of them, not even when I dug my ruby out of the satchel. It usually helped me to focus my scrying. For Teagan, I kept getting images of that locked door, nurses and doctors walking right by it or being repelled off to do something else. I gathered she was inside, protected by layers of her dad's magic; protected specifically from *me*, given that he had accused me of putting her in the hospital in those two hours I'd lost. The thought made me feel unwell. I couldn't imagine hurting her but I *did* have blood on my hands when my memory resumed, and it wasn't mine.

When I looked for Declan, I got nothing at all.

The hours dragged by and the gamers in the room slowly left. What I wanted *most*, even more than confirmation that Teagan, Declan or Emmanuelle were alive and alright, was to hear from Renatus. I was used to having his voice in my head, to knowing how he felt and what he was thinking, even when we were apart. I was used to being part of something more than myself, the tempering other half of an influential powerhouse who always knew what to do next, or at least was willing to make decisions so I wouldn't have to. Now that door was bolted shut from both sides, and in the silence of my own mind, I felt small and alone.

The most I could get was a faint impression of feeling. Mentally I curled up against that metaphorical door, wishing I could open myself to the mind behind it but not daring to, and I concentrated. There were always cracks, and my Empathy was not tied to my magic, nor to my bond with Renatus. It took a few moments before I detected the tendrils of his faraway presence.

Wariness… uncertainty… conflict, confusion… missing, mourning…

Knowing that he was okay enough to be feeling anything at all, especially the complex mix I would have expected after what happened to his best friend Emmanuelle and the shock sighting of his thought-dead sister, filled me with such relief that I had to sit up to suppress a sob. The only people left in the room had headphones on and no one noticed as I hugged myself and got my breathing back under my control.

By morning I couldn't say I'd slept, but I maybe dozed a little and did feel somewhat rested when I felt Hiroko's presence approaching the building. I had hardly moved. Neither had Jackson's blockade. As the sun there eventually dipped to the horizon, men and women tagged out, to be immediately replaced by new, fresh strangers. Their purposeful enthusiasm did not waver, even when Nastassja left, when Jackson left, when Nastassja returned and sat cross-legged on the hill opposite the gate, gazing at her childhood home with her usual complicated mess of heightened emotions.

Teagan's hospital door didn't open.

Declan didn't materialise.

Angela continued her day.

The one-handed guy in the field ultimately gave up, but an image of a different stranger later came to me from the night market in Thailand.

The message was clear to me long before I accepted it. I wasn't going back to Morrissey Estate, not any time soon, and no one good was coming for me. Renatus was pinned. Bad people who wanted this stupid, blank ledger were inching closer along my trail. I had to move on, away from Hiroko, and I had to be prepared to stay missing for as long as Jackson was prepared to guard that gate.

Hiroko had clearly gotten some sleep, like the sensible girl she was. Her hair was brushed smooth and her fresh clothes were neatly pressed. Meanwhile, my long hair had dried overnight, complete with kinks and knots that had no excuse for forming when I'd hardly even moved. I was sure I looked dreadful, especially sitting in the middle of my satchel's contents like a crazy hoarder, but as we'd shared a bedroom since March, she'd seen me worse.

'What is the situation at home?' Hiroko asked, all business because she knew I would be. She sat elegantly on the edge of my sofa and picked through the paperwork I'd taken from Renatus's desk. I shook my head.

'Not good. Magnus Moira are guarding the gate. I can't get back in without facing them all down, and the council can't get out.'

Hiroko angled her gaze up at me, worry rising inside her. 'And our friends? Addison? The twins, Iseult?'

'No one's getting through that gate,' I assured her confidently, my thoughts touching on those four teenagers I cared for most in the student population. She relaxed and went back to reading.

'I know you won't stay,' she said, not bothering to keep her voice down. No one was left but us. 'And… I don't think I should come with you.'

She said it tentatively. I understood the conflict perfectly and hurried to put her at ease.

'It won't be safe for you,' I insisted, closing the blank ledger on my lap for the millionth time. 'Emmanuelle might be dead. Teagan and Declan might be, too, and I almost lost Renatus yesterday. You've done more for me than I should ever have asked. If anything happened to you or Angela…'

'I know.' She instinctively touched the string at her neck, and I thought of the crumpled paper crane hanging on that under her cardigan. Her soft feelings confirmed that she was dwelling on Garrett, the boy who'd taught himself origami to have an excuse to talk with her before he'd been recruited by Magnus Moira. The boy who'd saved her life in that theatre yesterday and then disappeared. For all we knew, he could have been caught – I was too afraid to scry for him.

She swallowed the thoughts away and presented me with a backpack filled with necessities: toothbrush, hairbrush, hair elastics, a bar of soap and an outfit.

'I don't want you to be alone, even less without a plan,' she explained, 'but if I help with your plan, and anyone catches up to me, I could put you in danger just to know it. And then this morning when I woke, I knew what we must do.' She reached for the little bowl I'd used to cast yesterday's memory spells, and my stomach dropped. Still practical and businesslike, she continued, 'What do you need?'

'What for?' I asked uncomfortably. 'For an ill-advised memory adjustment I'm not qualified to make, or for my upcoming penniless fugitive phase?'

There was a momentary pause, a lapse in our well-synced comprehension. Despite thick accents, Hiroko and I generally understood each other exceptionally well – my Empathic abilities possibly helped. Still, she wasn't a native speaker, and I occasionally let terms slip that needed definitions.

'What is "penniless"?' she asked curiously, and when I quickly explained, her eyes lit up with understanding. 'Oh, I don't think you'll be *penniless*.' She put the bowl down and tapped the paperwork in front of her. 'You signed this? You know what it entitles you?'

'Aye, I signed it…'

'But you didn't *read* it.'

Her disapproving expression said it all, but I knew she wasn't really surprised.

She Displaced us to an unoccupied hotel room so I could shower and get dressed. I lightly toyed with the cute collar of the cardigan she'd included in the backpack and knew, with a sense of deep warmth and gratitude, that these were her clothes. We wore the same size and though our styles were different, I kind of loved the idea of dressing as Hiroko for a day in her home city.

When I stepped out of the tiny bathroom, she smiled to see me in her outfit.

'Are you ready to try the best breakfasts in Sapporo?'

chapter three

The chaos faded but the tension didn't. From the moment Renatus pulled the gate shut and heard the clang of iron on iron, he knew logically he was safe. His pursuers, close on his heels, collided with the gate and rattled on its posts, even tried to reach their hands through the bars and cast spells at him, but the house had stood against this for centuries. Spells bounced; hands welted and reddened until they were withdrawn. Breathing hard, backing away up the path toward his home, he wasn't paying attention to them. He was looking over their heads at the woman yelling at them to stop.

Ana. It was impossible, unacceptable, but the evidence was there, a distant figure dressed in black on the hilltop opposite him, where she'd just moved on Aristea and Hiroko. For months he'd known *of* her, but she'd been the shadowy bitch Nastassja who'd attacked Aristea in a forest – he hadn't seen her, he hadn't known, he hadn't even guessed, because why would he? His sister was dead. Powerless to stop it, he'd watched as she'd died, broken and bleeding, in his arms eight years earlier.

How could she be alive after that? She couldn't. Equally as disturbing, then; if she was alive, which she evidently was, who was the dead girl he'd mourned for almost a decade, buried in his family cemetery in the orchard at the lower edge of the property?

His thoughts were a wild mess, a spiral of questions and horrors around a pit of silence where normally there was an anchor – one he hadn't realised he'd come to treat that way.

Aristea was in the wind, blocked even from his mind, and *he had sent her away*. He could still see the look of fear in her expressive eyes as he'd grabbed her shoulders and told her she had to leave. He almost thought he could feel it the way she did, but the shock and fear were probably his own, given the situation. Given what he'd done.

Panic seized his chest. She was alone, she and her friend Hiroko. They could be anywhere. Anyone could have caught up. Anything could have happened. And Renatus had just closed the gate, leaving nine, ten, maybe more dangerous adversaries between the girls and their safe return, and closed his mind off from his apprentice, like he did when he was mad with her. Leaving her in silence. Alone.

How could he do that to them? To Aristea, who'd just risked her life and broken the conditions of her house arrest to come to his rescue in Belarus? Who'd taken the fall for him only an hour ago when–

No. Across the span of distance he was trying to put between them, his gaze met the bright, alien gaze of Nastassja – *Ana* – and he quickly clamped down on his disordered thoughts. *'Scrier, Telepath, it's a very special mix,'* Ana had said. *'Sharing a mind. Sharing eyes.'*

Telepathy. This was why he'd cut his apprentice off. Eye contact helped initiate it. Wards blocked it. Or should. Rattled, he ran his attention over the layers of magic he wore, but fatigue and stress made it difficult to know whether to trust in their solidity. He'd never had difficulty shielding his mind; perhaps he'd gotten lax with overconfidence, or perhaps his sister transcended more magical rules than just returning from the dead.

His sister. Renatus turned away in an effort to break her gaze, but then he was looking up the hill at the house he and Ana had grown up in. The house he'd been running for when he'd turned back to see she wasn't following, and had realised something was wrong, so wrong...

And at the front door, just now slipping inside, Qasim, carrying Emmanuelle, as motionless as Ana in the orchard...

Overwhelmed by a sudden wave of ill-feeling, he retched and

dropped to one knee. Nothing came up, not even when his stomach heaved a second time. No doubt, his enemies outside the gate were watching this show of weakness, but he couldn't care about that right now. Everything was backward. Em was dead. Ana was alive. Aristea was gone. His vision started to go black at the edges.

In a parallel with the past, a firm but gentle hand took his elbow and righted him.

'It's alright, it's alright.'

Lord Gawain, high priest of their council and leader of most of the magical world, had appeared from inside the house. How depleted was Renatus's energy if someone so powerful and so familiar could get this close without him even sensing his presence? Before leaving here, barely twenty minutes ago, he'd been weary but thought he could handle whatever the day threw at him – after all, he'd survived whatever had happened at Shanahan's, if only barely.

Apparently he'd grossly underestimated this day.

'Breathe,' Lord Gawain instructed, distractedly glancing down at the gate when a chorus of boos and excited yelling swelled at his appearance on the hillside. Magnus Moira, a movement they'd mistaken for followers of Lisandro's rhetoric, was quickly proving to be more a combination of free magic activists and opportunistic anarchists that Lisandro had found a home with. As the leader of the White Elm, the pacifist Welsh barrister in his seventies represented their one common enemy. He refocused on Renatus as the younger man tried to follow his order. 'That's it. Breathe, you're safe. What happened? Aristea and her friend aren't here – were they with you?'

Was there a more confronting question?

'They're... I don't know,' Renatus admitted truthfully, ashamedly. He wanted so badly to be able to answer, and normally could, easily. Open that door in his head. Reach out to the universe and get an image of where his apprentice was. But even thinking of how to find her was dangerous, and he quickly changed the track of his thinking before he could do more damage. 'She's gone. I can't think about it. My head... She's...' How to explain? His mentor, the same man who'd pulled him away from Ana's body when he'd found the siblings after the storm that had killed their parents, was staring at him without comprehension. So Renatus turned, helplessly, and gestured at the gate, at the woman calling others back from it. Across the distance, their gazes locked again. 'She's alive, and she's in my head.'

Gawain had not known Ana Morrissey – he'd met Renatus for the first time in the minutes after her supposed death – but somehow he knew her instantly. His light eyes widened.

'Nastassja is… *how*?' he clarified of his young friend, glancing between them for confirmation. Complex emotions crossed his face, shock and distress and disappointment, none of which made sense until he concluded, 'Your sister is Lisandro's wife?'

Renatus could have thrown up yet again, except he didn't remember the last time he ate. Yes, even worse, Ana was Nastassja and Nastassja was married to Lisandro. His godfather. Basically their uncle, growing up. Former member and self-declared enemy of the White Elm council. And murderer of Aristea's family, as well as his.

He swallowed the urge to retch. His sister had somehow faked her death to be with the man who'd killed their parents, leaving Renatus an orphan. This day could not get worse.

But it had. Aristea was gone. Emmanuelle, too, and maybe even Declan, that little shit.

'How is this possible?' Lord Gawain wondered, and Renatus didn't try to guess. The council leader looked between the siblings, searching for similarities he'd have no trouble finding, even at this distance. He distractedly rubbed his mouth and chin, deeply disturbed by his own thoughts. 'Is she wearing the ring? The Elm Stone,' he pressed when Renatus just blinked.

'I… I don't…' Think. Aristea had seen her before and had reported the stolen power source on Nastassja's hand. He looked out at the distant figure. Too far to tell. 'Maybe. How could that be connected to her reappearance?'

'Maybe it's not, but the first time Lisandro asked for it was after her supposed death.' Lord Gawain followed his gaze to the small crowd outside the gate. 'I knew her story wasn't finished with you, but this…' The old Seer gestured at the gate, apologetic for the limitations of his gift. 'Pieces are missing from the hints Fate sent me. I never imagined… I only knew she was there in your future, a shadow over every day of your life. And I thought…'

That was an apt interpretation for Renatus's life up to this point. Fair. His mentor was still gazing down the hill and past the gate, equal parts troubled and wistful. He finally turned back to Renatus.

'Tell me what happened. What do I need to know?'

The question made Renatus want to tear his hair out in frustration.

'It was a trap. Lisandro knew about Aristea's dismissal from the council waiting list–' stop thinking about her, stop thinking about her '–and she said we're linked, so somehow she's in my head. Everything I think, everything you say to me, everything I see…'

'Could be compromised,' the elderly Seer realised. In his mind, Renatus felt the gentle shutdown of his mentor's mind from his, and in the moments that followed, felt the other minds connected to his through the White Elm's telepathic link do the same. A wise precaution. Who knew if Ana, Nastassja, whoever she was now, could hijack other minds by going through his? Beyond the gate, eerily bright green eyes that weren't green when he knew her before held his gaze, and he wasn't prepared to put anything past her.

He couldn't trust her. She was back after eight years and he couldn't trust her, his own sister, the person who'd known him best. It was impossible. It was the truth. She was with *them*, and they were monsters.

The snap of Jackson's fingers and the sick sideward jerk of Emmanuelle's head repeated in his mind's eye, and Aristea's voice rang on repeat. *I think they killed Emmanuelle I think they killed Emmanuelle I think they killed…* Beneath the shock and ill-feeling, furious grief crept through his every cell. The desire to blow something up built quickly, and another memory surfaced: a drifter called Sean Glassner carrying Ana's dying body and dumping her on the muddy ground when he saw Renatus.

Furious grief flooding his cells, his aura, and a loss of control.

Lord Gawain didn't know about that part.

It didn't get to that this time, anyway, because Renatus's nerves responded differently today to his power. He inhaled sharply as white-hot pain, as searing as his fury, shot through the skin of his arms where his magic had been gathering, ready to cast. He hurriedly yanked up his sleeves. Thick black lines like poisoned veins were spidering through his skin, lighting his nerves with pain as they laced together and wove past his elbows, up his biceps, over his shoulders...

'Renatus! Let it go.' Was it just something he detected in Gawain's voice, or did he feel tendrils of the older man's worry? No one had ever seen Renatus lose control and lived to tell the tale, and few modern sorcerers had witnessed an actual burnout, which apparently Renatus had almost experienced earlier in the day. His blackened nerves and charred auric network – the usually invisible channels inside the body that move magical energy around – along with his almost zeroed energy stores were sure signs of his near miss, though he didn't remember what had happened. Lord Gawain was careful not to touch him. 'You need to calm down.'

'I'm trying,' Renatus bit out, and concentrated on breathing through the pain. With effort, he let the gathering energy disperse before he could do more damage to his nerves. Aristea had sustained a similar injury after casting a ward to protect a city square from a noxious wave of magic. But hers had been limited to just one hand, one forearm. What feat could Renatus have performed to do this to his whole body? 'It's just... Emmanuelle...'

'The others are with her,' the Seer assured him, calmer now that Renatus's energy wasn't building anymore. The black lines took longer to recede; Renatus let his sleeves drop, hoping the anarchists taking up stakeout positions couldn't see the marks from where they watched on. 'Fionnuala is doing what she can.'

Renatus failed to withhold a curse, emotion spiking again. 'Fionnuala? Did she come out? Did she see?'

He tried to extend his senses into the house to feel for his head of staff's distinctive presence but pulled back before he could find her. Could Nastassja read that, too? He couldn't be responsible for sharing an energetic map of everyone who was currently inside the house with the enemy.

Lord Gawain shook his head uncertainly.

'She went to ready Emmanuelle's usual room,' he said. 'Qasim met her on the way upstairs.'

Again, Renatus tried to breathe. His hands were still lined with fading charcoal-grey cracks and emotional regulation was not his secret power, so it was hard to do, but his mentor's words did help. He didn't want his childhood nanny to see the girl she'd raised on the other side of the fence. She'd helped him plan the funeral. She'd placed his letter on the casket on his behalf when he couldn't bring himself to attend. It was bad enough that he had to face this new reality – whether out of protectiveness or selfishness, he desperately wanted to keep Fionnuala free of it.

Lord Gawain was quietly watching the gate while Renatus got himself under control.

'I saw this,' he confessed. 'Months ago. I saw Morrissey House under siege.'

Renatus felt uneasy. Seers were the most common of the six classes of sorcerer, conduits of Fate and interpreters of some very sketchy messages. They foresaw future events and choices still to be made, as well as some of the consequences of different paths, though never all. Lord Gawain, along with three other Seer council members, was particularly powerful and perceived the webs of destiny that tied individuals and groups of people to specific places and points in time.

'I'm not sure this counts as a siege,' Renatus said, eyeing the crowd beginning to quieten beyond the gate. Jackson had arrived, calling out orders with the glee of someone too comfortable with undeserved leadership, and others were withdrawing from the gate to take up positions nearby. They didn't seem in a hurry to leave.

'Call it what you want,' Lord Gawain said heavily. 'They're not going anywhere. Weeks, months. An embargo, a chance to prove the magical world doesn't need our interventions. None of our other councillors can get in, and we can't get out. I just didn't know it would be *now*.'

He turned to look up the hill at the house, but his words kept ringing in Renatus's ears, threatening his newfound semblance of calm.

'Weeks? *Months*?' he repeated starkly. He was trying not to think about her but his apprentice leapt to his mind. A target for all their enemies, without him for *months*?! 'Aristea's out there!'

'Out where?'

The worried reply came from the gangly teenaged boy who'd just Displaced right beside them. Addison James was the tallest person on campus and, like the two girls holding each of his hands to hitchhike his jump through space, he was a close friend of both Aristea and Hiroko. Simultaneously, their attention slid to the commotion outside the estate.

'You shouldn't be out here,' Lord Gawain admonished immediately, beginning to shepherd them back toward the safety of the manor. 'You need to stay out of sight.'

Renatus's family home, too large for one person and a small housekeeping staff, was currently serving as the campus for the White Elm's first attempt at a magical skill-honing Academy. The best young sorcerers their world had to offer had been gathered at the start of the year to grow their powers through proximity to each other's magic and to tutor them in high-level skills like healing, scrying, spell-writing... talents severely lacking in their communities thanks to centuries of benevolent censorship and suppression on the White Elm's part.

Nothing like hindsight, especially given that the past year had been more challenging for their government than the past forty put together, and there were fewer competent sorcerers in their nation than ever before. Many of those who were, or showed promise, had been quick to side with Magnus Moira's enticing idea of free magic for all.

Since their arrival six months ago, the students had been almost painfully well-behaved, with most exceptions involving Aristea Byrne. Renatus had never seen any of the other teenagers answer back or disregard instructions given by a councillor. The relationship was not that of teacher and student; it was world leader and hopeful candidate.

So it initially surprised him when Addison James brushed Lord Gawain away and held his ground. He addressed Renatus staunchly and he could see they weren't kids anymore.

'Hiroko and Aristea came to help you,' he said. 'Did you see them?'

'They're together,' Renatus answered, hating that he couldn't be more reassuring. 'Hiroko got them out before anyone could hurt them. I don't know where they went.'

Iseult Taylor, the tiniest person on campus and the most promising of the students, frowned at that, unsatisfied.

'I thought you could always find each other, through your bond?'

Renatus resisted the urge to grab his hair and scream in frustrated rage at the unfairness. It *should* be that easy.

'It's complicated,' he said, with restraint, after forcing himself to swallow his feelings. Addison nodded once, ignoring catcalls from beyond the gate.

'It's been complicated here, too,' he said. His Australian accent sharpened with stress. 'Did she tell you? Some Magnus Moira bitch possessed Sterling and nearly burnt down your office.'

Renatus looked over his shoulder and met his sister's waiting eyes again, disappointed with himself. Aristea had warned him something was not right with Sterling. Last night he'd made changes to the magic woven tightly over the estate, and today, a powerful presence was able to slip through tiny gaps he'd left to steal Sterling Adams's body.

'Is she alright?' he asked immediately. The girl in question had been sleep-walking, weeks ago, when Aristea had come across her and recognised from the odd things she said that she wasn't the same person. Given that the estate couldn't be scried into by an outsider, he'd dismissed the possibility of a Haunting, but now he knew there was another Morrissey scrier alive and very capable…

'Aristea got her out, but she was kind of a wreck. Kendra's

with her now,' explained the other girl, who by process of elimination had to be Sophia Prescott if her twin Kendra was out of frame. Lord Gawain waved at them all again, bothered by the eyes of the anarchists outside the property.

'We can discuss this inside,' he insisted. They all began moving back toward the house. To the students, he asked, 'How did Aristea get the Haunter out of Miss Adams?' but it was Renatus who answered with the only logical reply.

'The pendant,' he assumed, and the Prescott girl nodded. 'It's a cursed object that locks the spirit inside the body and keeps other spirits out. I found it on one of my first days on the job and I, uh, kept it.' He cast an apologetic look to his leader but refused to apologise outright. His job, when it wasn't tracking dark magic and its practitioners, was studying illegal magic and dismantling unsafe or unstable spellwork, often anchored to physical objects. He hadn't expected to find genuinely useful cursed objects. 'In short, we all need one, *now*. If Nastassja–' it helped to call her that, to separate her from the girl he'd looked up to and adored '–can project her consciousness through the warding to take Sterling, she can do it to anyone. She can be any of us, with just a touch, and we may not sense her coming.'

'You didn't happen to withhold thirty of these illegal pendants?' Lord Gawain, ultimate line-toer and rule-follower, asked dryly. Renatus suppressed a frustrated sigh, coming to roughly the same total in his quick headcount of current residents. He tried to make himself think rationally, but it was difficult, especially with the slippery touch of another mind at the edge of his. Ana? He would have recognised her presence instantly a decade ago; now he could only assume, and fear it.

'All we need is a Crafter,' he reasoned, thinking hurriedly, hoping he could think faster than Ana could follow. 'They could copy the magic, anchor the copies to other objects.'

'We don't *have* a Crafter,' Lord Gawain reminded him, prompting another ungraceful swear from Renatus. They used to have three – Lisandro, Jackson, and later, Aubrey – and all of them had departed the council, enticed by the free magic movement, as those gifted with the ability to rework and create magic at its fundamental level would be prone to favour. Renatus had some experience with the process, but it didn't come to him as intuitively as to natural Crafters, the rarest of sorcerers.

'Yes, you do,' Sophia countered, a little affronted, and nodded at Iseult. Lord Gawain stopped in his tracks, realisation hitting him hard. The short statured Irish girl blinked her pixie-like eyes.

'You have three,' she corrected, and named two other students still inside. 'But I'm supposed to…'

Her gaze moved worriedly down the hill. She had negotiated to live at home with her family nearby and only attended classes on Thursdays. Just her luck, or maybe theirs, that Magnus Moira had made their move today of all days.

'Can you contact your parents?' Lord Gawain asked, implying telepathically. Everyone here knew that cell phones and other non-witch devices didn't work on the estate, surrounded by so much magic. Iseult nodded. 'Good. Tell them not to come for you, it's not safe. We'll look after you here until that blockade moves on. It might be some time,' he warned gently, then paused, distracted by telepathic conversation Renatus couldn't hear. The three teens looked at each other in ominous wonder.

'Kendra just said a few minutes ago that I'd be staying a while,' Iseult confirmed, mentioning their Seer friend. 'How can I help?'

'Find the Crafters and take them to Sterling,' Renatus directed, trying to fend off the presence attempting to infiltrate his thoughts. How many times had this happened in recent weeks, unnoticed? 'Don't take it off – she may be particularly susceptible. If any of you can replicate the magic in that pendant, you do it. I don't care what you have to do.'

Lord Gawain wasn't paying attention and so missed the knowing look in Iseult's eye as she nodded and Displaced away. Most of the magic Crafters were born to create was too bold and wild to fit within the White Elm's very limited scope of acceptability, and they were taught to restrain their power. To keep it clean. That restrained, rule-abiding magic was horribly inefficient by comparison to the styles that would have forged powerful and complex spellwork like the pendant. If they had to break some of those rules to get everybody in this house safe from his sister's influence, that secret was safe with him.

At least, safe from the good guys.

'Miranda says you're one of her top students,' Lord Gawain said to Sophia, who looked surprised to be addressed so forwardly. 'She and Teresa can't get here and we need help with Emmanuelle.'

'I don't... What happened?' Sophia asked, flustered. Renatus felt his insides twist at the mention of his friend. Dare he hope?

'Help with what?' he demanded. 'Is she–' He stopped himself abruptly, feeling the faintest flutter behind his eyes, like a tiny muscular spasm. *Sharing a mind, sharing eyes.* They'd never been able to do this as children, but she hadn't been undead back then, either. The feeling of vulnerability, of betrayal – from the theatre, from the last eight years – hit him hard, and before he could stop himself he'd already turned to the gate and screamed, '*Get out!*'

He must have backed it up with some mental force because outside on the gravel road, the lone figure of Nastassja took a surprised step backward. All over, his skin seared with the rush of emotion, and he searched his mind for that presence. If she was still there, she was hiding better.

Addison and Sophia had stepped away, too, and were watching him warily. Lord Gawain looked concerned, but tried to move things along.

'Qasim said it's a spinal injury,' he told Sophia, who was looking less than confident. 'Anything you can do...'

'Come on,' Addison said quietly, taking her hand. Renatus ignored them as they disappeared, and desperately took his mentor by the arm. The nervous glance down at where they made contact was harder to ignore.

'Emmanuelle?' he pressed, glad when Lord Gawain didn't shake him off. 'I can't feel her. I saw her go down...'

And he'd done nothing. He'd gone there for her but had been unable to act, his magic barred from him like never in his life. His wards disabled. His magic senses switched off. His powers, always reliable before today, neutralised. She'd still run for him, expecting him to protect her while she couldn't protect herself, but Jackson had caught up, and Renatus hadn't been able to stop him. Useless.

'Alive, but not good,' Lord Gawain admitted, his words the mildest form of bitter relief. Aristea and Hiroko might be dead by now, Declan might be dead, but Emmanuelle was not. 'Hopefully the students can do something for her – it's difficult for Miranda to diagnose from where she is.'

Yes, Germany was quite a way. Healers shared and used their magic through physical contact, making it extremely worrying to have two of their three Healers stuck on the other side of the stakeout. Not as worrying, though, as having their third one as the victim.

Lord Gawain's thoughts, blocked from Renatus's, were on a totally different track.

'Aristea hasn't contacted you?' he asked with concern. When the younger shook his head, he continued seriously, 'Qasim tells me she took the ledger from your office.'

That damn book. Renatus hadn't even wanted to *be* there at his uncle's penthouse, hadn't believed this ledger existed until Aristea convinced him just last night that such a record of Lisandro's illegal dealings might be real. Now everything was screwed up. Aristea was off the council's waiting list, expecting a *trial*, and everyone on the other side of that gate wanted to find her and take that book from her.

'She's making things worse for herself,' his mentor reminded him. 'Theft of evidence in her own trial? She already stole it once today, and we can't afford your uncle as an enemy. Not right now, while we're already divided.' He paused, listening. 'He's asked Oneida if you know about his bodyguard.'

'There was no bodyguard.' Not that he recalled.

Lord Gawain regarded him for a beat, then said, 'Could this be linked to her taking the ledger?'

'She only wanted to keep it from Nastassja,' Renatus guessed, his voice firm with certainty he felt rather than knew. Why else would she take it? 'She hasn't done anything wrong.'

'She wiped your memory with an illegal spell and is withholding information pertaining to a home invasion that resulted in another girl in hospital,' Lord Gawain countered flatly. Renatus swallowed his retort. It went down uncomfortably. Aristea wasn't withholding as much as everyone thought, and he felt like a coward to benefit from her silence. 'That much she's admitted to. So don't defend her. You don't know what she did, you don't even know what *you* did.'

The Seer eyed him with a frown, and Renatus dropped his gaze, ashamed. This was why Aristea had insisted on taking this fall, on letting the council believe she knew what had happened at Shanahan's earlier. It took the heat off Renatus and whatever he'd done to get into this near-dead state he'd woken in, effectively lighting her future with the council on fire to preserve his in the short term. He didn't know how long she expected it to last. As soon as Teagan Shanahan woke up, this could all fall to pieces.

'By rights,' Lord Gawain added, 'you shouldn't have left the estate today, either, but Aristea was made *explicitly* aware of her confinement and–'

'And good thing she didn't listen, or you could have lost four of us in that theatre,' Renatus shot back, feeling that slippery presence at the edges of his mind again, deeper this time. A cold shiver ran up his spine and he hurried to shut down his thoughts about Aristea. What was Nastassja looking for? How was she getting in through wards that had always protected him absolutely, and how was he going to keep her out? She seemed to simply ignore every measure he threw against her efforts. 'Can we not discuss this right now? Whatever I think on, she can see. Send Jadon to Angela Byrne's, and don't tell me about it unless something goes wrong.'

Renatus redirected his thoughts, hard, toward memories of his own sister as a child. Ana playing the piano in the ballroom, teaching him a song. The memory hurt but he hoped it distracted his sister from following the thoughts about Aristea's. He knew Aristea wouldn't have gone to Angela – he'd told her to go somewhere he wouldn't guess, an explicit direction he felt she was more likely to follow than "stay home, you're in trouble" – but knew that he wouldn't be the only one to look at her family home.

In his mind's eye, his sister's hand danced up the ivory keys and his followed; when he turned his real eyes to the figure outside the gate, he saw her chin lift and knew she'd seen the same.

The idea made his throat tighten. But the distraction had worked.

It must have been what she was waiting for. Nastassja broke formation and approached the gate, watching him the whole way. Intrigued, Renatus took a step closer. Lord Gawain caught his arm.

'That's not a good idea,' he warned as Renatus shook his hand away. 'She might look like your sister but she's a darkness you don't need. Don't give her what she wants.'

The reminder was well-intentioned but painful. 'And she's in my head whether I stand here or go talk to her. At least this way,' he added coldly over his shoulder, already walking away, 'I might find out *what* she wants.'

The feeling of his mentor's worried gaze on his back stung but he refused to turn around, and within a few steps he felt him Displace away into the house. Good, his senses were starting to settle. Barely. He felt overwhelmed, terrified. He was walking, alone, toward a stranger who looked like his older sister, and a dozen or so other strangers who, five minutes ago, had been trying to hurt him and his companions. And they would have been successful if Aristea and Hiroko hadn't been there. Magnus Moira held their positions – he heard Jackson call for them to do so – but eyes glittered in unfamiliar faces, curious and eager for a confrontation he wasn't in any state to give them. They'd seen him vulnerable, the White Elm's big power card, the weapon they no longer had to fear, and they were all high on the excitement of their near-kill.

Through the gate, they couldn't sense his low energy, but they might have before he got inside. He touched the ruby bracelet encircling his wrist and probed it for confirmation that its energy stores were available. Aristea, thoughtful to a fault, had half-charged it this afternoon and offered it as assistance for his recovery. Neither had expected him to genuinely need it. He'd been told so many times that Lisandro would never dare kill him, but today in the theatre with his godfather's minions grabbing him and no way of stopping them, he'd truly been afraid for his life. Maybe this was the purpose behind that show – breaking his reputation. If the goal was to dismantle the White Elm, it would go a long way.

Nastassja, who was unmistakably once Ana Morrissey, didn't hold her position, and her eyes didn't glitter with that feverish recklessness. Instead she looked like he felt. Nervous. Hopeful. Guarded. Sick. Sorry. Ana had been a fiery and volatile child, never able to control or hide emotions that seemed too big for any one person to carry around. She wore them now as she did back then. She reached the gate at the same time that Renatus did and stood opposite him like a warped reflection in a very broken mirror.

So much the same. So much different. Eight years had passed and she wasn't a girl anymore and he wasn't the little boy she no doubt remembered, either. They inhaled in shaky unison. He had a thousand–

'A thousand questions,' she finished, her voice hitting him like it did to hear it in the theatre a few minutes ago. A lifetime ago. She had the unfamiliar notes of someone who'd been living abroad all this time, but underneath, that Irish cadence they shared was hard to shake. 'I'll try to answer.' She smiled, some of her uncertainty falling away, replaced by something warmer. Pride? 'You're so grown up. Your hair… you grew it out. And you're so tall.'

Where to start? *Why? How?* Even articulating those questions threatened to break him, let alone the inevitably heartbreaking answers. He was aware of the gazes of the sorcerers on the other side and let his drift across their faces, memorising them. More than one man was missing a hand; he knew what they'd done to deserve that. It was spiteful and unbecoming but most certainly true that if he was at his full strength right now, he wouldn't have to hide behind this old gate. His nerves tingled uncomfortably with the flush of emotion he hid better than his sister ever could, and he looked past her at Jackson. Smug eyes were waiting for him.

It wouldn't do to have the black cracks burning under his sleeves lace their way up his neck with all these people looking on, so Renatus worked hard to keep a cap on his hatred. If he had his power, if this gate and its wards were open, if he wasn't supposed to be one of the good guys, there'd be little to stop him clicking *his* fingers like Jackson did to Emmanuelle. Except he wouldn't be snapping necks. He'd be setting people on fire.

All of them.

He dragged his attention back to Nastassja and took a step back from the gate. 'I don't think I need any answers from whoever you've become.'

She stepped closer to maintain their proximity, looking desperate.

'Ignore Jackson,' she urged, and he eyed her suspiciously. Her face was as he recalled, though older, more filled out. Her black hair looked at least as long as before, though it was difficult to tell, coiled atop her head, and she was as overdressed as ever. But she seemed less tall than he remembered – no doubt a perspective thing, since he'd grown considerably since he was fifteen – and her figure had changed to imitate their mother's silhouette. And her eyes were wrong. The warm brown she'd been born with had been replaced, somehow, with eerie green. She shot a quick glare at Jackson over her shoulder, a glare that said she knew him well and she'd talk to him about this later. 'I'm sorry about your friend. I didn't know she meant so much to you.'

'You're sorry?' Renatus repeated, incredulous. 'For what *he* did? Or for Lisandro turning a theatre full of fanatics on my apprentice?'

She'd come after Aristea before so it didn't much surprise him when her expression closed down at the other girl's name. She was jealous and possessive as a child, prone to aggressive tantrums when forced to share anything she perceived as hers by rights. He didn't remember her ever lashing out at him – though rose-tinted memories could blur a multitude of sins – but certainly toward their cousins, the Shanahan girls, and other society visitors' children.

'They weren't going to hurt her,' Nastassja muttered sourly. She visibly tried to shed her resentment when she shifted gears to ask, 'Where did she go with Uncle Thomas's book?'

'Like I'm going to tell *you*,' Renatus sneered at her, the brazenness laughable. He shut down any remaining worried thoughts about Aristea and gestured at the staked-out Magnus Moira followers watching on from their positions behind his sister. 'You're with *them*.'

'And you're with *them*,' she retorted, dropping her voice to keep it between them. 'The White Elm? They're against everything we were raised to believe. You should be standing on this side of the fence, Ren.' No one had called him that in nearly ten years. He was sure his face didn't react but his chest tightened and he must have acknowledged it in his thoughts, where Nastassja was still listening. She took the last step, right up to the gate. 'Whatever they've told you, you and I don't have to be enemies.'

'Fine. I'll come out when you send your little army away.'

She looked again at the people waiting in the wings, at Jackson, watching on.

'They won't go,' she murmured, and Renatus closed the gap to be able to respond at the same volume.

'Tell Lisandro to call them away from my front door, or I – and the White Elm – will interpret this as an act of aggression on the part of Magnus Moira,' he warned, but she was already shaking her head. He frowned. 'What? Do you expect me to believe Lisandro doesn't still jump at your whim, Ana Morrissey?'

The name he hadn't meant to give back to her slipped out and she smiled a little, wistful. He wondered how long since she'd last been called that. Then she swallowed whatever feelings it stirred in her.

'It isn't that simple,' she intimated quietly with another

guarded look back at her silent companions. 'It's exactly what it looks like. They are here to stay, and I can't move them. This is a war a long time coming, little brother. But it doesn't have to be that way for you and me.' She lifted her gaze to the house behind him, the house where they'd grown up together in a previous life. 'Let me come in and we can talk. There's so much to tell.'

'Let you in?' Renatus repeated. 'To the heart of the White Elm after your side just declared war on mine?'

'Do they own this house as well as you now?' she responded fiercely, hands clenching at her sides. Fiery indignation licked at the edges of his aura, more external emotion he could almost swear he felt rather than read in her posture or face. 'You let the White Elm decide who comes through the gate? It's ours.'

It was certainly true that, growing up, there would never have been any talk of harbouring the White Elm at Morrissey Estate. Family friend Lisandro's affiliation with the council was tolerated because he fed information back to their parents and worked to scale back the Elm's tendency toward raiding old families like theirs. But if Renatus had ever voiced an interest in joining? Generations of Morrissey magic had been invested in keeping prying eyes and figures of authority off this land – his serving on the council was a betrayal to his ancestry as serious as opening the gate to Nastassja would be to his sworn family.

'It isn't that simple,' he parroted finally.

His once-sister surveyed him in silence for a very long moment, eerie gaze holding his, and he felt her mind this time, a presence behind his eyes. Seeing what he saw, looking back at herself through his vision. It was the strangest thing. Together they watched her take the last step up to the gate and close her hand around one of the iron bars.

'Yes,' she said, 'it is.'

No one else saw; only the two of them. Her fingers wrapped around the cold iron, the stolen Elm Stone that had arguably started half this mess in full display on her ring finger in its new setting. But that was the least of Renatus's concerns. Her skin didn't welt like her companions'. The same way the magic of the house responded to Renatus, to his bloodline, the touch of her hand to the iron and her will was enough to unlock the impossible knotwork of spells designed to keep him – to keep any Morrissey – safe from incursion or unwanted visitor. Except the house didn't know she was meant to be dead. It didn't know she wasn't wanted. So the magic unravelled without complaint and the gate's latch softly clicked open.

Renatus felt his heart seize in his chest at this unexpected threat and the faces of everyone inside the house – elderly Gawain and helpless Emmanuelle and dear Fionnuala and all the students he was meant to protect – flashed through his mind in the wave of his panic. He should have anticipated this. He should have known this wasn't over.

Nastassja, Ana, whoever she was, tightened her grip on the iron post and, just as softly as the latch had opened for her, the keyhole clicked again.

Locked.

She took a step away again, point made.

'And no, it isn't,' she agreed quietly. She watched – through her own eyes, through his, he didn't know or care – as he anxiously grabbed the gate as well and shook it to check. It was indeed locked once again, nobody getting through, but *she could*. She'd been careful to make her show of power to him alone, keeping it from all of Magnus Moira, from Jackson. Why? Wasn't she on their side? Wouldn't she want them to have every advantage over him and the White Elm in this "war a long time coming"? Was she just biding her time? Or was she trying to communicate that she had no intention of being his enemy, as she'd said, and wanted him to see her restraint?

It isn't that simple.

Nothing ever was. Feeling overwhelmed and out of his depth, Renatus backed away and started back up the hill toward the house.

'Tell Aristea she won't be hurt if she brings us the ledger,' Jackson called, raising his voice to be heard as he kept walking. 'If she presents herself and hands it over, we'll let her inside with you. You can be together, safe. But this is happening. Might as well help it along, before we need to go looking.'

As nice a prospect as that was to his rising fears, Renatus only replied over his shoulder, with absolute confidence he did not feel, 'You won't find her, and I won't help you.'

'I'll be waiting,' his sister called after him, voice loaded with meaning that he didn't have the energy to decipher. She wasn't breaking in with her army, that much she'd demonstrated, and she'd said they weren't moving, so by that logic, the gate was staying closed. But the fortress he'd relied on was no longer safe. He was no longer the only key.

He wasn't the last Morrissey after all.

Sweat prickled behind his neck, under his hair. Everything was messed up. Emmanuelle... Declan, maybe... Half the council locked in here, the other half elsewhere, split up... Ana, not dead, on the wrong side of this brewing civil war... and Aristea, missing. Behind his eyes, a slithery presence he was finding harder to block, his sister was inside his head, able to see what he saw, know what he knew. As afraid as he was for his apprentice, he could not scry for her. He couldn't open his mind to hers and check in. He hadn't felt this alone since he'd lost his parents and Ana in the same afternoon, and the dark months afterward.

Elijah, teleporter extraordinaire, appeared beside him as he strode up the winding path toward the house. Like the other White Elm minds usually linked with his, the New Zealander's mental voice was silent, but he fell into step beside Renatus and asked him what there was to report.

'We need a constant watch on the gate,' he replied tensely as he walked, trying to outthink Nastassja, trying to come up with any workaround that might change this increasingly hopeless situation. 'We don't know what she's capable of, and they're settling in for the long haul. Do you have a pen?' he added abruptly, cutting off the beginning of an idea before his sister could read it.

'Alright.' Elijah materialised a ballpoint pen from elsewhere in the house into his outstretched hand. 'I'll take the first watch. You should visit Emmanuelle now that she's stable.'

'Why?' Renatus asked warily, taking the pen and rolling his

sleeve up without letting his eyes stray to what he was doing. He glanced back at the gate. Still closed. Nastassja had withdrawn to stand with Jackson. 'What's her prognosis?'

'Probable paralysis,' Elijah admitted after a reluctant pause, gesturing to the higher storeys of the old house. Stomach heavy as lead, Renatus left his side to trudge indoors. He pressed the nib of the pen onto his forearm as he walked, trying not to concentrate on the feeling of the ball rolling ink across his skin, or on the messy letters he was no doubt forming, or the subtle spell work he was weaving. He thought hard about Emmanuelle and what might be done for her, and seemed to feel Nastassja's attention stray from him, moving to the familiar features of her childhood home.

Message composed, eyes fixed on where he was going and *not* on his arm, he closed the spell and wiped his hand across the words, sending them away. He could only hope the recipient was alive, regardless of how many times today and in the past week he'd wished to strangle him, and that Aristea was not as predictable as he'd grown to assume. Or that she was. He couldn't decide. He'd told her to go where he'd never guess.

Which was perhaps why he was more disappointed than surprised when, on his way up the second staircase, his arm briefly burned and the reply came through. He chanced a quick glimpse down.

No, but kind of you to check in.

chapter four

Our plan was far from solid, but certainly stronger than what I'd come up with on my own. A day of idle sightseeing in Sapporo gave us time to talk through my options, whether my exile was temporary or for the remainder of the year. Each time I scried Morrissey House, I saw Magnus Moira sorcerers around the gate, occasionally swapping individuals out for others but never relenting on their presence all through the Irish night. My hopes for a quick resolution sank lower. Every time I felt that wavering pressure at the edge of my heavily warded aura, alerting me that someone, somewhere, was scrying for *me*, my mental image of returning through those gates faded a little more and my resolve to stay hidden hardened. It hadn't been a bad dream and nobody who wanted this stupid ledger had lost interest in finding it.

'Be certain that I am in position before activating the spell,' Hiroko reminded me several times as we browsed shops after lunch. My exhaustion was starting to set in, but my well-rested and ever-sensible best friend was on top of things. She handed me a strong takeaway coffee and sipped her own bubble tea as she led the way across the street and into a dense park. I recalled that she'd learned Displacement in parks like these, practising small Skips through space as a girl with her father, away from fearful, non-witch eyes.

'Or you'll know something's amiss, I know,' I replied, tasting the hot drink. It was stronger than I preferred, but I needed the jumpstart to my attentiveness for the next few hours. I could crash later. 'I'm almost surprised the council haven't come for you already.'

Almost, except I knew they had bigger problems to contend with. I let my mind's eye touch on the house; as usual I couldn't see inside but I could see the crowd sitting outside, little fires between pairs of fanatics as they enthusiastically conversed through the night's stakeout. Dawn had cracked not long ago. I wondered if Renatus had gotten any sleep. He'd have to be exhausted, but his yesterday was arguably worse than mine – plus he'd just dismantled the anti-dreaming magic cast over his house. The prospect of facing his demons in his sleep could never have looked less attractive than it did right now.

Once we were out of sight of pedestrians, Hiroko chose a damp park bench and waved her hand over it. The wood dried impressively in a puff of soft steam. The showy spell reminded me of Renatus, who wielded magic like it existed for his own convenience. Need a tissue? Materialise one. Rain cramping your style and your park bench? Dry it out instantly by super-heating the water molecules in the first few layers of timber. I hadn't developed my grasp of magic to be able to use it so playfully, focusing my studies on big stuff – defensive wards, scrying – but Hiroko had spent her time at the Academy learning a wider variety of spells.

I'd admit readily that she was always a better student than I was, more disciplined and studious, and further along in her learning journey when we first met.

'You are sure we have done this correctly?' she asked, practical as ever as she consulted the recipe we'd written out this morning on the back of a receipt. We sat down together and took the bowl from the backpack she'd given me. Most of the ingredients were already in there, the herbs and salts and petals all ground up the same way Declan O'Malley showed me, a plastic bag wrapped around it all to keep the mush from spilling out. I set it on the bench between us, feeling uneasy.

'No,' I confessed, 'but those are the exact steps, and these are the exact ingredients and exact amounts, for a spell that's worked at least three times. Twice on me, and twice *by* me, apparently successfully.' I looked up at her as she produced our most recent purchase. 'We do *not* have to do this if you don't want to risk it.'

'Of course we do,' she dismissed, tipping the magnetic hematite bracelet into her hand and squashing the paper bag into her coat pocket. 'I'm a loose end.'

'This is super illegal,' I made sure to remind her, though when she snapped the elastic and the stone beads scattered, I still counted them and lined them up on the wooden bench.

'Worse than harbouring a fugitive?'

Even though it was the furthest thing from funny, I lifted my gaze to hers. I was sure our smiles were mirrors of each other. She really was the best friend I could ever have asked for and I still couldn't tell you what I'd done to deserve her.

Someone's irritating attention brushed off my aura for the millionth time and I used a larger rock to smash the shiny grey stones into little powdery chips. I broke up more hematite than I needed, much of it falling between the slats of the bench, and carefully pinched the fine dust into my other palm to weigh before sprinkling it into the bowl.

'Now,' I said, wiping off my hands, 'all that's left is the new memory, the fire, and...' Careful to check no one was watching, I withdrew the knife from the backpack apologetically. Hiroko swung her own bag from her shoulders.

'And the hair,' she finished for me, producing a pair of nail scissors. 'We aren't in the highlands now.' She gave my knife a disdainful glance and shook her sleek hair over her face to get a look at what she was doing. 'I am certain that any genetic material would suffice—'

'Blood magic expert, are we?' I interjected slyly, though this, too, wasn't funny. The White Elm, with whom we'd both studied and who wrote and upheld all the laws we lived by, endorsed an energy-only magic style. Many of their policies in the past fifty years had been aimed specifically at eliminating exactly the kind of magic we were playing with. Neither of us were experts. Neither of our families would have let us try this at home.

But Declan O'Malley, the least trustworthy person I knew, had heavily insinuated that the council *practiced* this magic they'd outlawed, and though I knew his word was only as good as his motive, I'd had trouble shaking this possibility. It made sense – small time magical crimes, not worth hardcore punishments like stripping powers, exile in the Russian prison or manipulating the non-witch legal system to get them into a regular prison, needed a simple solution. Was the council really so hypocritical?

Dumb question. They'd placed Renatus in the secret position of Dark Keeper, and his *literal* job was to collect, study and stay apprised of dangerous and illegal magic. They'd kept this tradition despite that the role had more than twice the turnover of any other council position, and that more than half of history's Dark Keepers had burnt out, suicided or gone bad.

Would a council who'd put their own twenty-two-year-old prodigy on such a disastrous path even blink at a few little off-the-books memory wipes? Screw them.

'*–but,*' Hiroko continued, getting a lock between her fingers to minimise the damage to her newly cut style, 'as this is a very delicate spell, and as it's my mind we are tampering with, I am happy that we do it exactly as you remember.' I caught the clippings in my palm to add them to the bowl. Her dark, shapely eyes focused close on the freshly trimmed lock. 'Perhaps not *happy.*'

I let my own hair tip across my forehead, regretful of the rough chop I gathered I took with the knife yesterday. Almost double the length of Hiroko's, I had a lot of affection for my wavy brown hair and had spent many years growing it. Whatever happened at Shanahan's, it must have been bad for me to *hack my hair*.

We mixed the clippings in and Hiroko dropped the little paper scroll on top. We'd written out the new memory, or rather the conditions of the wipe – the time period to be hidden under a patch of forgetfulness in her mind – on scented notepaper from the depths of Hiroko's backpack and wrapped it in string, binding the intention. Such a slow but elegant form of magic-making. I hadn't had time to consider it before, or simply didn't recall thinking it, but there was really something beautiful to having all day to leisurely go about spell-weaving, getting it all just right.

The White Elm liked to call our kind sorcerers, channelers of clean, objective, tracible energy. Working this memory spell with

Hiroko, I felt like a witch.

The coffee was really kicking in as we rewrapped the bowl with the plastic bag. I felt oddly pepped and ready when Hiroko took my hand and began the series of jumps we'd agreed would be necessary to get to my destination. I clutched the bowl and held my breath as she pulled me into that slippery, clingy blackness on the other side of reality.

It always held on just that fraction too long to be confident you were going to survive the experience.

Our feet landed in some alley, and the first breath of air I drew in was smoggy and humid. Hiroko turned to close the invisible hole we'd left in space and I looked up at skyscrapers that blurred into dirty low clouds. We didn't stay long; yesterday's haphazard travel behaviour had been successful in deterring attention from other Displacers, who could sense big jumps if they were on the lookout for one. Little Skip, cover, little walk, little Skip, cover... The sun crept back across the sky with every leap into a new time zone, until we'd rewound the whole day and emerged into an Irish morning somewhere in the south.

The end of our road together, for the time being, and we were, ironically, at the end of some dirt road, surrounded by farmland, outbuildings and beside us, a green post box. I inhaled the thick smell of the place, so different from the smoky air of the French town we'd just left, and finally dropped Hiroko's hand as I turned on the spot, getting my bearings.

'Dublin is sixty kilometres in this direction,' Hiroko advised with a precise gesture between two distant barn things, bearings never lost. She turned and nodded to her left. 'Renatus's house is two hundred, two hundred ten, maybe, almost due north.'

I had no intention of going back there, however I might want to. I unwrapped the bowl for the last time and looked dubiously at the mush of ingredients with the little paper scroll slowly soaking up moisture in the middle. I felt deep unease and had to voice it.

'Look, are you sure...? I mean, if I screw this up–'

She replied by hugging me tightly, wrapping both arms around my neck and shoulders and holding me close. I returned the embrace, tears stinging my eyes as I grasped her coat. I knew it was the right thing, but I so, *so* badly didn't want her to leave. I didn't want to risk damaging her mind. I didn't want to break any more rules. But more than any of this, I didn't want to be alone.

'I'm scared,' I confessed into her shoulder in my tiniest whisper. I was so close that I felt her swallow, fortifying her voice.

'Me, too,' she said, 'but don't be. You are strong and capable and resourceful. Do you think Renatus would have sent you away if you were not? Would your sister leave you at the school if she did not think it?' She pulled away and held my shoulders supportively. 'Have you not heard? You are formidable.'

I snorted, adequately distracted by the ridiculousness of her claim. Despite my efforts with sai training and my studies, I didn't think I'd hit any level close to "formidable", though the legends that had sprung up around my name and the number of high-level scriers still looking for me suggested it might be a matter of how the story was told.

'Well, if everyone is saying it, it must be true.' I took a hesitant breath and tried to channel some of the confidence Hiroko and my other favourite people seemed to have in me. I held out the bowl. 'Shall we break some more rules?'

She smiled the familiar, sly smile I was going to miss immensely. Before yesterday, I hadn't seen her in weeks and weeks, but the intensity of the last twentyish hours had reminded me how much she meant to me.

'Why not?' she agreed, removing the string necklace she wore over her head. I raised an eyebrow.

'There are like a hundred good reasons why not.'

'I will not remember them,' Hiroko said with a shrug, and I groaned at the reminder. If I got this wrong, the result would be just a little short of melting her brain. She held out the string with its crumpled paper crane. 'Aristea, we have few choices. There is no value in you hiding if someone like me, with minimal telepathic training, knows where you are. The White Elm will contact me soon. It is better I have nothing to share, and that they move on quickly, before other factions can take note. You have constructed the spell exactly as you remember. You have sent the recipe to Renatus...' She pulled the envelope from her pocket and poked it through the post box slot before I could change my mind. We hoped he'd be able to reverse-engineer the spell. 'You have even safeguarded my house, and I am grateful.'

'That was nothing,' I muttered, because of course I had accompanied her earlier today and coated the building in wards. No one but me was going to see inside, and I'd know immediately if someone magical was trying to breach the place. I'd gotten the idea from Emmanuelle, who'd instructed me in wards at the Academy.

'You have done everything already to protect me,' my friend explained, 'and now I must protect you. It will be okay.'

She placed Garrett's precious paper crane in my palm. I could feel its warmth from her body, but also its magical afterglow. Over breakfast, she'd meditated on the memory she'd be giving up, writing details into the folds of the aging paper, and now I'd be taking it with me. Keeping it safe. I cast a tiny ward over it, sealing her impressions inside where my feelings couldn't alter them.

'I'll take care of this,' I promised, mirroring her watery smile. Briefly, she linked her little finger with mine. Our silver rings clinked together. Last time she left me, I was too selfish to say what I should have. '*Sayōnara.*'

'Be careful,' she insisted, and then she Displaced away, leaving me alone at that dead end in the middle of nowhere. In my mind's eye I watched her trek back across the world for a few minutes, covering each Displacement as she went. I watched her land in the parking lot under her building. Exactly as we'd planned, she let herself into the apartment she shared with her dad, locked the door behind her, and went to her bedroom.

A breeze whipped around me in Ireland while I watched Hiroko move a few items in Japan, then settle herself at her desk with a novel. She removed the bookmark, placed it deliberately on the desktop, and flicked back a few pages.

She looked up. She couldn't see me, but she knew I could see her. Everything was now as it was at two-thirty yesterday afternoon in her bedroom, before she'd come to Morrissey House to comfort me, before the ambush in the theatre, before our escape and everything that had happened since. We were winding back the clock by exactly one day. Sure, she'd question where the day had gone, how it was suddenly Friday when she'd thought she was living Thursday, but it was, we'd agreed, the best point in time to reset her memory to. Getting days mixed up was less confronting than escaping a riot with a friend and then waking up at your desk with no idea of the outcome. We wanted to minimise digging, let the covered memory settle so she could go back to normal life.

'Thank you,' I murmured, summoning the magic, weaving my intentions through the mush in the bowl and the words in the scroll and the string that held it shut. Preparing for what I hoped was my only high-level crime for the day. 'Thank you for everything.'

I *pushed* the energy gathering in my hands through the copper and ignited the spell. In a violent little puff that made me start, the contents of Declan's bowl lit on fire, quickly burning itself out.

On the other side of the world, Hiroko Sasaki blinked. In my hands, thin tendrils of grey smoke sailed upward. I watched Hiroko anxiously. She was still, frozen. Gods, what if I'd broken her?!

But then she frowned at her page and checked the one after it, finding where she'd been up to, and settled back in her chair to keep reading.

'Thank you,' I exhaled, not sure who I was talking to, and after a few minutes of observing her seeming perfectly normal, I released my view of her. Scrying was natural to me, now that I'd tapped into the latent talent, but it still drew on energy I was low on. I shook the smoky remainders of the memory spell out of the bowl into the grass, criminal evidence as it was, and dropped the bowl back into its plastic bag. I'd clean it later.

For now, I had a plan to enact. I looped Garrett's crane around my neck for good luck and tucked it under my clothes.

'Stage one,' I murmured, checking my wards were secure before my first jump on my own. I mean, I'd done it before, but not since running away with Hiroko. I had a spotty record with teleportation, preferring to rely on better Displacers, so I allowed myself the time to breathe through my anxiety at taking this step without her. Concentrating on the Fabric that she saw intuitively as a Displacer, I found it and took hold with my mind. It's a complex matter of choosing a destination and bringing the two points in space together, forcing the formation of a wormhole that connects the two places through the void.

The Fabric split at my prompt and I made myself swallow a deep breath – I still didn't know if there was air in the void, had forgotten to ask Hiroko.

The grass and outbuildings of my country setting slipped away.

The void slid over me, or maybe I through it, I was never sure.

It lasted too long. The slick blackness of nowhere spanned on and on, and panic seized my chest. You could get lost in here, never land on the other side, never be found, like Sean Glassner…

My foot hit solid ground and the world emerged, or I emerged into it. I inhaled hard and stumbled forward, out of the wormhole, and let space close behind me.

Ugh, I was never going to get used to that.

Uncomfortable as it might be, nothing could beat Displacement on convenience. I was standing in someone's green backyard, between a whitewashed garden shed and a tall wooden fence I couldn't quite see over. Out of sight of the house, out of sight of the street, but it didn't matter. My heart leapt with excitement to see that non-descript shed up so close.

I remembered helping to paint it.

'Angela,' I whispered, hovering my hand over the wood panels of the boundary fence. There was magic threaded into this fence that wasn't there when a different version of me first moved here and the street's residents pitched in to get our elderly neighbour's home ready for sale so he could move into an aged care facility. Carefully I felt out the new spell work, but it was quickly obvious it was powerful warding, anchored into the ground and multilayered, and whose impeccable work it was. 'This better mean you're still alive, Emmanuelle.'

I felt no change in the magic as I climbed the fence – Emmanuelle Saint Clair, wards extraordinaire, would never weave a hyper-sensitive protective web over my house that treated *me* like an outsider – and I perched on the top to get my first view of my home in months.

The flat Angela had been renting for us since our parents and older brother died was quite tiny, or maybe I'd just spent too long living in Renatus's stupid-huge, four-storey manor. Stupid because the Morrisseys hadn't had more than two children per generation going back at least two hundred years, so it wasn't like they needed the space. Ange and I hadn't needed much space; this block was so small that when I pushed off the fence into the yard, it was only five paces to the back door where I froze, hand raised to knock.

My sister was inside. Safe and oblivious. I closed my eyes and let my forehead touch the door, heart aching with longing. I could sense her, a glowing presence on my mental radar, just metres ahead of me. In the kitchen. Possibly steeping tea. Watching the end of the morning news, which I could hear through the door.

I *wanted* to knock. I hadn't seen Angela in person since March. She'd be so overjoyed to see me; she'd probably take the day off work to spend it together. It would be wonderful.

But it would also be sabotage. Renatus told me to go where he'd never guess, and this was the *first* place anyone who knew me would look. I couldn't stay. It was as dangerous for Angela to have me around as it was for Hiroko, except at least Hiroko could defend herself. If I let Angela know I was here… I touched the scar running down the side of my face. I'd lost my peripheral vision when I'd been struck in the eye with a bad spell, and though I'd learned to live with the impairment, I'd never found a way to explain the situation to Ange. If she saw this, I'd have to tell her what happened. She'd never let me leave.

Eyes still tightly shut against my reality, I extended my senses beyond the house, out into the street, into the neighbouring houses, as far as they went before I felt the stretch, and I brushed the edge of another familiar presence. This one, unlike my naïve sister, was warded, but not as well as I was. Tuned into emotionally energy more than most sorcerers, I detected his wired mix of anxious boredom. Only someone who knew him and knew to expect him would have picked up on his presence.

My quiet "thank yous" were not done for the day. Of course Renatus would not leave my family unprotected. Jadon, one of the few White Elm councillors even younger than my master, was nearby, holed up alone in a cottage further down the street. Perhaps the owners were away. I didn't care how he'd managed to secure the proximity; I was just grateful, even if his presence was just as much about catching me as it was about protecting Angela from becoming collateral damage.

Jadon wasn't a natural scrier, but he was a Telepath. I had no way of reliably shielding my sister's thoughts from him if she saw me. He'd be here in under a minute. He'd have to bring me in and that didn't suit me at all. I liked Jadon and didn't want to put him, myself, or my sister in that position.

I opened my eyes and let my gaze fix softly on the tidy herb garden where the spare key was buried, but I wasn't really seeing. My attention was inside, watching Angela in my mind as she perched on the sofa to tie her sneakers. She was dressed as I'd expected, loose shirt and tight sports leggings, earbuds dangling ready around her neck. Her fingers deftly wound shoelaces into bows while she watched the news story about a decommissioned heritage theatre in Belarus burning down yesterday. Some of those free magic enthusiasts losing control of their ill-considered spells, perhaps? My sister's eyes, bluey-green like seafoam, appeared concerned, though she couldn't possibly know what had happened. She switched the screen off, then picked up her mobile phone to compose a quick text message. She wandered to the front door as she typed, stretching out her neck in preparation for her run, grabbing her house keys without looking.

I'd counted on this morning ritual of hers, knowing she'd be leaving at precisely six-thirty for at least half an hour, rain or shine because she was a crazy morning person, but I still regretted it immensely to see her pocket the phone, open the front door and check her high golden ponytail like she always did before she left the house.

I followed her energy down the street for her warm-up, and waited until I felt Jadon's attention shift to her too before I hurried to the herb garden. The soil was moist with dew, and my fingers found the peppermint tin exactly where we'd buried it.

I doubted my very responsible sister had ever locked herself out. Like most spare keys, it was in case either of us forgot or lost our own one, but she was neither forgetful nor prone to losing things. It was buried here for my benefit, like nearly everything Angela did. Shaking it out of the tin and unlocking the back door, catching the screen as it swung predictably toward the wall where it liked to slam, I felt a wave of guilt.

I was breaking into my own house. I was sneaking in while my sibling was out. This was wrong.

Some scrier's attention bounced off my aura and my own mind's eye skimmed automatically through the other places I was concerned about. Angela was jogging, music turned up loud. Hiroko was still reading at her desk, oblivious to how instrumental she'd been to me in the past day. Renatus was unscryable, of course, but I got a good view of the encampment outside his gates. And my attempts to scry into Teagan Shanahan's hospital room were still met with an image of her closed door. I so badly hoped she was okay and that whatever had happened to her wasn't truly my fault.

Everyone I cared for was in some awful situation I regretted deeply. My family was the one exception, and missing Ange for a bit longer was a worthwhile price for keeping her safe.

Resolved, I slid the key out of the lock and went inside, determinedly avoiding anything that would give me pause – photos on the walls I'd love to gaze at, rooms Angela had repeatedly rearranged. In case she shared my talent for picking up impressions, I resisted touching anything I didn't have to. I went straight for my bedroom, which she'd left nostalgically untouched, and raided my drawers and wardrobe for clothes and the real prize: my soon-to-expire, never-used passport.

On my way out, I might have paused a little in the doorway of Angela's bedroom, where I could just detect her perfume on the cold still air of our empty little house.

chapter five

Stage two was more difficult. Hiroko, impromptu financial advisor, had insisted that this top my list of priorities, so with bus money I'd found in my drawers, I was two towns over by the time the banks opened a few hours later.

Displacement is convenient and fast, but if I could avoid that clingy, cold grip of the void and had hours to waste, I was happy to take the bus.

Even still, I was third in line to be seen by the teller in the beautifully refurbished foyer, and in the extra time waiting I counted six attempts to scry me. I was sure I felt the eyes of the security guard who'd opened the doors, as well as the lens of the camera in the corner, and the anxiety I'd been keeping largely at bay began to build.

I really didn't think I was going to get away with this. I had no right. Everyone here knew it.

When the teller called, 'Next please,' it took all my false confidence to smile, step forward and place the stapled photocopy on the counter.

'Good morning,' I said, heart hammering in my chest at the brazenness of this move, 'I'd like to access my account.'

It took a lot of explaining and the teller called her manager over to take me into another office so she could continue serving proper customers. There, I sat as calmly as I could in the plush modern seat opposite his desk while I explained again what I wanted and he pored over the document I'd taken from Renatus's office.

The one that had infuriated Nastassja.

The one that identified me as his heir in all respects, and entitled me to act on his behalf in legal and financial matters. When I'd signed these documents on my eighteenth birthday, he'd said it was for insurance, but this was much more than that. Why he'd give me this much power and access, I did not know for sure, though I suspected it was about his mother's cousin, Thomas Shanahan, who had tried in the past to use family tragedies to control the Morrissey fortune. Even in death, should that befall him, Renatus didn't want his villainous uncle to best him.

Mature, I know, but Renatus was like that. Let's say strategic.

And rich. Holy hell, his family had accumulated some *serious* funds, as I understood it, through their services as spies and from brokering sales of illegal magic between other sorcerers. I'd seen some of the numbers before, in storage boxes, but those statements were old. Renatus didn't have anything to spend his money on except food and paying staff – he handled most property maintenance with magic, he never holidayed or dated, and his inexpensive hobbies involved hunting bad guys, plotting in his office and playing around with cursed objects – so the accounts just sat there. And grew.

It seemed a well-known account to the bank staff, enough that they made me sit and wait while they exchanged meaningful glances. The bank manager eventually confirmed that they'd received the same paperwork back in July, and my passport, though old, showed I was the same as the person named in the document, but it was bank policy to require more than a single item of identification – especially when trying to access the kind of money I'd walked into. They should have sent me away, but there must have been some understanding around this secretive client, because they didn't.

'Do you perhaps have a driver's licence?' the manager asked hopefully. 'A learner's permit?'

I shook my head. 'I don't drive.'

I mean, I could *drive*, if push came to shove. Angela had been giving me lessons, but true to form, my life as a slack student extended back to a point well before my time at the Academy.

I'd never gotten to taking the test or putting in an application. Buses had gotten me around just fine, and my indulgent sister and aunt had been on call when I'd been stranded after finishing work late or something. It hadn't seemed like a priority. Yes, I was regretting past Aristea's lethargy right about now.

The bank manager sighed and rearranged the papers on his desk for the twentieth time.

'The thing is, it's bank policy…'

His fourth iteration of the bank's policy was interrupted by a sharp knock at the office door, accompanied by a highly strung employee.

'Uh,' she said eloquently, glancing between me and her boss, '*Mr Sullivan* and his associate are here about the Morrissey account?'

Did she seem more nervous when she looked at me? And did the manager's unease skyrocket at that name before he quickly got it under control?

'Show them in,' he encouraged the employee, pasting a quick smile over his face. I sat forward with interest, trying to place that name. It didn't take me long. Martin Sullivan, the same friendly lawyer I'd met on my birthday, strolled in and spotted me immediately.

'Miss Byrne,' he said comfortably, 'very nice to see you again.'

But he wasn't alone. I didn't detect his companion until Mr Sullivan was already shaking my hand warmly, and then two polished shoes clipped through the doorway after him. Recognising the self-assured energy, I turned to behold a slick foreign detective who could blow my cover in an instant.

'We're sorry we're late,' Gabriel Winter said before I could decide whether to bolt. He swiftly introduced Mr Sullivan to the bank manager as representing both the client and the law firm that had filed the paperwork, and they confirmed they'd had dealings together before, and everyone shook hands. Winter managed to avoid giving his name or any explanation for his presence, and like oil, their attention slid straight over that detail. I didn't detect any magic to prompt that. The banking staff seemed to genuinely not want to know. 'We understand there's an issue confirming Miss Byrne's identity?'

The bank manager looked only briefly surprised, then nodded with a glance at me. He thought I'd arranged this. Not sure when I was meant to have made that phone call, yet here they were, supposedly on my side. He accepted it. I wasn't so ready to do the same.

'That's her,' Martin Sullivan stated automatically while I sat slowly back into my seat, warily watching the newcomers, two men I wasn't aware knew each other. Did Renatus know? Wholly non-witch Mr Sullivan presented the manager and me with a business card each, and rolled out his copies of the paperwork I'd signed. 'Aristea Byrne has been added to this account. I can confirm that my client wishes every affordance be made to accommodate the needs of his heir.'

Everything suddenly happened a lot faster. Falling over themselves to oblige, the bank staff disappeared with Mr Sullivan to process things while I turned the card in my fingers, finding a handwritten post office box address on the back. I spread my attention out thinly, far beyond the card. No other sorcerers in my vicinity. No change at the gates to Morrissey House to indicate they were coming for me.

'You're in league with Renatus's lawyer now?' I asked Winter cynically when we were left alone, tapping the card on my knee. Renatus was going to flip out. 'Any other part of his life you'd like to infiltrate while you're looking for ways to fulfil your daily quota for pettiness?'

The only Avalonian I'd ever met smiled at the floor, an expression without any warmth.

'Is it possible you're vastly overestimating the interestingness of the man you call your master?' he wondered aloud. Bank staff walked straight past the open office door without taking note of either of us. In the normal mortal world, I wasn't that attention-grabbing unless you saw my scarred face, but Gabriel Winter, with his expensive suit, sharp eyes, unlined face and shocking white hair, was quite distinctive. 'Tipping off Mr Sullivan seemed the most effective means of helping you.'

'Why would you want to help me?' I asked. He hated

Renatus, and the feeling was intensely, civilly mutual.

'Avalon and the White Elm are allies.'

Not an answer. I fidgeted with the business card, eyeing the exit, contemplating my situation. He was right, they were allies, which meant he would probably report my position to Lord Gawain at the first opportunity. But they were also strained, strange allies of necessity, with the isolated island nation prone to spying on White Elm citizens and keeping secrets of varying significance. He'd kidnapped a witness to the Prague attack to give evidence at a trial and seemed to have been instigating a breakdown in relations between White Elm and Valero after the death of their shared councillor Anouk, only to turn on a dime at the end and provide illegally obtained surveillance that saved that alliance.

Not the most trustworthy ally, you understand, and not someone I expected to be very helpful.

'I'm not White Elm,' I said finally, testing the waters. I didn't know how much he knew, or what he wanted. He nodded, drifting silkily over to the manager's desk to pick up a glass paperweight as if out of interest.

'I am aware,' he agreed. 'I am aware of many things, Apprentice Byrne, including the sheer number of people you may be hoping to avoid, friend and foe alike, to keep that pesky old book safe.'

His knowing gaze lifted to my face, and I felt my hand tighten on the armrest of my chair. I had been working on recovering my tact, but Renatus's dislike of the Avalonian had long since soaked into me.

'Why are you here?' I asked bluntly. Outside the door, banking staff were in conversation, and I didn't know how long I had. Winter's bland smile widened. Always so smug.

'Lady Miranda reached out to us, through our friends at Valero, asking for our help in finding you. They're all indisposed with this unfortunate Magnus Moira mix-up, and worrying about their missing council apprentice, lost out in the world. Not so lost, it turns out.'

My stomach felt cold. My whole plan, ruined, by this prissy jerk.

'I don't know what–'

'No one knows you're here,' he drawled, his usual cool calm as infuriating as ever despite the relief his claim brought. 'If your next pointless question is to ask how I found you, I'll remind you I'm a detective, and as a former citizen, Renatus is a person of interest to my nation. Naturally, I am aware of where he banks, and which law firm his family employs. Our scriers saw you depart Morrissey House. The number of places you might choose to go is limited by your minimal life experience and very few meaningful connections.'

A reminder that I was all but friendless and helpless in this world, and that I was even more predictable than I'd imagined. Great. I was still playing with that card, and I must have touched a patch of it I hadn't yet, or perhaps I was just distracted.

Thin hands… Detective Winter, writing the address…

I flicked Sullivan's business card in the air with all the disdain I could muster.

'Now I see why Renatus likes you so much,' I deadpanned. I eyed the card; he'd caught it in mid-air with a twitch of his finger. It hung, suspended, in the space between us, along with a lot left unsaid. I decided to finish clearing the air. 'Are you telling him where I am?'

I mean, he'd have to, right? Gabriel Winter idly turned his hand; the card twirled in the same direction, just as casually. I sensed a carefulness in his next words.

'I'm not sure how much he's told you about Avalon,' he said slowly, 'and I'm not sure how much of what he's told you is *true*. The island is home to most of the world's best Seers. Advice that emerges from their communion with the Fates informs the Steward's decisions. Some of it seems questionable, but it is always accurate. This morning's advice was that the preservation of your estrangement from the White Elm council, at this time, is more important than the terms of our alliance with them. As you can imagine, it was surprising advice. But we are not the Fates.'

I stared at him, processing that. 'Did you just say that keeping my location a secret from the council after they asked you to find me matters *more* than abiding by a centuries-old, legally binding agreement?'

'Some of the advice is questionable, but it is not our place to voice those questions.'

'Your whole society acts on the advice of these Seers?' It sounded like a terrible way to conduct life, if my experience with Seers was anything to go by. Their understanding of what mattered seemed warped, too many different outcomes and consequences for too many participating parties moving around in different futures. Maybe nobody was meant to know as much as they did, let alone have to decide whether "right" meant best for an individual who deserved a good outcome, best for the most, or best for the self and those they loved. I didn't know anyone else from Avalon, but the impression I'd gained from Winter and what I'd heard about their culture gave me a good idea as to whose interests their Seers served. 'When you say it matters *more* than the alliance, how does Avalon benefit from me staying off the council's radar? And how will it disadvantage the council?'

'Questions a wiser apprentice might have asked before running off with the evidence her council needed to repair their alliance with Valero,' the detective noted delicately, and I narrowed my eyes. He plucked the lawyer's business card from the air and held it out to me. 'Suffice it to say that the White Elm has a challenging path ahead of them regardless of your actions, and none of that is your fault. I was told this morning to find you and to make sure you had what you needed to stay on your own path, and that's what I'm doing. My duty. I'm sure you're doing the same.'

It was maybe the most straightforward the detective had ever been with me, and the sense of honesty he was giving off prompted me to warily accept the card.

'What's the address?'

'I've been out of this world for some time but I'm sure they aren't going to hand you a card today. You're welcome.'

The manager and Mr Sullivan bustled back in, all much more chipper now that the right papers had been put in the right in-trays and the right hands had been shaken. The stack of cash I'd requested withdrawn – based on a generous number Hiroko and I found in a web search at an internet café – wouldn't be ready until late Monday, and as Detective Winter had predicted, the bank card needed to be posted out. With him watching on, I gave them the post office box address, and he procured a key from his pocket and slipped it to me. I thanked him without thinking. He gave me a sidelong look of wry surprise that said more than I liked about his opinion of Renatus's general lack of diplomacy.

'Maybe there's hope for you yet.'

The manager had me sign a few things and let me withdraw a more reasonable amount for the weekend. Mr Sullivan stayed for the remainder of my bank visit, overseeing the staff's excessive helpfulness, and together with Gabriel Winter, saw me out.

'The Morrissey family is a valued client,' the lawyer told me as we stepped out into the sun. 'Please call the number on that card if there's ever anything more I can do for you, Miss Byrne.' He turned to Winter and shook his hand. 'Thank you for the tip, Mr Winter. Appreciated.'

The frosty smile I associated with him summoned enough brief warmth to fool a stranger into thinking he wasn't a horrible person, and Mr Sullivan got in his car and drove off. I waited for him to turn a corner before looking suspiciously up at Avalon's liaison.

'Who does he think you are?'

'Your business partner,' he answered without hesitation. I raised my eyebrows, about to ask why the lawyer would believe such a ridiculous cover story. He knew I was eighteen. 'He represents much more dangerous people than Renatus Morrissey – he knows better than to ask questions.'

I tried not to reflect on the kind of people Mr Sullivan worked with, or what kind of people he, and the bank, assumed Renatus and I were. I extended a hand to Winter.

'Well, partner, I think our business ends here.'

He smiled his cool smile and accepted the handshake. 'I doubt that very much. Fate has business plans for us both, I am sure.'

He Displaced away. He didn't offer me a way to contact him if I needed it and I was glad. It was bad enough that I'd needed help from him in the first place. After a glance up and down the street, I opened my satchel to admire the envelope of money inside. Time to buy myself some lunch.

And that's the story of the day I got rich. You wouldn't think it, but it was also the day I first experienced sleeping under a bridge.

The nights were cooling down so I quickly regretted the choice, but didn't see a better option that satisfied my paranoia. There were two hotels in town, and Thomas Shanahan, the man who'd placed a price on my head, owned a chain of hotels across the country and Europe. His sons owned several more. Except the big one in Belfast where the family was based, I didn't know the name of a single establishment they owned, and until I did, waltzing through a hotel door seemed unwise.

Cars rumbled noisily over the bridge as I settled against one of the concrete supports. It was sturdy but the pillar still vibrated with every passing vehicle, making me nervous. I holed up in what passed for a corner, ensuring no one could sneak up on me, and worked new wards, fixing them to the location. These wards were a relief, drawing energy from the earth rather than from me, and allowed me to release some of the other shields I'd been powering all day. No one would be able to scry me, see me, sense me or hear me… provided I remained right here.

I silently thanked Emmanuelle for the thousandth time for her instruction in this area, and wished desperately that I had a way of finding out what had become of her.

I arranged my clothes and backpack as blankets and pillow on the gravelly ground, glad that Angela couldn't see me. She'd be mortified. Past me, in fact, would be mortified to see me now, virtually homeless, technically on the run, literally falling asleep under a bridge. As my heavy eyelids dragged down, I fetched my sai blades from the satchel – it seemed prudent to sleep with weapons close by if you had them, especially if you were sleeping under a bridge and people were hunting for you – and the ledger. My clumsy gloved fingers flicked through the pages, hopeful, but they were all blank, as before.

'You are not worth all this trouble,' I grumbled at the book, and hugged it close as I finally, blissfully, passed out.

You wouldn't think the ground under a bridge is that

comfortable, and it's not, but if you're exhausted enough, turns out you can sleep almost anywhere.

Seashells on a distant beach…

A tropical rain shower in a humid jungle… death, bodies, trees blasted bare…

Two hands on a glassy ward, the wrong side…

A ring of unimaginable stored power changes hands…

Signatures…

Opulent hallway, vault-like door… screaming, panic… magic lacing up tensed arms, illuminating skin… another arm blocking my path… 'No! Don't touch him!'…

Rain lashes the windows… lights flicker, a hand grabs mine, too tight… terror, cracks above us… outside, the tree falls… no escape… the roof caves in under countless branches, upstairs furniture falls through onto a glass dome… thunder rolls…

I sat up, gasping. I opened my eyes to rattling iron supports and cracked cement about a metre from my face. Panic clutched my chest, personal wards sprung from my skin and I automatically reached for the mind connected to mine.

The door was firmly closed and Renatus was silent.

Oh, right. Bridge, isolation, fugitive times. I sighed as the memory of the last day or two rushed back, and I let my eyes adjust to the gloom of my hideout. I'd slept right through to morning, and woken, disorientated, to the loud ambling of a truck over my bridge. Not thunder. No killer storms.

'You said somewhere you'd never guess,' I murmured, missing Renatus intensely in that moment. I'd like to say my instinct to check with him was purely concern for him, but in reality, however hard I'd been working to equal him, to be strong enough to match him and protect him from the path he didn't even know he was on, my automatic response to fear and loss of control was still to reach for *his* protection.

Kind of pathetic.

Anyway, that needed to change if he was going to be off-limits for the next umpteen days or weeks. I'd survived my first night without a roof or bed, and there were plenty more to come. I felt stiff and cold, but also rested. Powering fewer wards had probably helped in that department, lending weight to the argument that I should look for somewhere more permanent to hide out until this all blew over.

First, I needed to get out of Ireland. Regular Displacement without the option to restitch what Fabric I disrupted was non-preferable, especially as I inched closer to my seekers. Every time I used magic, I was leaving a mark on the energetic world that could potentially be followed. In Sapporo with Hiroko, lost in crowds of strangers, we'd agreed the best place to hide from any hunter was wherever the hunter did not have home advantage, or better yet, where I did. For me, that was in the mortal world. I grew up aware of magic, but living the non-witch life – homework, cars, cartoons on television… The experiences of the people hunting me (that I'd met – I was working off assumptions) aligned better with Renatus's childhood. Their society seemed to have had trouble assimilating with the last century of progress, and took from it only what they needed. I doubted many of them knew how to plot a trip with a bus timetable.

Before I was Renatus's legendary apprentice, I was queen of taking buses.

That's how I spent my Saturday, after a visit to the public bathroom in town near the bank and a bite to eat at a small café around the corner. I caught a bus heading south and sat in the seat behind the driver to ask questions about the best interchange stops. Like most drivers, he was chatty and happy to help. At the interchange, he hopped off and got a handful of paper timetables for me from a fellow driver, and waved away my thanks with a smile.

I had my ticket and was heading for the next bus when I felt myself being scried *again*. This time, though it deflected, it was immediately followed by a second glance of targeted attention, then a third, and a fourth… I stopped where I was.

'Watch it,' some guy snapped at me when he had to go wide to avoid a collision, but I ignored him. What was happening? Each attempt to scry me seemed to *scrape* at my wards, seeking me – that wasn't unusual, though the consecutive attempts had an effect I'd never experienced. Their efforts built on each other's, the friction of their will to find me wearing on my wards, little by little.

If they kept this up, they'd break through. They'd find me.

Emmanuelle hadn't covered this in my warding lessons. I clutched the straps of Hiroko's backpack and tried to breathe through the initial dread. My wards had never failed me before; in fact, this particular talent had saved my life on numerous occasions, as well as Renatus's and thirty-odd strangers in Prague. The truth behind that tragic political stunt was exactly what Shanahan's ledger was supposed to prove, and was ironically also why I was now being hunted, my wards being tested out by baddies and opportunists.

I didn't know the magical theory behind what was happening, but I had to assume that this was an organised effort of several scriers exploiting the fact that no one's power capacity is infinite. With enough pressure, eventually my armour would have to crack.

Could I weather them, backfilling my spells with energy I channelled and with energy from my own body, longer than they could sustain their focus? I had to try. I closed my eyes tightly and told a kind old man who checked on me that I was experiencing a migraine. It wasn't far from the truth. Wave after wave of searing attention grazed over me, different intensities, different people. I counted five distinct patterns as they cycled on repeat. I didn't know who they were, or what their abilities were like. Most sorcerers weren't natural scriers – there were no others at the Academy; I'd outlast any of my classmates – but those few who were, in my experience, were damn good at it. Renatus, Qasim, Declan, Nastassja… If literally the only four scriers I knew, who all despised each other, had teamed up to find me, I was so screwed.

The ridiculous thought prompted a humourless laugh from me, and I pushed back against the digging, pushed and resisted, and it got me across the line. Their focus broke, and the pressure on my aura fell away. I breathed deeply like I'd just surfaced from underwater, and I opened my eyes.

My bus was pulling away.

'Wait!' I bolted across the turnaround area, waving my ticket urgently. I felt tireder than I did before, and under my hair, my neck was damp with the exertion. I caught up with the sluggish vehicle and slapped my hand on the bifold door. 'Please! I have a ticket!'

All my work buttering up the other driver scored me no points here. She stopped the bus and let me on, but she was resentful and made no secret of how little she cared for my excuse when I apologised. Zero sympathy. People who don't get migraines rarely understand how debilitating they can be.

'How far are you going?' she asked gruffly when I held out my pass. She started the bus again and I lurched, grabbing for a handhold with my free hand. My fingers brushed the steel support post behind the driver.

'...a better way?'... Arthritic fingers with swollen knuckles grasp the post... A young man with his head down catches the woman's elbow supportively... 'Quicker isn't better if you land in the sea trying'... A teen girl with dark red hair follows closely, eyes on her game console... 'Like you'd ever land us in the sea'... 'Don't tempt Fate'...

I whipped my hand away and got my feet back under me. I should have expected that. Impressions, leftover energy from past contact and intense moments in time, frequently came to me as a scrier, and more so when I was distracted or my wards were weakened. I swallowed and adjusted my backpack and satchel, trying to regain my composure.

'All the way,' I answered the driver, checking my ticket for my seat number. I glanced down the aisle and hoped it wasn't the spot next to snappy guy, who had fixed me with a glare for inconveniencing him for a second time. 'I need to get to the ports.'

The guy was lucky I was trying to contain my magic, because the nasty look that followed me made me wish Renatus's mind was open to mine, and not because I wanted someone to complain to. The Dark Keeper's head was a repository of spells ranging from flashy to handy to genuinely savage, and I'd been guilty of drawing on them in confrontational situations.

I settled for holding his gaze steadily as I approached and passed, which seemed to do the same job of unsettling him, at least. It would have to do. I was at my personal limit for law-breaking in a single week, and I still wasn't done.

It was almost two hours later that my bussing and walking adventures brought me to Belfast Harbour, within mere blocks of Thomas Shanahan's hotel home where I'd apparently cursed his sweet ditz of a daughter and almost gotten Renatus killed via burnout. Allegedly. I figured no one would expect me to be stupid enough to walk straight into enemy territory and I wished I didn't have to, but it was the only place I knew I could get what I needed to function in the non-witch world. My own identity was dangerous.

The city was noisy, busy in a different way to Sapporo, and the port smelled like salt and brine and the cold. I got my gloves out of my bag and wrapped a scarf around my neck and mouth. I detected a handful of magical auras in the crowds, but no one paid me much mind, their eyes passing straight over me. Not invisible, just too slippery to catch attention.

I paid for a locker near the passenger terminus and stashed the ledger, my backpack and, regrettably, my sai. I wasn't looking for a fight. I didn't know what *to* look for; I'd never been here before. All I had was a surname. Somehow, though, after trawling each marina and peering at the signs over each building I passed, I came across what I'd been sure Fate would lead me to.

Murphy and Nephew Distribution.

The door squeaked. The foyer was unheated and uninviting, low-lit and timber-heavy, with an unattended counter and old, illegible certificates and grimy plaques on the walls. A tarnished gold bell sat in the middle of the counter, daring visitors to summon whatever passed for staff in this place. It didn't appear very magical, but my senses immediately dampened upon entry, the space warded and woven tight with anti-scrying and protective spells. The right place. I tugged the hem of my gloves, ensuring I wouldn't make skin contact with anything, and dinged the bell.

They gave me plenty of time to wonder how big a mistake I'd

made coming here.

I couldn't sense presences in this magic-dense space, but I heard the attendant's unhurried footsteps coming down the hallway behind the counter. I carefully arranged my features into a flat expression of confidence. I'd been learning the ways of this world, and the sweet, honest routine that had won over my first bus driver and the staff at the bank wouldn't do me any good here. If the Murphies were like the Shanahans, the Raymonds, the Morrisseys or the Quinns, and I had no reason to think they weren't, girls were for marrying, for forging alliances with other families and for keeping a home.

I was not for anything or anyone, and I reminded myself of that before unwinding my scarf to face the man who stepped in and paused at the sight of me.

'I think you're in the wrong place,' he said, a little slowly, regaining his composure and moving behind the counter. I dropped my scarf to hang around my neck and stood my ground.

'I don't think so,' I responded. I watched his eyes taking in my scar and my messy hair, tousled by a rough night and my windy walk around the docks. I was terrible at judging people's ages, but I could see, at least, that he was older than Renatus by about ten years. He had sandy, straight hair that fell over his face, and the stubble on his thin jaw was reddish. I stamped down on any remaining nervousness and lifted my chin. Time to play. 'Admittedly, this establishment is less impressive than I was led to believe.'

The man blinked – women in his society didn't trade barbs with powerful men – and took the bait.

'And what were you led to believe?'

I fixed him with my best level look. 'That the Murphies control these ports, and they're the kings of what they do.'

His face relaxed into something close to smug. I'd seen this rapport-building dance between underworld sorcerers at Teagan Shanahan's engagement party. Insult, compliment, deflect, repeat. A game of asserting power, destabilising others, and impressing everyone with your skill at polite nastiness. I really did not have time for it and thought it was thoroughly stupid, but if flexing was the path to respect, I'd take it.

'I'm here to employ particular services,' I said, getting to the point as bluntly as I dared. I hardly knew how to ask outright for fake IDs from strange sorcerers, but he didn't need to know how green I was.

'I see.' He rested his hands on his counter, regarding me. I didn't even know who he was, though he certainly knew my name and reputation. 'I'm not sure you're our particular clientele.'

I'd been afraid of this, though I tried to keep that out of my voice as I said, 'Because?'

'Because it may not be in my family's interest to do business with such a controversial figure,' he replied diplomatically, winning that round of polite nastiness, but then he slipped up when he added, 'After all, you have been blamed for the misfortune of my sister-in-law, Miss Shanahan, and her missing bodyguard.'

Bodyguard? I dismissed that before I could get bogged down, and instead raced through the information I had on these families. Teagan was the youngest of several Shanahan children – the eldest, Caitlin, had been married to the Murphy heir to cement the friendship between their fathers, and the middle sister Keely had made a scene at their wedding over being promised to Declan O'Malley. I'd read a letter from Uncle Thomas to Renatus's parents, thanking them for the suggestion of Caitlin's betrothal, and in my mind I pictured the handwritten document, trying to remember the boy's name.

I got it, and I raised my chin, ready for the next round.

'So you know what happened,' I stated evenly, not a question, and left it hanging for a long moment in which he held my gaze and said nothing. No, the specifics of the events at Shanahan's hadn't gotten out, not even to extended family, and no one knew that *I* didn't know, either. That was to my advantage, the possibilities of what I might have done best left to the imagination. Add to that the uncertainties around my departure from Renatus, Lisandro's public attempt to recruit me to Magnus Moira, and this first mention of a missing bodyguard... I could, theoretically, be anything from a total nobody through to the formidable witch princess some feared. 'I'd have thought it would be in *anyone's* interest to do business with someone who could tell you what Shanahan has written next to the name Reilly Murphy.'

It was a long shot, but it paid off. The attendant pursed his lips, confirming his identity, and I detected his discomfort. Shanahan really was some piece of work, a spider in the middle of this society's noxious web. Even his son-in-law had reason to believe he'd find himself in that stupid ledger, in debt and with unfavourable notations. Either that, or the Murphies were as deeply involved in Shanahan's dealings as the mobster himself, and stood to lose as much power if that record went public.

'And what would you want in exchange for something like that?' Murphy asked finally, a concession I wasn't expecting. I held in my urge to sigh in relief. I wasn't out of the woods by any means.

'That isn't for sale right now,' I answered firmly. I couldn't provide it even if I wanted to and wasn't prepared to play out that bluff any further. 'Before I could even begin to negotiate, I'd need assurance that our business here is between us.'

He read my meaning perfectly. 'No one knows you're here. Though I'm sure you know there's a fine price on you.'

'I have an inkling,' I confirmed. I tread carefully going forward, relying on my read on his emotional state to inform my every word. Though initially unsettled by my presence, he didn't feel threatened or stressed, so I didn't think he'd sold out my position yet; instead, he seemed discerning, intrigued, which suggested he wanted to see where this went. 'I'm confident we could come to an arrangement where you felt comfortable ignoring that opportunity.'

Reilly Murphy smiled. He was a good-looking man, as Declan had alluded when he'd said Keely got the rawer deal of the sisters, but the expression was caught somewhere between amused and condescending.

'I don't think you can afford to match that opportunity, let alone cover my services on top. And if that's the case,' he pushed away from the counter and gestured to the door, 'we're done here.'

Jerk. But I didn't know where else to get fake IDs and passports made up, so I was going to have to make this work. I dug into Declan's satchel and dumped a handful of bills on the counter.

'I have Renatus Morrissey's bank account,' I said flatly, capturing Murphy's attention. I slapped a sheet of Hiroko's scented notepaper on top of the money. 'That's what I need. I imagine that Renatus would consider it a personal favour if you'd accept my custom, and a personal *slight*,' I left the word hanging long enough for him to remember who we were talking about, because if I had a reputation, it was nothing compared to my master's, 'if I were to find myself in unfriendly company as a result of doing business with your family.'

Reilly Murphy leaned forward to read my short list of required documentation.

'As it happens, we have an opening on our books for a new client,' he said smoothly, withdrawing an expensive camera from a drawer under the counter with one hand and offering a slip of paper to me with the other. I opened it while he continued speaking. 'I think you're right, and we can come to an arrangement that works for us both. Perhaps the first transaction of an ongoing business relationship.'

I hoped not, and maybe my silence implied that, but he still waited patiently as I read the unreasonable price he was offering. It was almost a third higher than Hiroko and I had estimated as the upper limit from our forum research yesterday. Amazing what information people will divulge on the internet as answers to "how much should I expect to spend on fake identification?" I considered the wisdom of trying to barter down when the forger's silence was part of the deal. I nodded once and extended the slip back to him.

'Payment upfront,' he added sleekly, reaching for the price, and I whipped it back.

'Deposit upfront,' I disagreed, nodding at the small pile of cash between us. 'The rest on collection. When will this be ready?'

He didn't argue; in fact, I detected a certain satisfaction at my refusal, and realised it was a test I'd accidentally passed. He picked up my list off the money to read it again.

'It won't be an overnight service. We don't work on Sundays. This should be ready, oh, Tuesday. Wednesday at the latest.'

'Then I'll be back Tuesday afternoon to inspect your work,' I said boldly, and he smiled again, warming to me despite my best efforts to channel Renatus's characteristic wordiness and detached, superior rudeness. 'If you include a trace of any kind, I'll know.'

'We wouldn't dream of it,' Reilly Murphy answered immediately. 'Our family prides itself on our customer service and integrity. Where you go with what's yours is your business.' He held out the camera while I pocketed the slip of paper that stated the agreed price. 'I'll need a photograph. After that, we're done for today, and we'll see you again on Tuesday.'

I didn't know him well enough to trust his word or his family's honour or whatever, so I looked both ways when I stepped out the door ten minutes later. My senses felt replenished to remove myself from that energetically dampened space, but I half expected to find myself surrounded by bad guys. It was a pleasant surprise when that wasn't the case. I tightened my personal wards, wound my scarf over my mouth and throat again and strode for the bus stop.

I'd felt sorcerers in the crowds on my way to the harbour, but on the way back, they seemed more numerous. Maybe it was just more people getting out of work or finishing lunch. No one caught my eye or seemed to notice me – and so they shouldn't – and I knew it was mostly paranoia that drew my attention to them as I hurried. Anxiety clawed threateningly at my heart when, a few times, I felt scriers looking for me, though they were only one at a time, totally manageable. I had to remind myself this wasn't new and I had no reason to think it was linked to my visit to Murphy and Nephew Distribution.

Still, I was glad to board my bus out of Belfast, even if it meant yet another bridge for tonight.

chapter six

Impressions had come to him most easily when he first learned to scry, and it was the same now as Qasim ran his fingers through the air above Renatus's disordered desk.

'Aristea held her own here,' he commented as he glanced up at the ruined ceiling, not expecting an answer from the hunched figure in the corner. 'She had one advantage and she used it.'

'Stop talking.'

Renatus had dragged an armchair to the corner, facing the walls, and had now spent four days between there and his bedroom. Sulking. Qasim was trying to be patient with the younger scrier's irritating withdrawal behaviour, since, on this one occasion, it was warranted and even necessary. The Dark Keeper exuded misery. If his Empathic apprentice were here, she'd be unbearable, soaking in all that negativity, but she'd also stand a chance at knocking him out of it. So long as he was stuck in this spiral, he wasn't working on fixing the issues that made her departure necessary, which meant another day of her out in the wild, off their radar, and another day of miserable Renatus.

Qasim preferred any annoying version of Aristea over this version of Renatus, and would happily do a trade. The last four days had felt like the longest of his life.

On the first day, he searched for Aristea and Hiroko without luck, and took inventory of the resources they had inside the house in case this was long term. Enough food to last six months, or so the head of staff approximated. Sixteen of the thirty-seven students who'd turned up in March to be instructed in high level magic remained, most by choice, not that they had one at this point. Most were Healers or Seers, the two most common classes of sorcerer, with a handful of Crafters, two Telepaths and one Displacer. Nine of Morrissey House's usual staff of fifteen were trapped inside, too, along with six of the White Elm's twelve councillors. The council deliberated what to do, and Qasim assured himself it wouldn't be long.

On the second day, his patience frayed when Renatus wouldn't come out of his room. The council met without him and suggested that the severity of their situation – the lockdown, and the appearance of a dead Morrissey – should be suppressed from the public. Qasim's opposing position was outvoted. When he visited Emmanuelle and discovered no improvement, he marched to the gate to demand an audience with Jackson. The overbright eyes of Magnus Moira watched on as his former colleague appeared and sauntered closer.

'What do you want?' Qasim asked bluntly. 'What are you doing here?'

'They want what they've always wanted,' Jackson replied after a luxurious yawn to illustrate that he'd been woken up for this. 'Freedom to do their magic, freedom from the White Elm's oppression.'

'Freedom to commit acts of violence and terrorism, freedom to snap the spine of a woman as she ran from you. And they're fine with fighting oppression with more oppression, under the leadership of former councillors?' Qasim countered, grimly pleased to see several activists in the listening crowd share uneasy glances. 'What will it take to get rid of you?'

Jackson was awake now, and annoyed.

'Nothing short of the White Elm's unconditional surrender.'

The third day brought news that the council's most powerful allies had been contacted by Lisandro.

He's denying Magnus Moira involvement in the events at Prague, Lady Miranda reported, tired from the political back and forth with Valero. *That's all they'll tell me but he must have given them something quite compelling, because they're meeting with him today and my request to sit in has been refused.*

Avalon is being cagey, Lord Gawain responded, *but we know he's contacted them before. He's using our inaction to move his pieces around the board.*

Then why are we wilfully skipping our turn? Qasim asked, and the conversation started over with all the ways in which their hands were bound, locked inside Renatus's family fortress, ironically trapped by the same spelled walls that kept them safe and the one gate guarded by Renatus's supposedly dead sister.

By the fourth day, Qasim was frustrated enough to willingly choose Renatus's office as a distraction when he found its door open. Stop talking, he'd said.

'Come and make me,' Qasim responded flatly to the Dark Keeper's characteristic rudeness, 'if it will get you out of that chair.'

Renatus settled deeper into his seat, refusing to engage, and Qasim wanted to tip the armchair over. Despite the constancy of familiar voices in his head – locked-out councillors Teresa, Oneida, Susannah, Jadon and the council's high priestess, Lady Miranda, were as connected to their counterparts as ever – these past few days had felt unusually quiet.

No Renatus, dry and unfeeling until he wasn't, with his unwelcome suggestions he gave like orders.

No Emmanuelle, yet to regain any level of consciousness they could discern with only student Healers anxiously working on her, to interrupt mental discussions with her classic mix of frustrated English and angry French.

No Glen, who'd been silent to their minds since the death of his fellow White Elm Telepath Anouk, to offer kind and reasonable alternatives.

And voices in his head aside, after four days trapped in Renatus's pompous Irish manor home, Qasim was madly missing his own family. His wife Nasira. His children. His much warmer home, his bed, his kitchen, his favourite meals. He'd gotten a message to Nasira through Miranda, thankfully, but Qasim was finding every hour of Lord Gawain's vague complacency and Renatus's sulking more irksome. He knew the council's leader was an impressively powerful Seer – he'd worked with him for decades and had lived by Gawain's visions with complete faith – but since when did an unwelcome series of future events mean lying down and simply taking it?

Which brought Qasim back to the main reason he was frustrated with Renatus, who was much easier to be mad with than Lord Gawain. For all his irritating faults, the younger scrier was, generally, a self-appointed action hero. Sitting still and being patient were not skills he had ever honed, and in the past, whether for better or worse, caging him up like this had reliably resulted in delinquent behaviours like arguing with authority, sneaking out and running headlong into danger, usually with an overreactive demonstration of combat abilities.

No such luck this time. Where was that self-righteous energy when Qasim needed it?

Perhaps he'd used it all up on Thursday, when he'd apparently found his limit in some forgotten altercation at Thomas Shanahan's penthouse. According to Teresa and Oneida, who were administering continuous care to Shanahan's critically ill daughter, the altercation had not been forgotten by the other party.

'Those two almost killed my child, they stole from me, and no one's heard from my head of security since he responded to the alarms,' Qasim heard the large man ranting as he scried Oneida trying to calm him down in a hospital hallway. *'If my people catch up with them first, I won't be sorry to hear they've taken care of things for me.'*

This head of security business was new, and not something Shanahan had mentioned in his initial complaint against Renatus and Aristea. He'd refused to give the employee's details to assist the council with a search, but insisted the young scriers had enacted some treachery upon this nameless staff member.

'Will you please get me a pen?' Renatus spoke up, while Qasim was crouched under the desk.

'What for?'

Renatus's hand was extended over the arm of his chair, waiting. 'Does it matter?'

Exasperated, Qasim complied with fetching a fountain pen

from the mess that used to be Renatus's immaculate desktop. More evidence that he was not in a good place. Control freak Renatus had always ruled this space, at least as long as Qasim had known him. Then Nastassja, formerly Anastasia Morrissey, had commandeered Sterling Adams' body. Qasim kept tapping into impressions of the confrontation that broke out when Aristea had caught her in here.

'Renatus must have lined me up as his heir in more ways than just writing'… A snarl, fingers curling instinctively for something with which to lash out… A handful of pens bouncing off an automatic ward just shy of Aristea's face… 'You're nobody'…

It was fortunate that Aristea's wards and reflexes were so sharp, because Nastassja's spellcasting and repertoire of dangerous magic had proven, even in that short exchange, far superior to what the Academy's only scrier student had to offer. Ash and chunks of charred plaster still littered the desk and carpet where Nastassja had blasted holes in the ceiling – flaming holes that would have gone through Aristea if she'd not been so quick.

Two teenaged girls, keeping the desk between them… 'It must kill you that I'm here'… Black crackling ball of energy and a scream ricochet from a close ward into the ceiling… Fire, crashing, raining grey and orange… 'He didn't love her!'… Aristea feinting left, forcing the other's hand, getting her close…

Qasim touched his fingertip to the fresh stab wound in the beautiful oak desktop, feeling a sense of irritated pride. Aristea's reckless arrogance had paid off when she'd tricked her opponent into extending a hand for the ledger so she could slam her sai down, trapping her wrist and distracting her into catching the pendant that would expel her from Adams' body. She'd gotten her opponent angry. He might have felt frustrated with her lack of tact and precision, except that Aristea was an Empath. The only advantage she'd had in this conflict was her ability to sense the other's emotions and motives.

He was relieved she'd thought to use it, and begrudgingly relieved also that she'd broken the law in her first few weeks here, Haunting into this office. If she hadn't, Renatus wouldn't have realised how fascinatingly talented she was. He wouldn't have bent the rules to keep her and loaned her the pendant and she wouldn't have known how it was used when they needed her to. Now, thanks to the very busy work of Iseult Taylor and her Crafter peers, everyone on the campus wore an adapted copy, protected from Nastassja and any of Magnus Moira's other immoral scriers. They knew the free magic movement had at least twelve who were exceptionally gifted – enough to possess all those people they'd stitched up as murderers in Prague.

All this knowledge they owed to Fate, and to Aristea, but right now, both felt very far away to Qasim.

'Are you bringing me that pen?' Renatus asked, a moody prompt. Qasim looked up, unhurried.

'Am I slowing you down?' he replied. He stepped over pieces of ceiling to bring the spoilt scrier his pen. 'Have you found Aristea yet?'

'I'm not looking for her,' came the usual reply, 'and you shouldn't either.'

This part, he'd refused to elaborate, and Qasim had had enough of asking why. He'd tried arguing. He'd tried demanding. Renatus was not talking about Aristea.

'Then that would be two of us not doing our duty.'

Renatus's expression gave nothing away but he took the pen without a word, unamused. His impassive face and his fixed gaze also didn't falter when, at that moment, Qasim's mental eye on the gate showed movement. A shift change. A few sorcerers got to their feet and dusted themselves off, exchanged pleasant conversation with their replacements, and left. Nastassja replaced Jackson.

They're there for the long haul, Susannah confirmed when Qasim updated the council and Lord Gawain said nothing. Meditating, again.

It would be handy to have Aristea around so we'd know what they intend, Elijah mentioned a little gloomily, accent ringing clear in Qasim's mind. Aristea's ability to determine feelings and motives had never been more useful than right now, when they didn't have her, and an embargo of anarchists were camped outside their walls, including a very powerful scrier gazing up at the house.

'She says she's interested in reopening negotiations,' Renatus spoke up flatly without breaking his eerie, unblinking eye contact with the wallpaper. Qasim shot him an angry look he probably didn't catch.

'How nice for your dead sister,' he spat, getting the first flinch out of the younger scrier in days, making him blink. Good, he needed a decent jolt. 'What are you, their message boy now?'

'Of course not, now be quiet,' the other replied, leaving Qasim feeling tired. And he *was* tired. Tired of this house, tired of worrying about those people outside, tired of wondering what was going to happen next and nothing ever eventuating.

As ever, he was tired of Renatus, who should be better than this, and of the risk that their council, which had stood for five hundred years, might be losing their strongest weapon to domestic dramas.

'She's just living in your head now, is that it?' he demanded, yanking on the back of the armchair hard enough to turn it away from the corner. It startled the sulking Dark Keeper into smoothing his sleeve down, but Qasim saw in his face that his eyes were clear, the earlier comment having already broken the spell. 'I thought you were *trying* to block her.'

'I *am*,' Renatus argued, standing abruptly so they were eye to eye, 'and she keeps finding new ways in. *I don't want to talk to you!*' he shouted in the direction of the window, something he'd done enough times lately that Qasim wasn't moved. The first time, he'd mentioned it to the collective of White Elm voices in his head, but by now he didn't think it worthy of note. The younger scrier turned on the elder, seething with helpless anger. Charcoal cracks spidered across the back of his hands. 'I was working on it and *you* keep interrupting.'

'How am I to know that? You don't say a word and all your expressions look the same.'

'You know I'm not possessed,' Renatus snarled, yanking on the dark silver chain dangling from his neck. The pendant Iseult had created for him spun on the end of it. 'You know I'm not doing anything at all with this thing on me.'

'I'm sure it's only that pendant stopping you from doing

anything useful,' Qasim retorted. 'If it was really crushing your magic, you wouldn't be experiencing *this*.' He grabbed for the other's hand, and caught only the pen as Renatus swiped away, but the point was made. A few decent nights of sleep and some good steak dinners, and he was almost back to his full strength after a burnout episode that left him comatose. Now the magic was back, pulsing under his skin as charred lines when his emotions flared. 'Pull yourself together and quit choosing weakness. Kick her *out*. You speak for *us*, not for them.'

Renatus went to step away but his chair obstructed him. Pressing blackening hands to his ears, he closed his eyes tightly like he was blocking something out. Outside, Nastassja was watching the house with a conflicted, purposeful expression. She was more expressive than her brother, but clearly his kin, their faces carved in the same smooth angles, their power surreal. Neither of them should exist, but they did, and one was on the other side with the council's coveted Elm Stone on her ring finger, while the younger one was here, cracked and maybe broken.

However damaged, he was the one they had. Frustrated into impulsiveness he normally resented in Renatus, Qasim grasped the other's temples between his hands and *pushed* his own will through the mind that lived there.

'*Get out!*' he growled with both his voice and mind, and outside the gates, the other Morrissey heir flinched sharply at the rebuttal she clearly felt. Shoved out of her brother's head, shaken by her unexpected exit, she took a hurried backstep and vanished, Displacing away somewhere. Renatus's eyes shot open, freed from the constant tragic battle Qasim should try harder to pity him for, and the Scrier dropped his hands and gave him back his personal space. 'You need to be firmer with her.'

Renatus stood frozen for a moment, perhaps as he checked as much of his mind as he could for that unwelcome presence, then he yanked up the sleeve of his left arm to read the text that was written there.

'That might not work next time,' he commented instead of thanking him. 'She'll adapt. She keeps finding new ways to get in, to see what I see, to hear what I think. I'm trying hard not to think.' Qasim noted that the text on his forearm didn't look like his usual spidery handwriting.

Still no, he thought he read through the receding black veins. *What makes you think I'm looking?*

'I hadn't noticed a difference,' Qasim replied calmly, earning a reproachful glance. Aristea was onto something – both Morrissey siblings were most easily manipulated when provoked. But this time he laid off. 'While you're clean, what can you tell me? What's that?'

He gestured at the writing fading on Renatus's arm.

'It's from–'

'Renatus, you have to stop her.'

The two scriers both looked to the door as their leader, Lord Gawain, approached from the stairwell down the hall. Renatus hid the writing under the sleeve of his shirt, confirming that it was something he shouldn't be doing, and Qasim caught the edge of his querying gaze. He could feel the elderly Seer's presence growing closer, but, excluded from their telepathic network, he had to be wondering what he was missing.

'Your guess is as good as mine,' Qasim admitted in a low voice, then raised it to be heard from the hall. 'We're working on it. She's out, for now.'

'Out where?' Lord Gawain appeared in the doorway and hurried inside the office. The door had been left ajar for days; strange, considering Renatus had almost always kept this space very private, enjoying the unique magical locking mechanism that kept anyone but his blood out. 'Not Nastassja. I'm talking about Aristea. We need to find her, right *now*.'

Qasim felt alarm bells ringing in his head at the urgency in his leader's voice.

'Why? What's wrong?'

'Is she alright?' Renatus demanded, desperately. Lord Gawain stopped in front of them, shaking his head, breathing hard from taking the stairs too fast.

'She's on a path I never saw for her before,' he explained in a rush. 'I don't think she knows what she's getting herself into.'

Like he had dozens of times already, Qasim extended his thoughts out into the world, seeking the familiar energy of the girl he'd considered apprenticing before Renatus jumped the gun. He kept one steady mental eye on the activity, or lack thereof, outside the gate, and another, perpetually, on his home; it was nothing to split his attention this way and view multiple times and places simultaneously. But Aristea did not want to be found. The awful alternative was that she had been killed, but Lord Gawain's worry about her future disproved that, at least for now. His attention reached and reached and never settled. He let the energy drop. A sustained attempt might wear on her wards, depending on the type she was using – she'd learned from Emmanuelle, who taught the strait-laced and legal kind, which meant that they'd drain quickly.

'What is she getting herself into?' Qasim asked. The girl frustrated him, but he also cared for her wholly, as protective of her as his own daughter. She'd come far from that naïve girl he'd scried with forty-nine other potentials, standing at his back to fight alongside him in that trap of a theatre last week even without her powers.

Did we find her friend yet? Lord Gawain was still coming out of his trance; Qasim saw it in his glassy eyes and his shaky hand as he reached for the back of the nearest chair for support. He took the Seer's elbow and guided him to sit. Renatus hovered at his shoulder, in conflict – too afraid of his sister harvesting knowledge from him later to ask anything specific, too invested to walk away without knowing.

'Is Hiroko involved in what you saw?' Qasim prompted, attempting to keep the conversation verbal for Renatus's benefit, though others in the circle had heard the question.

Miss Shanahan is stable, Oneida told them from Belfast. *Teresa or I could visit Miss Sasaki.*

How many times has she relapsed now? Lady Miranda, a surgeon and a brilliant Healer, asked them worriedly from Germany, where she was continuing talks with the White Elm's tenuous Russian ally. Teresa, a much younger Healer still finding her confidence, had been thrown in the deep end with this Teagan

Shanahan business, and spoke up now as the girl's treating physician.

Every few hours. I think I should stay, she agreed in her thick eastern European accent.

'I didn't see Hiroko, but she is the best lead, isn't she?' Lord Gawain said. 'You said they're not together…?'

Aristea's wards were keeping his eyes clear of her actions, but Qasim had spotted her more bearable friend Hiroko Sasaki going about her normal daily business at home in Japan several times over the weekend. Alone. He'd reported on that, but between the Shanahan girl's dangerous condition in Belfast, the tense political situation they'd left hanging with Valero and the lockdown on the rest of their council at Morrissey Estate, the White Elm hadn't had the manpower to do anything more than keep an eye on the teen Displacer.

There's still no action here, Jadon complained from near Coleraine. *I can go.*

'Not Jadon,' Qasim said instantly. 'He stays where he is.'

'What's going on?' Renatus asked, looking between the older men. 'Is this about Angela?' Qasim waved him back irritably when he leaned forward to ask again. For once they were on the exact same page.

'Angela Byrne mightn't have noticed him but Jadon's presence in her street is unlikely to have been overlooked by anyone watching her house,' he said firmly. 'Removing him could provide our enemies with an opening, if our theory is correct and they're looking as hard as we are for Aristea.'

'It's not just a theory,' Renatus insisted. 'She – Nastassja – wants to find her, and we saw the way everyone came for her in the theatre once she showed the book.'

Lord Gawain was blinking himself clear of his vision.

'Yes, the book,' he agreed thickly. He looked to the messy desktop where they'd left the blank ledger last week before everything fell apart. 'That was when this all started. She's not what we thought. She was supposed to save this council. That's what I saw. Partnering her with you… it put us on the right path, the path to preserving our legacy.'

Beside Qasim, Renatus frowned and folded his arms, disturbed.

'And that's why you approved our partnership,' he said warily. 'You said it was the only way that might lead to a victory.'

'Now it's leading somewhere else,' Gawain insisted. 'This path she's on, she has to be stopped. Everything she does brings us closer and there can be only one outcome.'

'What are you talking about?' Qasim asked. 'What outcome?'

I'll try to find her, Oneida told the collective when no other instruction came regarding Hiroko. Qasim focused part of his mind on the girl and let the Native American Seer access the images that came to him.

'There are still exit points,' Lord Gawain was murmuring, looking up at the air like he was reading a map on the ceiling. 'If she comes back, if she never finds the cave, if she sits her trial… But something's missing. I've forgotten…' With effort he broke eye contact with Fate and looked into Renatus's drawn face. 'If you open your mind to her, would she come, knowing she'll be put on trial?'

'We're not putting her on trial,' Renatus rebuked without hesitation. Lord Gawain regarded him.

'Is your memory coming back?' he asked, and the younger closed his mouth tightly, swallowing whatever else he wanted to say. The council leader tiredly rubbed his clean-shaven chin, always too willing to back down when Renatus's stubbornness reared its head. He'd say it wasn't worth pushing, that his Morrissey obstinacy wouldn't bend, but Qasim scoffed at that, even in thought. Push hard enough and Renatus would always snap. He couldn't help himself. Lord Gawain just didn't like to fight him. Usually Qasim considered that too great a concession from a man in Gawain's position – Qasim certainly wouldn't be giving the Dark Keeper this much rope – but on this occasion, he was oddly glad for it.

'Aristea's got no reason to come back, and no capacity to, even if she wanted to,' he said firmly, hoping to get the conversation back on track. 'If *we* aren't brave enough to step outside this gate, we shouldn't be entertaining the idea of asking Aristea to try to get *in*. She's a smart kid – she'll be keeping her head down somewhere. Why does it matter that she isn't here?'

'It's one of the conditions of the only acceptable future,' Lord Gawain tried to explain to the two scriers. That was always hard. Scriers saw the present as it was; Seers saw the present as a shifting set of stepping stones that needed to be arranged *just so* to facilitate the ideal future. 'Aristea's trial needs to be arranged and she needs to be judged. It sets her on a whole new path.'

The trial. Qasim didn't believe for a second that whatever had gone down at Shanahan's was Aristea's doing, but she'd insisted, and while Renatus had started off vehemently opposed to her claims, he'd since gone quiet on the issue. What seemed undeniable, at least, was that Aristea had conducted a dangerous memory spell, using crude pagan blood magic on Renatus to cover up the events at the hotel, and Teagan Shanahan wouldn't stop bleeding long enough to wake up and set things straight.

'What's the outcome of that trial?' Renatus asked. Lord Gawain hesitated. 'You know already, don't you?'

'She shouldn't have run. It doesn't support her case.'

'She didn't *run*–'

'You weren't there,' Qasim told Gawain before Renatus could say something he'd regret. 'It would have taken a miracle for Aristea and Hiroko to make it to the gate from where they landed. Renatus was lucky to push through. Sending her away was her best chance.'

'If we don't bring her back, if we don't proceed with the trial, it's all been for nothing,' the council leader claimed. 'She isn't what we thought.'

'What does that *mean*?' Renatus demanded. 'If you want me to believe–'

'Whatever she's about to do in the next few weeks, it brings about the end of the White Elm.'

It was a huge proclamation, met with silence. Qasim stared at his colleague. Renatus blinked, thrown.

'Well, I don't believe that,' he responded after a beat. Qasim scratched his tightknit hair, uncomfortable with this claim as well. Lord Gawain was a powerful Seer, but his visions usually showed *very* distant futures, with a lot of grey in between.

'Something she's going to do,' he clarified slowly, 'is going to set events in motion that will, eventually, see our council come undone?'

'That's right,' Lord Gawain confirmed, relieved to be understood, if not believed. 'I'm sure she doesn't intend it. It's not something she's seeking. She's just a catalyst, and she *can't* catalyse this future if she's here, and if she's charged for her crimes.'

'She can't join the council as a criminal,' Qasim pointed out. He glanced at Renatus, not liking where this was going. 'What have we been training her for, if not to prepare her for the council?'

Lord Gawain must have still been partly in his trance, less perceptive than usual. 'Apprenticing her with Renatus strengthened him, gave him perspective he didn't have before. It's benefitted the whole council.'

Qasim knew it was the wrong thing to say. Renatus's hand tightened on the back of the armchair. Finally, the righteous anger he'd been waiting for.

'And now?' he asked incredulously. 'You're asking me to call her back here, through a blockade that will certainly capture or kill her for some stupid blank book, to face a trial she'll certainly fail, because she's served her purpose? Because I've...' The righteous anger threatened to choke his words. 'Because I've used her?'

Qasim looked down, unexpectedly ashamed. He had accused Renatus, many times, of treating Aristea's apprenticeship as being about him and his needs instead of hers. He hadn't realised the other scrier had come to fear it to be true, and he hadn't realised *he* had ceased to believe it himself.

Lord Gawain softened, apologetic.

'I shouldn't have said it that way,' he agreed gently. 'I meant, sometimes the best outcome, the one we work toward as the White Elm for our hundreds of thousands of nationals, has a cost we don't perceive at the beginning. Unfortunately, this time, it might be Aristea's future with the council. It's possible to get her back through the gate – I've seen it, one of ours breaks through, just once. And she isn't destined to fail. She did make her own decisions, but perhaps Fate will show us more during the trial, or perhaps failing it will put her on a new, better path for her life. We don't know. Regardless, the alternative is letting Lisandro win. Letting the council fall, like he said it would.' The old Seer waited, appealing to Renatus with patience. When there was no reply, no resistance, he prompted, still gently, 'Call her back. We can get her through the gate. We can avert all this.'

Qasim slid his hands into his pockets, conflicted, and Renatus turned away to stalk over to the window. He glared out at the embargo beyond the gate.

'You're asking me,' he said finally, very darkly, 'to choose between her and defeating Lisandro.'

'I'm asking you to choose to back your council,' Lord Gawain corrected.

'Is this an order?'

The question seemed to surprise Lord Gawain who, in Qasim's experience, had very rarely issued his favourite with explicit orders. 'I'm sorry?'

'Then no.' Renatus kept his gaze on the gate. His posture was straighter than Qasim had seen in days, and even with his unbrushed hair and the rings under his eyes, he looked calmer and more collected. 'I'm not betraying her. Vote on it, discuss it among yourselves, I don't care, but I'm not helping to bring her in. I'd rather see Lisandro win.'

'You?' Qasim repeated. 'Would let Lisandro *win*?'

'I didn't say I'd be happy about it.'

'This council has gained you everything,' Lord Gawain argued. 'You'd let it crumble?'

The breath Renatus drew in looked painful, but his voice didn't shake. 'If that's the price for integrity, I'll pay it.'

Lord Gawain looked lost for words, and he turned his helpless gaze on the Scrier. Qasim took his own slow breath to buy himself a moment's thought. In his mind, he watched Oneida crossing paths with Hiroko Sasaki on her way home. The girl's smile was polite and warm, hardly the look of someone who'd narrowly escaped a supernatural riot a few days earlier. Her greeting and the first few sentences the pair exchanged offered no indication they'd worked in tandem to break the balance of power in the Belarusian theatre, Hiroko Displacing in with a spell of Oneida and Teresa's that activated right behind Lisandro and sent the crowd running.

I don't think she remembers, Oneida shared with the group. *It's as though she wasn't even there.*

Aristea had spelled away *Hiroko's* memory of Thursday, along with Renatus's. She'd risked the minds of two of her most beloved people, and hadn't yet turned up at her sister Angela's house. Whatever she was hiding, she was keeping the people she loved clear of it. Was it really just the ledger and what happened to Teagan, or something more?

'Qasim?' Lord Gawain prompted meaningfully. 'This is another cross against her. You know what this means. Can you find her?'

Renatus didn't know about Hiroko, and looked across at them, frowning. Qasim sighed, finding it hard to accept the side he found himself on.

'Maybe this is how she manages to break our council,' Qasim said finally, 'because I'm refusing, too, for the time being.'

It was an awkward silence for the ages.

'You don't believe me?' the old Seer asked. 'About the path she's on?'

'I believe that's what Fate showed you,' Qasim corrected gently, 'but it wouldn't be the first time it's shown you a worst-case scenario to prompt alternative action. And you know I never accept a solitary outcome until the moment arrives.'

Lord Gawain nodded for a moment, then struggled tiredly to his feet.

'Yes,' he said, wavering. The trance had taken more out of him than Qasim had seen before, and he looked unsteady. 'I thought... Perhaps you're right, and this is a schism of my own making. There are factors still missing... I think I'll lay down. No, I can manage,' he insisted when both scriers reached out to help him shuffle toward the door. 'In my vision I saw myself, too, a stepping stone, playing a part I would never play. Perhaps it was less literal… Perhaps it won't come to pass. Or perhaps you'll come to see.'

Qasim nodded graciously as the elder sorcerer left the room. Renatus said nothing, but his dark expression spoke volumes. He was not changing his position. He hadn't been more fixed on anything in days.

As soon as he left, Renatus let his head tip back to stare at the ruined ceiling. 'I shouldn't have been part of that conversation. She'll be back to look for what I know. She could be in there now, digging quietly.'

'Then weed her out,' Qasim snapped. He'd had enough of bad news and complacency. 'Lay some bait, learn her patterns. Your apprentice won *this* round,' he pointed up at the ceiling, at the messy desk, 'against her with wards and a pair of swords she barely knows how to wield. I'm sure you, our Dark Keeper, should be able to take her on in a metaphysical plane.' He glared at the other when he didn't reply. 'Unless you don't want to?'

He hadn't meant to voice this suspicion, though he'd been feeling it for days. As a boy, before the White Elm had met Renatus, he'd idolised his big sister, and her apparent death had derailed his life for many years. Now, with her back from the beyond, where did Renatus stand? After almost a year as enemies, Qasim found himself half-wishing he could just ask Lisandro about it at the next circle. Renatus's continuing commitment to Aristea gave Qasim some confidence in his loyalties, even if his devotion to Lord Gawain was on shaky ground – after that exchange, Qasim could hardly comment on that.

Renatus took a long time in answering.

'She used to be taller than me,' he mentioned, dropping his gaze to look out the window. But he wasn't looking at the gate. His eyes fixed on the orchard, an overgrown plantation of old apple trees that took up the lower fifth of the estate. A path through the middle of it led to a family graveyard, where Ana Morrissey was meant to be buried with their parents. Who or what was in that grave? 'She was always taller. That she isn't anymore should make me feel stronger, more capable, maybe, but I don't. She scares me,' he admitted, surprising Qasim, though he tried not to let it show. 'She completely evaded notice while I grew taller than her and I don't know what she's done or who she's become in that time. We don't even know each other. But I do know that every day that's passed, she's chosen something, some *life* over me. It must mean a lot to her. But she didn't pick me.' He rubbed his wrist, where the tattoo that matched his apprentice's was marked into his skin. 'Aristea did. She took a fall that should have been mine. She's risking *everything* to protect *me*. So don't ask me whether I want to keep my sister out. As long as she's coming after my family, she's not part of it, and if giving her a single inch poses any risk to Aristea...'

Qasim joined him in looking out the window.

'We're not going to let anything happen to her.' The pair fell into a long stretch of silence, strangely in sync, and Qasim let his attention flit through images of the past and present. They touched on a room one floor down. 'I'm going to visit Emmanuelle. Are you coming?'

'No, I can't see her like that.'

'You're a coward.'

'Yes. Sue me.'

The Renatus he knew was back, though with perhaps more of his apprentice's sass than he needed.

'You're a coward,' Qasim said again as he turned to leave, 'but at least you're out of that goddamn chair.'

chapter seven

Time was playing tricks on me. Watching three places in two different time zones in one exhausted head was already a minor mathematical challenge every time I scried for one of my three favourite people, but as the week wore slowly onward, I got the distinct feeling I was running out of time. It was an illusion – I had nothing *but* time and no clue as to when my life would return to normal, if ever – but a pervasive and uncomfortable illusion, nonetheless.

A deep sense of unrest seeded in my chest long before I arrived back at Belfast Harbour for my new IDs, one that had nothing to do with the bridges I'd slept under until I'd found an empty house with a "for sale" sign pitched out front. Thanks, Jadon, for that idea. It was to do with the long hours I spent lying awake or sitting in parks eating store-bought sandwiches I'd have made better myself, my brain aching with tension as my magical energy sapped away into maintaining wards I never thought would fail me. The bombardment of attention from scriers hadn't stopped. Usually it was just the one, bearing down and then flung away by design of my wards, but four times in as many days I was stopped in my tracks by the sickening crush of multiple people concentrating on me so hard that I could barely resist.

I didn't know how much longer I *could* resist, and on Tuesday night after exchanging a generous pile of Renatus's money for a fake passport I was *never* telling my sister about, I began to wonder about the viability of my plan from here. Would leaving the country help me at all, or just put me further away from people who might help when my wards inevitably shattered?

I wasn't even out of the harbour before I had my answer. Stepping through the Murphies' doorway into the salty evening air, I felt another wave of brief attention as someone tried to find me, and a few paces away a short man with a wool hat and an aura that identified him as another sorcerer was peering in a nearby window. I stopped to tighten my warding and watched as he looked around intently, eyes sliding straight over me even as I zipped my jacket up against the wind right in front of him. His gaze wouldn't, couldn't focus on me, but the feelings of curiosity and low-key excitement I detected from him prompted a healthy stride on my way back to the lockers. He'd felt on the verge of finding something, and I was all too certain that I was that something.

On the path to the well-lit but empty passenger terminus, attempts to scry me were deflected by my wards, and two more magical people passed me with intent looks that set me on edge, but while I punched in my locker code and yanked open the door, someone Displaced *right* beside me. Just stepped out of somewhere else, planting her foot hardly a metre away and looking around for witnesses. I had only half a second of warning and there was no one to see her but me. Heart leaping up my throat, I clutched the bag to my chest and jumped back against the wall of lockers. She'd had her back to me but the noise made her spin, and for a breathless moment I was sure I was caught. Wildly I wondered how quickly I could wrangle my sai out of the bag to fight her off.

As with the others, her eyes slid across me and fixed on the open door of the storage locker. In a swish of a worn trench coat and a burst of anticipation, she stepped closer to inspect the offending detail, and I sidestepped out of her way, trying not to breathe, trying to keep my possessions from clinking in my arms. As quickly as I dared, I backed away and then, when I didn't think she'd hear, I turned and bolted through the doors. I didn't slow down until I was out at the road and waving down my taxi.

'The airport, international,' I requested in an uneven breath as I clambered into the back seat. The driver warned me it'd be half an hour and I let my head fall back against the headrest, relieved to be moving and not responsible for watching where I was going. My energy and sanity were both wearing very thin. My wards, too, it seemed; or perhaps Reilly Murphy had sold me out now that our business was concluded. I had no way of knowing and didn't want to wait to find out from whoever caught up with me first. At least on the continent, there were fewer obvious places to look for me.

If only my luck would hold out that long.

I tried to use the taxi ride as a rest, to conserve energy, but I had two more "migraines" before we were halfway. Sweat gathering under my scarf, I felt again like I was running out of time, and though the rest of the ride was uneventful, I was back to questioning my plans when I handed the driver another handful of Renatus's money. I looked up at the imposing terminal and doubtfully watched a family as they dragged suitcases behind them, enthusing in bubbly tones about the trip they were about to take. I was almost at the end of my rope. I ran a mental check over my wards, through my body, and came up disappointed. I was running on empty, exhausted.

What would happen next, if this last-ditch effort didn't get me into the clear and out of everyone's laser-sharp focus? Getting caught by one of Shanahan's underworld associates, or even one of his enemies, simply wasn't an option. "Uncle Thomas" had told the White Elm he wanted my head, and given what his father had instigated against the O'Malley family fifty years ago, I couldn't be sure he didn't mean that literally. My next best choice was capture by Lisandro and Magnus Moira, which included any number of untrained and unsympathetic magic-users with a deep hatred for the White Elm. What one of them might do to me as a message to the council could push even my overactive imagination. Lisandro himself had hurt me in the past – burned my arm and neck to rile up Renatus, blasted my face with a twisted spell of his own making when I got too close, and, you know, murdered my parents and brother. And his wife, Renatus's psycho sister, seemed bent on taking me out. Their family made me grateful for my comparatively simple relationship with Angela. Sure, I'd lied about my near-death experience in Prague on my birthday, hadn't told her about my scar or my tattoo, and had kind of broken into her house last week, but we had nothing on Renatus's family.

That made the White Elm my best-case scenario. This assessment didn't shock me, since I was technically allied with them and did genuinely like almost everybody on their council, but being "caught" by them meant coming back before them as a runaway. It meant facing the music for whatever Renatus and I did at Teagan's to get hold of the stupid ledger and running the risk of being found guilty of crimes I couldn't remember, as well as new ones like spelling away Hiroko's memory. I'd never join the council with a criminal record. I might be separated from Renatus. It did already feel like that, an uncomfortable silence in the back of my mind where there should have been a reassuring constant presence, but a magical separation was a permanent punishment for masters and their apprentices whose futures no longer aligned, or who abused the power they had over one another.

I joined a line to the front counter and swallowed, unsettled. Did my future still align with Renatus's, or had I taken us in different directions? I didn't know my own fate, but I knew his – Renatus was destined to kill Lisandro one day. He'd lived for this, wanted it for so long, and I knew he believed that if he could pull it off, he'd be free of his cloying, painful past. But what he didn't know, and I sometimes wished I didn't know, was that executing his godfather wasn't Renatus's salvation. It was his undoing. From there, Susannah had warned me, he would begin his descent into someone just as twisted, just as dark and terrible, or maybe worse. Renatus was impulsive where Lisandro was controlled. Renatus was less stable, less experienced, and more powerful than anything the living White Elm had encountered before. I didn't want to believe the young man I cared for so deeply could become someone I could be afraid of, but I also knew him too well to fool myself.

And though I thoroughly disliked Susannah, and didn't like to put much stock in what Seers thought they saw, she had an excellent track record as a Seer, and this warning was too dire to simply hope it wouldn't come to pass. Lisandro had taken it seriously, and had murdered almost my whole family to prevent Renatus and me from ever meeting, hoping to derail this future.

No such luck.

The line moved up, and I stepped forward. There was no certain way of avoiding Renatus's horrific future, if it was even to happen, but as the only person who cared more about him than the repercussions, I couldn't let our futures diverge so much that I wouldn't be around to prevent it. I'd decided months ago that I'd be the one to kill Lisandro, if I could only work out how a girl of eighteen with less than six months' formal magic training was going to take on a lifelong sorcerer, natural Crafter and former Dark Keeper for the White Elm; I still didn't have an answer to that, but I did have a slip of paper with a message written in my own handwriting. I slid it from the satchel hanging from my shoulder.

Whatever it takes.

So I couldn't let the White Elm catch me if it meant being separated from Renatus, the both of us losing the connection and power boost that made a victory against Lisandro and Magnus Moira viable. My only option was to stay alive and stay free until Renatus's mind was his own again and he could contact me to say the coast was clear, and we could determine the next step together.

'Next, please,' the smiley woman behind the counter called, and I hurried forward, slipping my fresh new passport from my coat pocket. Time to test out Reilly Murphy's word and risk becoming the next star of an airport security show. 'Good evening, what can we do for you?'

'I'd like to book a seat on the next flight to Prague, please,' I said, placing the illegal document – *so* illegal, how was I going to get away with this? – on the counter as calmly as I could. Like it wasn't a damning piece of evidence more terrifying to me than the empty book in my bag that dozens of people were stalking me for. 'Doesn't need to be direct, I just want the soonest one.'

'You're in luck,' the attendant said with a bright smile that

made me feel even more exhausted, and she gave me the details
of a plane going via Heathrow, which I was *just* in time for. She
asked me for checked luggage – I had none – and she scanned
my passport while I watched with a tense chest, barely breathing.
It didn't scan on the first go. I think my heart stopped for a
second. She smiled and bent the spine, opening the front cover
with more force. Nothing about her emotional state indicated
any suspicion. 'I love the feel of a brand-new passport. So many
adventures yet to be had. They're just…' She pressed it again to
the scanner, and to my wobbly relief, it beeped. 'They're just
hard to get flat enough to scan up.'

Tickets clutched in hand, fake passport back in my
possession, I headed for customs, but didn't feel totally ready for
that next obstacle just yet and I had a little time, so I had dinner
at the overpriced café. The people at the tables around me were
chatty, excited about where they were going, and I let a little of
my guard down to let some of that positive emotional energy
influence mine. No scriers for the last while. Maybe it was getting
too late for them. I had noticed fewer attempts at night. That
supported my theory that most of my seekers were based in the
time zone I was trying to escape.

I hoisted my backpack and satchel over each shoulder and
froze to hear the clink of the metal *swords* I was trying to *bring
through customs*. I blinked, realising the glaring hole in my plan.
How was this only occurring to me now? Hello, metal detectors.
Hello, security guards.

Slowly I walked my rubbish to the bins, buying myself a
moment to debate my next move. I had my ticket out of here. The
sai were going to make that difficult, but the possibility of
leaving them behind didn't sit well. Yes, I had magic and could
defend myself without them, but that was while I had wards. I'd
been working with Tian and Renatus on using my beautiful
swords for the weapons they were. It seemed silly to go without
them.

And, frankly, they were gifts from Renatus, and I felt far
enough from him right now without ditching another
connection. Somehow, I was going to have to make this work.

I took a big breath and started for customs. I wasn't going to be arrested. I'd Displace out if this didn't work. Try to get across the Channel myself and just take the risk. I'd landed in Prague on my own before, by accident; I could do it again if I was desperate enough.

Keeping the bags in my personal space and under my warding solved the problem of the first metal detector, but then there was the x-ray machine. I swallowed my nervousness as the line ahead of me thinned.

'Right here, miss.' A bulky customs officer with a thick accent waved a plastic basket at me. I stepped tentatively closer. I'd previously formed wards around external objects, no problem, but not while this strung-out, and not for the express purpose of obscuring metal shapes from machines and computer software. I didn't know if it would work or how the ward would affect the visual on the screen.

That feeling of time running out was back.

I put my things in the basket and reluctantly let the conveyor belt carry them toward the big box that would look inside, and stepped through the human archway when waved forward.

An alarm beeped and I nearly burst into tears. My jumpy reaction, and the way I whipped myself away from the customs officer who reached for me from my blind spot, was apparently more concerning than the fact that I had metal on me somewhere, because I felt the flat energy around me spike.

'Miss, could you please step to the side?'

'Why?' I demanded, unreasonably defensive. I glanced quickly at the big x-ray box and saw my bags hadn't gone through yet. I might be able to get back to grab them before anyone could catch me. Displace somewhere, anywhere, and hope I landed in the right place. My hands curled with the restless urge to snatch up my things and bolt. The frowning man showing me his open palms noticed.

'We're going to use the wand,' he explained, deliberately patient, and for a delirious moment I thought he was talking about the magical instrument I'd brought with me to the Academy and rarely used. Renatus sometimes used one – I

assumed to channel and direct some of that wild raw energy –
but for me, emergencies requiring big leaps in magical learning
had never coincided with days I'd had my grandmother's
handmade wand on my person. Today included.

Then I saw the metal detector paddle the officer reached for,
and I tried to make myself relax.

'It's… It's probably my buckles,' I said, more to myself than
to him. I wiggled my foot, silver buckled boots glinting in the
unforgiving lights. 'I'm sorry I jumped. I didn't see you.' I
gestured at my face and he softened, noting the placement of the
scar through the corner of my eye.

'Not a problem.' He ran the wand over my body swiftly and
confirmed it was my shoes causing the issue. He made me sit to
take them off. I complied, eye still on my bags. The first, the
backpack, had just gone inside the x-ray. A seed of interest, and
then concern, began with one of the security officers watching
the screen. She stopped the conveyor belt and signalled to my
wand-bearing officer, whose gentle demeanour shifted subtly.
'Can I see your passport?' Numbly I withdrew it from my coat
pocket and he opened it with the same practiced force as the
front counter attendant. He read it quickly. 'Confirm your
name?'

You know, I'd read it maybe ten times inside Murphy and
Nephew Distribution's foyer, committing to memory the false
identity I'd paid for, but right then, it totally fled from me.

'It's written on there,' I said instead, and earned myself the
exact look of suspicion I deserved. He looked down at me as I
got my second shoe off.

'I need you to confirm it,' he said firmly. I stared up into his
hard, dark eyes and felt my chest tighten with certainty. I'd run
out of luck. This was the end of the line.

'It's…'

'Ivy?'

Both the customs officer and I looked at the speaker, a shock
eleventh hour saviour squeezing between the people in the line
with polite apologies. He was the last person I expected to see
and his presence had worrying implications, but the shock of

seeing him alive and his mention of the name he shouldn't have known gave my brain the kickstart it needed.

'Ivy Jane Callahan,' I recited to the customs officer. I pushed myself back to my feet so I could look at him levelly. 'Birthday twenty-ninth of May. What's wrong with the bag?'

I nodded at the x-ray scanner and the officer reread my passport, still exuding scepticism.

'Did you pack your bags yourself, Miss Callahan? Hey!' He lost interest in me and turned to fend off Declan O'Malley, who'd just dumped his bag on the conveyor belt and stepped right through the metal detector archway to reach me. The beeps started again. 'You need to wait—'

'Sorry I'm late, sweetheart, I got caught up. You alright?' With false concern so convincing even I almost bought it, Declan inspected me closely. Rugged brown hair fell into the first familiar face I'd seen in days. 'Why were you on the ground?'

I should have stabbed him. Maybe I would have, if I had anything sharp handy, but instead I answered, 'My shoes set the alarm off.'

'Sir, you need to wait on the other side of the arch,' the customs officer instructed, and Declan's face broke into a practised apologetic smile. He lifted his loose shirt to unclip the chain belt that had set off the metal detector.

'Right, right, sorry, it's these bloody chains,' he agreed, starting back the way he came, then paused as though just noticing the behaviour of the scanner operators. 'That's not one of our bags, is it? Is this about the bowl?'

The scanner operator looked up at him as he finally went back through the arch to await being called through.

'That, and somethin' rather more concerning,' she said, sharing a glance with the customs officer who waved him back. Declan handed them the belt to add to one of the plastic baskets and stepped through again, with no alarm. 'Can you explain a small, sharp object in this bag?'

I let the customs officer wave the wand over me again, keeping an eye on Declan as he stepped over to act innocent with the security people at the scanner. As soon as I was pronounced clear, I hurriedly pocketed my new passport and rushed to Declan's side with my shoes still in hand. The satchel, with my very incriminating sai, was now going through.

'So this is *your* bag?' the woman officer was asking Declan, opening her hands over the cute backpack from Hiroko. He nodded, and she looked across at me. 'You two are travelling together?'

'No,' I replied flatly, at the same time he confirmed, 'Just married,' with one of his easy smiles, one tooth missing, and I *so* wished I had whatever small, sharp object the security officer had spotted in the backpack. He shot me an affectionate look that I met with an acidic one. He explained, 'She still hasn't forgiven me for doubling up my band tour with our honeymoon.'

I bit my teeth down hard so I wouldn't speak. The scanner operator blinked.

'He invited his band on your honeymoon?' she asked me, incredulous. She glanced at Declan as the satchel came through. 'I'd kill my husband for doin' that.'

I looked at him too. I hadn't seen him since Shanahan's, and in my experience, his appearance in any critical situation had always preceded a turn for the worse, however much it might look at first like he was there to be helpful. Where had he been, and what was he doing here now? I checked my wards, specifically those around my thoughts, and felt his slippery presence at the edge.

'What a good idea.'

He smiled patiently at me and laid a deliberate hand on the edge of the machine. The security officer, in a much better mood, asked us to open the bag, and I did, feeling tense. Bowl. Herbs. Clothes. And the stupid little knife I'd cut my hair with. I let her go through the things I shouldn't be bringing through an airport.

'Nice pen,' she admired, picking up what was very obviously a small knife in her gloved hands. I refocused my tired eyes and saw the soft glimmer of magic around the objects – Declan casting an illusion. 'That must have been it. This all looks fine. The next one yours as well?'

She leaned back to look at the screen. I prepared for the

inevitable wave of surprise to see the distinctive shape of two sharpened swords, for the blaring alarms and for the rush of security guards to arrest us.

'Just clothing,' Declan told her, and she nodded complacently. The satchel came through without stopping and I grabbed it before he could. It made an incriminating *clink* but the officer seemed not to notice. No one did. I swung it over my shoulder and Declan removed his hand from the scanner once his bag and chain came through. Whatever he'd done to fool everyone, even an x-ray machine, I needed to learn it; but not from him. Lessons from Declan tended to cost me time and dignity, and I was low on both.

Miraculously, we were sent on our way, and we wove through the remaining queues in absolute silence. My mind was spinning, but mostly, I was seething. We passed the final checkpoint and I made straight for the first restroom sign I spotted. He followed me without prompt, unhurried, so when I stormed to the end of the service hall and spun to face him, he was still passing the door of the men's room several paces behind me. Glancing around at the signs with mild interest, smiling amiably when he caught my eye, you'd be forgiven for assuming he didn't know me well enough to read the burning dislike broadcasting across my features.

I wished I could say I didn't know him at all.

'You take me to the nicest places,' he commented pleasantly, extending a hand to trace his fingers along the wall leading to the bathroom, no doubt absorbing impressions of those who'd touched it before he did. I'd seen him do it before, and I felt incredulous rage surge through me to see him acting so normal, as if everything were fine.

'What are you doing here?' I demanded through clenched teeth. Declan slowed, letting a father and son exit the bathroom, sharing a charming smile of acknowledgement, and then crossed the distance to stand opposite me.

'Catching my flight,' he responded as though it were the most natural thing in the world. I folded my arms, mainly so I wouldn't hit him out of frustration. Almost a *week*, I'd assumed him dead or underground somewhere, the cockroach that he was, and now he showed up like he wasn't the key factor to my life falling apart at the seams.

He had put the idea of the ledger in my head, setting me on this path of disaster.

He had shown me the man in his basement, a "contractor" hired by Thomas Shanahan to infiltrate my sister's life to get dirt on me, and told me the White Elm had illegally wiped his memory and *let him go.*

He had shown me how to cast memory spells, had in fact cast one on *me*, and had left all the ingredients in this satchel I was even now clutching close.

And *he* had disappeared without any trace, leaving Renatus and me to take the blame for the ledger and whatever had happened to Teagan.

I should have started off asking him about any of that, but I went with, 'Why would *you* need to catch a plane?'

'Why would you?' he countered easily. 'Unless you were avoiding Displacement that might be picked up by anyone with their ear to the ground, and not able to utilise the services of anyone else who might usually do it for you. Speaking of...' He looked around suddenly, a theatrical impersonation of a man expecting to see someone he already knew wasn't here. 'Where is Renatus? Is he– whoa!'

He'd backed up two automatic steps when I took an unintentional one closer, tight fists falling loose of my folded arms.

'Leave him out of this,' I hissed, trying not to wonder what part Declan had played in Renatus's near-burnout, 'and leave *me* alone.'

'*Leave* you?' Declan repeated, turning on the spot as I strode around him in a wide arc. 'What kind of friend would I be if I left you alone at a time like this?'

The ridiculousness of that statement, the nerve, was enough to make me stop, choking on a single breath of laughter.

'At a time like this?' I clarified, facing him again. He looked exactly as I recalled from the last time I saw him, unruffled and tidy if you could call grunge tidy *ever*, but with the faint sense of magic about him that told me this was an illusion to hide a deteriorating appearance. 'How is this time different?'

'Well...' He spread his hands helplessly, looking about the service hall again. 'Your other allies are looking thin on the ground, baby doll.'

'I do not need help from you,' I made sure to state very clearly, choosing to ignore the epithet, 'and even if I did, I still wouldn't want it, not after you *left us* at Shanahan's–'

'Is that how you remember it?' he cut in smoothly, and I clamped my mouth shut before I could do any further damage. His brown eyes, set into a deliberately innocent face under an artfully confused frown, were dancing. He was there. He *did* remember. For me to say anything more would betray that I didn't, and I wasn't sure whether he knew that or what he could do that with that information. He continued to feign confusion. 'And here I was, thinking I'd helped you escape certain death and torture. My mistake. How's his head?'

He pointed sympathetically to his own hairline, reminding me of the injury Renatus had come back from that misadventure with – an injury neither of us could remember him sustaining. I subconsciously wrapped my hand around the strap of the satchel, aware of the weight of the ledger inside.

He wasn't just here to rile me up, though I'd long suspected he got more enjoyment out of that than was decent. I had something else he wanted. It used to be easy to be charmed by his playfulness and forget Renatus's warnings, but not anymore. Declan was dangerous, and well above my paygrade.

'Say, is that my bag?' he mentioned, deliberately offhand, with a nod at the satchel. I nudged it behind myself with my elbow, lifting my chin determinedly.

'Finders keepers. I want you to stay away from me, Declan,' I warned him as I backed off. I felt for my wards, hoping they'd hold against someone like him, clearly well-rested and much more knowledgeable about magic than me. He made no move to chase me or grab me, not that I expected him to, but I still made sure to spell it out. 'Do not follow me, do not come near me. Just... stay the hell away.'

I turned and marched back down the corridor, determinedly ignoring his call after me.

'That might be difficult...'

I turned the corner and refused to glance back. His aura was hidden from my radar but his emotions, or at least the emotions he chose to portray, remained in place. I knew I needed to get out of sight of him and regroup, but his appearance here had shaken me up. As far as I knew, Declan O'Malley was the reason I was on the run in the first place. How had he found me? If he'd managed to track me down despite all my efforts, how poor was the condition of my wards, and who would find me next?

The feeling of time pressing in on me increased as I went looking for my gate.

chapter eight

I had almost half an hour's reprieve. I was one of the first to board my plane, and handed over my ticket with tight relief. Relief to be getting away; tension because I hadn't been on a plane by myself before, and because I didn't know for sure if I was any safer in that tin tube than I was in this departure lounge. I couldn't sense Declan anymore but I didn't know who or what awaited me in the minutes, hours, or days to come.

Declan was, to use Renatus's words, scum, but relatively loyal scum. There were worse people I could run into.

I idled down the aisle between seats, browsing for the number to match my ticket, and stashed my backpack and satchel in the overhead locker while I had the space to do so. I took my spot in the cramped little seat beside the window and stared out at the harshly lit runway as the plane began to fill up. My wards were still as tight and secure as I could manage, but I'd never sustained warding this intense for this long before. What would happen when I no longer could? Would they weaken or just break, or would they stay strong at my expense, beginning to burn me from the inside out like my big shield ward in Prague did to my arm? Like whatever Renatus did at Shanahan's to almost kill himself? Tentatively I rolled my left wrist in my lap, channelling a tiny bit of magic down to my hand to see the grey cracks light up under my skin. It wasn't as bad as it had been at first, but the thin lines like cracked porcelain were hard to miss. I released my hold on the magic and let the cracks fade.

'Ah, this is cosy.'

I gave a start as my neighbour dropped down into the seat

beside me, and I honestly and immediately wanted to stab him.

'*What* did I just *tell* you?' I hissed, beginning to stand. We were not having this conversation again, here on this increasingly crowded plane, and we were not about to be flight buddies for umpteen hours. But Declan made no effort to move out of my way, pulling his tray table down and reaching into the seat pocket to find the evacuation instruction sheet.

'Bit hard to stay away when I bought the seat right beside yours,' he said reasonably. I stayed half-standing, poised ready to make the escape I wanted to enact but couldn't work out how. I couldn't really teleport with all these people watching, and I couldn't count on getting my things out from the locker above me by the same method. I could shove Declan out of his seat, make a scene, but that would require either touching him, which I'd made a point never to do on very firm advice from Renatus, or using a forceful push of wards I was already feeling strained with.

Given my options were limited, I opted to try once more the power of words, as if they'd ever worked with him before.

'We seem not to be understanding each other,' I said, very plainly. 'I don't want to travel with you.'

'You hurt my feelings, Miss Aristea. But luckily for you, I'll live.' He smiled. His missing tooth stayed hidden behind the playful curve of his lips, and I knew he wasn't going anywhere. 'You don't have to travel with me. You're travelling alone, I can see that, such an independent young lady, and I'll just travel alone beside you. You should put your seatbelt on,' he added seriously, showing me the instruction card. 'I don't think they'll take off unless you do.'

Frustrated, I looked up and down the plane. Most other passengers had seated themselves, a few still packing the compartments overhead, and the flight attendants were moving gracefully between all this, handing out colouring packs to children and confirming details with elderly people. Out my window, when I lowered myself slightly to look, the luggage carriers had finished their job underneath and had driven away. Boarding had closed.

It was now or never.

'Move,' I instructed Declan, glaring when he only looked up at me in pretend surprise. 'I need to get off this plane.'

'That's a terrible idea,' he argued. 'Every degenerate I know is looking for you – you can't backtrack, that's inviting them to catch up.'

'Well, one of them did,' I reminded him sweetly, gesturing again. 'Move.'

But the insult only made him grin. He turned back to his instruction card like it was the newspaper.

'Don't you want to know how I did it?'

'How you found me?' I should have just pushed past him, ignored him, but for some reason I always gave his words real estate in my head. 'How?' Were my wards laxer than I thought? Was I leaving some kind of trail?

He smiled and cast his gaze at my loose seatbelt. 'Sit.'

Ugh, nothing was ever a simple, straightforward answer with him. I wanted to tell him where to go, and I think I opened my mouth to do that, but another voice cut in, politely.

'Miss, is everything okay?'

The flight attendant had arrived at Declan's side and was smiling at me. I looked around again and saw everyone was seated now, and I'd missed the announcement advising of impending take-off procedures. I was still halfway between sitting and standing, my neck bent under the curve of the aeroplane's side, and I was still only halfway to making up my mind on what to do.

'I'm...' I didn't know what to say. I'm being followed by this crazy man. I'm feeling trapped and scared and I want to be let off this plane. I'm leaving. But none of it came out in time.

'She's a nervous flier,' Declan intimated to the attendant with one of his winning smiles. He clipped his tray table back up before she could ask. 'We're just talking through her exercises. Air travel is extremely safe,' he said to me with the exaggerated calm of a caring boyfriend talking through a script. Ugh. 'In fact, it's the safest way to get where you want to go. No one can get to you when we're up in the air. You'll be totally safe, unreachable, you might even say.

And besides, you'll be with me.'

The flight attendant's smile warmed at his apparent care and I really, really wanted to stab him, but something in what he said caught my attention. *Unreachable.* Was he suggesting what I thought he was?

I weighed up my options. Declan was a well of information, though I always paid dearly for it; there might be something to be gained, and lost, if I stayed here with him. Going back meant buying another plane ticket, later, and though I didn't want my decisions influenced by his words, Declan's warning about backtracking inviting my pursuers to catch up made too much sense. And while Declan was not my favourite person right now, it was impossible to ignore the most basic fact of the moment: Declan had never tried to kill me, nor had I ever feared that he would, and as dangerous as I knew him to be, I still wasn't scared of him.

The people following me? Some of them genuinely scared me.

I had my mind locked down, impenetrable, but Declan must have read my thoughts in my face.

'You're with me,' he repeated.

Slowly, reluctantly, I slid down into my seat. 'How… reassuring.'

'He's right, it really is very safe,' the attendant said kindly. 'I need to ask you to put on your seatbelt before we can depart.'

'So that you're safe,' Declan reiterated sensibly, watching as I irritably did as I was told, and shot his brilliant smile back once more at the attendant as she reminded us to call her if we needed her. He relaxed in his seat as she moved on. 'What a delightful lady.'

'What did you mean, unreachable?' I asked, tightening my seatbelt. I could hardly believe I was strapping myself in for a plane ride with Declan O'Malley. I imagined Renatus's disgust when he heard about this. 'Can we not Displace that high?'

As much as I hated having to ask him for information about our world, our magic and the way those both worked, and hated even more the feeling of him knowing how much I didn't know, I really wanted this knowledge and was prepared to admit I wasn't an expert Displacer. It wasn't much to give this trader of secrets – I was a student, new to magic, and using a plane, so the fact that I wasn't a strong teleporter probably wasn't news he could do much with.

To his credit, like usual, he acted like it was no big deal to part with the answers I wanted, and as usual he behaved like he wasn't judging my ignorance.

'A good Displacer isn't much affected by altitude,' he said easily, leaning past me to get my safety card out of the seat pocket. I tipped instinctively away, not wanting to make physical contact, and he didn't breach that boundary, keeping his hand and arm clear of me. 'Speed, though, that's the big factor. You might have noticed that whatever momentum you Displace with, you maintain on the other side?'

He paused while I considered. When Hiroko and I ran through one of her wormholes, we arrived at the other side midstride, our speed maintained. When she took hold of me outside of Shanghai, we weren't moving, and we arrived at a standstill in the photobooth in Sapporo. I remembered the Displacer students discussing this over lunch one day, a million lifetimes ago when life was more normal – when I just attended a magic school, wasn't on the run from one – and nodded to Declan to let him know I understood.

'I'm not a physicist or anything fancy,' he reminded me humbly, dropping my evacuation instructions on my lap, 'but somehow or another, the Skip's relational to the gravity and rotation of the Earth, so if you jump through a wormhole at ten kilometres an hour anywhere on Earth, you'll pop out at the same speed – more or less, excepting minor shifts for altitude and whatnot – provided you're landing on Earth. No one's ever come back from experiments trying to land elsewhere. Must have good beaches to keep them away so long.' He cast me his grin. I determinedly kept my smile to myself. He'd burned me before, pretending to be friendly, pretending to be harmless and helpful. Not again. 'Now imagine your landing site is moving at eight or nine hundred kilometres an hour, and you rock up at your measly ten.'

I stared at him, not quite comprehending. 'Let's pretend I'm not a physicist or anything fancy, either.'

He pointed over his shoulder. '*Splat* on that back wall, if you're a crack shot Displacer and spot-on with your target; for the rest of us, probably falling through the air some dozen kilometres behind the plane. In flight, it's moving too fast for a Displacement from the Earth's surface,' he clarified. Under my seat, I felt the soft jerk as the plane began taxiing toward the runway. 'Same reason all those pioneers couldn't land on distant alien planets. The speed's too different. So yes, to answer the question you're trying not to ask: this plane is about to be the safest place possible for a pretty little witch tired of bad guys teleporting into her personal space. And until take-off, my sweet, you fortunately find yourself in the company of *me*.'

'How *fortunate*,' I replied scathingly, grabbing my safety card to pretend to read it when I heard the announcement prompting me to do so. Eyes fixed on the diagrams, I heard rather than saw Declan's smile.

'Very fortunate,' he agreed quietly as the attendants began lining the aisle for the demonstration. 'How many times have you been attacked in the past hour since I turned up?'

I shot him a dark look but fell silent for the presentation. Our flight attendant was only a few seats ahead of us and she smiled warmly at me as she and the others began to point out the nearest exits in case of an evacuation. I smiled back out of habit, but now I was thinking on what Declan had said. My time at the airport had been peaceful – no sudden appearances, except his, and no sense of strain on my wards. Was his presence somehow deflecting attention or was he doing something to keep my enemies away?

A million years ago, just last week, he'd promised me a favour. Was there any merit in the idea that he might be honestly trying to help me?

Not likely.

I forced myself to relax into my seat and lean closer to Declan so I could drop my voice and not interrupt the demonstration.

'Okay, I'll bite,' I murmured. Smirking playfully, he turned his head so we were facing each other. Too close – boundaries weren't his strong suit. But backing down when I'd initiated always felt like a failing or a sign of weakness, and I hated to be weak in front of him.

'Oh, please do.'

'Don't start,' I warned with a finger in his face that only made his smile widen. 'What did you mean before? How no one's attacked me since you turned up?'

'What did you think I mean?'

'I think you owe me so many favours by now that giving me a straightforward answer should be automatic.'

'I thought that's what I just did?'

'Declan—'

'Are you sure you don't want to listen to this?' he whispered with a worried frown, indicating the line of flight attendants now raising life vests above their heads. 'It sounds terribly important. It might help your anxiety, knowing how to protect yourself in the event of—'

'I'm not experiencing anxiety,' I argued in a fierce whisper. 'I'm experiencing the low-key murderous rage I have come to associate with being in your presence.'

'Oh, that.' He smiled again and turned back to the presentation, settling his shoulders into the cushioning of his seat. 'That's just our latent sexual tension. To be expected, in close quarters like this.'

I bit my tongue, hard, and leaned back into the corner created by the curved inside wall of the aeroplane, disengaging before I could make a scene. This boiling fury inside me was not entirely Declan's fault – I knew, had always known, that he liked baiting a reaction out of me, and I had responded to every irritating and provocative thing he'd said since he sat down, playing into his games.

So I went silent and stoically watched the remainder of the demonstration, determinedly ignoring my companion. My seat vibrated with the rumble of the plane's building engine noise as we waited on the tarmac for our turn on the runway. I felt the same unsettled vibration inside my chest, the apprehension and excitement and nervousness of my fellow travellers permeating my aura and affecting my own reaction to the impending take-off.

What if Declan was wrong and someone Displaced in here, and I couldn't get away? What if someone had worked out already that I was here, and sabotaged the plane? They could rid themselves of me, the ledger and Declan in one move without having to face either of us. What if, what if, what if?

The flight attendants finished and moved away to ready themselves for take-off. Declan leaned forward to get a hand inside his jacket.

'Your wards are bloody good,' he mentioned casually, as if I wasn't ignoring him, as if we were still in the middle of a conversation, 'but they're not intended for long-term like you've clearly been doing. You've had these up since the day at Shanahan's?' He nodded at the air around my head, implying he could see the energy there, shielding me. I refused to answer. 'That might be a record. Not good for you, though. Magic like this, it's meant to be anchored down to something. You, you're anchoring to yourself, like a good little White Elmer because that's the only way to stay inside their narrow painted lines. That's why you're under strain. That's why they're starting to fail.' He caught my look of surprise with a kind smile. 'And that's how they're finding you.'

The plane got moving, turning onto the runway, and I ran anxious attention all over myself, scanning for gaps in my warding. How had I not noticed them failing already? How was it that even now, they seemed fine?

'The lapses are only temporary,' Declan explained, withdrawing a packet of gum from his jacket. 'Mere seconds, less. Only someone looking for you in those exact moments would catch you with your guard down. Unfortunately for you, you've got enough people on the lookout that half the time that happens, someone will be looking. And they've been turning up, I gather.'

'And that's how you found me?' I guessed. He unwrapped a piece of gum and popped it into his smiling mouth, shaking his head.

'No, sweet Miss Aristea, I found you because I know how you

think.' He offered me the packet. I declined, recalling Renatus's warning when I first met Declan – never to accept any food or drink from him, and never to let him touch me. I didn't know what would happen if I did, but I'd chosen so far not to find out. 'You're resourceful, but limited by connections. It wasn't hard to find out whether you'd followed my advice with the Murphies, and to learn you'd asked for a passport. What would a girl on an island do with a passport? Hmm. And how patient is that girl? Not very. I figured you'd be here sometime today or maybe early tomorrow, at latest.'

The pilot had angled the plane to face down the long runway, and now the engines kicked into overdrive, accelerating fast. I grabbed the armrests automatically, nerves fluttering, and dozens of unwanted images of past passengers slid through my defences, all of them doing exactly what I was doing now. I should be wearing gloves, keep those pesky impressions out. I found them in my pockets.

'Take-off is perfectly safe,' Declan reminded me, swapping the gum for a ballpoint pen. I closed my eyes against the roiling of my stomach.

'I have two swords in my bags and I will impale you with them.'

'Funny, they didn't show up in the scan?'

The weightless sensation of lift-off stole my breath for a moment, and I opened my eyes to the brightly lit cabin without seeing it. Elsewhere on the island I was leaving, my sister slept soundly with her cell phone on the bedside table, well within reach; outside Morrissey House, the encampment of Magnus Moira hadn't budged, and I hadn't seen anyone come and go through the gate. Far from here, across seas and cities, Hiroko was starting her day like usual.

And in lieu of the constant wearing attentions of scriers on my wards, I felt the tension in my chest loosen. I felt like I'd gained a little reprieve – a scrap of extra time.

'How long are you planning to be away on this nice getaway of yours?' Declan asked me, unbuttoning the cuff of his jacket to get at his wrist while I swallowed to clear the pressure building in my ears.

'Not your concern,' I answered coolly. My ears popped and the plane gently banked. 'We're parting ways at London.'

My companion smiled patiently and began scribing something onto the skin of his forearm. 'Not according to my ticket, and judging from the shadows under your eyes, better I don't. Why don't you get some sleep? Drop some wards, recharge while you can.'

I scoffed. 'Fall asleep, so you can assault me and steal my stuff?'

'Where would I go?' he asked rhetorically, stopping in his writing to wave the pen at the cabin full of buckled-in passengers. 'I've already explained the impossibility of Displacing on or off this tin can, yes?'

'I'm only taking your word that that's true,' I countered, and he shrugged delicately, resuming his writing.

'You're welcome to test my word for yourself, but know I will mourn you deeply. How would you describe your current state?' he redirected, nodding at his arm. I couldn't see what he'd written because of the angle. 'I've got "radiant as ever". Would you say that sums it up?'

I frowned and leaned closer, holding tightly to my armrest when turbulence threatened to tip me into Declan's lap. In script I'd recently seen on a different arm, I read the words: *Vital and radiant as ever, think we're in love. Might take a trip somewhere quiet.*

My heart leapt with sudden and explosive hope that had nothing at all to do with the provocative wording.

'Renatus sent you?' I breathed, almost too scared to voice the possibility aloud. Hiroko was right. Renatus wouldn't leave me alone to this, not if there was *anything* he could do to help me. Declan wavered.

'*Sent* is a strong word,' he answered. He put the pen away and swiped his palm over the ink. A tiny injection of magical energy into the act, and the words were gone. I'd seen Renatus doing the same thing, communicating with Declan. Sorcerer instant messaging. 'Pestered, maybe, with repeated assumptions?'

I didn't quite know what that meant, and when he didn't

elaborate, I pestered, too.

'Well, is he alright?'

'Usually. How should I know? I didn't ask. His right hand still works, though his penmanship's taken a dive. Must be the stress of all those fanatics camping out at his front gate.'

'You've seen it too?'

He spared me another patient smile. 'Scrier, sweetheart. Read your new name off your passport when I was still a hundred metres away, negotiating customs. It's a horribly inefficient way to travel, this, isn't it? Too many lines. And everywhere we land, different money. More lines. Yes, I have noticed the small blight that others call Magnus Moira occupying the moors. A dozen in view, and a dozen more you can't see. You're right to stay away.' He took an interest in fiddling with the reading light above his head. 'You're inside my warding right now, you know. You can take a break.'

I flopped back in my seat, re-evaluating. My first instinct was to get as far from Declan as possible at the first available opportunity, but the prospect that Renatus had sent him – or pestered him into finding me – changed my outlook completely. Renatus had always been plain about neither liking nor trusting Declan, yet had counted on him in several critical scenarios, belying his words. And I, too, was lying to myself. My *logic* said to get away from him; my instincts were what I'd followed back at the x-ray machine, right to his side to let him handle the security people for me.

I was as bad as Renatus. Or perhaps he was as bad as me, taking on my naïve and gullible qualities as our personalities continued to morph, wanting more and more to trust people when he should know better. When *I* should know better.

I extended my awareness and tentatively felt for Declan's warding. When I cast wards, they were like glass: bubbles, plates, mushrooms, temporarily solid energy holding a shape I wanted to protect me, others, or external things like my bags. There was always a faint thread left between me and my creation, an umbilical cord that allowed me to keep pushing energy in or to cut it off. Declan's magic didn't feel like glass. More like... basket weave? A net? Originating from... where? It didn't seem connected to him at all. It reminded me of the rope-like magic knotted over Renatus's estate.

It had never occurred to me that I'd been sleeping under illegal magic there, but of course, that's what it had to be. Old magic. Blood magic. Though I had only a fraction of the same trust in Declan, he wasn't lying when he said that the magic surrounding him was also encapsulating me.

Reluctantly, hoping my trust wasn't as misplaced as usual, I let down some wards, one at a time. My physical barriers. The defence against scriers. The walls I usually maintained to keep others' emotions at bay. I kept up my telepathic shields – *don't even try me, Declan* – but consciously stopped surveying my surroundings for magical energies.

I gave it a wary second, tensed in case my companion tried anything.

'So suspicious,' he complained. I rolled my shoulders back into my seat, trying to relax. I found I felt better already, no longer straining my attention and efforts like I had been.

'Everyone I care about is in danger because of me, and I'm stuck on an aeroplane with the dodgiest crook I know. Can you blame me?'

'I think you overestimate your part in everyone else's danger,' he said, my insults sliding off his back as always. 'I can't speak for the rest, but I promise, Renatus would find plenty of trouble even without you in the picture. He's just that way inclined.'

'And Teagan?' I challenged. 'Would she be in hospital right now if it weren't for me? If it weren't for *either* of us?'

He visibly backed off at my mention of our mutual young friend. I honestly had no idea whether Declan cared about me, but the soft remorse I felt coming from him felt sincere. He quickly hid it behind a scoff.

'Unlikely, since I'm the one who dropped her off there, and you're the one who... you know,' he said with an infuriating shrug, since we both knew I did *not* know. 'It seems she'll live, thanks to your council Healer pals, and the danger she faces henceforth has less to do with you than it does her family's past choices. And you should stop doing that,' he added, a warning edge to his voice that I wasn't used to. It pulled me back from the now-familiar image of a closed door at an unfamiliar hospital, which I'd been watching in my mind's eye. My real vision blurred briefly as I adjusted back. 'I thought Renatus was meant to be *teaching* you? Use a tool when you're low on energy. It draws less on you.'

I considered this new information. Qasim, my scrying instructor, had never put it that way, only said that using a scrying tool – like a mirror, candle flame or crystal – was easier, a step on the way to scrying with the mind. It was true that I usually had more success with tool-scrying when I was tired or stressed.

'I'm not saying light a fire in an aeroplane,' Declan added hastily when he saw me patting down my coat pockets. He pointed up at the "no smoking" sign above us. 'I feel like they'll take issue with that.'

'I'm not lighting a fire.' I had to awkwardly twist my wrist to get my fingers around the ruby without bumping my elbow into Declan. These rows were not built with personal space in mind, and I was trying hard to maintain mine. Large, priceless stone free, I cradled it in my gloved hands and stared into its depths.

It didn't take long. The same vision of Teagan Shanahan's hospital room door appeared in the smooth surface of the crystal. At first it stayed as it always had, closed fast, but then the handle turned and someone stepped out. It took a moment for me to recognise the small frame of the dark-haired young woman who carefully locked the door behind her, stretching kinks out of her neck and blinking exhausted eyes. Teresa was a councillor with the White Elm, and a Healer. She looked like she hadn't rested properly in a week.

'Hmm.'

I blinked and lost the vision. Declan was eyeing the ruby with a look of recognition. I wondered what he knew of it and opened my mouth to ask, then realised how lax I'd gotten around him. Yes, objectively speaking, he'd been perfectly helpful – and a little infuriating, though no more than usual – but I had to remember he wasn't my friend. He wasn't here to be helpful. He wanted something from me, like always, and I had to keep my wits sharp or risk making everything even worse than they already were.

'I'm going to get some rest,' I announced, slipping the ruby back into my pocket and shutting my emotions down, with effort. 'Don't try to touch me.'

'I won't say I wouldn't dream of it,' Declan said cheerfully, materialising a worn paperback from somewhere and settling back in his own seat, 'but I'll refrain on this occasion.'

He was as good as his word, which made one of us. I couldn't rest, much less sleep. The vibration of the plane's engines rumbled loud in my ears, making sleep impossible even when I clenched my eyes shut. The reprieve on my wards was a welcome relief, not that I'd admit that to Declan, but it was too short to make much difference to my energy levels. Too soon, we were landing in London, and then we weren't moving at nine hundred kilometres an hour anymore and I felt my anxiety clawing at my chest. My stomach dropped like lead to feel the plane's wheels hit the runway, and I gathered my weary wards back to me.

'You could just let me take care of it,' Declan sang, leaning too close while the plane was connected up to the terminal. All around us, passengers were restless, unclipping their seatbelts despite the announcement telling them to stay seated until the lights went off. Their restlessness was influencing mine. 'Give your wards the day off.'

'I could do a lot of ill-advised things. Don't you dare!' I threw myself forward to catch him but was held back by my seatbelt. The light had blinked off and Declan was one of the first standing, popping the overhead locker open.

'Don't what, *Ivy*?' he asked over the noise of the cabin. He was tall, and handed a bright purple overnight bag down to an older lady in the row behind us. She thanked him warmly and he gave her his most charming smile. He looked back at me as he reached back into the locker, daring me to make a scene. 'Don't retrieve my own bags?' He swung Hiroko's backpack over one shoulder and the rucksack he'd brought with him onto the other. I hurried to unlatch my belt. 'Don't fetch my dearly beloved's? How ungentlemanly.'

He grabbed the satchel – *his* satchel, admittedly, though I'd since claimed it – and held it out to me. Worried, I snatched it away. It felt the same weight as before, but I'd seen Declan perform sleight-of-hand magician-style magic in the past and didn't trust for a second that he hadn't slipped the ledger in the same smooth move. I dropped it on his seat to throw it open and dug through its contents. Sai, check. Clothes to cover them, crumpled documents, and there: the ledger, buried where I left it.

I closed the bag up and lifted my gaze to meet Declan's, aware I'd just revealed the book's location like an idiot and determined not to appear apologetic for mistrusting him. His eyes were bright, his smile sly, and I knew it didn't matter whether Renatus had sent him to check up on me or protect me or whatever. I still couldn't trust him as far as I could throw him. But he wasn't going anywhere, so when he said, 'Shall we?' I silently shouldered the bag and joined the crush of passengers disembarking.

We had a few people between us on our way up to the terminal, and we didn't end up near each other again until the departures lounge where we were to await our connecting flight. I kept the satchel close, one hand holding it shut, and tried not to make it obvious when I glanced down every passage, hoping for some opportunity of escape. Declan was more than I could handle and definitely going to screw me over – it was just a matter of when. I did not need another pressure on my limited sense of time.

My attention snagged on an empty, cordoned-off corridor that seemed to lead deeper into the airport, and I slowed down, letting the stream of fellow passengers overtake me. When I sent my attention down the corridor, I sensed no life, just a series of quiet corners and some tins of paint.

Exhausted hope rose in my heart. I could hide out. I could buy a new ticket, go somewhere else. I could shake Declan off my trail if I was smart about it. And quick.

'Going somewhere?'

I didn't feel his approach and leaned away from his breath in my ear, but he caught me by surprise when he crossed our established boundary and grabbed my hand. I began to protest when his fingers twined with mine and I resisted when he pulled me behind him into the corridor, away from the stragglers from our plane. Maybe I should have shouted. He had space open in an instant and tugged me through it with him.

The void dragged over us both and I wondered if Angela and Renatus would ever find out what happened to me.

We emerged in a field somewhere, and I gulped down a breath of air to give my lungs what they needed to yell at my kidnapper. I shook my hand free of his and stepped away, furious.

'What *the hell* are you doing?' I demanded, elbowing the satchel behind my back and channelling energy as fast as I could into the layers of warding around me. I couldn't win if he decided we were going to fight it out for this stupid book; I could only deflect and hope to escape. 'How many times do I need to say "don't touch me" before you *fucking* hear me?'

'Language, language,' Declan chided, rolling his eyes and waving his hand at me to show me what he'd donned while I wasn't watching. 'Relax. We're both wearing gloves. Renatus can last another day without my head mounted above his fireplace for *daring* to touch you. You wouldn't have come with me otherwise and I have to prove a point you won't like.'

'What point?'

'You're vulnerable,' he replied bluntly. It was my turn to roll my eyes. 'You were about to run off, and I can't help you if you leave.'

I actually growled with frustration, running my fingers through my loose hair. It was still knotty from the sea air at Belfast Harbour.

'I. Don't. Want. Your. Help,' I spelled out with as much contempt as I could muster. 'I don't want it, I don't need it, and you don't really intend to give it, so drop the friendly act and leave me alone.'

He still had Hiroko's backpack but I wasn't about to ask him for it and it didn't have anything vital anyway. Overhead, a large aeroplane was accelerating away from us, up and up on a steep angle, and when I looked behind me, I saw the distant lights of the runway. Beyond that, the massive sprawling terminal. I spread my awareness toward it, feeling for presences and trying to gauge the distance. I wished I wasn't already so strained.

I barely noticed the soft dismantling of Declan's weave-like warding around me – in fact I exhaled a breath of relief, figuring he was finally getting the message and preparing to leave – but the effect was clear. It took less than a minute. I'd decided I would walk some of the way back to the terminal to reduce the distance before Skipping, so I was a good forty paces away from Declan when the first scrier's attention grazed over me.

Forty-five when I felt the second one.

Sixty when space contorted beside me and a man stepped into being, almost on top of me. My invisibility wards came to life and I sprang away, digging in the satchel for my sai before panic could take over. When was this going to *stop*? He was the same man I'd seen tracking Hiroko and me on our first hasty escape from Morrissey House. The man with one hand.

Time squeezed in on me as the man spun on the spot, seeking me. I wasn't ready. I couldn't get my weapons fast enough.

But he froze halfway, attention catching on Declan O'Malley still standing sixty paces away with a backpack slung over each shoulder.

'Works for me,' the man sneered, summoning magic to his one hand. I stared in fright, preparing a quick ward I could throw between them to protect Renatus's irritating relative, but Declan was faster than us both. A reddish tangle of magic struck the one-handed man in the throat and he collapsed with a strangled scream, clawing at his neck as the magic sparked and spat. I backed off, and Declan appeared at my side. He offered his leather-gloved hand.

I suppose I took it without further question, and he Displaced us away immediately. We stepped out between two towering sheds that, once I identified the shrieking howl of jet engines, turned out to be aeroplane hangars.

'Sorry for the demonstration,' Declan yelled over the noise, jerking his head to indicate that I should follow him out into the open. I blinked as we moved into the bright lights of the airfield, watching out for cameras or onlookers, but I couldn't feel anybody around except those inside the hangar. 'I didn't think you realised how fried you are.'

He cast an apologetic look back at me that seemed genuine. It would be nice to think he hadn't wanted to put me on the spot like that. I debated whether to believe it, though it hardly mattered much.

'Will that guy live?'

'Unfortunately, yes,' Declan confirmed with a heavy sigh as he yanked off his gloves and pocketed them. The sound of our feet scuffing the ground changed as we moved from cement to soil. He stopped and knelt down, and I copied, feeling like I had nothing left to lose at this point. Declan's wards encompassed me once again and it didn't seem I was capable of doing this without him right now.

'He was looking for me,' I said slowly, rethinking the exchange we'd just escaped, 'but he was willing to take you instead.'

'Think you're the only one with a price on their head?'

Sly dark eyes flicked up at me as he dumped his backpack on the ground between us and began unpacking a strange assortment of materials. He paused with his hands on the zipper, letting his façade waver before my eyes. Unblemished skin shifted into tightly bandaged fingers and a few recent cuts on the backs of each hand, and I recalled seeing him reopening wounds like these when I visited his house, wiping traces of blood onto the locks of his doors. He'd said something similar then, too.

'Who's after you?' I asked, looking up at him. The illusion of perfect health was returning, though I caught shadowed eyes like mine and ravaged brown hair that was chopped at all haphazard lengths and angles.

'Well, who isn't?' he replied pleasantly. He swiped his bag

aside and began tearing leaves, humming a discordant tune. He heaped the leaves and petals together and began tracing unfamiliar symbols into the dirt around the pile. 'Watching? This is why they can look all they want.'

Planes whizzed overhead and droned past on their way to the runway but no one saw us. It occurred to me how bizarre my situation was, to be sitting on an airfield with a sorcerer I'd just tried to escape before running into an even worse option, and feeling bewilderingly safe, as I usually did with him.

I made myself face the facts.

'I know why you're really here, Declan,' I said. He kept drawing symbols, kept humming. I tightened my grip on the satchel's strap. 'You want something.'

He stopped what he was doing to give me a steady look.

'Sweet Miss Aristea, everybody wants something,' he reminded me kindly, and I really felt he was being sincere this time. 'All of them, the ones looking for you, they want to get paid, or they want to satisfy some imagined need for justice. You're in luck, though, because what I want directly aligns with what *you* want.' He smiled his lopsided grin. 'I just want to live, baby, and I'd prefer you did, too.'

I considered this carefully. 'You're not going to steal the ledger from me?'

'Not today.'

No promise of the future, but I shouldn't have expected much more from him. I slowly nodded, seeing no better choice.

'Then I suppose for today, we're allies. Or until our interests no longer align.'

His smile widened. 'My thoughts exactly.'

chapter nine

It seemed he didn't eat or move for days, though he must have gone through usual motions. Sleeping. Drinking from the glasses of water left beside him, because soon enough they were empty and new ones took their place. Attending the bathroom. Ignoring people, mostly Qasim, who began joining him in his solitude to work at Renatus's own desk each day. He kept to himself, except to occasionally make a snide comment or to forcibly clear Renatus's mind of Nastassja's presence when she got too deep a foothold. It had happened three times now, though only twice by accident. On yesterday's occasion, Renatus had deliberately let his guard down to test a theory. She'd taken the bait, and he'd used the opportunity to observe what weaknesses she exploited in his mental barriers, what senses she could access and what neural pathways she followed to reach them. Qasim had seen Renatus struggling with her, and had again kicked her out, ranting at him for being weak and without will. But whatever. Today, Renatus felt more prepared to deal with her. He knew now what she could see when she dug into his head, and what she couldn't.

He could finally think without her overhearing, provided he kept his thoughts to one very guarded area of his mind, and he was also quite sure he could now listen without broadcasting that to her. His eyes, though, his not-dead sister seemed able to tap whenever she pleased. He was yet to work out a means of blocking his vision from her, including images he summoned to his mind.

So he stared at walls, the floor, his hands, keeping his visual thoughts blank, keeping her frustrated.

'Who is she?' Fionnuala asked darkly, peering between the curtains after dropping him something else to eat. He swallowed the uncomfortable truth.

'Lisandro's wife,' he said, and his housekeeper looked back at him in shock. 'We thought she was Keely Shanahan, but now...'

He couldn't lie. She would detect it. So he tried to steady himself to be honest, something he was new at, but she spoke before he could.

'Goodness, Keely,' she said, very seriously, turning back to the window. 'And we all thought she was dead for sure. You know, I had been thinking she looked familiar. So odd how these things work out.'

She smoothed the curtains into place and squeezed his shoulder affectionately on her way back, too accustomed to his moody behaviours to question why he was sitting alone for days on end, or to notice his shaky breath of guilt as she collected the last meal's dishes, checking over what he'd actually consumed. He knew he'd regret that omission later.

'She wouldn't want you to do this to yourself,' the former nanny chided. Momentarily his stomach clenched, until he realised she was talking about Aristea, or maybe Emmanuelle. Then he felt guilty for not thinking of Aristea first, or Emmanuelle, for not attributing this miserable apathy purely to them.

'I miss her,' he admitted, and he didn't know which one he was talking about.

The now-conspicuous presence of Nastassja touched the edge of his consciousness. He still didn't know what she wanted, or what her intentions with him could be. He resisted whenever she tried to force her way into his thoughts, and conceded when she looked through his eyes since he couldn't stop her anyway, and when she spoke to him, though he rarely replied, he always listened.

You don't have to be afraid of me.

It doesn't have to be this way for us.

Please just come to the gate. We can talk, the three of us. I can help you understand.

The White Elm is finished. Free magic is springing back to life, everywhere. You and I can be part of it, and your apprentice, too. She can come home under a government that will actually protect her. You don't belong with them. They don't deserve you.

The words rolled around in his head for hours after, resonating more than he liked. He *was* different from the other White Elm. He *did* want to understand who Ana had become, and why. He *was* hurt and frustrated by Lord Gawain's stance toward Aristea. The Seer had overlooked a hundred warning signs and errors of judgement on Renatus's part to support him into a man of principle and integrity, or so he hoped. How could this same compassionate, wise man not offer the same patience to a girl as good and righteous as Aristea Byrne? How could he really believe his own interpretation of Fate when it suggested that *she*, not Renatus or Nastassja or Lisandro or Jackson or any more obvious culprits, was on a path to bring down their centuries-old order?

And how could Renatus possibly be certain which side was right when both were hunting his apprentice and both wanted him to betray the other?

'She's going to be alright,' his housekeeper told him warmly as she gathered the cutlery. 'She's strong, and special.' True of all the women in his life. She paused for a long moment, loving gaze resting on the side of his face where he could practically feel it. 'So are you, and you'll know the right thing to do when you see it.'

Fionnuala didn't truly understand what was troubling him, but wasn't one to push, and as her footsteps faded, he steeled himself with thoughts of Aristea and Emmanuelle. She was right, whether she knew it or not – whatever Ana's reasons, whatever her explanations for opening the gate and choosing not to tell her own people, Ana had *left* him, and was now on the side of people who had *taken* from him.

The right thing to do was obvious, if not comfortable. Wasn't it always?

He stood and forcibly drove that presence away. As he began

down the long staircase, he kept his gaze locked onto his hand on the handrail. A fine layer of warding kept impressions at bay so he wouldn't see them and share them with Nastassja. He'd never avoided them before, not the way Aristea did, and felt numb and blind without his usual level of sensory stimulus.

He followed the sense of disquiet he detected from the ballroom, a feeling that increased as he descended the stairs. His colleagues could feel him coming.

It was like being fifteen again, pushing that door open. He didn't meet any of their eyes but he could feel them on him. Wary. Uncertain. Mistrustful.

'Renatus,' Lord Gawain said calmly, though perhaps guardedly. He sounded more present today, having recovered from his trance. 'You're here.'

You don't belong with them. They don't deserve you.

'*Should* you be here?'

It was Qasim who asked, and Renatus felt grateful for his sceptical tone. Nothing out of the ordinary there, just business as usual.

'I think I know where Lisandro is, or at least where Nastassja's based. I've been able to block her from using my ears, so as long as I don't look...'

He tried not to swallow when he trailed off into the silence. He wasn't fifteen, and he wasn't the child Lord Gawain had picked up at the scene of an accident and kept around despite the misgivings of the rest of the White Elm. He'd proven himself enough that he shouldn't be praying for their acceptance.

Qasim, luckily, was not so fickle.

'Then it sounds like you should be here,' he said coolly. 'What do you know?'

'I've been tracking the times of day Nastassja attempts to contact me or turns up outside the gate,' Renatus explained, stepping away from the doorframe and watching his feet cross the vast floor. 'She's active roughly when we are, but busy, probably with whatever politics Lisandro is so focused on that he can't help in the effort to pin us down.' He reached the grand piano in the corner and lifted the cover, revealing the black and white keys underneath. 'She only tries to contact me when she's outside the gate, suggesting our telepathy is affected by distance. Wherever she goes, it's too far, but you've seen her power. I think she's a couple of hours ahead of our time zone.'

'Belarus?' Lord Gawain asked with interest. 'Lisandro's had a base there for a few months, at least.'

'That's where Aubrey took the boys,' Elijah confirmed, 'and two of them, maybe more if Magnus Moira caught up to Garrett or Joshua, are likely still there. But it's not the only–'

'You're confident she can't hear us?' Tian checked as Renatus sat down before the piano. The councillors trapped inside the house with him were using the ballroom as an unspoken meeting place – the students didn't use it, thanks to the association with Peter's funeral. The disarray of Renatus's office, along with his segregation from the council's collective thoughts, made this the most functional private space in the house.

'That's what he said,' Qasim said, a little irritably. Renatus carefully spread his fingers across the keyboard. It was strange to still be feeling traces of what others exuded, including his colleagues' tetchiness with each other. The combination of close quarters, high stakes and strong personalities tended to yield this result.

'I've blocked the aural pathway she was using before,' Renatus elaborated to put the group's minds at ease. He felt through his own. 'She's not in there right now. You've warded the room against her. She can't scry us. All she can do when she checks in is scroll my surface thoughts and look through my eyes. At that,' he finished, gesturing at the piano keys in front of him. He pressed the keys and felt notes echo and resonate through him. It was hardly music but the vibration in his veins was invigorating, like waking up to sunlight on his face. Under his skin, he felt his magic singing back. It was there once again, fully rejuvenated but out of his cowardly reach. Even small exercises of magic brought those cracks to the surface, and without an experienced Healer onsite to advise him, he'd opted to avoid it altogether.

It was like having an amputation. The ghost of his magic

hung in his aura, every other action a careful decision to go without what had always come so naturally. Was this how non-magical people experienced life? Flavourless, colourless, everything a chore you have to do with your own hands and efforts? How did late-blooming sorcerers like Qasim or Aristea get by for so long?

For Renatus, it was beyond frustrating. All this power, and he couldn't do a thing with it.

'Alright, well, Renatus's intel matches mine,' Elijah's voice said, eager to prompt the discussion along. 'There's still no movement outside the gate. They're continuing to Skip in from the same handful of locations, which we can assume are Magnus Moira safehouses or hotspots.' The crumply sound of a large sheet of paper being moved around told Renatus that he'd marked these on a map. He concentrated on his fingernails to avoid the temptation to look over. 'Of course we don't have the manpower to canvas these positions with half of us locked in here. Maybe that's what they want.'

'Locking us in here is Lisandro delivering on his implicit promise to Magnus Moira,' Qasim answered sourly, and Renatus tipped his head to listen closely to the other scrier. 'In the theatre, he invited them to imagine a world without the White Elm. Now they don't have to imagine.'

'If they struck an hour earlier, they would have had all of us, not just half. We were all here,' Tian reminded them. 'Ready to meet Valero and Avalon. Either they didn't know that, or what happened at the theatre didn't go as planned and we forced their hand.'

Renatus was inclined to believe the latter, and considered this while the others listened to the voices in their heads. The Fabric of space around the Belarusian theatre had been stretched into a funnel, directing nearby Displacements straight inside, and a precisely crafted spell had been active in the building, disabling only White Elm sorcerers from accessing magic, which included their ability to warn each other telepathically. The perfect trap. They would have continued to dogpile in one at a time, blind, unable to escape, and it had been going that way. Lisandro could have had Magnus Moira dispatch the entire council at once.

They didn't account for Hiroko Sasaki.

'That's a valid point,' Lord Gawain agreed with something that all the others had heard in their heads. There were several noises of assent. 'It's not a secret that our skillsets and talents vary widely, and Lisandro knows them better than anyone.'

Renatus played another frustrated handful of keys.

'What's a valid point?' he prompted. Being cut off from the discussions was necessary but irritating. Lord Gawain started explaining that Oneida had mentioned–

'Everyone Lisandro would consider a threat is either down and out, or in here,' Qasim summarised, not bothering to hide his lack of patience. 'Glen is catatonic, Anouk is dead; they were a powerful team. It's likely that what happened to them was deliberate.'

'Emmanuelle was a deliberate blow, too,' Tian concurred softly. Again, the others hummed their agreement. Renatus watched his hands curl and tried not to rewatch the scene of her head snapping to the side, her body falling mid-step. His own hands useless, too far away and disconnected from his magic. 'It was not only Jackson's fixation with her.'

'How did that benefit Lisandro?' he bit out. 'Emmanuelle's a Healer, not a threat.'

Qasim scoffed.

'Not a threat to who? She's your first choice for backup when you don't have your apprentice. He's your godfather – he knows you too well. And hasn't he played you perfectly into your corner? Take away two women, replace them with the one you thought you wanted back–'

'Can we try not to self-destruct this council before Lisandro has his chance?' Lord Gawain interrupted the antagonism tiredly. 'Let's make him work for it. I think we can agree that the way he's manipulated this situation, he feels free to forge ahead with his agenda without us interfering. Any word from Aristea?' he redirected, casting his voice over to Renatus.

'Not as long as we're one of the parties hunting her,' Renatus replied coldly, then scaled back the attitude so he wouldn't lose his temper. 'I don't know where she is. She's alive, that's all I know.'

Vital and radiant as ever, think we're in love. Might take a trip somewhere quiet.

The words had long faded from his forearm but he'd memorised them late last night when they'd arrived, deliberately recalling them in Declan's voice so he could forget the image of the ink on his skin. Harder to forget was the warm relief to read the long-awaited reply. Aristea was alive and well, and Declan was getting her to safety. He was too appreciative to feel appropriately annoyed by the provocation. His shady childhood companion, though hardly a friend, was still the most desirable option of all the people who could have caught up to Aristea – no declared "side", no family or formal associations to dictate his loyalties, and as much reason to avoid Aristea's enemies as she did. At least for now.

'I've stopped looking,' Qasim brought up staunchly, his tone leaving no room for argument or question. 'She's warded, but those will fail soon. Sooner if I keep wearing on them. She'll be forced to let them down, or resort to another style of protective magic. I'm not playing a part in driving her to lawbreaking or capture.'

Renatus had known heavy silences before but had never understood what made them so weighty. Now he felt the faint tendrils of his colleagues' emotions. Unease. Pride. Having his magic stripped to the bare bones last week, he'd noticed for the first time this fledgling ability to detect undercurrents of energy. Baser than magic, lighter than air, thick enough to change the way time flows through space, he wondered how long ago Aristea's natural Empathy had started to bleed across their bond, and how long it would have taken to notice if not for the unfortunate situation at Shanahan's and the consequent silence in his head.

Lord Gawain eventually nodded in acceptance of Qasim's principled position, just as they were interrupted by a knock at the ballroom door. Renatus looked over before he could stop himself. Three girls stood there, radiating various degrees of apprehension.

'Go on,' one of the Prescott twins prompted the strawberry blonde at the front of the trio. 'Tell them.'

The poorly guarded thoughts of Sterling Adams had made Renatus uncomfortable since the students had first arrived, and had been a major factor in his initial distance from them all. She'd gotten better at keeping her enthusiastic inner monologue to herself thanks to a semester of work with Glen on telepathy skills, but now her bright eyes roamed the ballroom and landed on Renatus at the piano in the corner. Her cheeks flooded with colour and her nervousness skyrocketed.

'I... I think I saw something,' she managed in a small voice that swelled in the large room. 'We were meditating.'

Lord Gawain nodded patiently. 'Good, as we discussed.'

The girls nodded too. Seers, all three. Sterling's friend Xanthe, Aristea's schoolyard nemesis, stood wordless at the back, and the Prescott girl – Kendra – encouraged Sterling with a meaningful look. Renatus assumed this meditation was some activity assigned in place of classes, since everything had been at a standstill for a week, and he admonished himself silently for his laxness. He was the headmaster of this Academy. He should know what the students were learning, should be ensuring it now more than ever.

'I keep... It might be nothing,' Sterling offered hastily, fidgeting with her pendant, 'but I keep seeing the gate. In my meditations. People using the gate.'

The image of his sister's hand on the iron, the Elm Stone empowering her unnaturally, and the remembered sound of the latch clicking open came back to Renatus with ease, and he stood.

'People coming *in* the gate?' he asked Sterling, facing her properly. They'd hardly exchanged words before and she looked as though she might faint at the solid attention, but this was important. 'Her?'

She knew who he meant and paled at the memory. She shook her head.

'Going out,' she corrected as bravely as she could. Her eye contact was intense, unblinking. 'Not all of us. Ideas and words, too, but I'm not sure what that means.'

She got overwhelmed and dropped her gaze. Kendra spoke up.

'We think it might be today,' she explained firmly. The Canadian Seer's determined confidence, Renatus thought, had been a good influence on Aristea in the short time they'd been friends, just like, however much it had hurt her, the breakdown of her friendships with Xanthe and Sterling had toughened his apprentice and helped forge her independence, as well as her loyalty to Hiroko. Without these girls playing their parts in her journey, Aristea wouldn't be in such a strong position to survive out there without him. 'Some of the omens from Sterling's original vision have appeared today.'

Renatus didn't mean to but his gaze shifted to Qasim, and he knew they were on the same page. "Omens" sounded like some watery melodramatic garbage, but neither wanted to voice such an offensive opinion. *Seers*.

'It wasn't really a full vision, you said,' Xanthe reminded Sterling, perhaps interpreting the beat of silence in the ballroom as disbelief. Renatus tried not to wince, hoping his prejudice wasn't so transparent. Kendra Prescott flared with dislike.

'Nobody asked for your input,' she informed Xanthe, and Renatus recalled the incident a few months ago when Xanthe had weathered a broken nose.

'What omens, Sterling?' he prompted before this could escalate. Immediately wished he hadn't used her name. The rush of shaky emotion was even more embarrassing than the sharp breath she drew, though after a second he remembered the breath was all anyone else detected.

'First the soap, in my shower.' She went even redder, if that was possible, and she closed her eyes briefly to steel herself. 'It went down the drain in the exact shape as I saw in my vision. Then at breakfast, I dropped my cutlery, and the knife and fork landed in a cross. And… It was a couple more things like that,' she summarised hurriedly, embarrassed. It certainly sounded as nonsensical as she'd just realised. Tian had left the huddle of White Elm to approach the girls, and he tugged lightly on the modified pendant Iseult Taylor had made for him.

'May I touch this?' he asked, nodding at the one hanging

around Sterling's neck. As Renatus understood it, Tian's gift worked best when guided by physical objects, usually weapons, and he closed his hands over the black ornament when Sterling held it out to him. Renatus glanced again at Qasim, from whom a thoughtful curiosity had begun to stir.

'Words and ideas through the gate,' the Scrier repeated, then ventured a guess. 'Letters? Doesn't the mail come today?'

Renatus had to count the days, realising he'd lost all practical track of time.

'Do you think they'll allow it?' Elijah asked. 'Controlling the flow of information and silencing us here is in their interest.'

'It seems they will,' Tian said, releasing Sterling's necklace, 'if we target the right ears. Magnus Moira is not a homogenous movement. Different sects speak and act through different voices. There's a man in crimson,' he told Renatus in a serious tone. 'No hair, small. He wants Magnus Moira to be taken seriously as a viable replacement government. It has not fully occurred to him yet that they are keeping the children of his intended future nation from their parents.'

Renatus glanced around the group, then back at Tian. 'Why are you telling me?'

'You're the only one Lisandro's personally sanctioned,' Lord Gawain agreed. 'It needs to be you that asks.'

Ugh, negotiation was hardly Renatus's finest skillset. But Qasim advised that he could detect the mail carrier's truck ambling up the road now, so without waiting to be sent, Renatus dropped his gaze back to the floor to head off for the gate. The three girls slunk out of his way and he was mindful not to capture their faces again.

'Let's test your omens,' he said to Sterling as he passed her, fending off her building emotion at his nearness.

The sunshine was much sharper outside than through his bedroom curtains. He kept his eyes locked onto the gate and the people beyond it as he strode down the hill. Jackson had been sitting with a handful of others on a grassy hillock, but upon someone calling out Renatus's approach, he stood hurriedly, dusting himself off and moving to the front of the group.

Posturing, always. But Renatus mostly ignored him, using him only as an image for Nastassja when she was notified and jumped into his head. He felt the stretch of her attention – he'd been right, it was harder for her at a distance.

Jackson also made a useful anchor for Renatus's attention, which was tempted to stray across to the orchard. Thoughts about his sister had only a handful of end points. Who was buried under Anastasia Morrissey's tombstone? What circumstances had allowed his real sister to escape the death that had come for their parents? And he never let this question arise before shutting it down, but what part did Ana play in the storm Lisandro had taken responsibility for? The only people he could ask were the two people he hadn't decided whether to speak to again.

Don't go there.

The crowd visibly tensed as he approached. Last time they'd seen him, admittedly, he'd been a wreck, but today, if they were looking properly, they'd see his power fully restored, an aura to rival Nastassja's. They weren't to know it'd hurt him to use it.

At least his power was good for something.

'You look healthier than last time I saw you,' Jackson commented, folding his arms and smirking. But this talent of Aristea's was exceptionally convenient, even at this fledgling stage he was at, because Renatus could sense through the smirk and careless posture to the wariness beneath, and it filled him with confidence.

And satisfaction, of course. Aristea's gift had come with her pride, something he'd already had in spades.

'I'm here to collect the mail,' he responded flatly. 'Are we going to have a problem?'

'I guess we are,' his former White Elm brother replied. He eyed the noisy van now ambling up the track. 'Nothing goes in, nothing goes out. That's how an embargo works.'

'How nice that you've learned a fancy new word. That's not the arrangement I've been offered.'

Renatus left that hanging, wondering whether Lisandro's lieutenant would catch the implication that Nastassja had been speaking to Renatus behind his back. Not far behind him, a young bald man in a crimson cloak – the uniform of the truly dedicated Magnus Moira followers – broke away from his position to come closer where he could hear. Curiosity killed the cat.

'This is an educational facility, as you well know,' Renatus said to Jackson, then shifted his attention to the crimson man. 'It's not just my home and it's not just White Elm you're locking up here. There are sixteen children studying inside, and your political stunt is preventing them from contacting or returning to their parents.'

'They chose their side when they came here to work for you,' Jackson retorted. 'We don't owe them a thing.'

'They're minors, they don't work for us, and their parents have been made aware that you are the reason they can't see their children,' Renatus countered. He kept an eye on the crimson man. As Tian had suggested, this one was listening intently, his resolve wavering. 'If you're also going to deny these families the right the communicate…'

The mail van stopped and the older gentleman driver stepped out uncertainly, looking around at this hippie encampment. Crimson cloak took another step closer to ensure he could speak to Jackson in a low voice.

'Did you know about this?' he asked, tendrils of discomfort accompanying him. 'The children are not our target. It's the White Elm we want–'

'Not now,' Jackson snapped. Renatus opened his hands.

'You've got us pinned. We aren't going anywhere. But these kids, some of them are frightened. They want to go home. Let's start with the letters,' he suggested, gesturing the mail carrier over, 'and we can talk about a handover for the families later.'

It was reasonable, and he could feel the faintest traces of agreement coming from a few of the men and women in the background. Wariness still, too, but not as much. Jackson's reaction was more severe – the response of a man losing face. He extended an arm to block the mailman from approaching the gate while he sneered at Renatus.

'You think we're stupid?'

What are you doing? His sister's voice was strained in his head, demanding, and he sensed her all through his mind, checking for motives. She'd find none. He wanted the letters. He wanted the concession, the first backward step, to come from them. It was that simple.

'I think *you* are,' he agreed, ignoring Nastassja, eliciting exactly the flavour of resentment he'd been aiming for, 'but I think the rest of your organisation is noble enough not to use innocent families as pawns.'

It was the right wording. Crimson cloak nodded, and the bobbing of his bright, shiny head in the sunlight was hard to miss. Several others in the background nodded too, or at the very least dropped some of the animosity they'd been subconsciously harbouring. A leader's influence often extended thus, but it didn't extend to Jackson.

'Suddenly this is all about *families*, is it?' he demanded.

Renatus looked across the flat at Nastassja as she stepped through the Fabric. Her eyes met his as he replied, 'Hasn't that always been the point?'

She strode over to stand with Jackson and Crimson cloak, acting unruffled but Aristea's gift suggested she was oddly thrown by what he'd said. Touched, maybe?

'They want their mail,' Jackson reported irritably, and she nodded tightly, indicating she knew. She'd been watching. The bald man was thinking hard, his determined stance here challenged.

'My faction won't support the suppression of children's rights to contact or return to their parents,' he insisted. Jackson sighed, annoyed but also surprised by the other's boldness. He was more measured than Renatus expected in his reply.

'For all we know, he receives intel by mail,' he explained as patiently as he was capable. It gave Crimson cloak something to consider. 'It would be an excellent ploy by the councillors on the outside.'

'We're already in communication with the councillors on the outside,' Renatus answered in irritation. 'You know that from when you were a White Elm. We are constantly connected, constantly sharing. All you're doing is withholding letters from scared mothers and fathers, and from lonely children.' He extended his hand to the side, hoping Qasim was watching and relaying the conversation to the others. He nodded to the delivery driver. He realised he didn't even know the man's name. Fionnuala probably did. She'd always collected the mail for him. 'How many letters do we have today, and how many have international stamps?'

The driver counted through the thick envelopes in his hand.

'Nine in total... only two are local,' he reported. Renatus nodded. He didn't need Aristea's gift to recognise the failing levels of resistance in Jackson's crew. Some weren't moved, but others, those connected with Crimson cloak, had been converted, or at least nudged a little closer. Jackson opened his mouth to reply but closed it quickly when Nastassja leaned close to whisper a warning. Renatus detected their mutual dissatisfaction.

'Surely no one here believes I have seven international friends writing to me?' he asked rhetorically, rolling his eyes, not caring if it added to an impression of a spoiled teenager. That would only add to the effect of his next words. 'Is this some sort of punishment? Has Lisandro changed his mind about me? Someone fetch my godfather and tell him Renatus wants his *mail*. It's really not that much to ask.'

It only took a beat of whispered conversation and a meaningful gesture at Crimson cloak. Nastassja turned back to him.

'Lisandro has not changed his mind,' she said. 'Give him his mail.'

Renatus didn't wait for anyone to argue, confidently unlatching the gate and extending his other arm through the gap to wave the driver closer. This time, Jackson didn't attempt to stop him. Nobody else made a move, though all the eyes did stay, unblinking, on the opportunity presented by that open gate. The incoming letters were handed over, and in Renatus's other hand, stretched back inside the estate, a neatly tied stack of unsent envelopes landed perfectly in his palm. He twisted his arm against his back, as though retrieving this stack from a pocket, and gave them to the driver. 'Thank you. Please ensure these are sent. Do you need to check through the children's letters to their mothers?' he asked Jackson coolly as the driver hurried back to his vehicle. Though arguably a good idea on their part, the implied pettiness represented a challenge in front of their followers, and Jackson and Nastassja both said nothing. Renatus held his ground in the open gateway as the delivery truck drove away, unobstructed, and didn't go back inside until it was safely out of sight. 'We'll know if you interfere with that truck's progress.'

He locked the gate and accidentally met Nastassja's waiting gaze once again.

Feel like you won a round, do you? she asked sourly. He turned away, giving her a view of the house. It did the trick; she withdrew a little.

Feel like I've got better things to do than argue with your imbecile friends, he answered flatly. Something must have stung, because her reply was more of a retaliation.

I hear your precious apprentice is getting around with your old friend O'Malley, she said, almost a snarl, hurled like it was meant to hurt. He kept his thoughts carefully arranged so she wouldn't detect the spike of panic that ran through him. How did they know already?!

News to me.

Declan couldn't have been the first or the only one to catch up with Aristea. Chances were good that the other scrier had found it easier to track the trackers than rely on breakdowns in Aristea's warding. That's what Renatus would have done, anyway, and Declan was nothing if not efficient. And reliably unreliable. And a lot of other things. If he'd reached Aristea, and Renatus knew now that he had, it probably hadn't gone down cleanly.

So it was unsurprising, he told himself, that Magnus Moira knew that Aristea had been spotted, and who with, because between them, the scriers had probably dealt unfavourably with the tattler.

And you're okay with your little girl running about town with that dirtbag? Nastassja provoked, her meaning clear. *I hear he's as untrustworthy as his ancestors, and half as decent.*

Worse, Renatus agreed wholeheartedly, *but my apprentice is no little girl and my bar for her suitors is set remarkably low after your example.*

There was never going to be a comeback for 'you married our uncle'. Whatever she wanted to say, she didn't, and he felt her give in. A glance back at the gate showed her arguing with Jackson and Crimson cloak, adequately distracted.

Just inside the doors, Sterling Adams' enthralled face wasn't anything new, but his White Elm colleagues' impressed expressions before he dropped his gaze were irrationally warming after the frosty reception he'd received in the ballroom only minutes ago.

'Nice landing,' he complimented Elijah, handing over the stack of envelopes. 'Your precision never ceases to astound.'

'Collecting it up fast enough once we worked out what you wanted was the real feat.' Elijah swiftly shuffled through the letters, then paused. 'These two are yours.'

He was holding out a pair of envelopes, which Renatus accepted without a glance. He wasn't sure yet how he'd manage to read them without risking sharing with Nastassja.

'Tian's right,' he told the others. 'They're a fractured movement, with different reasons for being there. We can use that.'

He felt the inspiration that stirred in his colleagues. Another hand briefly landed on his elbow.

'Well done,' Lord Gawain said simply. It meant more than anyone else knew. Renatus nodded – they weren't okay yet, not if his mentor still meant to arrest Aristea, but he felt the distance melting. The high priest moved off with Tian, discussing other concessions Magnus Moira might be manipulated into making, now that they'd caved to this first step.

The three Seer students hovered near Elijah, looking over his narrow shoulder at the names on the other seven envelopes, and Renatus chanced catching Sterling's eye. It wasn't hard.

'Your vision was valuable,' he told her before he could let her contribution slide. Her cheeks went red again, and he nodded after Lord Gawain and Tian. 'You should all go with them. I'm sure you've got more to offer, and,' he added when the two councillors overheard and looked back, 'while you're stuck here, we could use your help. Time for lessons to start back, I think.'

Sterling had no words. Xanthe answered for her.

'Thank you, sir,' she said finally, and grabbed her friend's arm to drag her into the ballroom. Kendra hung back and even fell into step with Renatus when he started in the same direction. She had an envelope dangling in her hand.

'Sir, do you know when my sister's shift finishes?' she asked curiously. He kept his eyes on the floor, counting steps across the reception hall, but angled his head toward her to indicate that he was listening and unsure what she meant. She elaborated. 'With Emmanuelle?'

He had been selfish, ignorant, self-absorbed this past week. Qasim had told him the Healer students had arranged an informal roster to ensure Emmanuelle always had a caretaker, in case she woke up, but the teenagers were yet to see any improvement. Renatus hadn't been to visit her, telling himself he was afraid of sharing her vulnerable state with Magnus Moira through his traitor sister.

A cowardly lie he told himself. If he could still be a councillor, still be some sort of negotiator, still be a spiteful brother, he could find it in himself to still be a half-decent friend.

'Shall we check?' he invited, changing direction for the stairs. Kendra kept pace, eager but unsure.

'I haven't knocked in case I interrupt her work,' she confessed, fidgeting with the letter she held, hopping onto the bottom stair alongside him. 'Though, she's said there's not a lot she can do…' She stopped herself with a wince. 'I know they're doing everything in their power.'

Everything in their *power*. Renatus squeezed his hand into a fist, feeling the power under his skin. He'd never been capable of healing, an anomaly among sorcerers in more ways than just his power, and the inability to heal the women he loved – Ana when she'd died, he'd thought, in his arms; Aristea when Lisandro had almost taken out her eye in Prague – haunted him endlessly. The addition of Emmanuelle to that list had kept him away, and he felt for the Healer students trying, around the clock, without result. He knew the weight of failure intimately.

Kendra filled his silence tactfully by tearing at the seal on the letter from her parents. He held out his two, taking care not to let his eyes catch the names or the stamps. If they were from his apprentice, everything he'd done to protect Aristea from Magnus Moira could be immediately undermined.

'Before you do that, could you read these to me?' he requested. 'Just who they're from.'

'Is something wrong with your eyes?' Kendra asked, concerned. He shook his head, turning onto the next landing. How best to explain, when the council had agreed to classify a lot of this information?

'Outside the gate, they have an extremely strong Telepath who can see some of what I see. The one who possessed Sterling.'

Kendra hesitated, not wanting to answer back but curious. 'I thought she was a scrier, and that was how she got Sterling?'

'She's a lot of things.'

'She sounds like a virus,' the young Seer muttered, turning the first envelope over obediently as they continued up. 'Alright, one isn't for you at all. It's for Aristea, from A. Byrne. Her sister?'

'Angela,' Renatus concurred. He'd never met her and had recently given in to the reality that when he finally did, it was going to be an unpleasant experience revolving around him articulating excuses for all the misfortunes that had befallen her little sister under his negligent care. Aristea's first encounters with *his* older sister had only gone slightly worse.

'And this one…' Kendra made a noise of pleased recognition. 'Hiroko! She's alright.'

'When was it sent?'

Renatus knew that Hiroko's memory of their escape together had been obscured, but a few days ago the Displacer had been made aware that Aristea was not here.

'Uh, Friday,' Kendra said, checking it over. 'Not through Japan Post, though. Same timestamps as Angela's.' She offered it back as they reached the door to Emmanuelle's usual room. 'It's addressed to you.'

She knocked gently while Renatus slid the two envelopes into his jacket, deep in surprised thought. Hiroko Sasaki had written to him. About what? Aristea was safe-ish with Declan, and reading what Hiroko had put to paper could jeopardise that. Perhaps it was worth sharing its contents with Qasim to learn what was inside.

No one answered. Renatus leaned over Kendra's shoulder to push the door open. The house's complex magic responded to his blood and any locks or latches gave way without protest. The dark room beyond was distinctly miserable, and it took a moment for his eyes to adjust. Looking like a slumbering fairy tale princess, still wearing the corseted velvet dress she wore when Jackson took her down in the theatre, Emmanuelle was laid out on the bedspread. No pillow. Limbs straight and rigidly placed. Glassy box of magic encasing her head and shoulders. Wards built into a brace, and the Fabric stretched to keep space around her perfectly still.

Asleep and curled up in the armchair beside her, the other Prescott looked worn out. Though unable to do it, Renatus understood the theory of healing – best practice was to repurpose the energy of the patient into their own directed recovery, but when the patient had none left to give, or like Emmanuelle was not replenishing her energy stores by eating, the Healer gave small amounts of their own. Too much and they wouldn't have the power left to guide the process, so it was slow, undertaken over several attempts or with numerous Healers.

The Healer students at the Academy were talented, he was sure, but they were no Lady Miranda, real-life surgeon, and they were not Emmanuelle. The ratio of magic they could give to their patient versus how much they required for themselves as they developed their stamina could not be very high.

Renatus bumped Sophia's shoulder and she woke with a start.

'I fell asleep,' she muttered thickly, sitting forward and pushing her hair out of her face. 'I'm sorry.'

'You've nothing to be sorry for,' Renatus corrected, circling past her to attend to the drapes. Better to get some light in here, vitamin D or whatever. He wasn't usually for that sort of thing, but Em was, and the mood in this room left a lot to be desired. He kept his gaze on the arguments outside the gate and off his fallen friend, carefully avoiding his own aching sadness. He kept his tone brisk. 'How is she?'

Sophia groaned a little when the sunlight blared in through the window. 'Uh, about the same. They told you the prognosis?'

'Tell me again.'

'Clean break between the vertebrae, with a few small bone shards, and a severed spinal cord,' Sophia explained. 'Given that it didn't kill her instantly and there's no other damage, she shouldn't still be unconscious, from a medical standpoint, so we know she's in a trance. But by now she's used all her own energy up staying alive without food, she's locked down, we can't get any energy in, and Lady Miranda's told us to stop pushing. She said she'll take what she needs.' The girl sounded doubtful, and she paused to drag an appraising look over her patient. 'She hasn't taken anything at all. I don't even know if she knows we're here.'

An empty shell. What a horrible concept.

'Have you tried talking to her?' Renatus asked, tone entirely objective. Sophia kept her surprise out of her reply but not the hesitation that preceded it.

'Sometimes. I don't think she hears. I'm… I'm afraid we're failing her.'

Her twin said something reassuring, about being sure that wasn't true, and Renatus found similar words slipping out of his own mouth. The girls blinked – he wasn't usually the uplifting type.

'You're doing everything you can,' he added, then nodded to the door in a polite dismissal, he hoped. 'You should go and rest. I can take the rest of the day.'

Hardly anyone knew he couldn't heal, and the brief grateful smile from Sophia confirmed that it wasn't something Aristea had passed on to her friends.

'Thank you,' Kendra said to him, with feeling. She took her

sister's hand and showed her the envelope from their parents, closing the door behind them. Renatus kept his gaze off Emmanuelle in the silence that followed, looking everywhere else. Listening. The harder he concentrated, the more certain he was that, even from where he stood at the window, he could hear the softest sound of breath. Steady. Slow. Shallow. But constant.

'I think she's wrong,' he said finally. He twisted the bangle on his wrist, looking without seeing at the window frame, at the wallpaper, at the carpet. 'I think you can hear us. I think you know exactly who has been around and what it would cost them to really help you.'

Still careful where he looked, he turned to approach the bed. His house had many beds, more than he had any use for, but since offering the house for the White Elm's Academy, he'd come to be glad for the excess of bedrooms. The students could board here, soaking in each other's magic and getting stronger, instead of returning home each day after their tutelage. His colleagues could stay on campus, rather than return home around the world between lessons and council meetings, and on this occasion, one could reap the same benefits as the students.

But passive strengthening wasn't enough. Not until she'd dealt with the dire injury threatening her very life.

'It's very noble of you, refusing what's being offered by the students,' Renatus continued, watching his knees as he sat in Sophia's vacated armchair. Still warm. He laid the ruby bracelet aside. 'Dignified to the last, even at risk of being plainly stupid.' He extended a hand to the bed and felt for Emmanuelle's. His fingertips touched her rings first, and it discomforted him to find her skin just as cool, cooler even than his, and he was always cold. Loosely, he enclosed her hand in his, and let his eyes fall shut. 'I'm sure you'd agree, it's hardly a mark on your integrity to exploit me in the same way.'

It wasn't immediate. He had to work against his own instincts to bring down his emotional and energetic walls if he was going to let her in. For almost a minute there was no reaction, just her limp hand in his. He tried not to doubt his plan.

'Come on,' he urged, his voice an irritable mumble even to

his own ears. 'Whatever Shanahan's spell did wasn't enough to kill me, I doubt you could.'

Was that spark of irritation his own, or...?

There is a special kind of surprise, a wondrous moment of fright, associated with touching a seemingly lifeless chrysalis and feeling it twitch against your skin. Renatus felt that surprise when he felt a sudden pull on his life force. The instinct was to cut off the stream of energy flowing through his hand, but he fought that and let it go. The power that naturally built up inside him, which he'd been unable to find a useful purpose for, drained straight out and into his friend, through every skin cell of hers that had contact with him. He'd never done this before, and on a certain level he wasn't doing it now, either – Emmanuelle was in charge of this, directing the energy, taking what she needed. More than her teenage students should give up. More than any sorcerer should relinquish.

Renatus flattened his palm against her skin, adding his other hand to her wrist, getting more contact points, thrilled by the reckless danger. The black cracks that had been recovering under his skin flared back to the surface on the back of his hand and wrist, and he could feel the burn up his forearm, past his elbow, over his shoulder... She was draining him. But he was *healing*. If it would bring her back from this state and back to fighting beside him, he could be generous. He had so much to give, after all. Or did. He felt his eyelids growing heavy as the cracks fled down his legs, over his back, along his scalp... Her aura, which before was so empty he'd hardly been able to sense it, was now swollen with magic he could feel against his skin, and his was shrinking back.

He was joking before when he'd said he doubted she could kill him. If she wanted to, she was capable, but it wouldn't be this way. Her body and her aura didn't have the capacity to hold what he could, so to drain his entire energy into her would have devastating consequences. He wasn't trying to set her alight, and didn't want to see her cracked like he was.

Emmanuelle was an expert with energy and knew her own limitations and requirements. She cut off the flow when she was restored to full strength, leaving Renatus with an energy level that most sorcerers operated with as their maximum.

Still, putting his wards and barriers back up felt like a chore by comparison to his usual ease, and when he stupidly stood to leave, the abrupt motion sent a rush of dizziness through him, and he hit the floor.

Bewildered, he blinked at the ceiling.

'Did… you just… faint?'

The question was slurred through unmoving lips, heavily accented, and hardly louder than a breath, but sounded so good even through the receding vertigo that he choked on a laugh.

'No,' he insisted, lifting one heavy arm to slide the tight bangle over his hand. 'And it's about time you woke up.'

Other than a single noise of scepticism, Emmanuelle said nothing else, slipping back into her trance to start real work on all the severed nerves of her spine. Renatus listened to the lengthening of her breaths, like someone falling asleep, and soaked up some of the energy left for him by his apprentice. He made no further attempt to get to his feet. He just lay there and stared at the ceiling, feeling beaten and exhausted and better than he had in days.

Maybe he could be good for something after all.

chapter ten

'Again? How many times do we need to do this?'

Declan had jumped down from the train platform onto the tracks that were still vibrating with the movement of the receding train, and with a tired glance over my shoulder at the mid-morning crowd that was totally ignoring us, I hopped down after him. He smiled back at me and slowed to let me catch up.

'How many times have you heard the phrase "you can never be too careful"?' he countered, handing me sweet-smelling leaves to tear up. My fingers still had the scent of the oil from when I did this earlier this morning. 'That's how many. Your white magic wards have the disadvantage of being bound to your own energetic capacity – one of your White Elm's lovely control mechanisms, ensuring nobody is messing with magic above their station, classist much? – but the benefit of being renewable in the moment. If it's broken or dismantled, you can recast a replacement immediately. This is stronger but slower,' he conceded, stepping off the tracks once we'd wandered far enough. He glanced around for trains and knelt. 'It's also more easily undone. Someone can literally trip over my spell and ruin it, the bastards. No magic or intention required. Solution?'

'Rinse and repeat?'

'Provided you can pay the price, magic this way is limitless,' Declan concurred, drawing quick symbols into the dirt. 'Who's going to find *fifty* of these hidden around the world? Each of them doing virtually the same job as your wards, except costing you nothing more than the initial price. Neat, hey?'

I watched closely as he repeated the process he'd performed in London and again when we'd landed in Prague, burning what smelt like sage and mixing essential oils into the pile. I could feel the magic starting to build as he kept humming, a strangely beautiful form of wild magic I wasn't used to wielding or experiencing.

I was also starting to appreciate why the White Elm's ban on this style of magic was so controversial and, in their eyes, so necessary, at least in the era when the laws were passed. Unlimited magic with no natural limitations except how much blood someone was willing to let? An oversimplification, maybe, though if this was all Magnus Moira stood for – and how was I to know there weren't people within the movement who felt that way? – I would find their position more sympathetic.

Or perhaps I wouldn't, because Declan, a criminal, was my first real introduction to how this magic I'd always assumed was "bad" or "dark" could be used for good. I'd grown up in a pro-White Elm household, raised on white magic rhetoric, and I'd never questioned authority.

Until, ironically, I met Renatus, White Elm councillor and bad influence.

Declan drew a circle around the spell and I threw the leaves on, earning a nod of approval for paying attention. I still wasn't thrilled with my travelling companion, but the fact remained that I had no other options. Though I was still tragically under slept, the hours spent unwarded in the air and since landing were more refreshing than I'd admit. It might be illegal, it might be dirty, but it worked.

He finished the first stage and reached my least favourite bit, retrieving a pocketknife from his boot.

'Time to pay the ferryman, princess,' he reminded me, and with a flick of the sharp blade, carved a tuft of his own hair from his head. His façade slipped momentarily, showing me how little of his hair he had left, and then it was back, and he sprinkled the strands into the spell. He didn't even wince as he dug the point of the blade into the back of his wrist, where I knew an unseen wound was barely beginning to close up. Blood welled forth, and he patiently let it drip into the messy circle. 'The more you give, the stronger the magic, obviously.'

Dubiously I got out my own knife, or rather the knife I'd taken from Renatus's desk, and let my hair fall forward over my shoulder. The three locks I'd already shortened seemed to stand out starkly from the rest, though I knew this was irrational me speaking and it was unlikely anyone else could tell.

The bloodletting was less traumatic. I pricked the edge of my hand and squeezed a fist a few times to get the blood pumping. The bright drops joined Declan's in the dirt.

'The first time I saw one of these, there was one thing different,' I mentioned cautiously, thinking back to a forest in Scotland late at night. A bloody, messy pile on the ground, marked out by esoteric symbols like Declan had drawn around this one. 'The man had cut off his own fingers.'

The memory of his infected, still-bleeding stumps and the exaggerated sound of the drips onto the leaf-littered forest floor made me shudder, and I pulled my hand back. Declan nodded.

'Anything that can't be replaced has a higher value and strengthens the spell,' he explained in a conversational tone while I looked about for something to clean my hand. I thought briefly of Renatus, and channelled magic quickly to my other hand. As expected, a tissue materialised, and I used it to stem my bleeding. 'Fingers are a high price to pay to stay hidden.'

'Too high,' I agreed, 'especially when the spell can be undone so easily.'

'I take it Fingerless didn't stay hidden?'

I shook my head, regret stirring in my stomach. The runaway from Magnus Moira's Belarus compound had been so desperate to stay clear of Lisandro – and Nastassja in particular – but in trying to track him down, Renatus had destroyed the protection spell. He'd just knocked it over with his hand, like pawns off a chess board. And days later, the White Elm had found the nameless Scot dead, tortured, and nailed to a tree.

Declan was right. There was no "too careful" here, and it wouldn't pay for us to leave all our eggs, or fingers, in one basket.

'Fingers aren't a good choice,' Declan advised as he finished off the spell. I found I recognised the steps now. 'It limits future options. Toes can affect your balance but if you get decent shoes…' He shrugged, like it was something he'd give fair consideration in the right circumstances. 'Teeth are really effective. I hear.'

He grinned, and I saw that gap in his smile differently than before. Regretting I said anything, I swiped my thumb, hard, over my little wound. I wasn't an excellent healer by any means, but it was a skill I admired, and I'd succeeded at closing off the last two cuts I'd made.

Focus, intention, and a little *push*; those were the ingredients of the white magic I'd been taught, and they worked for me now. Under my guidance, the cells either side of the cut found each other, and I was able to seal the skin.

I felt the activation of the protection spell around us at the same time. A brief spark, then a settling of energy. Declan stood and dusted his knees.

'Lovely city,' he said idly, which was true, though from here behind the train station you wouldn't know it. Lightly he kicked at the train track as he led the way back to the platform. 'What are we doing here?'

I realised that he'd come this far with me, two flights, half a continent away from home, without ever asking me why I'd picked this destination.

'I don't know what *you're* doing here,' I retorted without hesitation, then did pause. It had made a lot of sense when I planned things out with Hiroko, but that seemed so long ago now. Measuring time with "bridges slept under" as the meter has that tendency. 'I had some, uh, trouble here, a few months ago.'

Two hands, slamming into the glass of my ward… locked out…

I swallowed the memory of Anouk's death, and my part in it. I was getting better at living with that guilt, but being back in the city where I'd saved thirty-something other people but not her, it was much closer to the surface. My exhaustion didn't help.

'Trouble,' Declan repeated, glancing at me dubiously. 'Yeah, that's what I call it too, when my bestie's godfather tries to take my face off.' He waved his fingers vaguely at the left side of his face and accepted my frown graciously. 'Hate it when that happens. So, what? You figure no one expects to find you at the site of your strife? Smart, I suppose,' he conceded, 'but that's not really why you're here.'

We reached the platform and hoisted ourselves up. No one spared us a glance. It was such a relief to only need the one ward, the visual deflection kind, though I also kept my mind tightly shut down. Declan's good behaviour for the past ten hours was no indication of how he'd behave if circumstances changed in the next five minutes.

'This is where everything started to go wrong.' I shrugged uncomfortably and adjusted the straps on the backpack and satchel. How many times did I need to do that before I found a new tic? We joined the streams of people leaving the station. 'Anouk. Lisandro and my eye. And then a few weeks ago, I tried to Displace home, because that guy from your basement was with my sister...' Shanahan had hired him. It was best not to wonder whether he was still down there, tied up, or if Declan had let him go before running off. 'I ended up here instead.'

"Here" was easily the prettiest place I'd ever been. We emerged from the station into the main street and were treated to the sight of the majestic Czech capital. Under the springtime sun, every building looked golden, and the medieval spires of the roofs gave the skyline more visual interest than any city I'd seen back home.

My companion nodded as if he agreed, though I was reasonably certain my thoughts were locked down.

'There are worse places you could land in a botched Skip,' he admitted. 'So we're thinking Fate wants you here? Have you dreamed about it?'

Scrier. One of our traits was the tendency (curse?) of scrying in our dreams, prompts sent from the universe to direct our waking attention to details that had gone overlooked. I hadn't known about it until recently, and apparently neither had Renatus, who'd been so confronted by the repeated nightmares of his family's deaths that he'd spelled the whole *house* to disable dreaming on the premises.

'No,' I confessed. We walked aimlessly down the street, unfamiliar languages being spoken all around as tourists and locals wove past. 'But that doesn't mean much given where I've been living. The whole thing with Magnus Moira and the scriers and the ledger… which we're not discussing,' I added firmly, wanting to kick myself for bringing it up on my own. Declan raised his open hands in helpless surrender, but still smirked. 'All I mean is, this seemed a good place to start.'

'Start what? Unsolicited investigating?'

I shrugged. We stopped at a crossing and waited for the lights to change. 'Like always, you seem to know more than you should, so you're aware the White Elm is hunting me?'

'Their best and most unique asset that isn't my sulky cousin? Yes, I'm aware. But that makes sense, everyone knows that,' Declan reminded me, and we crossed with the crowd. 'The part I shouldn't know is that if they catch up with you, they're going to put you on trial. Which means we aren't here because Fate suggested it; we're here to clear your name.'

Untrustworthy semi-villain or not, it was touching to hear him say "we". The solidarity was stabilising.

'Not so much. I definitely did some of the things they want to charge me with. But if I can find evidence to prove Lisandro was behind what happened in Lennon Square…'

I couldn't finish that idea out loud. If I could prove that, maybe I could undermine Lisandro's influence over Magnus Moira, and maybe the White Elm could arrest him without Renatus needing to confront him in a fight to the death. Maybe if I could prove he set that attack up, I could understand why he chose this place, that moment, and work out where he was hiding and what he was planning, so I could confront him.

I could kill him myself, saving Renatus from the ending Fate had written for him.

Declan couldn't hear my thoughts, but maybe he read my determined expression, because he stopped me with an arm across my path. I pulled up before we could make physical contact.

'This is about Renatus,' he gathered, tone serious. He watched my face when I didn't reply. People milled either side of us, their eyes sliding past. 'It doesn't take daily mopey check-in messages for me to know he hasn't asked for this.'

'That's because he doesn't understand the stakes,' I snapped. 'He doesn't know what I know, what he'll do, what he stands to lose. I'm the only one who can help him, and I can't tell him or I'll just make things worse.' I took a deep and shaky breath, realising what I almost let slip. 'I might only have this one chance.'

Declan was staring at me like I'd grown an extra head, but he still asked me very steadily, 'To do what?'

'To...' I shook my head, the words not coming forth, and I ran my fingers back through my hair as I looked around at where we were. Such a beautiful place, but so loaded with pain and uncertainty. 'To... understand. Understand what Lisandro's trying achieve, to head him off, before...'

Panic was climbing my throat so I stopped talking and focused on calming down. I knew it made zero sense, and Declan's slow nod seemed to confirm that.

'Before,' he repeated, but didn't prompt elaboration. He looked around as well, taking in the city while he processed my outburst. 'Okay. I can get behind that. But promise me this isn't your vigilante moment.' His eyes slid back to me suspiciously. 'Say you're not looking for Lisandro to try your hand at taking him on.'

I didn't like his perceptiveness. Hearing it like that, sounding so ridiculous, I felt my panic subside, and I stepped past him to keep walking. Of course he fluidly kept pace.

'I don't owe you promises, Declan.'

He sighed dramatically. 'That's an odd way of saying "no, of course not". I know you to be markedly brighter than my dear cousin with his charming death wish so I'll sleep peacefully, reassured you know better.'

We walked the busy streets for a while in silence when I couldn't bring myself to answer. He was right, as usual – I *did* know better. I'd faced Lisandro a grand total of four times, five if you counted the day he murdered my parents and brother, and of those encounters, the best I'd ever come off was severely shaken. Twice he'd put me in hospital, and last week he'd sent me running yet again. I was no match, and I'd rather never see him again. But I needed to. I needed to learn his weakness, understand my opponent, like Tian had taught me in my swordplay lessons. My enemy was stronger, older, more experienced... but if I could get inside his guard, so to speak, maybe I stood a chance.

Maybe I could be that "unless" Susannah had alluded to.

At the next corner, Declan directed me to take a left downhill. 'To clarify, we're going to be in this city for a wee while, yes?'

'I intend to be, yes,' I agreed cautiously as our strides naturally lengthened. Though I accepted that he could turn on me in an instant, I took a moment to acknowledge that I'd basically just told him I was planning a murder and he was still sticking with me.

'Because we want to understand Lisandro's endgame, and we're talking about a complex man, so we're expecting a complex, time-consuming endgame,' Declan elaborated. 'Do we have a starting point, at least? Something more substantial than a certain ledger, of which we will not speak?'

I pressed my lips together tightly, unnerved. 'I might.'

He didn't push it. He led the way around the block, telling me which hotels belonged to Shanahan's family or other hotelier associates. For a city so far from the United Kingdom and Ireland, where that community was based, there were a surprising many.

The possessed sorcerers whose bodies had been used to wreak havoc on the youth democracy rally had Displaced into Lennon Square from a handful of local hotel rooms. Coincidence?

I'd long learned there were few of those.

We stopped across the street from a nondescript sign advertising vacancies. My senses, when I extended them forward, immediately detected the unchecked magic left all over the building.

'Relax, I know the owner,' Declan advised, shaking his forearm from his sleeve like he did when he wrote to Renatus. 'Just give me a sec to confirm we're welcome.'

With his pen he scribed *I'm upstairs*, and sent that with the usual swipe of magic. The ink disappeared. There was a low stone wall behind us, and Declan tiredly lifted himself to perch on the top. Grateful for the break, I leaned back beside him and rested the bags I was carting around on the wall. My string of rough nights and my lack of sleep on the flights was catching up hard, and the thought of a real bed was decadent.

'A few logistical questions while we wait,' he said conversationally, producing the Czech phrasebook he bought at the airport and flicking it open. 'When we say "a wee while", and we struggle to communicate in broken English and Czech, how many nights are we actually booking for?' I blinked, startled by the reasonable query. 'Start with a week?'

I nodded quickly. I hadn't counted on having access to a safe hotel so hadn't thought about what information they'd ask for. I went through my bags and then pockets for my passport.

'And how are we funding this abscondence? Poker? Hustling pool? I'm *very* good at poker.'

'I bet you're *very* good at cheating,' I countered, though good-naturedly. Staying cross with Declan was too exhausting.

'Beggars can't be choosers, baby.'

'Who's begging?' I asked, showing him the bank card. 'Certainly not Renatus's heir and her unsavoury companion.'

An affectionate smile warmed his face. 'See, this is why I love you. Behind that sweet, good-girl façade there's an unprincipled felon just waiting to happen.'

He didn't mean those words the way they were supposed to be used, but I didn't miss the lack of energy flicker after he spoke them. They mightn't be true, but they weren't a lie, either. I think that's why I decided to do the next dumb thing I did.

'Here.' I thrust a crumpled, dirty page of paper at him from the depths of my bag. 'My starting point.'

Despite its unimpressive appearance, Declan treated the offering with the appropriate interest, lowering the guidebook to his lap and taking the list delicately. He traced his fingers across its creases and the names written in old ink, soaking in whatever impressions were left.

'Lisandro wrote this? Hit list? Nice to see one without my name on it.'

'I've never known what it's about,' I admitted, 'except that he wrote it, Peter Chisholm kept it, and Peter delivered it back to his one remaining friend on the White Elm before Lisandro drowned him. We don't think it's a hit list because Lisandro's missed plenty of opportunities to kill Renatus and me—'

'That doesn't mean anything,' Declan argued. 'You're uninitiated, a child as far as magic's concerned – think he wants that karma chasing him through life? See how long you last past twenty before you rule that option out, because I have it on good authority,' here he bowed to me theatrically in thanks for the intel, staying seated on his little wall, 'that half these crossed-off names are people he personally assisted into the afterlife.'

'What a lovely way of phrasing "the bastard murdered my parents".'

'Ah, well, who doesn't have murdered parents these days?' Declan asked cheerfully. 'It's all the rage. What about this Peter guy? What's his connection?'

'He was a Seer. I figure that means he believed this was important for us to know about.'

'I figure the fact that your and Renatus's names are featured makes it important for the White Elm to know about, but I see your point. Have you touched it?' He offered it back. 'Without gloves, germaphobe?'

I let him hold onto it for now. 'I got something the first time, nothing since. What about you?'

'Hmm,' he answered noncommittally, going back to reading it. 'If not a hit list, what do you think is the connection between all these people?'

I leaned closer to read, though I'd seen it before. 'They're all sorcerers. We're all... I don't know, entwined with each other. Like Asheleigh, that's got to be Asheleigh Hawke, and for a while we were treating her like a missing person until we realised she was aligned with Magnus Moira. And I mean, they,' I pointed vaguely at the names of the people I kept seeing in my visions, my grandfather and his four closest associates, '*are* Magnus Moira. The founders.'

I'd managed to surprise him. I felt it spark from him, and I felt it in the way he pulled back from me.

'And you know this *how?*' he demanded, intrigued, and I rolled my eyes.

'Scrier,' I reminded him, and he closed his mouth. Impressed.

'Mánus Morrissey started Magnus Moira,' Declan marvelled after a while. 'I always knew Renatus was an immense disappointment, but this changes my understanding of the bar. And you, too. You two are *literally descended* from the founders of today's biggest magical liberalism movement, and like the goody-two-shoes you are, you're with the White Elm? At least *you* have the good sense to be an outlaw.' He thrust the list back at me, and I tucked it away again. 'Doesn't seem like a helpful starting point to me. I bet you whatever money Jakub's being offered right now that I find us a better lead by this time tomorrow. Before you get your hopes up too high,' he added, opening his book again, 'I'm hoping he's a loyal lad and that number's zero.'

We sat there for another ten minutes – him people-watching, me reading the guidebook he handed me after about three pages – before the door across the street opened and an unfamiliar sorcerer stepped out. He couldn't see us thanks to our warding but it was evident he was looking around for someone specific in the thin streams of people milling by. Declan leaned closer to me.

'Empath girl, do your thing,' he prompted. 'Does that seem like someone who wants to exchange me for piles of money? It's a credit to him that hordes of bad guys haven't shown up yet, but what do we say?'

'You can never be too careful,' I concurred quietly, tuning into the balding hotelier. It was an effort to filter out all the people between us but before he could go back inside, I had latched onto his distinct emotional signature.

Intrigue... mild annoyance... bewilderment, concern...

He shut the door and I was cut off, but I got enough. I didn't detect any duplicity, any sense of urgency that might suggest he was waiting on someone to turn up, and I reported this to Declan. He hopped down from the wall.

'Well, if you're wrong, at least we'll be captured together,' he said cheerfully, handing me the satchel. 'Now let's go in and see if they'll fulfil my dream of being trapped in a foreign hotel room with my cousin's beautiful apprentice and *only one bed*...'

'Oh, Declan,' I said fondly, showing him the page I had just read, 'there are more than three hundred bridges in this city. You and your one bed don't stand a chance.'

chapter eleven

Like all hotel beds that have been slept in by a thousand previous people, the mattress was lumpy and sunken in all the places you'd like it to be firm, but I melted into it when I gave it a test run.

'It's been too long,' I muttered dreamily. All my muscles began to relax hopefully, and either side of me, the bags I'd dumped felt heavy and warm. I wouldn't even need to get under the covers. This was fine.

'Mixed signals,' Declan called from the other end of the room, and reluctantly I sat up, 'though if that's an invitation…'

'You're sure about this friend of yours?' I redirected, rolling miserably off the bed to slouch back to my travel companion. He waited at the door, playing with his own room key – obviously I was not rooming with Declan O'Malley – and shrugged. I felt like I'd seen him do that a lot in the past day, and me, too. There was a lot to be uncertain about.

'Jakub was a client of my father's, back in the eighties or something when his first wife ran off with an Irish backpacker,' he explained, pocketing his key. 'He followed her there, then hired my da when he lost the trail. He's sent work our way ever since. In short, no, but you're not even sure about me, so given the scale, Jakub's fine.'

He proceeded to demonstrate the spell work he used to strengthen ordinary locks, but in my tired and distracted state, I didn't pay much attention. My thoughts stuck on what he'd just said. His grandfather, I knew, had operated in a similar line of work to Declan, trading secrets he could pick up as a high-level, natural scrier, but had died for choosing the wrong side during the White Elm's crackdown on blood magic. I didn't know much about Declan's father, except that he was still in the womb when Lorcan O'Malley and his extended family were massacred. Declan had intimated that there were no other O'Malleys, and it had never crossed my mind to wonder where his parents were.

'Again, you pay the price,' he narrated, scratching a recent wound with a fingernail and wiping it across the lock of my door, making me cringe at the way his words fit my errant thoughts, 'and hair won't do for this one, it's blood or nothing.'

'Declan, I've never asked you about your dad,' I brought up, tactful as any tired person. His perfectly unsurprised reaction told me I'd taken him quite by surprise and I wanted to put my foot in my mouth.

'No? I've never asked about yours, to be fair,' he answered after a beat. Voice perfectly even. I'd touched a nerve. And something else. A knowing sparkle in his eye. 'Are we sharing now?'

The way he said *no* was so loaded that I knew I was missing something. Maybe from those two hours I erased or the sixteen minutes he took the time before. Whatever it was, I wasn't qualified to play guessing games with him, and I withdrew.

'You're right, I'm sorry,' I said hastily, nodding at the door handle. 'Continue.'

'That's done. But it only lasts as long as it's locked.' He closed the door to show me. On an energetic level I was becoming familiar with, I felt the spell activate. Then he turned the handle and I felt it break. 'The second you open the door, it's all undone, but the traces stay, and you have to reconnect these.' With a wave of his hand, faint strings of magic like spiderweb brightened into the visual spectrum, and I saw that they were all cleanly snapped through the centre. 'Even if you were thinking about dead parents instead of watching, you can't get this wrong. Just follow the threads I left.'

He reopened the door and stepped out without a single inappropriate comment. His room was across from mine, and in the quiet of the third-floor hallway, he patted his pocket for his key. Despite everything else he was, despite everything decent he didn't know how to be, he was here, and had made sure I got this far, too. Had made sure I was safe. Had watched my back. Had taught me the magic I needed to protect myself and answered all my unreasonable questions, until now.

Now he paused in the hallway, looking at me with that calculating expression, the one when he was trying to work me out. Unusually hesitant.

'My da swindled people,' he said finally. 'You'd have liked him. Taught me that coin trick, you know the one? And… other things. O'Malley was a respectable name before him. Not his fault of course, no one to teach him the way. I don't know how much I look like him, but I inherited his reputation.' He paused again, then asked, more seriously, 'You don't remember anything from Shanahan's yet?'

I'd avoided admitting that, but I'd been carting Declan's own satchel around and he knew what he'd packed in there, so who was I kidding? I shook my head.

'Did a neat job on yourself, did you? Must have had a good teacher,' he couldn't help quipping, casting me his infectious grin as he finally found his key. I half-smiled back.

'He was hardly memorable,' I shot back, and his smile said he appreciated the effort. He unlocked his room and turned away, and I felt my smile slipping. 'Declan, wait.'

'If you're that scared to be alone…'

'Thank you,' I said before I could forget later. Later, he would sell me out, or piss me off, or do almost anything to undermine the rapport we'd worked up, but right now I was alive and free because of him. And he was here under false pretences. 'There's something you should know. About the ledger we stole.'

I had his complete attention. 'I thought you didn't remember anything.'

'I don't. Not that, anyway. But I can infer.' I sighed. I knew I'd regret admitting this. 'It's empty. I know that's what you're really here for, and I don't want you to ultimately screw me over for something that's worthless.'

'What do you mean, empty?' he asked, putting his key back in his pocket. I shrugged one shoulder exhaustedly.

'Blank. Kind of,' I amended, seeing his eyes go wide. 'When I looked inside it at the house, it was full, but I can't read it anymore. I've flicked through all the pages a heap of times; there's nothing. Maybe it wiped itself, timed out? I don't know if that's possible.'

Declan appeared mystified, folding his arms in serious contemplation.

'Wh… No, I doubt that,' he answered, still thinking. 'It'll be a defence mechanism, yes. It's blank,' he repeated, 'except when it was *at the house*. The place was the key?'

I thought back. 'I don't think so. Renatus couldn't read it, even straight after I did.'

'Yes, well, he doesn't count; he's White Elm.' Declan rolled his eyes. 'I told him that was a mistake. And as we know, Shanahan's magic is especially intolerant of his kind.'

Screaming, a sound to tear at your heart… terror, confusion… half of it mine… white fire…

I flinched at the momentary flash of… memory? Where had that come from? Unlike scried images and impressions, it had come from inside my own head, but I had no context to place it.

Declan was asking something, and I shook that disturbance from my thoughts.

'…did it look like? Did you get to read any of it?'

'Nothing specific. It was ruled up by hand into columns, with names and details down the left-hand side, but they were hard to read, and it had dates and amounts. Big amounts, thousands. In and out, with calculations and percentages. Maybe interest?'

I expected Declan to demand to see the ledger, but he actually took a step back from me. The unguarded emotion I gleaned in that brief second said he hadn't meant to react.

'Trust Shanahan to keep track of interest,' he recovered quickly, pasting his easy smile back in place and retrieving his room key. 'Doesn't miss a dime, that old scrooge, and he's got plenty of them. Have you heard what he's offering to anyone who brings *you* in?' He unlocked his door and let it swing inward. 'You remember how to do those locks?'

Disorientated by his odd comments, I grabbed the edge of the door to close it enough that I could see the traces of magic he'd left on the doorknob.

'I'll work it out.'

'Good, grow some of that magic back with a big sleep, and tomorrow we'll start investigating.'

I frowned. 'You're staying?' Even though the ledger was useless?

'Renatus's money paid for this nice room,' Declan pointed out innocently. He closed his door and I closed mine, choosing to interpret his reply as one of solidarity. It was reassuring to pretend I had someone reliable on my side.

I think I slept about sixteen hours straight, and I think that to start with, I was too tired to even dream. But that blissful stretch ended sometime early in the morning.

Heavy rain slashing at the windows… lightning, cracking thunder, the flickering of living room lights… a hand grabbing mine, and my sister's voice, high-pitched but firm… 'You have to stay with me'…

Two hands… black magic in an uncontrolled wave… screams and running feet in a beautiful city… regret and fear from inside the killers, a second soul… regret from the end of the square…

Brightly lit bedroom with lace curtains… seashells threaded into mobiles over a basinet…

Blood on the grass… ten sorcerers in a circle… columns of light, frying five of them from the inside… 'Long live Magnus Moira'… a woman raising her hands to the sky, rain pelting down… manic exaltation at her own power… two men I recognised, alone with the charred proof of their choices… 'Some legacy'…

Brightly lit bedroom with lace curtains, this one my own… seashells on the shelves, on the windowsill…

Warm sun on extravagant hats… a christening party on the lawn… two friends striding down the hill, joined by the woman Moira… 'White Elm. Another raid'… Lorcan O'Malley with Tom Shanahan the first, waiting near the gate… dismay, dread… 'But I had thousands…'

Night, quiet except the rhythm of the sea… a cave mouth under a ridge… vagueness, loneliness, numb anger, regret… all of it familiar…

and seashells…

Funeral in the rain… an older lady with a teen grandson and a little redhead girl… wildflowers in the mud, grief… Lisandro, youngish, offering a replacement rose…

Renatus hitting the plush carpet, unconscious… blood seeping from under his hair…

I opened my eyes to the darkness and let the customary disorientation pass. I was in a hotel room in Prague. I was alone. I was safe. My life was a mess and so were my dreams, but what else was new?

I was also undeniably refreshed. A full day without straining against scriers and a decent night's sleep had done me a world of good, despite my disturbing dreams.

'Now just imagine how strong you'll feel after a hearty breakfast,' Declan said on our way out into the city later that morning. We butchered our way through ordering in an out-of-the-way little restaurant that he insisted upon, and I sat opposite him by the window while we ate. The images from my dreams turned over in my head as I became more focused. Blood and hands and seashells, repeated throughout time without any apparent connection except for a handful of sorcerers and their modern-day descendants.

A pair of police officers came in for coffee, speaking amiably in their rich-sounding native language. I loved listening to it, but didn't understand a word, and I looked out the window instead of looking at Declan, who sat up straight and watched them with interest. My destiny and Renatus's had countless overlaps spreading back and forth through time, but how did Declan tie in? His grandfather, Lorcan, was Mánus Morrissey's first cousin, and with my grandfather Cassán's unwitting help, they'd betrayed each other. Lorcan's whole family was slaughtered. I really didn't want to believe in history repeating itself, especially as all the roles were notably twisted this time around, but the thought was still there.

I had to remind myself he *couldn't* read my mind, that I would *know*, when he dropped his napkin and announced our first agenda item for the day.

'Time for our morning bloodletting,' he said brightly, getting to his feet and digging in his pockets for money to leave as a tip. 'I have a special surprise for you. From your granddaddy.'

'From my… what?' I pushed my chair in and followed him. He held the door for me and we stepped out into the morning sun. Images of Cassán from my visions swam in my mind.

'When the White Elm started cracking down on, well, everything, it became useful to be able to shield certain activities from their sight,' Declan explained as we walked. 'Specifically, from their Scrier. You know, the capital "s" one. If a protection spell's going to wear out and a vision's going to slip through the cracks, you can bet whatever contraband you're trying to hide that *he's* the one that sees first. Luckily in the early sixties, the council's shiny new laws burned the legitimate career of a gifted magical theorist, and he wrote the anti-White Elm wards. Blocks *only* them. Bless that man.'

I thought back over visions I'd tapped into from Cassán's life.

'That's what Mánus was brokering for him,' I mentioned, making the connection. 'You can sell spells? There's a market for that?'

'Sweet Aristea, there's a market for everything. Let's find a secluded garden somewhere so I can share your legacy with you – surely the council's got some loophole for lawlessness when it's your *grandad's* spell? – and then we can get started on our day.'

Curious to see Cassán's spell and feeling increasingly unconcerned, maybe even a little exhilarated, by all this freedom, I stretched my awareness beyond my body, beyond my immediate surroundings. Quick images of the next block over, and the one after that, flashed behind my eyes, and I found what I was looking for in mere heartbeats.

'This way,' I directed, leading Declan to the next crossing. 'Will a park do? And what's this about us getting started?'

'Aren't we investigating?' he asked, feigning confusion, pointing back over his shoulder. 'And weren't those the same fine officers who attended your "trouble" back in July?'

I pulled up short, startled, and he grinned when I had to apologise to an older lady who ran right into me.

'Wh… how would you know that?' I asked, trying despite the sick feeling in my stomach to think back to that day. Were there police? People were calling for them, yes, because they'd mistaken the danger as a bomb threat – closer to the truth than anyone had wanted – but I didn't remember seeing any.

'You worry about all the wrong things. Who *cares* how I know? Who cares how I knew to pick that spot for breakfast? If it matters, their minds are the usual garbled mess left behind by overbearing Telepaths, and a little bit of picking reveals the trauma they're happy to forget. Park,' he prompted, waving me on. 'You got paper in that bag?'

'I…' I checked the satchel for a notepad. He leaned closer to look at the contents, but had already withdrawn innocently when I defensively covered it back up.

It was hard to argue with Declan's worth when he recited a list of hotels from the policeman's memory faster than I could write them down.

'He was hooked into someone else's brain, basically, when the Displacements were being traced, and his knowledge of the city was accessed to speed up the process,' Declan explained flippantly. The park came into view. 'The Russians, I'm guessing. Good of them to leave us a starting point.'

Cassán's spell turned out to be much more involved than the relatively simple protection spell Declan had already taught me, and considerably more specific. Particular words. Precise timing. Weird ingredients. Exactly thirteen drops of blood. Declan confirmed that my grandfather had been a scholar of many forms of magic, and as a Crafter had been skilled at weaving them together into something new and unique.

'Whatever the White Elm might suggest, the whole world is not divided neatly into "white magic" and "bad magic",' he said with more firmness than I was used to from him. 'Blood magic is messy and dangerous, sure, but there are countless ways to summon magic without sacrificing bits off yourself, or without using yourself as a vessel for the whole spell. Songs. Runes. Arts. Dance. Spirits. Potions and cooking. Some people do that knitting thing.' He gestured with his hands but the motion was too vague for me to decipher. 'Point is, no matter how you bring magic to the table, once it's there, you don't have to stick to the one plate.'

I liked that analogy, and slid my ruby from my pocket. A bit like scrying – just because I'd moved on from tool scrying didn't mean I couldn't still utilise crystals and flames to take some of the energy demands off myself. I could see why Renatus and Declan, and probably thousands of others, enjoyed the flexibility of employing multiple magical styles in their approach to sorcery.

As I did every hour or so, I checked in on all my precious people. Angela at work. Hiroko eating dinner. My aunt and uncle in their spare bedroom, discussing potential renovations. Renatus… presumably inside Morrissey House. The crowd was still outside, though the faces in it continued to revolve daily. I didn't see any I knew. I focused harder, shifting my perspective to look to the edges of the widespread group, but then Jackson reappeared in the centre of the crowd. He flicked up the collar of a new jacket as he nodded an acknowledgement to some Magnus Moira groupie, and I realised he'd ducked off to freshen up. His hair looked clean and he'd clearly been away long enough that there had been shift changes at the house. Until now, at least one of Lisandro's lieutenants had always been onsite when I looked. Was their watch loosening?

Declan closed off the spell with a flourish and I felt it working; an extra layer of concealment, a lead blanket between me and the council. I felt wildly safe, even when I first got the feeling we were being followed a few hours later.

The feeling continued for days after, on and off but never coming to anything. I tried not to be paranoid, especially as I found myself relaxing into a daily routine with Declan. Wake up, breakfast somewhere new, disagree about something, head off into the city, get mad with him about something else, illegal magic lesson to pile onto my list of crimes – a record stuck on the one track, but never once in that week did I sense the attention of scriers. With my invisibility wards and his illusory faces, we systematically worked our way through the list of hotels to confirm that *all* were connected with Shanahan. In two of the buildings we even made it into the room the attackers had stayed in.

'You didn't tell me this involved Benny O'Callaghan,' Declan said with careful non-surprise, fingers freezing on a drawer. I likewise had my gloves off and was running my hands over every surface within reach, picking up hundreds of useless impressions of strangers being boring. I was on my knees at the wardrobe, exploring the little bolted-down safe and getting nothing helpful. We were trying to be quick – a cleaner was turning down the rooms on this floor – but I stilled.

'Where have I heard that name?'

'Maybe from me. Society heir, very political. Total prat. He joined Magnus Moira earlier this year.' Declan shifted aside when I got up and came over to check the drawer for myself. 'His father wouldn't shut up about it at first, but no one's heard anything in a while.'

I traced my fingertips along each edge, mental barriers as low as I dared in the company of Declan O'Malley, though to his credit he'd been relatively well-behaved all week. Image after image of tourists idly checking this drawer washed through my awareness until:

Bored fingers tug drawer open… young man, high energy, magical aura… impatience… high forehead with brown hair gelled flat to the side…

'That's because he's dead,' I said as I pulled away, deeply uncomfortable. The ringleader of the Prague attack had gone down with his ship, killed by the same shockwave that ended Anouk and the possessed Finnish coven the scriers had been wearing. I'd never known his name, but I could still hear his voice in my head.

'*We heard there was a soapbox here and we've got a message to spread, too.*'

Unlike the twelve crimson-cloaked hostages puppeteered there by Magnus Moira scriers, Irish – Benny – had wanted to be there.

'Hardly a loss,' Declan advised. He closed the drawer. 'I'm sure his parents think he died a hero's death. How *refreshing* for them.'

'He didn't. He instigated a terror attack.' I followed him to the door when we detected the cleaner in the hallway. 'I suppose his parents can hardly admit to that.'

'Hence weeks of silence. It's like he just fell off the map.' Declan and I both went silent as we slipped past the cleaner, though over the noise of her headphones, she mightn't have noticed us anyway. Outside on the street, when we were clear, he said, 'Speaking of falling off the map, or onto it, what about this Nastassja? What can you tell me?'

I took an interest in our list of hotels – that was our last one – to buy myself a moment to think. Declan had been unusually good with boundaries since our arrival in the Czech Republic, staying out of my room, mostly avoiding probing questions, and this one was innocent enough. Why wouldn't he wonder about a new scrier on the block? But she wasn't just a new scrier. The story behind Lisandro's wife was tied into my master's vulnerabilities and hurts, and though I trusted Declan more than I should, that was with *my* vulnerability.

'Renatus says you're the informant, not the other way around.'

'Does he?' Declan delighted in that comeback. 'How characteristically obnoxious of him. And how adorable of you to be parroting him.'

I felt his eyes on me as I shrugged. I also felt his focused curiosity, his certainty that I knew more than I was letting on. We walked for a while before he artfully redirected.

'You know, the first I heard of her was about a fortnight before we saw her at Teagan and Geroid's engagement,' he said idly. 'Whispers, rumours, then a name, a reputation, and then she was centre stage, and we haven't been able to shake her shadow since. Before June – nothing. Kind of like Lisandro, no family line, but let me tell you, power like hers isn't easy to keep hidden.'

I didn't want to discuss this with Declan. He was clever, so of course, he knew something was off about Lisandro's sudden wife. His words stirred my uneasiness – I'd thought she was just sudden to *us*, we the people she was hiding from. Wasn't it odd that Declan O'Malley, knower of things he shouldn't, with his ear to the ground and his fingers on every surface anyone influential had touched, hadn't heard a word about her until the White Elm did?

We were most of the way to Lennon Wall, the vibrant but dreaded site of the July attack, when I began to suspect we were being followed. I spread my attention back through the streets and alleys but couldn't find anyone or anything out of sorts.

'Why did you say they picked this square?' Declan asked me conversationally, though I didn't miss his casual glance over his shoulder. In the short time I'd been stuck with him, I'd learned a lot of his subtle body language, so when he tilted his head like he was stretching his neck, I knew he meant to take the next corner, and I followed him automatically into the cobbled alley between bookshop and pharmacy.

'There was a rally on the day,' I responded, though he knew this. 'A pro-democracy rally, run by a group of teenagers who'd been talking online.'

'Right,' he said vaguely, skirting around a display of flowers outside a store, careful to ensure his stray hand touched as many as he could. 'And that morning, didn't you receive those things clinking around in your bags?'

I understood what he was signalling, and lifted the flap of the satchel, tensed for impending conflict. I still couldn't detect anyone, but the certainty that I was being watched did not abate as we wound around corners, further from the main street and into narrower alleys.

My instincts did not let me down. We turned into a long service lane that I recognised from my first visit here with Renatus – this was the way we'd approached the square, and we were closing on the same spot Lisandro must have stood while he watched the chaos he'd unleashed. Up ahead, at the final bend before the square, an unfamiliar man strolled into view, hands in his pockets like he was cold. Under his thick jacket, his shoulders looked broad and strong, but his energy signature felt dull, blurry. Non-witch? He didn't *look* threatening, but I instinctively slowed. He nodded in acknowledgement like he'd just spotted us.

No surprise registered, only satisfaction, readiness.

My hand closed on the cold of metal in the satchel.

'Byrne and O'Malley?'

North American accent. Energy masked, probably, just not as well as we were. I wished we'd stayed invisible. Declan stopped ahead of me.

'Don't know them, but they sound like quite the dynamic duo,' he replied pleasantly. 'Sure you'd like to mess with them?'

I sure cast him an irritated look for unnecessarily poking the bear, but my highly tuned attention was captured by movement behind me. I turned swiftly. The woman who'd followed us into the alley froze mid-step with one foot still in the air.

'Miss Seidel,' Declan said with the genuine-sounding delight I now recognised as entirely false. 'It's been too long. How nice of you to join our party! Do you know each other? Mr…?' With more of that falseness, he gestured back at the first interloper as though his name had just escaped him. The American leaned around us to be seen by the woman.

'I had them first, you can go.'

'I think not,' she replied in a German accent, then turned her gaze back to Declan. 'O'Malley. This is she?'

She'd jerked her narrow chin at me. He looked at me with theatrical surprise, like I'd appeared out of nowhere.

'She? No, just some cute thing that followed me off the street. You know how it is, Hanna.' He winked playfully. I was, by now, accustomed to the compulsion to stab him, and my grip on the hidden sai did not help matters. Hanna Seidel did not seem moved, but at least did not seem as irritated by Declan as I was.

'This does not need be difficult,' she said, straight to the point. Her emotions felt the same. Flat. Purposeful. Unafraid. A subtle magic was at work around her, too. Something to do with the Fabric. 'Some friends are looking for this girl. They have a rumour that she is with you. It seems they are right.'

'Oh, yes, friends are good things to have,' Declan said warmly, idly clutching at the opening of his jacket and sighing. 'Magnus Moira, right? Your aunt told me you'd joined.'

'You should too. Before the White Elm can eliminate our

culture completely.' She cocked her head, regarding him. 'We are at war, with everything to lose. We could use you.'

It was the thing anyone would have said, but as an Empath, I was the only one who felt just how strongly Declan rejected those words. It didn't show in his placid smile or his apologetic shrug.

'You see, that's the sticking point,' he explained. 'A lot of people seem to think they could use me. You got a better offer over there, lad?'

He turned back to the first man, still holding position at the other end of the alley. I kept my eyes on Hanna Seidel.

'All I want's the book, and the girl,' the man told Declan blandly. 'Don't really care what happens to you. Hand them over, and we're square. I won't watch where you run.'

'Well, that does sound better,' he agreed, 'though I don't have the book, and the girl might have something to say about being handed over like property.'

'She may not have a choice,' Seidel warned, producing a nasty-looking serrated knife and nodding at me. 'Over here, please. Lisandro is waiting.'

Losing patience, the first interloper pulled a sleeker, longer blade from one of those pockets. 'Screw your politics. Mr Shanahan's paying a mint for this little thief; she's mine.'

They argued briefly, and I glanced at Declan. His minute headshake confirmed what I feared; we couldn't Displace out. The woman was a Displacer, and she'd stretched this space too tight for us to manipulate. We were going to have to push past one of our captors and make a break for it.

Fine. The sooner the better.

'Actually,' I interrupted, 'I'm no one's.'

I withdrew the twin blades Renatus had given me for my birthday. Both mercenaries reconsidered upon seeing their meek teenaged mark transform into a determined-looking sword-wielder with *two* kickass blades. In truth, I'd had only a handful of lessons, but it was enough that I knew my forms and stance, and from their faces, I knew I looked the part.

I hoped it would be adequately off-putting. I didn't know how useful Declan would be in close combat versus knives.

Maybe we didn't need to fight.

'Warned you,' Declan reminded them pleasantly. Hanna Seidel seemed to recognise the futility of arguing with her logical ally.

'We can decide what to do with her once she is detained,' she suggested to the man behind us. 'We can take her together.' She waited for the other's approval before looking to Declan. 'O'Malley, where do you stand?'

'Me? Here, I suppose.' He looked down at the cobbled stone beneath his feet, and she shrugged, moving in. No love lost there, obviously. She came for me, and from the other end of the alley, the American ran at Declan.

The last time I had to fight for my life in this city, I used a massive dome ward, and though that'd keep us safe from these adversaries, it would also keep us locked in place, allowing them time to call in reinforcements. So instead I slashed at the oncoming woman before she got close enough to strike, channelling magic down my arm. A brief, hard ward burst from the edge of my blade and slammed into her middle like a heavy breath of wind, sending her sprawling several metres away. I spun to Declan in time to see him duck the American's first hack. When he straightened, he'd released that grip on the lapels of his jacket and he had two short knives in his fists, pointed down and sharp.

Not sure why I'd doubted his capacity to take care of himself.

The fight that followed was quick and dirty – punches and elbows and the brick wall behind them, and these three knives amidst it all – but much too tight for me to assist with the same kind of blast I hit Seidel with. I'd only knock Declan on his arse, and he looked like he was winning.

I'd worked hard on my periphery senses when I lost vision in my left eye, so I sensed Seidel coming. Her knife hit the glass-hard energy of my ward a good twenty centimetres from my shoulder, and though my vision was dark where she stood, I knew innately that she'd made the overconfident mistake of putting her all behind that move.

I took a leaf from Declan's book and thrust my elbow back into exposed tense flesh. The heavy exhalation over my shoulder said it wasn't expected. I fell into one of Tian's lessons. Every move was two-step. One: I spun to face her with my dominant hand ready. She'd closed her arms down over her middle so my sai struck her solidly in the elbow. Her hand sprung open, dropping her knife. Two: I twirled the other sai in my hand, and as Seidel leaned in over her vulnerable areas, I jammed the pommel up as sharply as I could.

I wasn't strong enough for that to break her jaw, but the crack was still awful. She stumbled back, radiating with the shock of it. I kicked the serrated knife away and quickly backed off before I could think too hard on how naturally I'd resorted to violence.

Declan and the other were still locked into their brawl, and both were bleeding. Two knives had been dropped already. When I got a look at my companion's face, I saw that his eyebrow was split, and that he was *grinning*.

I couldn't possibly roll my eyes hard enough. They broke apart briefly and circled each other like animals.

'That all you got?' Declan mocked, I supposed because he couldn't go twelve seconds without causing trouble. The illusion hiding his bandages had slipped away and he looked like the wild unpredictable mess he really was. He adjusted his grip on his little knife and addressed me. 'You see your gap and you run, hear?'

The American was faster than Declan seemed to expect, and grabbed him by the front of his jacket. He slammed a surprised Declan into the wall and swung a huge punch at the side of his head.

'Declan!' The crack of my companion's skull on the brick made me forget all about Seidel's jaw. Heart thudding with adrenaline, I wasn't quick enough with the first little ward, but got one in before the American could hit him again. It was an instantaneous distraction, the man hissing and shaking out his fist, but plenty of time to get that final knife in the forearm for his trouble.

The mercenary's grip loosened, and Declan took full advantage. He spat in his opponent's eyes, and before the other could pull back to clear them, he slammed his head forward into the unsuspecting face. A sharp knee to the groin got the other off him completely.

We had a clear run to the other end of the alley.

'Declan, come on,' I urged, hurrying closer while he panted in place, but there was less time than I realised. Crunched over his pain, the American strummed with red-hot fury and, with a growl, launched forward in a tackle. If he'd been happy to just take me and let Declan go before, priorities had changed. His shoulder caught Declan's gut and his hands found his jeans. With a savage yank, he ripped Declan's legs out from under him, and then they were on the cobblestones, rolling over each other and yelling, punching, trying to choke each other, and I no longer felt confident that Declan was winning. Especially when the mercenary got on top and tore that little blade free of his forearm. Aimed it down. It felt like I swallowed my heart, but it's hard to remember. The next twenty seconds went by in a disjointed blur of horror. They were so close, I could hardly make out who was who. *Declan!*

A loud wet sound hit my ears and a burst of sticky warmth hit my face and chest. I processed the facts out of order. Blood. Declan. Knife. Neck. Mercenary. Shock. Someone else.

Then it came right and I backed up with my sai raised, wiping my eyes clear with my shoulder before any blood could drip in. I blinked a few times and saw wide-eyed Declan wriggling free of the dying man collapsing on top of him. The mercenary gulped, wordless, as blood spurted vibrantly from the serrated knife buried deep in the side of his neck. Declan clambered to his feet beside me, shaky with emotions I didn't usually feel from him, and we both looked back down the alley at Hanna Seidel.

I should have restrained her, not turned my back. She was on one knee, just lowering her arm from that disturbingly excellent throw, though from the feel of her, I wasn't convinced she'd been aiming specifically at the American. Either target would have sufficed.

I think Declan knew it, too.

'Are you stupid?' he demanded, voice higher than usual. He pointed at me. 'The council's looking double-time for this one and you commit murder right beside her?'

Seidel smirked. 'Thanks to you, the council doesn't see all in this town. And you were the last one to touch him, yes?'

If there was blood left in Declan's face, it seemed to be draining. He stepped back unsteadily into my blind spot. I got a grim sense of determination from him. A decision being made.

I was still getting my bearings, fighting off the dying American's terror and confusion, and jumped in fright when I felt rough hands grabbing at my satchel. I turned automatically, already spinning a blade, then froze.

'Dec... What are you doing?' I asked stupidly, and as I watched, he did exactly what I'd been waiting for him to do for days. Blood all over him, all over his hands and arms, he flipped the satchel open and swiped the ledger out in a single practiced move.

'Until our interests no longer align, sweetheart,' he reminded me, backing up. My hands were full with my sai so I couldn't grab it back, and it didn't occur to me to stab him like I'd been considering periodically since Belfast. I stepped after him, dazed. It shouldn't have been a shock, but did he just *rob me*? Eyebrow dribbling blood, hair shorn crazily, jacket askew and undershirt torn and stained red, he grinned apologetically. 'Didn't I tell you to run? I meant from me.' He raised the book at Seidel. 'Don't leave me hanging, Hanna. I'm going to burn it. Kisses.'

And he turned and bolted, faster than anyone who'd just taken such a beating should be capable of. Just before the bend ahead, presumably where the Fabric relaxed, he opened a swift wormhole and disappeared.

With my ledger. Without me.

'Declan, why do you have to be such a predictable *jerk*?!' I shouted after him, enraged. Behind me, emotions settled in the same way his had – a decision made – and a blur rushed past. My wards must have been back up; either way, she didn't even try me.

'Choose your friends wisely,' she called. 'Mine will see you soon.'

She leapt into the same space he'd vanished, the way only a

Displacer can, and when she didn't bounce straight back, I knew she'd gotten through before he could block her.

I was left alone with my own heavy breathing, and the final rasps of the man twitching on the ground. Blood had formed an unreasonably wide pool around him in the twenty seconds since he took that flying knife to the neck.

Logic hit me like cold water. Declan was gone. The American was bleeding out, fear fading into something vaguer, something sadder. I was watching him die, and I was the only one here. With swords. With his blood on me. How would this morning's officers solve this one? Someone must have heard the scuffle, our raised voices. *Mine will see you soon.* Seidel's friends were Magnus Moira. They'd be onto me quicker than any non-witch police.

I needed to get the hell away from here. Hastily I stashed my sai in the open satchel and concentrated on the ward magic around my face. Renatus had shown me before how to manipulate it into an illusion, like what Declan wore over his dishevelled features. I repeated that hurriedly, stretching it in the hopes of disguising the blood spatter across my upper body, and turned to leave, building wards up layer by layer. So much for Declan's protection spells.

I hesitated an extra moment, looking back at the mercenary dying on the ground. I was about to run from the scene of a crime. Of a *murder*. Who *was* I? I wasn't at fault, but I was a witness, and this man was about to die alone in a tangle of fright.

I responded without realising, something I'd never tried before. I tuned into the fragmented distress he was radiating and thought about reversing it. I forcibly brought positivity into my centre, and, I don't know, *pushed*. Contentment and calm and acceptance and warmth and happiness and all those sorts of things that don't quite have names.

It's hard to know if it worked. Empathy is about receiving people's emotions, and in that stranger's final heartbeats, I felt the change, receiving soft contentment and calm and acceptance and… then nothing.

Maybe it was a swap? Suddenly I felt small, without the delusion of Declan's protection. I tried to shake it off, tried to stay strong and alert as I stepped out of the alley into the sunny street, but all I felt after that was afraid, and alone, and shocked, and betrayed, and hurt, and shaken, and like nothing was fair.

chapter twelve

Life had never been fair, and didn't Angela know it?

'These are nice,' her aunt said with interest on one visit, pausing to smell the flowers in a vase on the table. 'Someone special, hmm?'

Code for: something you haven't told us about?

'Oh,' Aunt Leanne commented with surprise on another pop-by, inspecting the glassware her juice was served in, 'these look new!'

Code for: where are the ones I bought you?

'Such a dear,' she said warmly, *all the time*, admiring photos of Aristea on the wall. 'You know, she's just doing *so well* there. They're really bringing her into her best self.'

Code for: the White Elm, a bunch of strangers, was doing a better job parenting Aristea than Angela had, and Leanne, who knew what it took to be a real guardian, had taken it upon herself to go see. She could barely hold in reminders of her knight-in-shining-armour moment, when she'd fronted up at Aristea's school to demand she come home. She'd returned empty-handed, thrilled with the living conditions and her niece's learning, and had decided things were, after all, best left as they were.

She'd *decided*. Like it was her choice. Angela bristled at the thought. Nobody *decided* for her, or for her sister. People *decided* for young women all the time, and Angela had decided for herself when she'd first applied for custody of Aristea that she wasn't going to be that kind of guardian. Boundaries, but no decisions. Aristea's life, future, and body were her own, right?

Maybe that was the naïve and freshly orphaned twenty-year-old talking, but still, her sister must have been mortified when Aunt Leanne arrived and tried to tell her to come home. Yes, Angela missed her. Yes, Angela's life felt empty without her. But Aristea had *friends* for the first time since their parents died. She had purpose. She was learning and experiencing things their family would never have been able to give her otherwise. It made Angela envious and a little resentful to hear it, over and over, but the way Leanne told it, Aristea even had a big brother in her master, Renatus.

So she had left things alone, even after months apart, birthdays spent separate. She'd thought that she was being strong, but as the weeks wore on between replies to her letters, and funny rumours started to seep into her conversations, Angela began to feel less comfortable with her stance.

Aristea was eighteen, and her decisions were hers to make, but if Angela wasn't making them, how could she be sure no one else was? Her aunt's comments were beginning to undermine her confidence.

'That's another month,' she worried, leafing through the envelopes on Angela's counter like her niece's mail was her business. 'It's not like the Elm to go so long without a newsletter. It does make me wonder. They still haven't clarified what happened in the Czech Republic all those weeks ago.'

'It was a gas explosion, and I'm sure they've got enough work on their hands without typing up a newsletter every month,' her husband said, ever at ease. Uncle Patrick smiled over his book at Angela, a knowing expression. Though he'd been closer with her brother and sister, whom he'd tutored and home-schooled, respectively, Angela had always gotten along well with her only uncle. He was a retired teacher, a fair few years older than his wife, and the kind of quiet, self-assured soul who carried a novel with him everywhere he went and did not care what anyone thought of him opening up to his bookmark whenever conversation lulled. As her parents weren't huge readers, Angela suspected her sister had secured her love of reading from him.

'They've got Aristea and a bunch of other kids to watch, after all. Couldn't pay me enough.' Their daughter, Kelly, was applying makeup from her compact for the second time since their arrival twenty minutes ago. Angela nodded as though she agreed, and tried not to make it obvious when she checked the time. Her late father's family visited at least once a week, worried that she was lonely, which, admittedly, she sometimes was, but not for this. Kelly was still talking, holding her eyebrow pencil very precisely as she shaded in perceived gaps. 'Anyway, they're probably still on damage control. I heard again that the White Elm set that whole gas explosion thing up to frame Lisandro. And now they're saying this theatre fire last week in, where was it? Belarus? They're saying that's connected and there was some brawl there. Like the White Elm got into a punch-up and didn't like the outcome.'

'Who told you that?' Angela asked sharply, thinking over what she knew of the Prague incident. The councillor Qasim, someone she innately trusted, had said it was a set-up by Magnus Moira, and in their handling of it, another councillor had died. She didn't know who, but she was certain it was a great loss to their already finite resources as a council of thirteen.

'Uhh...' Kelly concentrated on her eyebrow more than her memory of the gossip. 'Lydia, I think.' Like Angela knew who that was. 'She's been spending lots of time at that old bookshop that's just reopened. The new owner's a witch and she's restored the whole place the way it used to be in the sixties. I haven't been there,' she admitted, closing the compact, 'but she says there's always a crowd, lots of interesting people around. People who know things.'

Doubtful, Angela thought, but she kept that to herself.

It took another half hour before she could rid herself of Aunt Leanne's family, claiming she had an appointment.

'I'm so proud of you for sticking with your counselling all this time,' her aunt assumed warmly. Code for: I didn't think you would see it out. Angela smiled tightly.

'I'll see you next week?' she redirected, not at all interested in discussing this sore point. Formally seeking help with her personal demons was how she'd secured guardianship over Leanne's assumed right to the sisters when they'd both made applications to the family courts, and she'd only ever intended to go along for the required number of sittings. But five years later, she was still seeing the same therapist, and still seeing slow improvements to her sense of control over her life.

When they were gone, Angela took immense satisfaction in turning the lock and letting her forehead fall against the door. A thousand times in these past five years, she'd reflected on what a huge mistake she'd made in seizing her sister's custody from her aunt. Aunt Leanne had automatically made room for her nieces in her life when her brother Darren died, suppressing her own grief to support the sisters however they needed. Everything would have been easier if Angela had just left things alone. If she hadn't overreacted.

But when Angela heard the judge's unexpected decision – insert here the realisation that she was twenty years old and responsible for a traumatised minor, and that her aunt was *livid* and she'd probably just torn her family up right when they most needed each other – she'd only had a moment to regret her actions before Aristea squeezed her hand and whispered, with so much heart, '*Thank you.*'

Her little sister didn't understand what had prompted the choice, nor what had incited the huge argument between aunt and niece that she'd witnessed, but she understood the sacrifice on Angela's part. She'd never let Angela wish her away, never done anything to be more of a burden than she could manage, other than be characteristically untidy as she drifted through life.

Was she untidy where she was, too? Was she safe to make her own choices, the way Angela had dropped everything to ensure for her?

The house hadn't been messy even once since Aristea left, and being surrounded by her own cleanliness and unsettled thoughts made Angela not want to be here. She grabbed her purse and her keys, and left without thinking where she wanted to go.

She ended up in town, parked opposite that bookshop Kelly had mentioned. It looked very happening, with more people moving in and out of its doors than any of the shops nearby.

Angela wasn't a reader the way Aristea and their uncle were, but the bookshop and its customers had the witchy vibe Kelly had implied. It might prove a good distraction from worrying about her sister.

From the instant she got out of the car, she seemed to catch more attention than she usually got, but that may have been because she compulsively checked both doors were locked before she would leave her vehicle. Crossing the street, she saw two of the customers enjoying an armchair's view of her through the window, open books in their hands and looks of interest on their faces. She hesitated, waiting for her instincts and their close friend, paranoia, to kick in and tell her she should leave. She faked looking through her bag before committing to going in. The readers inside went back to their books, interest lost, and Angela's rarely used magical senses whispered to her that she was in the presence of other sorcerers. Quite a few, including the armchair readers. She could sense them, and now that she focused, she pinpointed more, scattered through the store, which she now realised was deeper than she'd suspected from the front. If she could sense them, they could sense her. Hence the interest.

Angela shelved her resting paranoia and pushed the door open. A soft bell announced her arrival, though inside, it didn't seem to matter. Despite a library-ish aesthetic, the atmosphere was more café-esque, chatty and vibrant. The elegant store was indeed deep, tall dark shelves stretching for the ceiling in eccentric arrangements either side of a mostly clear central walkway. Customers in yoga pants and gumboots stood at a refurbished timber counter with their armfuls of books, and wicca enthusiasts with shiny pentagrams on proud display over deliberately black outfits took advantage of the ladders that allowed them to explore the top shelves like people who knew what they were looking for.

'Merry meet!' a shop assistant that was mostly piercings called from the counter, waving brightly. Several cheerful customers throughout the shop chorused in response, 'Merry meet!' in some fevered attempt to contribute.

So not Angela's crowd, but now that she'd tuned in to her

latent magic, she felt a need to stay. A soft fluttering in her stomach, in the veins of her arms, somehow, urged her onward into the funny old shop. More than one person glanced up at her but she paid them little mind, especially when the feeling intensified the further she walked. Past a section on crystals and geology. Past a boxed-in corner about ghosts. Cringe. But that feeling was stronger still as she reached what looked like the back of the shop, only to find it extended narrowly to the right, behind its neighbouring store. It was quieter back here, less brightly lit, the shelves heavy with aged and second-hand tomes rather than the new commercial editions out the front. There were only a handful of patrons back here, and they moved silently in the aisles. Angela took care to step softly as she wandered closer to whatever was causing the oddly magnetic pull in her.

The idea that something was manipulating her, directing her, pulled her up short. Only a few weeks ago, her workplace's regular courier had developed a sudden interest in her and offered to drive her home. In his presence she'd felt strangely complacent and trusting, not her natural mode of operation, and she'd felt compelled to answer his prying questions, even let him inside her house. The whole time, her instincts were waving urgently at her through the haze to wake up to herself and take control. When she did, Dan had locked her in her bedroom and searched Aristea's for information. Emmanuelle and Qasim from the White Elm had arrived within a minute of her phone call, but the memory of being out of control, of being complicit in endangering her sister, still made her feel shaky.

This was not helped by the fact that Emmanuelle had not answered her messages, nor by what Kelly said earlier today.

But, keying back into the sensation she had right now, it didn't feel the same as whatever Dan did. In his presence, she'd felt dulled, overly content. The pull to the back of the store was kind of opposite – she felt very present, very aware, very alive. Choosing an aisle, Angela slowly inhaled the smell of old paper, grounding herself in the moment, reminding herself she had come here by choice. The place really was lovely, even if too-happy echoes of 'Merry meet!' sounded off in the store's front half *every time* someone walked in, and it served as the distraction she needed from the many things that were outside her control.

Her aunt. But Leanne did love Angela and had long forgiven the custody issue. The verbal slights were Angela's interpretations, as the counsellor reminded her.

Aristea. But her sister would write when she remembered.

The White Elm. But Emmanuelle would text back when she left the estate, and they knew where to find her if something was wrong.

This section was markedly less organised than out front and Angela indulged briefly in the whimsy of tugging occasional books out by the spines to flip through them without intent. Some were older than they looked, still unread after decades; others looked ready to fall apart. All the while, that frenetic awareness of magic vibrated throughout her, a suspenseful eagerness that built and built until some unspoken instinct prompted her to look to the very bottom shelf.

The vibrating stopped, or stilled, like a held breath. Angela got comfortable on the wooden floor, curious, and ran her fingers along the spines. She paused on the smallest.

'Ó Grádaigh,' she murmured in wonder, pulling it free and turning the damaged paperback in her hands. The front cover had been torn off, the tatty imprint page censored by hurried black ink, but what was left of the spine identified the author's surname, spelled the same as her maternal grandfather's. He was a writer, and a researcher of magic – she'd read one of his early manuscripts many years ago when she still felt connected to her witch heritage, before bad dates and big storms and paying bills took centre stage. Was this his work, too? The other was a beautiful text, drawing connections between love and Fate and magic, positing the theory that they were different faces of the same force. Intrigued, Angela turned the first page.

She couldn't properly describe what happened next. The vibration in her chest, momentarily still, pulsed suddenly, and on the new page, an intricate geometric design flashed brightly.

Startled, Angela dropped the book onto her knees. Even through the trashed front page, the design shone with a slowly ebbing pale gold light. More cautious now, she turned the page back and examined the glowing *thing*. A circular design the size of her palm, made of loops and points that repeated around the circle to create a sort of mandala. It was very beautiful, and perhaps even more so when she realised it was hand-drawn, though what ink could have done this, Angela had no clue. She compulsively began to trace the shape with her fingertip, awed by the prettiness. This was a spell, she gathered, and not a standard feature of the book from the publishers. She wondered who'd put it here, and what it did, and thought she should probably refrain from touching it further.

Someone rounded the corner and Angela looked up at a shop assistant, who seemed momentarily surprised to see her.

'I'm sorry if I'm not supposed to be back here,' Angela said automatically. There was no sign, nor was it empty of customers, but that didn't mean necessarily it was open to the public. The assistant smiled.

'Real witches always find their way into this section,' she intimated, putting some of the books she carried back into their shelves. 'It's taking us longer than expected to sort through it all. There's stock here from eons back, when the store was owned by the O'Malleys, and there's just no sensible way of categorising it. Plus half of it's probably cursed.'

She laughed lightly, and Angela looked down at the book she held. The golden mandala was gone.

'Do you think this one is?' she asked, holding it up. The assistant came to kneel beside her so she could look it over. She had fewer piercings than the one working the counter, and a definite aura of magic around her.

'Hmm, there's something to it, isn't there?' she agreed. She noticed the spine. 'Ó Grádaigh. Makes sense. Founding father of modern magical theory. Most of his work was blacklisted in the fifties and sixties.'

'Blacklisted?'

'By the White Elm,' the assistant replied. 'That'll be why the cover was removed. You would have been arrested if you were caught selling this back then. This looks like his book on spellcasting – *very* touchy subject in those times. The energy we're sensing could be an active protective spell to keep it from being scried during the burnings.'

Burnings, banned books, blacklisted authors... Angela's head swam with all this history she didn't know about her own culture. About the figures of authority she'd entrusted her sister to.

She swallowed her doubts. She hadn't known her grandfather. Neither had her mother. She *did* know Aristea, and she knew two modern White Elm councillors, and she trusted them.

'How do you know all this?' she asked finally, and the other woman gestured around the dusty shelves.

'I read.' She nodded at the book in Angela's hands. 'For someone taking an interest in spell casting, normally I wouldn't recommend they start off with Ó Grádaigh – it's high-level theory, and foundational to a lot of illegal stuff. But,' she added, glancing meaningfully at the air around Angela's head, 'you seem like you can handle yourself, and treated academically, it should be a fascinating read. Oh.' Angela had idly opened the front page again, and the mandala briefly flared to life. The assistant saw it too, confirming that Angela was not imagining things. 'I think this book wants to come home with you.'

Maybe that was their line with all gullible newbies, maybe the mandala was some trick of theirs to capture interest, and maybe it was all some ploy to sell tatty old books, but cynic or not, Angela still held out the book.

'How much?'

chapter thirteen

Even when all the blood was washed off, I still didn't feel close to normal. It seemed that suddenly the city was home to many more sorcerers than before, their auras constantly brushing past my shielded one. I used the city map in Declan's guidebook to stay off the main roads. I found a hotel that wasn't on our list, eager to avoid Shanahan's associates, and though I had no reason to trust his word, it was the only word I had to go off. I booked in at the front desk with some extremely poor attempts at the phoneticised Czech phrases I found in the book, and once inside my room I prioritised stabbing my finger so I could bleed generously over my locks while I worked the spell Declan had shown me.

Again, no reason to believe this would work, but I had nothing to lose from trying. When I felt the spell seal, I went straight for the bathroom, and upon seeing myself in the mirror, I turned promptly for the pristine toilet and threw up my breakfast.

'Ugh,' I muttered shakily when it was all up, and flopped against the wall while the toilet flushed. I felt boneless, clammy. Spliced with other awful memories, the American's graphic death played over and over in my head.

Two hands hitting the glass of a ward... too late...

Seidel's knife embedding in that man's neck... blood spurting... nothing I could do...

Declan's head hitting the brick... my ward too slow...

My hands, dried blood... Teagan's? Renatus in the orchard, pale, cracked, not waking up...

Screaming, white fire on skin...

The ward coming down, Renatus too far back... my breath stopping abruptly...

I ran my fingers over the tattoo on my wrist, then squeezed

my fist and channelled some magic, a distraction to focus on. Greyish cracks lit up under my apprentice mark, proof of my brush with burnout. Proof I had found my limits when it mattered most. That's what I had to remind myself. I hadn't saved Anouk, but I'd saved Renatus. And today, the people in that scenario weren't my responsibility. Seidel and the American wanted to capture me. Declan was a thieving prick. I didn't owe any of them anything.

Still. It's not every day you watch someone die and walk away wearing their blood. I wondered if the police had found the body yet, and who he was, and how his family would react to his loss. I wondered with remorse whether Cassán's anti-council spell would prevent Qasim and Renatus from tapping into today's events and whether that meant Hanna Seidel would get away with murder, or if Declan would take the fall based on the energetic evidence at the scene – because Seidel was right, he was the last one to touch the American.

The hot shower did a lot to bring me around. I stood under the water until I felt the temperature drop. When I was dry and dressed and had given up on my stained shirt, I re-evaluated my options.

Prague wasn't looking so safe anymore. Displacements would be monitored. I'd lost the ledger, I'd lost my ally – if he ever was one, let's be real – and Magnus Moira knew where to look for me. The only upside to my situation was that the American hadn't had a chance to tip anyone else off, so if he *did* have any connections I should worry about, they probably weren't onto me. Yet.

I reread the list of hotels Declan had rattled off and knew what I had to do.

I used the hotel's sole computer in the lobby to access the internet. I hadn't been to the website before, but a search for keywords like "white elm" and "prague rally" and "marcy pretoria" made the online destination very clear. The forum the sorcerer kids had met on and organised their party for democracy was basic enough, and very public. Links to the most prominent users' blogs revealed even more discussion, a lot of it worrying enough to make me question whether I wanted to contact these people. I sat and read the conspiracy theories, the counterarguments and the hate for the council with a sinking stomach for almost an hour before making up my mind.

A few voices, thankfully those of moderators (with the group's message *Peace, Freedom, Choice* quoted in their signatures, along with a link to an online petition), seemed intent on seeing reason, and their logical reassurances were influential in pushing the overall tone back to the intended neutrality. They all used online handles but also referred to each other by real names in the comments. These friendships had transcended this forum and moved eventually to real-world meetups over a course of, as far as I could tell, *years* of communication. I tended to forget that the White Elm and their policies had been a hot topic for much longer than my involvement with them.

I picked my mark and created a new profile so I could comment on a very popular post from last month, one I knew my photo had been redacted from.

Was nice to see you in Germany. I'm nearby and need to meet you.
AB

I had to vacate the seat and let other guests use the computer, but I checked back every hour until almost six, when I got my reply.

How near? Castle tour at 6:30?

It was lucky I saw it when I did, because by the time I'd refreshed the page from writing my confirmation, he'd deleted the whole thread. Better not to leave a public trail.

The hours since Declan's abandonment – bastard – had been nerve-wracking but uneventful. No scriers' attentions bouncing from my aura. No Lisandro knocking at my door. Apparently the protection spells Declan and I had crafted were still in effect. Going outside, though, felt like pushing my luck. Seidel knew I was in town, which meant Renatus's sister and godfather knew, too, and I still didn't know how Seidel had found me in the first place. I warded myself up heavily and headed for the most distinctive building complex in the city. It wasn't hard to find. The castle looked like a crown at the top of the hill, visible in the distance between buildings every now and then. Tourists were milling toward it, so I didn't need to bust out the guidebook and give my foreignness away.

Eyes fell away from me like wet snow from tree boughs. They couldn't stick. Nearly every block, I felt the presence of a sorcerer, sometimes even passing them right by, and my anxiety skyrocketed, but none noticed me. Every city has roughly the same population of magical people, so at least some had to be locals going about their business, but I wasn't taking any chances, not on the street, not crossing the iconic Charles Bridge where I'd skinned my knees in a rough Displacement a few weeks ago, not as I stepped through the castle complex's arched gateway and stopped just short of the ticket office, awed.

I wasn't alone. The visage of St Vitus's Cathedral is an impressive sight. In the late afternoon sunlight, a bride was posing on the front step, and a photographer was capturing what I assumed would be some of the most stunning wedding photos a girl could ask for. Enthralled, dozens of tourists were watching on, craning their necks back to admire the spectacular gothic building.

There was one sorcerer already here, though he couldn't see me initially, and through the crowd, I couldn't spot him either. I recognised the energy signature and altered my warding. I detected his wariness about this situation before I saw him near the corner, scanning the crowd with no regard at all for the beautiful church. That wariness dropped into relief when he caught sight of me, and I raised a hand in greeting as he approached.

'I didn't make it as far as the castle yet,' I admitted when he was closer. 'Or the ticket booth.'

'I figured,' he replied, holding two tickets out to me. 'You're a tourist. Minimum forty second pause at the sight of the cathedral.'

Grinning, I accepted the offered ticket with thanks to my only Czech friend. Jaroslav, whose surname I didn't even know, whose job, family, backstory and past I had no clue about, had been one of the organisers of the Lennon Wall rally. He'd helped

me shepherd the crowd out of danger when the Irishman's –
Benny O'Callaghan's – fear bomb had been set off above the
square, though when Renatus and I had first come upon the
street party that had kicked off their meet-up, Jaroslav had been
standing on a car, laughing and exciting the crowd.

That seemed like a long time ago. He'd cut his thick boyish
hair into something more sensible. His enthusiastic idealism had
been blasted away while he stood beside me under the glassy
ward that had left Anouk and three others out to die, and the
young man before me now seemed immeasurably sobered by
comparison.

'Thanks for meeting me,' I said with sincerity. 'I wasn't sure
if you would.'

'I *had* begun to wonder if you might be bad luck, but I thought
I'd give you one more chance,' he said generously. I smiled back,
grateful.

'I realise you're not exactly aligned with the White Elm, and
as a political figure, I'm…'

I tried to think of a less threatening description than
"dangerous to be seen with". He wasn't to know that the last
person to approach me had taken a fatal knife to the neck, but he
was a prominent voice in magical youth politics. His followers
ranged across the spectrum from staunchly anti-council through
to council-optimistic, but none fit the bill for "pro-" and I'd
already seen from reading his blog that, due to his censored
account of the proceedings he'd witnessed between the White
Elm and their allies Valero and Avalon, his neutrality had been
challenged by commenters. I didn't want to damage his
reputation. He smirked knowingly.

'Problematic? I'm aware. But that's the nature of being a
political figure, I suspect.' His smile slipped a little, and his
worry simmered underneath. 'I was surprised to hear from you.
I have heard… things.'

'Heard what?'

'That you left the White Elm,' he told me. 'At least two
sources have said you joined Magnus Moira. Sources I trust.
People are saying the theatre fire in Belarus was lit by the council,

and the names of the men who attacked the rally got out somehow. It wasn't me,' he insisted quickly, and I raised my hands to show I believed him. 'I left those details out, like Elijah said. But everyone knows now they were White Elm supporters dressed as Magnus Moira. And the White Elm has gone silent. No replies to my emails to Elijah. I'm not demanding an explanation or trying to blame you,' he added, perhaps seeing my expression falling. 'It is just… difficult to know who to trust.'

I looked down at my shoes, thinking, and noticed a few flecks of blood on the toe. Jaroslav's online community was made up of young sorcerers highly engaged in political goings-on, the kind of people who asked questions and looked for credible answers. If *they* believed these lies, what did that say about the majority of the magical population? It worried me, though I'd never felt responsible for the White Elm's public perception before – that was their problem. Wasn't it? My own love for the council had been tarnished, and I was hardly the poster child for White Elm rule and policy right now.

'I understand if you can't trust my word,' I said finally, 'but I'm telling the truth when I say I'm not with Magnus Moira, and I haven't *left* the council. I was never *on* it.'

Jaroslav smiled wryly up at the visage of the cathedral.

'You know, I study political science,' he reminded me. 'I don't trust anyone at their word. Don't think you're special just because you saved my life.'

He dropped his gaze to mine and I smiled back at the ghostly sparkle of the boy on the car rooftop I saw in his eye. He paused, deciding, and then nodded at the scar on the side of my face.

'That healed well.'

'This is kind of why I'm here,' I explained. 'Lisandro picked out this place, *your* rally, as the epicentre for his demonstration. That Finnish coven that attacked us, those names everyone's trashing on Marcy's website – those men were innocent.'

I felt Jaroslav shutting down at my claim.

'They killed a guy I'd been chatting with online for five years,' he reminded me, bringing back images of that boy whose throat had been sliced right in front of us, uncomfortably

219

reminiscent of today's unnecessary death, 'and I was there when *your* council shared their identities as the killers.'

I let the loaded comment about my political alignment roll off. I knew what he meant.

'They were possessed by Magnus Moira scriers,' I told him. 'They were awake and aware and unable to stop themselves. They were terrified. And I...'

I didn't recognise it. Two souls in each body, two sets of emotions, I was the one witness qualified to see that situation for what it was, and I'd failed.

'It was a set-up, designed to do exactly this,' I finished, pushing away my inadequacy. 'Spread misinformation. Make the council look petty. Undermine them right when they can't answer back.'

Lisandro's favourite game of late, I thought with disdain. Pulling the rug out from under the feet of his former brothers and sisters and giving them the chance to know how it felt to be powerless. Like he'd ever experienced it himself. Like he had the first clue.

Jaroslav was frowning at me, disturbed.

'Possessed by scriers?' he repeated. 'Can they do that?'

I nodded. 'I've seen it. As a host she was like a killer puppet. She had no control.'

'And you think that's how those Finnish sorcerers came to be at my rally?' he clarified. 'That's a serious claim. It would change everything. Can you prove it?'

I thought of the list of names of missing scriers I'd compiled with Renatus and Qasim, a list presented to Valero to prevent the breakdown of their alliance. I thought of the ledger that I'd theorised would contain those same names, proving they'd used Shanahan's services as a "disappearer" of people wanting to escape their troubles and his use of Magnus Moira as a launderer of these individuals. I couldn't guess where Declan would have taken that. And then I thought of my own memory of the rally, the feelings I'd gotten from the men as they caged us in and killed that boy and chased us down; a memory I couldn't share with anyone without risking the rest of my mind, because there was only one person I was prepared to share my head with.

But I needed to be able to trust others, and people can always be trusted to act in their own interests.

'Yes,' I said finally. 'I have proof. This is the last piece.' I tried not to hesitate handing over the rewritten list of hotels. I'd added details from Declan's musings about who owned which building and their financial connection to Shanahan. The ledger, I suspected, would confirm all this, if we could ever read it. Jaroslav took it without word. I swallowed. 'I can't contact them directly, but the council needs this.'

'You want me to post it for you?'

'I can't trust the post,' I explained. We both shifted to let a tour group pass behind us. Their awe soaked into me in continuous waves. 'I'm trusting you. I know you're still trying to get a dialogue going with the White Elm. I read your petition.'

Jaroslav read the page in silence but I felt his wary surprise. It took him a few moments to speak again.

'It's almost six-thirty. Would you like to go in?' he asked, gesturing at the other tourists who'd completed their obligatory stare at the cathedral and were moving around to the right. I didn't really need to stay that long, but it appeared that I was as safe here as I was in my hotel room, so we joined the slow-moving current. Jaroslav glanced over his shoulder. 'Your friend is not here.'

I opened my mouth to say that Declan was *not* my friend, but then I realised he had never met Declan.

'Renatus. No, I'm travelling alone. Things got… complicated. So freaking complicated,' I repeated, mostly to myself, trying not to think about it. Vaguely I touched the front of my shirt, feeling the crumpled crane shape under the material. 'I'm kind of… undercover.'

'Undercover reading petitions?' Jaroslav queried. We circled wide around tourists taking pictures of an old fountain thing.

'I skimmed it,' I corrected. I followed his lead toward a line of people waiting to go in. When I felt his expectant gaze, I sighed. 'And… I don't disagree. But they will.'

'Did you sign it?'

'Of course not. I'm a White Elm apprentice.'

'You,' he countered good-naturedly, 'are a hypocrite. You clearly care about justice.' He waved the hotel list. 'About being thorough, doing things the right way. Deposing a benevolent dictatorship in favour of democracy–'

'I am in enough trouble,' I interrupted, taking the page back and kneeling as though to tie my shoe, 'and they are not the enemy. Here. Give them this when you front up with your signatures.'

I opened the note and wiped it across the toe, transferring some of the blood. I hoped it would be enough for Qasim to break through the anti-council wards hiding that crime. I refolded along the same seams and held it out to Jaroslav.

Betraying the council because I didn't see a better way to combat Lisandro.

'You're my insurance policy,' I explained, seeing his reluctance. 'Just don't touch the blood. And don't get caught with it. It may link you to a murder you didn't commit.'

'Should I even ask?'

I shrugged. 'Magnus Moira.'

'Magnus Moira seems intent on killing you. Or recruiting you.'

'Yes, I noticed that too.' I watched him pocket the note, and then said, 'They haven't managed to sway you yet?'

Someone checked our tickets and waved us through to the next checkpoint.

'If the White Elm accepts my petition, they're welcome to campaign,' Jaroslav claimed, shuffling forward with the compressed crowd. 'Magnus Moira has an important message but they lack cohesion. Ultimately, their purists want *no* government, which we know would be chaos, while another faction wants to replace the council with Lisandro. That'd be fine, if I really believed he wanted that, except they're a subversive movement trying to gain power the exact same way the White Elm did – through dominance and force, not through democratic processes. I can't support either of them until they give us the vote, and I still think we've got more hope of that with the White Elm.'

It was an interesting premise, but not one I felt confident in.

'He might be a sweet bumbling old man, but I don't think you'll get Lord Gawain to lay down the mantle and leave the nation to a popularity contest. And I assure you, that's the way he'll look at it. They're not perfect,' I conceded. 'They're just better than the alternative.'

Jaroslav smiled thinly.

'I'm willing to be convinced. And I'm not the only one.'

Quietly I recounted the scene in the Belarussian theatre. I left out Hiroko's name and Nastassja's real identity, plus anything else I thought was probably state secret, and paused a lot, because we were admitted to the castle and I kept having to be amazed by the displays. But I got the story across, and hoped his retelling of it to his readers would help slow the dissent.

'So they're not ignoring you. They're stuck, with no phones, no internet. I don't even know if they're getting mail.'

'Unoriginal yet effective,' Jaroslav commented quietly as we stood at the back of the group being shown the throne room. 'Divide and conquer. And drives that point home about the council's power coming from their ability to take it away from everyone else. Lock them down and they're impotent.'

I had to wait until the guide wasn't looking our way before I could murmur my cool response.

'Sounds a lot like Magnus Moira rhetoric coming from someone supposedly committed to neutrality.'

Working with adults, I had an appreciation for the way people could shrug off indirect accusations when they weren't wrapped up in their teenage garbage. Jaroslav was a few years older than me, but I didn't know by how much. I was shocking at guessing ages and had to work off comparisons. Older than me. Younger than Renatus or Declan. He only smiled wryly.

'You must know you're not the only person of political interest I'm in contact with,' he said quietly. My wary glance tipped him off that I wasn't comfortable with this. 'Look, I haven't told anyone you're here. I mean to say if you're truly interested in understanding Magnus Moira, you might try listening to them. Wait.' He followed when I stepped away from the tour group into the empty passage behind us. 'Alright, don't listen to them. Listen to me. I might have something for you. An event, this whole weekend. Some friends of mine are interested in joining, and this thinly veiled recruitment drive isn't far from here.'

'Where?' I asked, voice low to match his. He felt his pockets.

'Outside of Minsk,' he said as he offered me a crumpled flyer. 'It's maybe the third such festival they have held there this year. I'm not sure why always this location.'

'Because,' I said in realisation, taking the flyer to read more closely, 'Lisandro has a compound in Belarus, and I think you just gave me the address.'

chapter fourteen

Jaroslav showed me the quickest way to the train station.

'If you're positive you want to go, you can take a train to Warsaw, then change lines to Minsk,' Jaroslav said, his knowledge of the rail service challenging my bussing skills for their crown. 'Are you sure you won't wait for tomorrow? I can come with you.'

'It's better you don't,' I advised. We strode across the street with the crowd. 'I'm politically problematic in all the ways that get my associates hurt, and I'd rather you weren't.'

'Is this why you're Renatus's apprentice?'

His question threw me. 'How do you mean?'

'The hero thing,' he pointed out. 'You know, big rally in Prague and a bomb's going to take out some people you don't even know, and you two swoop in from across the world and save everyone like it's nothing–'

'It wasn't nothing,' I protested, rolling my sleeve up while he continued so I could show him the grey cracks under my skin. He winced but was still talking.

'And you can't prevent murder so you send some guy you've met twice to deliver your evidence to the proper authorities to make sure justice is served. *Not* that I am complaining,' he raised his voice over mine when I went to argue and request the note back. 'I'm grateful, of course, that you chose the day I almost died to find your hero complex, and I'm grateful for a bargaining chip with the council, but this seems a recurring thread. Is that why Renatus chose you? A shared trait?'

I'd never thought of it that way, at least not about myself. Renatus, yes. I wasn't traditionally very brave, nor very civically minded. When had that changed? How much more of Renatus's personality could seep across our bond?

'It is, actually,' I said finally. We stopped at the entrance to the same train station I'd arrived at with Declan. I thought of the spell holding strong near the tracks. Jaroslav smiled again, with less cheer.

'Well, don't let it get you killed. We're here,' he added, gesturing at the ramp down to the subway level. 'When you reach the last stop, you'll need to taxi the last few kilometres unless you like walking across open farmland. The flyer is meant to help you Displace in, or so my friend told me.'

'I don't doubt it.' I'd detected the subtle spellwork woven into the paper. I patted my satchel. 'My phrasebook says I should say *děkuji*.'

Jaroslav blinked.

'If that is supposed to be "thank you", it's nowhere close. But you're welcome. And you didn't need to buy my help, by the way.' He looked up at the sign over the entrance. 'Did you get everything you needed in Prague?'

His question prompted a little sigh of malcontent, because no, my main reason for coming here had gone astray; but then I realised who I was talking to.

'It's true, I didn't come here for the castle tour,' I agreed. 'I came back to investigate the rally, to understand. Why did you choose Prague?'

'I live here,' Jaroslav said at first, then reconsidered. 'We used to talk about meeting in Athens, years ago. Birthplace of democracy and all. Then when Lisandro left the White Elm and things started shaking up, our discussions turned more seriously toward an alternative system. Someone said we should meet at Lennon Wall, he'd seen it on a holiday to Prague, and I said, I can organise that.' He frowned, a surge of memory and sadness moving through him. 'Bryce said it.'

'Bryce?'

'They opened his throat. That was Bryce.'

I thought back, careful to temper my own feelings. When the possessed coven had closed in on us, armed with knives, one boy had tried to run, and he'd paid with his life. Bad luck, tragic luck. Was it, though? The fear bomb had taken out all the loose ends at Magnus Moira's end, killing the Finnish puppets so they couldn't tell how they'd been used, how they'd been infiltrated. Their meeting notes said one member, Miro, had brought the Prague rally to the coven's attention – we'd surmised he was probably a plant – but who had brought the rally to *his* attention?

'The street party was just the kick-off,' Jaroslav said now. 'We had the whole weekend planned. We wanted to organise ourselves into something more cohesive. A real movement the White Elm would have to listen to, in time. It was a strategy meeting. Then you showed up.'

'But you were talking about avoiding a war,' I pointed out. 'What made you so sure those were the stakes?'

He thought back. 'Just… some guy. I was working a summer job, I handed him his change, and out of nowhere, he told me the White Elm doesn't vet its members closely enough. That they judge net good over character, and it was going to lead us all into a war with a rival group if we weren't careful. He said, "shouldn't we all get a say?" I don't know who he was. Young, some tourist with his grandmother and little sister. He sounded a bit like you; I thought he was Scottish? But what he said stuck with me.'

It had led him to where we stood today.

'If you'd been successful that weekend, if your petition is successful; could your end goal be interpreted as threatening to Magnus Moira?'

He was at a loss. 'They should be for it. A chance to face the White Elm on even ground and take over legitimately. Unless they don't believe they can win that way, or,' he reconsidered, mood darkening, 'they'd prefer the war.'

Those words were still dancing in my ears when I joined the line to buy my ticket.

The train ride took more than eight uneventful hours, and I managed to spend about four of them asleep, dreaming my usual dreams of darkness, death, and shells on the beach. Because I'm a nice normal girl like that.

Warsaw was a brief stopover not long after sunrise and far enough away from Prague to feel like I'd left its horrors behind. The station was harshly lit, underground, and modern to the point of clinical. Glancing at the steely escalators and scrying ahead to the upstairs foyer and its automatic glass doors, I had little faith in finding an appropriate patch of dirt nearby until I watched another train disappear into its tunnel. Bingo. The station cleared out before I made my move, sneaking into the tunnel leading from my stationary train's line.

'You didn't see me do this,' I informed the skittering rodents as I grabbed ingredients from my bags to weave a new protection spell. One that didn't rely on Declan. I tossed some magic above me – a sallow, sourceless light blossomed in the tunnel, a trick I'd seen Renatus do and had clearly memorised at some point – and found the little knife. 'If I lose all my hair because of his spell, I really will stab him.'

I went through the motions and cast the spell exactly as Declan had taught me. I hummed my own tune, drawing magic in with its mindless originality, and wove the elements together with the symbols whose meanings I couldn't guess. The magic sealed; I felt the spark and the settling of a new network of threads, deflecting dangers from anyone tied into the spell.

I sat back on my heels and considered my next move. I had a ticket all the way to Minsk. There hadn't been any sorcerers on my train, and there weren't any magical signatures around this station. Presumably my seekers were focused on Prague, but for how long? I got Jaroslav's flyer out and read it again. Printed at home, no design finesse whatsoever, it encouraged "sorcerers of every creed and class" to a festival to "awaken the magic within". It sounded lame until I realised the play on words; the magic embedded in the paper was encoded with the location.

Anyone truly looking would be led to their promised land. And nobody was going there looking for *me*.

I wandered the station until I found lockers to keep my extra bag. I didn't know what I was walking into – one of a thousand reasons this was a terrible idea – and didn't want to be weighed down. I stuffed my ticket in there, too. The extra hours to get to Minsk were extra hours I could be caught. The flyer should guide me the same whether I was here or there.

Theoretically.

Back in the tunnel, I took a few fearful breaths before my attempt. Anything could go wrong. I was considering walking into the belly of the beast. Stupid, stupid… But Jaroslav was right. I didn't really understand Magnus Moira. My enemy was Lisandro. Were they really the same thing?

I clutched the flyer. I reached for the Fabric. I felt the void as I stepped through. And then the tunnel was gone, and I was standing on a sandy creek bed and blinking at a rising sun. Some small explosion went off nearby, startling a ward out of me, and I ducked, expecting the worst.

Nothing happened. I was alone, but beyond a small rise ridged with trees, I felt a mass of energy – bodies, minds, emotions, magic, all of it. No one seemed to be focused on me. I hugged my wards tight to me and ran up the slope. Beyond was the field Jaroslav had spoken of, and it was not at all the barren paddock I'd expected.

Countless caravans, tents and temporary stages. Circles of sorcerers meditating in the early light. An unnaturally balanced pile of stones, twice my height, apparently sustaining itself against the ideas of gravity. A small pack of unusual-looking wolves racing between tents, emanating unbridled joy that felt human as they chased down a rabbit. And a large dead tree, gloriously aflame, a totem at the centre of the huddle of tents, with not one person concerned about it and no indication of the fire spreading.

The scene made me feel equal parts uneasy and inspired. As I watched, the earth at the centre of one meditation circle began to shake, then crumble, then surge upward. Grass and plants burst forth, flowers blossoming to full bloom in seconds before wilting and falling back to the dirt to be replaced with a second wave, then a third, until someone broke concentration to gaze upon their work with awe. Nearby, ignoring them completely and lost in her own world, a barefoot dancer spun, with purplish smoke streaming from her hands in ribbons that painted her arcs and spins in the air behind her before slowly, unnaturally slowly, fading away. Two young women with dreadlocks stopped an early morning runner to show him their empty cupped hands, in which, after several attempts at a concentrated click, a spark of red lightning flashed, exciting them all immensely.

I knew that excitement. I knew that joy whenever I made new magic happen for the first time.

I had found Magnus Moira.

Their camp was huge, and I was walking straight through the middle of it.

Infiltrating enemy territory sounded like a momentous task, but it turned out to not be that difficult. Lisandro and his minions weren't anticipating anyone problematic trying to get *in*. They had the most meddlesome of the White Elm locked at Morrissey House. This encampment was a standing invitation to sorcerers everywhere – the barriers were necessarily loose. Face and aura disguised with a thin illusion, I drew a breath and waltzed in like I belonged there.

Picture your garden-variety folk festival, crossed with two parts circus show and one part movie set during a special effects take. As the sun rose higher, visually fascinating busyness rose in tandem. Dancers, joggers, meditation circles, families cooking over fires and faulty camping stoves. As I passed, one such device sparked ominously under the sausages it was frying, and at the next tent, two young men had their eyes tightly shut and their hands joined over a cold saucepan of oats.

Breakfast would be a long way off at this rate.

But amidst all this, what stood out most to me was the inspiring emotional atmosphere. It ran high, and positive. Everywhere, everyday people with sorcery in their blood were experimenting with magic, and, seeing it right before their eyes, were *believing*. The focus, the persistence, the hopefulness, the awe... An electric current of potential charged through the very air, fritzing those conventional electronic devices and powering up the auras and confidence levels of every person in this crowd. Many of them, it appeared, were trying moderate to expert magic for the first time. The same way the White Elm's Academy fuelled its students by concentrating magic use in one place, these festivalgoers were suddenly finding themselves capable of things they weren't before.

Their excitement was intoxicating.

I stopped and watched a girl about my own age, lying on her back with her hands in the air. A playing card spun lazily above her fingers, looking effortlessly impressive, though from the expression of tight enthusiasm on her tired face and the muttered hiss of her personal chant, it was clear that the levitation trick was far from effortless and had taken much of the night to master. I admired her tenacity. With the one exception of scrying, which I'd always wanted to do, any magic that did not come to me easily had simply been relegated to the "too hard" basket and probably would never have been properly studied had I not fallen into Renatus's shadow as his apprentice. How stupidly lucky was I, really? I teleported here, hid my face and energy signature behind an illusory mask and could remotely view all over the world, and how hard had I actually worked for any of it? Most people didn't get bonded with a superpowered repository of magical knowledge like I did.

The three of clubs shook. I felt the girl's attention and her anxiety as she worked harder to keep from looking my way, and I hurried on, hoping I hadn't distracted her too badly. I slid between a robust-looking tent and the back of a temporary stage at the edge of the site, pulling my hood tighter over my false face as I extended my senses softly through the camp. Hundreds of souls, almost all of them magical, very few of concerning capability. Renatus was better than I was at judging power levels by the accepted scale, but I could make comparative judgements easily enough, and across this whole camp, only four – no, five; one now popped in nearby – auras that my mind touched had power close to mine. And the fact that I could sense them so easily made them less concerning again, because it meant they didn't know how to ward themselves. Or maybe all this excitement in the air was making me overconfident, and they just didn't feel the need here?

That latter possibility started to feel more likely as that fifth presence continued its trajectory toward me. I leaned past the tent to look down the row of flimsier ones behind it, feeling for that person though I couldn't yet see them. I checked the straps of my bag in case I needed to run and dug my trusty ruby from my pocket. The image I wanted appeared in its surface immediately, giving me flashes of top-down perspectives all over the encampment, narrowing to this location where I saw the top of my own hooded head and, two tents away, another hooded figure slinking closer.

I slid a hand into my satchel, feeling for the handle of a sai, but hesitated from pulling it free. I was thinly connected to the image inside the ruby, and it gave me a direct Empathic connection to the people it showed. One of them was me, and the other, staying out of sight, did not feel like everyone else here. The positivity and enthusiasm of the camp was not reflected in his nervousness and shame. He was skinny, hunkering down, not exhibiting ambush behaviour.

Still, we were both out of view of anyone else, and it paid to be cautious.

'I know you're there,' I called, loud enough that only my frightened follower would hear. His answer sounded warily relieved.

'You're Irish.'

I frowned, loosening my grip on my sword in my bag. It wasn't a lot of speech to go off, but didn't I know that strange mix of accents?

'You're... say something else,' I prompted when nothing solid came to mind. I felt the surge of fear and heard the hardness of self-talk – not so much the words, just the feeling – that it took for my follower to force himself to step out from behind the tent and face me.

I didn't know his face. I'd never seen him before and knew I wouldn't recognise him even if I had. I blinked, searching for something distinct. My eyes kept sliding from shapeless feature to shapeless feature, absorbing nothing, and from the way his eyes moved across my face, I gathered he was experiencing the same thing.

Illusions.

'If you're who I think,' he said carefully, keeping his hands out beside him, 'then we have a friend in common. She was wearing the crane I made her.'

The mix of accents untangled immediately in my brain – British mum, Swiss dad, upbringing in India – and I unconsciously grasped at the front of my shirt.

'Actually,' I said, pulling the crane into sight by its string, 'I'm looking after it.'

Despite his thin, wary hopefulness, I kept my distance. Garrett Fischer had saved Hiroko's life at the theatre but as a Displacer, he could have gone anywhere after his presumed defection from Magnus Moira, so finding he hadn't left the country was not promising. Sending an old friend to get close to me was a decidedly Lisandro move, but my instincts had always served me better than logic, and even logic couldn't help admitting that he looked skinnier and shakier than I remembered.

I could take him, if it came to it. But I didn't feel that it would. Slowly, I dragged my fingers through the magic covering my face, unpicking it and letting the mask fall away. Real relief flooded through the stranger in front of me, and he mirrored my action.

The real Garrett Fischer was about my height, with thick russet hair and milky skin, and *skinny*. He was thin when I knew him, but this was an underfed, strung-out, abrupt kind of skinny, exaggerated by unbrushed hair and unwashed clothes. Along with a yellowing bruise on his cheek and exhausted shadows under his eyes, he looked decidedly unwell.

'What are you doing here?' he asked, eyes still on Hiroko's crane. 'Is she…? Did they…?'

'She's fine. What are *you* doing here?' I countered. 'I thought you got away. Josh, too.'

'We did,' he said miserably, 'but they caught up.'

He looked down, embarrassed, and I saw that his hand was scabbed and greyish, and that he stood unevenly, like he favoured one leg. Injuries sustained when Magnus Moira "caught up"?

'So you're back on the side of the people who nearly killed your girlfriend?'

'No!' Garrett's indignation was almost strong enough to edge his shy voice. 'They don't know I'm here, and this is the last place they'll look. But I can't leave. They've got Josh. He followed me, and we were okay for a few days, but then they… I couldn't stop them. They brought him back here.' He looked around with the hopeless look of someone who didn't know what to do. 'I'm afraid for him. They're harsh on defectors.'

I cringed, thinking of the Scot who'd cut his own fingers off to stay free of these people, and still ended up nailed to a tree. I hoped Garrett was thinking of the same example, and not something worse.

'I've been watching the camp, feeling for the right moment,' he said finally. 'And right now, all of the big four are gone, and… you're here.'

'The big four?' I asked before I thought it through. Obviously he was referring to the four biggest threats. 'Where did they go?'

'Lisandro and Nastassja left together for Morrissey Estate about twenty minutes ago. Jackson's guarding the gate, like usual, and Aubrey's hardly ever here. But they could be back at any time. I was going to try…' He trailed off with the confidence of someone who had no idea what one person could do to rectify his situation. He swallowed. 'Then I sensed you landing. Most people who land here want to be seen – Displacement's a skill they like to show off – but you were already cloaked. I wanted to see why. I hoped… I didn't want to hope.'

I swallowed, too, equally ashamed. Garrett and Josh were among four of my classmates coerced into leaving the estate on a night that *I* was supposed to be guarding it. I'd insisted on the mission with Renatus instead, because I was stubborn and short-sighted. While logically I knew it was the White Elm's oversight, not mine, I still felt guilty for not being there to alert Renatus when supposedly dead councillor, Aubrey, had walked in.

The bruise, the gaunt cheekbones, the limp and the hollow eyes… what had happened to Garrett and my classmates was on my shoulders. He and Josh were part of my circle of friends at the Academy, Displacers like Hiroko and Addison.

In my head, Hiroko's wise words *Our friends are always our responsibility* did brief battle with Jaroslav's pointed queries about my hero thing. I wasn't sure which won, but I couldn't deny the fateful timing of this encounter with Garrett.

It was still a godawful idea, being here, but it felt less like I'd had much say in it.

'We'll need a better plan than hoping.' I raised my hand to my face to rework the visage spell. Garrett hurried to copy me. 'Where are they keeping Josh?'

He paused. 'Plan for what?'

'For getting him out,' I elaborated, sealing my illusion. 'No one else knows you're here, Garrett, and no one is coming. My only capable ally ran off and I'm cut off from the council. Long story,' I added when his eyes widened. 'Renatus is locked in the house and Hiroko's blissfully amnesiac. Suffice it to say that if you want help, I'm all there is on offer. And after the way you were taken… I was supposed to be there to stop it. I'm sorry.'

Hiroko's kind-of boyfriend blinked at me, emanating immense shame and discomfort.

'You don't need to be sorry,' he said after a moment, cheeks filling with colour even through the false face. 'I wasn't taken. I walked out. I still don't understand why, or how, exactly, and it took me weeks to realise it was a mistake. Josh knew. He kept trying to tell me something was wrong. If I'd listened to him, maybe I could have…' He inhaled, shaky and lost. 'I just want to do something right.'

I forced a sad smile. Like Lisandro and other Crafters, Aubrey had been able to manipulate the emotional atmosphere in the room the boys were in. Made them complacent. Made them trust.

'Something *was* wrong, but you got out,' I reminded him. 'You saved Hiroko's life in that theatre, and she saved mine. Now we can do something right, together, and save Josh.' I paused. 'What about the other two?'

'They'll all be in the main compound where it's secure,' the Displacer said uneasily, 'but the other two will still be in the rooms, where we stayed. We were very well looked after. They won't come.'

'And they're not in danger because they're not deserters,' I finished, thinking. Thinking this was *well* above my ability as a runaway apprentice but not seeing another option beyond Josh Reyes impaled on a tree.

'Josh, they took to the lock-up. Standard practice, two days without food and water before questioning. But... aren't you afraid I'll betray you... or something? Not that I plan to,' Garrett added with haste, blushing. He never could last sixty seconds without going totally red in the face. 'Only...'

'Only you wouldn't trust me if the situation were reversed,' I guessed. 'I've already been betrayed this week and I don't have room in my schedule for you to try it. If you do,' I tucked the paper crane carefully back under my clothes, 'I'll make sure she knows about it. And I'll end you. And you'd make your mum a liar.'

My words visibly shook Garrett, though I wasn't sure which hurt more.

'My... What about my mum?'

'She told the council not to come looking for you,' I told him awkwardly. I had never expected to be the one to explain, but he looked relieved, understanding even before I went on. 'She had a vision and said any attempt to rescue you before you came back on your own would get you all killed. She got all the other parents to agree. That's why... That's why no one came for you.'

'Mum and her visions. What exactly did she say?' he asked, getting more serious. 'Am I walking into the same trap by accepting your help in place of the Elm's?'

'I'm not White Elm,' I answered automatically, then thought back. 'She said *the council* couldn't interfere. She touched our hands, mine and Addison's. She said we'd see you again. She said you'd come back to the house with information that would make a difference–'

'Information?' He went unsure again. 'You mean about the

location of the compound, or the stuff I heard?'

'I don't know. I'm sure the council will appreciate either at this point. But aren't we working on short time here?'

My question snapped him back to attention, and he nodded urgently.

'What's our plan?' he asked, and I frowned as I leaned closer to straighten his hood.

'I had hoped you had one.'

chapter fifteen

One trait Renatus had always resented in himself was the vengefulness he could never seem to shake. His godfather had seduced his sister – basically dead to him. When promotion into the Dark Keeper's chair had meant being prepared to apprehend or even kill Lisandro, he hadn't batted an eye, and that was long before he knew about the deaths of his parents. The Avalonian detective, Gabriel Winter, had severely misrepresented the protected island nation when he'd recruited young Renatus and had humiliated him in front of his peers – Renatus had lain awake more than one night imagining vicious retaliations. For every time Qasim had put him in his place he'd had to stifle at least two ungracious thoughts about striking back in some petty way.

He was a person of spite, and he hated it, but until recently he hadn't thought he could *be* any other way. The slow blend across of not only Aristea's powers, but also her nature, had changed him, and he knew he was calmer, more measured, more forgiving than before. The cost? The blending was more of a trade. The lightening of his nature had meant a visible darkening of hers. It did however allow him to see vengefulness more clearly in others.

'Tell me… where 'e went,' was the first thing Emmanuelle said when she next woke up from her deep trance, and Renatus knew she meant Jackson.

'He… followed us,' he answered uncertainly, gently probing her aura for signs that she was afraid, 'but Qasim got you inside before he could catch up. You're safe.'

'I don't want to be safe,' she retorted. Her voice was weak and whispery but the anger was not. 'I want to find 'im. I want to burst every blood vessel in 'is brain and see 'is eyes roll shut.'

She slept almost constantly, which gave him plenty of time to deliberate whether to tell her that Jackson was *right there*, just outside the gate. Would it scare her? Give her something to focus on and work toward?

'Give her something to fixate on to her own disadvantage, more likely,' Qasim concurred sourly when Renatus told him in the same breath as 'Emmanuelle's awake.' He threw his napkin down and stood from the dining table with an abruptness that caught the attention of some of the students, sitting at the other table. Boundaries were breaking down – some of the serving staff had been coerced to join everyone else for meals, but the students were still not game enough to sit at the "teachers" table. 'What did you do to wake her up?'

'Nothing I wouldn't do for you,' Renatus replied coolly to the underlying accusation. 'It was really all her. So you don't think we should tell her?'

'I think once she's strong enough to reconnect to the council's minds, she'll work it out anyway. You told her about Peter after we all agreed not to. If she can handle that, she can handle Jackson skulking at the front door.' He paused, listening. 'I told Lady Miranda that she's woken up and she says, "It's a miracle". The sarcasm is tangible.'

Renatus shrugged. 'Healing is always a miracle.'

He felt Lord Gawain's eyes on him and couldn't help glancing back as he reached the door. The usual conflict rose inside him, prompted in part by his mentor's messy feelings. The council leader remained certain of Aristea's past and future guilt, but also felt sick with regret for putting Renatus offside. They hadn't spoken in days. Renatus felt regretful too, but just as certain that offside was the only place he could stand to be. That's where Lord Gawain had pushed him when he asked him to choose the council over his apprentice.

On the stairs, Renatus asked quietly, 'Can he hear us?'

'Can your sister?' Qasim countered, which Renatus took as a

no. He opened his jacket and handed two envelopes to his colleague. Qasim turned them to read the senders' names. 'Hiroko? Was this before or after–'

'I don't know. I haven't read it. I need someone else's eyes.'

Qasim rolled his and made a comment about not being a mail-reading service, but tore open Hiroko's letter anyway. Renatus kept his curious gaze on the stairs as they ascended. The other scrier was quiet, his attention distracted, and Renatus realised his own barriers against magic had kept him from tapping into impressions left on the paper. He clenched his hands a few times to keep from looking. *Aristea*.

'Reckless girl,' Qasim muttered with a shake of his head.

'Did you see where she is?'

'I saw where she *was*,' Qasim responded. 'Hopefully she's too smart to stay put. And this… I don't know if I'd call it *smart*, but it's oddly sensible. Sasaki's influence.' He sighed. 'These gallant children, too honest for their own good.'

'What does that even mean? What did Hiroko put in the letter?' Renatus asked irritably, glaring at the landing as they continued up.

'It's not a letter, and it's not from Hiroko. Aristea sent you a spell recipe, presumably the one she used for the memory spells. It's evidence I wish I hadn't seen,' he reiterated in annoyance, 'for a trial we're not going to stop if she keeps crossing lines.'

It wasn't just criminal evidence. It was proof of Aristea's desperation. She wasn't a confident spell-caster, and she'd been put in a situation *again* where spelling memories away had seemed like her best option. The recipe's arrival here meant she wanted to be able to reverse it, and didn't trust herself to manage it.

She wanted *him* to fix it. Like he should. She had grown up so much and was so capable, but she was also still a kid. His, in many ways. Qasim's, too, and others'. He slanted restless eyes toward his fellow scrier.

'And the other letter? From Angela?'

'I'm not reading Aristea's mail,' Qasim replied stiffly, putting the recipe back into its envelope. 'Maybe you should write to her sister and open a dialogue before she finds out on her own.'

'That can't be the first contact I have with her.'

'You've had *six months* to initiate a better first contact,' the Scrier chided, but he seemed to take Renatus's point. Aristea was stuck with both Renatus and Angela for the rest of her life; "I have completely misplaced your sibling" was not an introduction the apprentice was going to easily smooth over.

They knocked twice before letting themselves into Emmanuelle's room. Still lying flat on her bed, Emmanuelle hadn't moved anything but her eyes and facial muscles and couldn't do more even if she wanted to. Magic held her perfectly in place. Even an involuntary shrug at the wrong time could set the whole process back, Lady Miranda had advised. Renatus felt that it was probably an overprotective precaution, but as the least qualified person on the estate to question a Healer, he was sticking to the rules. Best to leave it until it was done, as Lady Miranda instructed, and with Renatus's donation of energy, that should come sooner rather than later now.

'So it's true, and you're awake,' Qasim commented as he held the door for Renatus. With her minimal control of her expression, Emmanuelle glared at the ceiling over her head. She seemed very present this time. Present and irritable.

'My nose itches,' she complained.

'So scratch it,' Renatus replied passively. She twitched her nose twice, attempts to satisfy the itch, but it was useless and her frustration overwhelmed her.

'*Va te faire foutre*, Renatus,' she snapped as he approached.

'I'm sure there was a *s'il vous plaît* in there somewhere.' But Renatus couldn't gather the same venom to his voice as she did. Qasim was right, he missed his two sidekicks, and losing her and Aristea in the same minute as he himself was benched was about as big a knock as anyone could take. He rubbed the side of her nose. 'Better?' She didn't respond, but her falling frustration level was answer enough.

'How do you feel?' Qasim asked. He invited the reply he got.

'Like dissolving Jackson's lungs in 'is chest.'

'On the mend, then.'

'Aristea and Hiroko,' Emmanuelle said, with less certainty.

'They were at the theatre, but I cannot sense them 'ere on the estate…?'

'They're both alive,' Qasim promised. 'Hiroko went back home. Her house is warded, even against me – wonder which of your students might be responsible for that?'

'And Aristea's missing,' Renatus finished, Emmanuelle's worry soaking into his. 'Alive. Staying safe, we hope. Everyone's looking for her, my mind isn't secure, and if she comes back here, she'll still be put on trial.'

'The trial.' She scoffed, dismissive. 'You don't remember yet what 'appened at your uncle's 'otel?'

Renatus shook his head.

'I'm not trying too hard,' he admitted. The flashes in his dreams were unpleasant, filled with white-hot pain and a panicked sense of drowning. He supposed this must be the event that nearly burned him out. 'I still don't know how safe that knowledge is in my head.'

Both Emmanuelle and Qasim were quiet for the next minute or so, and Renatus fidgeted with the bedspread's hem, letting the Scrier catch the Healer up on what else she'd missed. He could tell from her terrible poker face that she didn't like what she heard.

'That's ridiculous,' she said finally. Qasim shrugged.

'Anything more than agreeing would be bordering on treason, so I am doing nothing.'

'This connection you 'ave with your sister,' Emmanuelle redirected to Renatus, 'who sounds like a bitch, by the way; does it go both ways?'

The question disturbed Renatus, not least because it hadn't occurred to him first.

'Are you asking if I can infiltrate the mind of Lisandro's chief lieutenant?' he asked quietly, hurriedly wondering whether it might be possible, how he might go about it, thinking it through as fast as he could in case Nastassja came back and caught him at it. How many laws would it break? How dangerous could it be?

Emmanuelle was so limited in her use of her body but

managed to look decidedly unimpressed.

'Are you suggesting you're too noble to consider it?'

And he was back to the realisation that he was indeed a being of spite, because no, he wasn't too noble. Too conflicted, maybe.

Emmanuelle still slept most of each day, and the other councillors were busily back to teaching, which gave Renatus a lot of time alone to reflect on this concept. Each time throughout that day and the following night that he felt Nastassja behind his eyes, he blanked his thoughts and paid attention to how and where her consciousness entered his. Mostly she just touched base, like fulfilling a chore when it occurred to her, but before dawn the next morning, she surprised him with direct contact.

I need to see you, Nastassja said with a bossiness that took him back many years. Still in bed, he blinked at the ceiling in case she decided to hijack his eyes.

That's nice. I don't need to see you.

Frustrated, she withdrew for a few minutes. She withdrew the same way as before, establishing a pattern he'd follow later. Not now, she wasn't done; as a child she'd do this, circle away when brute force didn't work and come back afresh with some other strategy. Back then he'd thought it was cleverness. Maybe it was, but now he saw it was manipulation, too.

If I show you how I got out, will you meet me?

Renatus sat up, startled. How she got out? As in… how she escaped their locked-down estate on the day her forbidden lover killed their parents and faked her death? He'd run ahead of her from the storm, and she hadn't followed. She couldn't have used the front gate – he would have seen her pass him or felt the Skip through space – and Lord Gawain and Lisandro were already at the gate by the time not-Ana was dying in Renatus's arms. So… how *did* she get out?

That information was on the table, if he was willing to play the game.

But what were the rules? The stakes? The chances of him coming off worse? High, and indulging the idea that she just wanted to reconnect as family was a quick way to having his heart broken. He spread his awareness throughout the house, touching on the energies of everybody else. Qasim and Emmanuelle, who would slap him for entertaining this, and Lord Gawain, who would frown and struggle to understand the pull, were all fast asleep.

I'm sick of this distance between us, Nastassja claimed as if she wasn't the one who'd forged it in the first place. *Please? This is important.*

She pushed a mental image to him of the orchard, and of the stone wall that ran behind it, and… a door?!

It was an uncomfortable strain against the loyalty he'd been choosing each day, but intrigue pushed him out of bed. He felt his shoes dragging on the grass as he neared the tree line. Further from where he should be, closer to the last place he wanted to go. The orchard was once well-tended but those days were long past, and even from this distance, Renatus could see the branches in need of trimming and harvesting.

Proximity brought him to a halt halfway across the lawn, along with the usual dread. Down the hill, difficult to see but obvious once you knew it was there, the rugged tree line broke for a path that disappeared into the shadows of the fruit trees. At the end of that path, his parents and someone he'd thought was Ana were buried with their ancestors. At the path's midpoint, he'd been faced with an intruder called Sean Glassner who'd found out what the void looked like when he'd misjudged teen Renatus's impulsive vengefulness.

Yes, he had a problem; he was aware. So was everyone else who got too close to this spot's cloying energy.

The mouth of the path was as close as he'd gotten since, and even that was with Aristea to accompany him. Alone, disconnected from her and from his allies on the council, he wasn't pressing on that wound today. He veered off to follow the orchard edge in the opposite direction, all the way to the property line, and swallowed the last of his immense discomfort. They were just trees. He yanked a sweet-smelling apple from the nearest branch, and it snapped free. Easily defeated.

Are you coming? His former sister, whoever she was now, tapped at his consciousness. He shoved back automatically and felt her surprised withdrawal. He was growing stronger in their bond, more able to exercise his agency. He wasn't weak. He could handle this. Maybe later he could handle what Emmanuelle had suggested, too.

I said I was, he snapped back, though he couldn't remember whether he'd confirmed. He picked his way over fallen branches, many of them rotted and crumbling. No one had been through to clear the debris of the storm eight years ago. He had a gardener who came every Saturday, and the first time she'd come out to assess the place, she'd asked, 'That isn't part of the job, is it?' with a disdainful nod at the sprawling plantation. Renatus had said he didn't care if it all burned to the ground or died of neglect, and she'd started the following week, happy to have only the gardens around the house to worry about.

A decade's neglect hadn't killed the deep and shadowy orchard, and he couldn't hurry through it fast enough. Even as a child he'd thought it was distinctly *not* a fun place to play, although Ana had come here sometimes when she was bored or wanting to be left alone. Evidently, that was when she'd found this secret door, if it existed, though how nobody else in the family knew of it… that seemed suspicious. Or perhaps not? Their father Aindréas had grown up with a largely absent father – much of the house's secrets, passed down through the generations, may have been lost when Mánus Morrissey just stopped coming home, presumed dead after some murky underworld altercation.

Renatus rested his hand on a dead tree trunk as he reached the wall.

Wind whipping branches, leaves like razors… a man with a bloodied face clinging to the trunk… hair and clothes soaked through… 'I can't see you but I can hear you, thinking. You're my daughter. Of course I can hear you'… another presence, out of sight… lightning strikes the tree and he leaps aside…

He ripped his hand away from the unexpected impression and stumbled over a loose branch. Already breathing hard, Renatus landed roughly on his backside and had to physically clutch at the leaf litter either side of him to stop from scampering to his feet and bolting.

Breathe. He coached himself through the infinity of one second's shock, and then was okay, or as okay as you can be after tapping into a vision of your father about to die.

Renatus got up slowly, dusting leaves from his back and legs as he gazed at the cracked tree. It was long dead, bark visibly scarred in a few jagged lines to the ground, but even before its branches fell, it shouldn't have been tall enough to attract a natural storm's wrath. Was that how Lisandro had finished off his best friend? Renatus had never known, had never seen the bodies.

Only Ana's, but it wasn't really her.

Cautious, morbidly fascinated, Renatus extended his palm to touch the tree again. Nothing. The tree had released its long-held secret, or as much of it as it planned to right now. Was it coincidence that its cracks looked like those under his skin? Aindréas was here, standing right here, in his final moments, talking to Ana. What were they doing?

It was obvious once he was staring at it, but otherwise obscured by years of unkempt plant life. A weathered timber door, heavy and held in place with wide hinges, was set into a narrow crevice in the stone wall, slightly too narrow to be standard, like the rest of the house. He approached, still dusting off his hands, and tuned his attention into the magic of the wall. Generations of his family had poured their talents into this fortress. Where there should have been a doorknob, there was nothing. Even if he hadn't felt the sluggish, long-unused magic singing to his blood, he'd have known exactly what to do.

He pressed his hand to the wood, ignoring the quick flash of another hand – *pressing hurriedly, wiping tears, thunder crashing –* and shoving hard when he felt the magic give as willingly as the front gate.

The door swung outward into the wooded area behind the estate. An escape. He had a back door. Considering all the paranoid little wormholes and other escape hatches hidden in the house, it seemed obvious that there'd be an exit other than the main gate, but in their decades or centuries living in the mansion, the family had never come under siege, so it had just been forgotten.

Until now.

Renatus was no longer the last of the family, nor the most powerful. Nearby, amidst the first clump of wild trees, the waiting figure of Nastassja positively radiated unstable magical energy, and he had an instant to reflect on how very stupid this plan had been.

An unguarded doorway into his fortress where his council, a dozen students, his helpless staff and his vulnerable friend were trapped.

An untrustworthy foe with the face of someone he'd loved.

No backup.

Yes. Stupid.

'Don't leave!' she begged when he immediately began to close her out. 'Please. We need this.'

'You don't know what I need,' he shot back coldly, holding the door, ready to snap it shut. He extended his senses further, past her. Where were her Magnus Moira minions? Jackson? Nothing. He couldn't detect anyone, but Lisandro liked to use invisible scouts. Aristea's gift had been invaluable in weeding those out, since a conscious human can't help but experience emotions. He tuned his focus to that deeper level. *Not* nothing.

'We came alone,' his sister said, and the shadow beside her seemed to flex. Alarmed but ready, Renatus raised his hand, purplish spell crackling in his palm. A little nerve paralysis ought to sort out whoever she'd brought along, and would be worth the dull sting in his own nerves. But Nastassja reacted with the same flash of alarm, moving to put herself in his line of fire. 'No, wait. We only want to talk to you.'

'*We?*' Renatus repeated before understanding dawned. *Oh.* He cursed loudly, and the person he most wanted to fire that spell on materialised from the inky shadow. The temptation to throw it at the pair of them and let them writhe on the marshes for the next hour was strong, but Renatus overcame the vengeful desire with effort and tossed it on the ground at his feet. Grass hissing with steam, he grabbed the door again. 'No. Piss off.'

He almost had it closed when a brief bubble ward burst in the gap, pushing it open just enough that Lisandro could get his hand through. He yanked; fear spiking, Renatus held fast, leaning his lesser weight in opposition. The door quivered in a childish tug-of-war.

'Family meeting,' his godfather said, at least gracious enough to emphasise the irony. He pulled again. Renatus glared at his long fingers and willed himself to find the extra strength to snap this door shut and slam those fingers. To break them. Even if it broke his, too.

Vengeful, yes, sorry, no.

'Let go,' he ordered fiercely, refusing to give even an inch. 'Stay out.'

'Calm down. If we wanted to get in–' Lisandro huffed with effort, gaining that inch Renatus hadn't wanted to give '–we wouldn't invite you to stop us.'

True, they could get in with Nastassja's Morrissey magic any time, but what else would they gain by leading him here to this secret doorway? Renatus strained against his godfather's pull, disappointed to find the other's physical strength was still superior. Lisandro had always been attentive to his fitness and the aesthetic of his body. Strength training, weights, careful diet, things Renatus knew he'd be adding to his routine if he survived this confrontation.

'You don't have to be scared,' Nastassja called to Renatus, sounding closer, sounding worried. 'They've brainwashed you. He's not going to hurt you.'

'I think… you've missed a few pages.' Renatus's fingers had begun to ache and his breathing was laboured. He leaned back hard. 'And if I *was* afraid, it'd be of getting… impaled on… a goddamn *tree*.'

The woman who looked just like Ana went darkly silent.

'Listen, just give your sister a chance,' Lisandro suggested with that long-suffering brightness Renatus remembered from when he was little. The atmosphere of the marshy woodland lightened, calm and comfort and agreeableness settling all around, seeping through the gap he'd opened in the fence. He detected the emotions more distinctly than he ever would have before. He didn't think Lisandro was doing it on purpose, just instinctively reacting to a difficult conversation. 'You don't understand what she's been through.'

There was so much wrong with that statement that Renatus gave up his losing battle with the door and let Lisandro stumble back with it, and he came out at them, laughing hollowly.

'What *she's* been through? *I* don't understand? And whose fault is that? My faithless fucking family?' The laughter died as Lisandro caught his balance, and he glared at them both, feeling his hatred hot in every vein, every pore. 'I should kill you both, be done with you.'

Nastassja frowned, hurt, but Lisandro rolled his eyes. 'Don't be so dramatic.'

'Rich, coming from you.'

'Maybe, but we'd beat your ass if you tried, so don't.'

Renatus stood his ground, ready for a confrontation – they were the heads of Magnus Moira and fighting them was the very reason his position on the White Elm existed – but the two just glanced at each other. Something about the momentary eye contact took the wind out of his sails and cut him somewhere deep.

They'd always had this, and he had forgotten until right now. Not telepathy, nothing more or less magical than total connection. Their father's friend had never needed to ask how Ana Morrissey was feeling or ask what she was thinking, and she'd always been the apple of his eye, in direct contrast to their father's inability to see valuable qualities in her. Renatus recalled a thousand conversations where he watched on, quietly envious of their electricity and the way they just *clicked*. His worldliness, her provocative pushback against boundaries, his stories, her questions. Never a gap for a word in edgewise.

Not really that surprising, maybe, that she'd grown up to fall for him. Was there a more compatible couple? Too bad they had to break Renatus's world to be together.

'We're wasting our time. I told you this would happen,' Lisandro reminded her now, and she answered with a look that begged a little patience. Her eyes glowed that weirdly bright green. Her hair was loose, crimped from days tightly braided, and fell past her waist. She still had her taste for dramatic makeup and beautiful things, her dress more elaborate than anything Renatus had ever seen Aristea in and her lips painted plum. Lisandro seemed to have hardly aged in years, though that was harder to judge – he was already an adult, or near enough, in Renatus's first memories, and they'd never gone more than six months of Renatus's life without contact. His clothes were as form-fitting and expensively tailored as ever. Only the most modern and impressive attire for the man without a family, without a name, in a society where those were currency. Never cut, his black hair hung in its customary ponytail down his back, a political statement in itself.

'Then why'd you come?' Renatus spat, annoyed with their synchronicity and all they represented. 'What is this? Lord Gawain isn't interested in terms.'

'Gawain Harrington is poison,' his sister spat back, emotional hackles up immediately. 'He should never have interfered in our family's–'

'We're not here representing Magnus Moira,' Lisandro interrupted calmly before Renatus could retort, 'and you can stop looking around for them. No one's coming. This is between us.' The former Dark Keeper nodded at his wife, who was trying to calm down. *His wife.* It was incomprehensible. 'I have a proposition for you, and Ana wanted to clear the air.'

A proposition? For him, not for the council? Interesting, and certainly disturbing. Renatus replied, but only to give himself more time to think.

'Ana today? I prefer the made-up name. It matches all the other lies tied up with you.'

His older sister was always quick to anger, and his words sparked an immediate burst that he felt in the air. Almost a reactionary spell.

'You can set aside the snark for ten minutes and let her talk, surely,' Lisandro said with mild irritation, and Renatus turned to regard him.

'Why are you even here?' he wondered. 'You can't tell me what to do. You're not my family: I relieve you of the burden of godfatherhood. You're not even my superior on the council anymore. Shut up or go away.'

'As kind an offer that is, you aren't any more qualified to relieve me of that burden than I am to unburden you of Aristea.' Lisandro paused to withdraw a spherical object from thin air and offered it to Renatus. 'I can confirm with confidence that she's in terrible danger, and that you'd be best served by shutting your mouth and listening to me.'

Renatus hated to accept anything from this manipulator and even more to give him anything in return, but no degree of control over his reaction could keep Lisandro from reading the way his stomach bottomed out at this news. It didn't matter if it was true or not.

He wanted to scry her. Couldn't trust his eyes.

He wanted to reach for her. Couldn't trust his mind.

He wanted to reconnect with Qasim and ask *him* to look for her. Couldn't trust his council.

So he reluctantly took the crystal orb from his godfather's hand. A memory keeper. Colour and images flashed inside, indistinct. Non-witches had later developed video technology to replicate this, along with creating false and fantastical images, but they weren't yet able to channel imagery directly from the mind itself into a permanent record.

Power re-established, Lisandro smiled wanly.

'Your dear Uncle Tom has put a price on your apprentice's head, and it doesn't suit either of us if one of his cowboy mercenaries catches up with her. Luckily, one of the benefits of heading a cult is having plenty of eager lackeys at my disposal to send to bring her in. No need to thank me.'

'So you admit they're a cult?' Renatus quipped, hefting the crystal ball in his palm. The memory held within was similar to an impression, a scried vision waiting to be tapped into, though tapping it would be a distraction from his physical surroundings he wasn't sure he wanted to risk. Lisandro rolled his eyes.

'What else do you call a movement that actively recruits the vulnerable or lost and then discourages criticism or critical questioning? They're a means to an end. Stay focused. One of them reported in.' He nodded to the memory keeper. 'Your girl is resourceful, I'll grant that, but she can't keep this up.'

Renatus looked at the ball in his hand, worried curiosity warring with his better judgement. Lisandro could kill him with a click of his fingers. Nastassja may or may not let him. There were no other witnesses to dissuade them from betraying their word.

But despite that the two together were stronger, older, more experienced and more in-sync than any pair he'd ever faced, he wasn't actually afraid of either of them. Angry, conflicted, resentful, hurt, confused, all those, but Lisandro didn't scare him like he ought to, and neither did his sister. They could have made their move and beaten him in any of the last three minutes and hadn't, so why wait until his eyes were closed?

With one more glance around the area for other dangers, he gave in, diverting his attention into the crystal.

A truck stop bathroom mirror… harsh overhead light flickering… familiar woman with hair pulled back tight and high, talking to her reflection and holding the crystal… 'I'm on the trail of the ledger, which is now held by Declan O'Malley. But in Prague I had to choose between the ledger and the Byrne girl. She is more capable than we expected, and very reluctant to come in. I traced an anti-council spell to the city, but that may have been O'Malley because I have not detected this since. It was only chance I saw them at my hotel, our usual hotel. She has not yet Displaced from the city. O'Malley confirmed that the council is looking for her. Others are closing in on her, too. I will recommend teams of two or three to apprehend her.'

Renatus opened his eyes when the roughly hewn memory ended abruptly. *Aristea.* He swallowed the ill-feeling rising in his oesophagus. Prague. What the hell was she doing back there? Separated from Declan, with what looked like Hanna Seidel hot on his heels. Others closing in – sorcerers eager to cash in on Shanahan's offer? *More capable than we expected… very reluctant… recommend teams of two or three to apprehend her.* Meaning Seidel had tried and failed, forcing Aristea to defend herself.

He should be with her. He should drop everything here –

shut that door in the fence and open the one in his mind – and find her and go to her.

Bronze-brown eyes and unnatural green watched him closely, waiting for him to make that mistake. With all the effort in the world, Renatus handed the ball back with deliberate carelessness.

'And?'

'And I can bring her home,' Lisandro said smoothly, twisting his fingers over the ball so it vanished. 'I know it kills you to see her endangered.'

Renatus frowned, wishing the promise didn't sound so attractive. 'It's usually *you* endangering her, so forgive me for taking your word with some substantial salt. You nearly took her eye out.'

His godfather shrugged delicately, and Renatus felt heat under his skin, hatred burning at his frayed nerves and threatening to spark into magic in his hands.

'Regrettable. I was out of sorts after what had to be done with Anouk,' Lisandro admitted. Renatus tightened his hands against the desire to melt shut the mouth talking about blasé murder. 'Things have changed. *You* two have changed. Hasn't she become an interesting little player? A few little nudges and now she's on a totally new and fascinating path into a future I don't want to see accelerated.'

Renatus had gotten himself under control while the other man spoke, reminding himself he was talking to a psychopath, but the words still wormed their way into his ears.

'What path?' he asked before he could stop himself. He wasn't sure whether he managed to keep surprise from his face at the reply he got, but he suspected some incredulity made it through.

'She's meant to bring down the White Elm,' Nastassja told him cynically. 'I'll believe it when I see it, frankly.'

'That makes three of us, I'm sure,' Lisandro agreed graciously, American accent crisp and hard against the siblings' soft Irishness, 'but we're not Seers. And she's only a catalyst. Wonder whether old Gawain has seen the same thing, and whether he'd even tell you if he did?'

The query was directed at Renatus but he dismissed it, trying not to linger on the concept of multiple high-level Seers channelling the same disturbing news.

'Aristea might have been easier to recruit to your delusions before you drove her to me.'

'Perhaps not.' Lisandro smoothed an imagined crinkle from his sleeve. 'I saw her at the theatre. We underestimate that girl. *I* think she'd burn your precious institution to the ground as quickly as mine if she thought it meant saving you. But that's beside the point,' he diverted loftily, letting Renatus process that troubling interpretation of Lord Gawain's vision. 'Capable as she might be of enacting it, all of us here would rather she didn't.'

Renatus frowned, thrown. 'Ending the White Elm is all you care about it.'

'A gross oversimplification. One my cult likes to believe, though I'd hope you were brighter.'

'Ending the council can wait,' Nastassja spoke up. Her mood had darkened with Lisandro's talk of Aristea and her loyalty, and it flavoured her voice. 'There are more important things.'

'Like what?' Renatus asked. They both went silent, thoughts and feelings tightly shut down as they shared a meaningful glance. He looked around, now uneasy with their isolation from the crowd outside the gate. 'You said you aren't here representing Magnus Moira.'

'As I said, a means to an end,' Lisandro reiterated delicately. 'This is personal, not political. There's a certain… sequence I require to the events that are coming, and you and I can help each other.'

Sceptical, but unabashedly curious, Renatus said, 'Oh?'

'I can promise to leave the pair of you out of what's coming next, because you won't like it. This door stays between the three of us, and you can go retrieve Aristea yourself. No one will stop you. You can have Aristea back safely and never put her in another fight. Live here, bring her whole family if it makes you feel better, or disappear somewhere. Do whatever you want. Just agree to one thing.'

Since Lisandro's spectacular departure from Susannah's garden a year ago, Renatus had fantasised how their reunion would go. They'd face off and he would take his revenge and be the victor. But then they'd met at that bar and he'd hesitated to take his shot; he'd tracked Lisandro to that Magnus Moira hideout but his backup had outmuscled him into holding back again; he'd turned away from his next chance to exact that revenge when Aristea's life was in danger and that, or the necessity of saving face in high society, had been the theme of every encounter with his godfather since. In no iteration of his vengeful fantasy did Lisandro put forward an offer so seemingly innocuous.

Renatus was afraid to ask, but of course he did.

'What thing?'

'Renounce the White Elm.'

It was both shocking and really the only request that would have made sense. He had an automatic answer.

'Think before you say that,' Nastassja urged, and he mentally kicked himself for not maintaining his vigilance. He felt the tendrils of her presence on his head and fought her out. 'Please, just consider it.'

'I don't have to consider it. Oaths mean more to me than they do to either of you.'

'I doubt that,' Lisandro answered coolly. 'You're alive, aren't you? Just… find your apprentice, keep your heads down, and let Fate do its thing. Don't fight for them. Don't participate in their death throes.'

'We don't want anything to happen to you,' Nastassja said hurriedly, and Renatus scoffed with astonishment.

'You set a mob on me.'

'Not everything is about you,' Lisandro reminded him. Renatus bit back a reply, taking a beat to acknowledge the slyness, the smugness of his godfather getting something by him. Almost. *I saw her at the theatre.*

The ambush at the theatre had been carefully planned, a stage show fully scripted by Lisandro up until Hiroko's arrival. The audience had watched the White Elm's power fall away.

Lisandro had watched Renatus and Aristea. Like he always did, Renatus realised now. And like they always did, they'd performed for him. In Scotland and in Prague, Renatus had shown his hand, revealing what lengths he'd go to when Aristea was threatened, but Lisandro had never seen the reverse. So he'd set it up.

Renatus had to drop his gaze, sick with fury. Anouk, Emmanuelle… so many people hurt or killed as game pieces in elaborate social experiments. *You two have changed.* Because Renatus with Aristea was something Lisandro couldn't predict without new data, and Aristea was something else again.

'We weren't going to let them hurt you,' Nastassja argued angrily, confirming his theory. She held her hand up, an aura of unnatural emerald around the Elm Stone beginning to glow brighter and brighter. 'I can protect anyone now.'

'Are we pretending this is you two looking out for me?' He nodded at the wedding ring on his sister's hand. 'You turn up with a stolen weapon and meet me not thirty paces from where you murdered our father. It is *literally* my job to track you two down and take that thing back. You put me in a moral grey area just by being here. And on top of all that, you married each other, which…'

There were no words, and Renatus looked away briefly so he could breathe through the frustration. Unexpectedly shaken and glancing at her lifelong protector with uncertainty, Nastassja closed her left hand inside the other.

'You can't take this,' she argued with Renatus. 'I need it.'

He levelled her with an irritated look. 'The last thing you needed was more power. You and I were born with more than anybody should have–'

'It was gone!' Nastassja screamed, startling him into stillness with her instability. Her hands had clenched; her aura pulsed. 'All of it, stripped away. No answer when I called for my magic. No images behind my eyelids. *Nothing*. Father and Uncle Thomas and their *stupid* binding spells. That was the price I paid.'

She glared, but Renatus didn't feel that things were any clearer.

'What does that even mean?' he asked, lost. 'Paid for what?'

Her eyes narrowed even more bitterly. 'If you're being funny–'

'None of this is funny!' Renatus shouted, losing patience. 'You were dead! I buried you! I couldn't stop the bleeding, and you died, and I saw that *every time* I closed my eyes for *years*, and you think your price was steep?'

She moved fast, and his back hit the wooden door as she shoved his shoulders, getting in his face.

'You have *no* idea!' she snarled, anger and hurt curling around her so intensely they burned at his own emotions. 'You think this is the way I wanted it? My own brother on the wrong side, all these secrets? To find myself replaced, again?'

Her angry breath warmed his face. Her eyes blazed, an eerie glow to the irises that used to be dark brown. His shoulders felt hot where she'd made contact and he could smell a faint smokiness that he gathered was burnt fabric, though he didn't trust her enough to break eye contact, not while her feelings were still spiralling upward.

'Hey.' Lisandro laid a hand on her elbow, trying to smooth the waters as always. 'This isn't helping.'

He'd always had this talent, this way of whispering to the irrationality inside Ana Morrissey, and her anger began to drop, but it had a long way to come.

'He's being unreasonable,' she bit out. Lisandro nodded amiably.

'Well, what's new?' he asked. He pulled on her gently, and she stepped back from Renatus reluctantly. 'Take a break. I'll talk to him.'

She didn't want to do it, but she conceded, making sure to kick at a rock as she spun away and stalked off. Far enough from the house, she Displaced, leaving Renatus and Lisandro alone. Exhaling heavily, overwhelmed by the vacuum of her intensity, Renatus slumped against the door.

'What… what happened to my sister?' he wondered aloud. Lisandro looked around the marshy clearing.

'It wasn't me, but my oversight contributed. We thought we'd considered all possibilities. We were wrong.' He leaned back to rest against the estate wall beside him, regret in his features but self-assurance in his casual posture. Like he wasn't at all uncomfortable to find himself in the company of his best friends' freshly reunited orphans eight years after *murdering said best friends*. 'It was meant to be a separation spell to cut her off from your family's magic to make her untraceable; it backfired and cut her off from *everything*. I mean everything,' he repeated seriously, glancing at his godson. 'She was a mortal. That person you remember, that vital, creative, fiery girl we loved… She just slid further and further away. You know,' he went on conversationally, 'when the White Elm charges someone with a top-level crime, that's what we'd do to them – strip them back to mere human, or throw them in Valero where their magic was annulled. It's a direct path to madness, but what does it matter when they're the villain? To watch it happening to Ana…'

He trailed off, picking at his sleeve with a haunted expression. The story explained the heightened instability – Renatus wasn't misremembering. She was more volatile now than before.

Renatus watched the other man, thinking back to the days after the storm. Lisandro had been highly strung and lost-seeming, overbearing when he was at the house and then absent for most of the day. Grieving, Renatus had supposed at the time, for his lost friends, and maybe on one level he was; but the distraction of a struggling Ana accounted better for the behaviour.

And he could imagine the struggle, though he'd only experienced it briefly himself. The helplessness of instant mortality after a lifetime of intense power. Cut off from everything. No magic, no voices in his head, no impressions when he touched new surfaces, no visions… All the power she'd grown up with at her fingers, torn away.

'You were happy enough to do it to me at the theatre,' Renatus commented coolly, earning a reproachful look.

'It was a few minutes, and giving the council a taste of their own medicine seemed reasonable,' Lisandro dismissed. 'They left her in that state for almost a decade. No Healer could help me, no mystic had heard of a way to restore magic that's been ripped away, and when I found a spell that needed more power than I could summon, no ring guardian would share the Elm Stone with a Dark Keeper. Your beloved Gawain wouldn't bend the rules for me to help her. Magnus Moira was the key to the people who would.'

'What people?'

Lisandro smiled tightly. 'A story for another time.'

'What did you tell Lord Gawain?' Renatus pushed. 'When you asked for the Elm Stone? You didn't tell him who she was.'

'How could I? Back then, I wouldn't have needed the whole stone, just to siphon a fraction of its juice.'

'Why?' Renatus asked, straightening and moving away, having almost forgotten that he was outside his estate walls, alone with the murderer he was supposed to bring in. 'What changed?'

The way Lisandro answered after the slightest of beats said there were multitudes still unsaid.

'She was dying,' he said precisely. He didn't elaborate except to say, 'She got sick and I got desperate. I worked on Peter for months and then he had a change of heart. I thought I was going to lose her. Breaking an oath to an ineffectual government and raising another one from ashes didn't feel so wrong in comparison. A small price.' He looked across at Renatus. 'You wouldn't have done any different.'

Would he? It was an uncomfortable question.

'We'll never know,' Renatus said eventually, 'because you both kept me in the dark. I can't believe you couldn't find a way to just *tell me* in all this time. And I can't believe that I can't believe that,' he added, annoyed with his own naïveté, 'because actually it's just like you. Easier for you to send me away to be breeding stock for Avalon than to do the job you agreed to when I was born.'

They'd never discussed this before, Renatus's time in the isolated, all-magical community, but he was still unsurprised when his godfather averted his eyes, embarrassed. Lisandro and Gabriel Winter had sold Avalon to him as a reprieve from his troubles and an opportunity to learn and grow. Ironic that the cost of Ana's escape from the injustice of her societal trappings was to outfit Renatus with the same unsavoury fate.

'I told you this wasn't my story to tell.' Lisandro regarded him for a long moment. 'It's not a secret you joined the White Elm to spite me, and it's hardly a shock that you were keen to bury me after Avalon – which wasn't my idea, by the way, though it would have been better for everyone if you'd stayed – but I think by now it's obvious the council's not a good fit for you, however much you wanted it to be. They're not like us.'

Renatus bristled. 'You and I are hardly alike.'

'No? What have I done for Ana that you wouldn't do for Aristea?'

'Well, aside from sleep with her when I'm meant to be responsible for her?'

Outwardly, Lisandro let it slide off, but he didn't know Aristea wasn't the only Empath in their extended family circle anymore, and he didn't think to curb his discomfort at that dig he didn't expect Renatus would be brave enough to make.

'Love is love. We don't choose it.'

'What's your point?'

'The apprentice you took to aid in serving them is destined to be their downfall. You're hiding her from them even now, because you can't trust the people you swore yourself to.' Lisandro let that last part sink in, and Renatus hated that it was accurate. 'The White Elm will not go down gently, and if it's true that they've lined up a trial for her...' The Crafter carefully flicked a fleck of lint from the elbow of his tailored jacket, illustrating his point. 'You know Gawain, but not what he's done. He's not who you'd like. *You* aren't who you'd like. Noble as you'd like to be, you'd set fire to five hundred years of history before you let them light the stake they'll tie Aristea to before this is over. You're *exactly* like me.'

He pushed himself off the wall in Renatus's heavy silence and started to move away.

'Come and go as you please, just don't let any other councillors out,' he drawled. 'The cult will lose their shit. And come find me when you've made your mind...'

He froze, contacted from elsewhere, and turned abruptly back to Renatus with a flare of shock. Something had changed. Something big.

And Renatus just raised his hands helplessly, because he wasn't scrying, and he wasn't connected to the council, so he couldn't know what it was.

'You...?' Lisandro started to ask, but seemed to realise the futility. 'Well played.'

He left an instant later, still top of the scoreboard without a single blow, leaving his godson in the dark in all respects. Renatus slid down the old wooden door to sit on the marshy ground with his messy thoughts.

chapter sixteen

My ally wasn't the one I would have chosen – there was no substituting Renatus, and I missed him intensely – but Garrett was the one I had, and I urged him into a brief walk through the festival to shed some nerves while I milked him for information.

'Nothing, really,' he said when I asked what they did to him, blushing like this was the most embarrassing admission of all. 'They treated us well. They made us feel… special. Enrico said we were suckers for going to the White Elm first. It felt like we'd found our place in the world. We had our own floor and everyone we met showed us some new amazing magic we could learn. I met other Displacers like Elijah – Walt, Hanna, Erik… They could do things he'd never show us. I got really good at mapping the Fabric, you know, sensing when people were manipulating it, doing big jumps. And they encouraged that.' At his sides, his fingers flexed and fidgeted. I didn't like his shakiness, but at least it seemed to be settling the more we walked. 'That's what they wanted us for. That's what we did for them. And in return, we had *all this*.'

He gestured around at the magic on proud display, and I felt the buoyancy of it. It was like we could breathe it straight in. I looked sidelong at Garrett, who did inhale deep. His hands unconsciously relaxed. I didn't know if sorcerers could suffer from withdrawal from magic, but the way he leaned into the energy of this camp, I couldn't help thinking that's what he'd experienced since abruptly leaving. This was a *bad* plan, with a faulty team and no contingencies for when this inevitably went wrong. But Lisandro and his most concerning allies were absent, Josh was trapped, and I knew Garrett couldn't pull this off without me.

Maybe not with me, either, but that was another problem.

'The building we want's one of three refurbished warehouses Magnus Moira uses as a more-or-less permanent base of operations,' he explained as I pointed him between two camper vans. 'It's not far from here: six point three kilometres due south. But we should Skip. I don't know when they'll be back.'

'Six point three kilometres, hey?' I repeated, quirking a smile. Displacers and their precision. He didn't smile back, not seeing the humour, and nervously offered his hand. My smile slipped, too. 'You'd better be right about this.'

What colour was in his face drained.

'I'm right about the distance.'

'About all of it.' I looked about. Worst plan ever, but there was nothing else for it. I accepted his hand. 'Don't betray me, Garrett. You'll be sorry if you do.'

I saw his throat bob in genuine fear and felt the void slide over us instantly. I tensed at the uncomfortable sensation but then it was already over. Garrett hadn't even moved his feet. We were standing outside a red metal door set into the side of a large, bland building, with two similar warehouses behind us. There didn't seem to be anyone else around.

'I told you, I got really good at mapping the Fabric,' he confessed, blushing furiously and radiating with shame. I approached the door, feeling for magic and booby traps.

'You did what you had to, to stay under the radar,' I reminded him as I ran my fingers through the air above the door. Magic, layers of it, and I wasn't that good at dismantling spells. That was a Crafter skill, or that of a Dark Keeper with lots of spare time. In some increasingly unlikely future in which Renatus died and I wasn't expunged from the White Elm's records, that was meant to be my job, but at this stage, pulling villains' spells apart with any sort of finesse was above my paygrade. 'What do you think will happen if I touch this door?'

'Probably nothing,' Garrett estimated, tracing his finger

through the same invisible layers of magic. 'There's an energetic alarm woven into all the walls – this Scottish guy who started questioning things left, and we all felt it go off – but it's activated by breach, not touch.'

'So I can touch it,' I presumed, cautiously pressing my fingers to the red steel and exhaling when nothing discernible happened, 'but once I open it, it'll all be on.'

'Basically.'

Okay, so we had a minute. I told Garrett to keep lookout and to be ready to evacuate, and I closed my eyes and spread my awareness out as intensely as I could. Qasim could mass-scry *fifty locations at once*. Surely I could manage two or three together.

I locked my attention onto the barren courtyard we stood in, and zoomed out to be able to watch our backs from high above. There was no one particularly close, and those who were near had not noticed us.

I forced my attention through the metal of the door to see inside the room beyond. It was all concrete, a series of storerooms with cage security doors, and behind those, people. Prisoners.

I brought my minutest focus to the door itself, finding the lock mechanism inside the door handle and identifying its components. It was locked, obviously, and its innards were complex and modern, more sophisticated than the padlocks Qasim had given me to play with in scrying lessons. Garrett was right. A complicated twist of magic, a version of the crude spells Declan had put on my hotel door, was wrapped subtly through the lock behind the handle. A better sorcerer might have been able to lift those pegs and pins, manipulate them into the correct arrangement; one of many cool tricks Renatus employed regularly that had not wandered into my own mind.

But plenty of other skills had crossed that barrier.

'Six cells in two rows,' I reported to Garrett. 'Two people on the right, one on the left. Josh is…' I looked harder in the gloomy space and saw a familiar figure. 'Second on the right.'

I took a breath. No one was watching. The lock's alarms wouldn't be triggered until we broke through. How much time would that give us?

Not enough. *Such* a terrible idea.

'Be ready,' I advised Garrett, running my hands over the door to get the best position. I pulled all my warding to my hands and dropped unnecessary ones to increase its strength. With my energetic defences softened, impressions came through in quick succession – *unfamiliar hands pushing the red door, voices speaking in different languages.* I ignored them, fixed my attention on the lock mechanism I had no means of picking, and *felt* my way to the edge of the spell's knotwork inside the door.

The rest of the door was unspelled. I channelled power down into my hands, feeling the heat building in my palms, and I pushed that growing fireball into the painted red of the door. The thick metal brightened between my fingers, degrees climbing, and even through my dense wards I felt the wavering radiation of extreme heat that rose past my face. I leaned as far away as I could without breaking my connection.

Garrett edged closer, awed and afraid.

'Are you sure–'

'Shh.'

I was abrupt but couldn't afford the distraction, not when I was super-heating steel only millimetres under my vulnerable human skin. I kept my focus inside the door as I shifted my fingers, mindful that the concentration of heat was not too close to the doorhandle. I traced a wide semicircle around it, scuffing my feet back when the melting metal bubbled and threatened to spill down the front of the door. Luckily it didn't, viscosity holding, and, feeling sweat prickling across my forehead and down the back of my neck, I held out, too. My palms began to sting, primal heat energy finding the most miniscule cracks in my wards and seeping through, so I gave one last push before withdrawing, breathing hard.

A rough bright-hot arc encircled the door's handle. Garrett took one of my hands and turned it over. The skin was red and tender. I shook them out. No time.

'I said be ready,' I reminded him. 'How long will we have once the alarm goes off?'

'Ten seconds,' he said doubtfully. 'Maybe less.'

'Let's go with the assumption we have less,' I suggested, quickly replacing my usual full-body wards. I lifted my foot and put all my strength behind a solid kick that caved the ruined door in without the chunk surrounding the doorhandle. 'I'll take care of the doors. You go for Josh.'

Past me wouldn't recognise myself in this moment. I led a charge of one other person into a high security enemy prison and with illegal fireballs that came oh-so-easily, blasted the hinges off the three cage doors separating three human beings from freedom. The two on the right were already at their doors, drawn by the spectacle of the melting door, but the presence in the third cell had stayed back. Whatever – we weren't here for strangers – but words that weren't said aloud and made no sense at all caught my attention and made me freeze.

little girl little not-crafter heir for o'grádaigh…

I yanked the swinging gate from my path and, ignoring Garrett and Josh's loud and anxious reunion, stared into the lightless storeroom at an older man curled into a ball on a sparse bed. His face was hidden, but what I could see of him was small, skinny and bound.

girl o'grádaigh girl here after all this time here today when when when…

'How do you know me?' I asked of the huddled figure buried in the cell's shadows. He didn't answer, but definitely heard me – his mental voice went instantly quiet, curious – and I got the oddest mix of emotions from him. I instantly changed the focus of my eyes to view his aura, which was diminished with blurry black patches that looked too familiar. 'Can you travel?'

With a fidgety hand – the other was just a stump, amputated at the wrist, a common punishment for Magnus Moira – he tried to wave me away, some of that telepathic buzz reaching my ears as he began to mutter it aloud.

'Meddling Cassán girl, but not a Crafter, thinks and thinks and thinks… Sounds like him.'

I hesitated. Josh was the one we were rescuing. I was wasting precious seconds.

Outside, someone was shouting in a language I didn't speak, and with a jolt of fear that was a good fraction mine, I glanced at Garrett. He had just melted through a chain around his friend's ankle and was trying to arrange the bigger, weaker frame of a white-faced Josh Reyes at his side.

'Sounds like we're out of time to discuss this,' I informed the man I hadn't come here for, and I leaned down to grab his arm. He lay limp until I made contact, then shrieked like I'd hurt him, thrashing until I backed off. I looked him over; no ankle bracelet, which I figured was for blocking magic, but also no shoes, super basic hospital attire, and his forearms bound to each other. 'Last chance. I'm here to break you out.'

He moaned incoherently, and I made my heartless decision to leave him behind, overtaking Garrett and Josh's awkward three-legged trek back to the door. A small crowd was gathering, angry and disturbed but not beyond my capabilities to handle. Yet. 'I'm guessing we can't Displace out of here?'

'Wouldn't be much… of a prison if we could,' Josh said dryly. His voice sounded cracked and hoarse, and his leg was bleeding profusely, but when I looked to him, he gave me a smile that made this whole dangerous escapade worthwhile. 'Hey, Byrne.'

Forgiven. I don't know why I'd thought he'd be any madder than Garrett, when neither knew my role in their initial kidnapping, but it still gave me strength to have it confirmed. A loud noise indicated the moment the bound prisoner tried to stand and banged into his cage door.

'But Andrew said it was a line of Crafters, unbroken,' he complained, head lolling back as he tried to find an explanation on the ceiling or something. Garrett hoisted Josh's arm further over his shoulders.

'Who is that?'

'I have no idea,' I admitted. A third prisoner, ankle still chained to the wall of his storeroom cell, spoke up.

'The Dark Keeper's apprentice,' he commented in calm interest that did not match the situation in the slightest. Unusual eyes in a young and actually very appealing face looked me up and down. 'My destiny has found me.'

'Do you know something useful?' I asked irritably, and his mouth quirked in amusement. I didn't have the time to notice the dimples in his cheeks but somehow I still did. He nodded at the flimsy man who slid back to the floor.

'He's an informant,' he filled in, accent thick. Welsh? No, something close. 'One of the coven founders. Eugene Dubois.' I started at the name, recognising it immediately, and looked again at the man writhing bonelessly in his cell doorway. I couldn't see his face long enough to know if this was my grandfather's friend, but if it was true… if he was… The dimpled prisoner, halfway between rugged and adorable with his hair in a rough topknot and his pinchable cheeks, rattled his cell door to get my attention. 'Hey. Forget the lost cause. Help me out of here.'

He wriggled his leg to make the chain chink. I didn't know what he had done to find himself locked up but I wasn't in a good position to be judging. My instincts said the danger was outside, not in here, so I raised a hand. Topknot leaned away to clear my shot. Another little ball of crackling orange fire struck the chain and it dramatically shattered. He shook it off and let himself out of the cell.

'I'm in your debt, White Elm, as destiny must have known I would.'

'Does destiny have any ideas for getting out?' I asked, raising my voice to be heard over those yelling outside. This had blown so far out of proportion. Dubois rolled about weakly, muttering.

'Just how he said, just how he said…' He looked at me suddenly, gaze momentarily focused. 'Are you using *my* telepathy?'

'I thought you were the rescue team,' Josh retorted with more attitude than his state of health suggested. He looked around. 'Where's Renatus?'

I was saved from having to explain that, unfortunately, he was stuck being rescued by the A team's B side, because beyond the melted door, a new presence Displaced into the courtyard.

'Aristea.' We all froze at that New York accent, that familiar cadence. 'Breaking and entering – not very becoming of a future White Elm.'

chapter seventeen

I was ready for a fight, but I wasn't going to get one. Outside, in the narrow courtyard between the two warehouses, Lisandro calmed down the crowd and switched on the charm. I felt it, a growing sensation of complacency and relaxation all around me. My stomach bottomed out.

'Come on out, White Elm sheep,' another American voice called in mockery. Younger. Regionally different. Familiar? I looked back at Garrett.

'You remember Egan?' he asked quietly, and in surprise I took my attention out of the storage locker to scry outside. Egan Lake? Standing at Lisandro's elbow was the first student to depart the Academy. He looked to have aged more than the five or six months since his mother had been duped into calling him home by Lisandro, but I was sure he'd think the same of me. He had the beginnings of a beard around the mouth that had called Renatus a liar the day I'd first staked my trust in the Academy's headmaster. I changed focus to view his aura. I frowned. Was he that strong before, or was I misremembering? Everyone invited to study under the White Elm was superpowered. I had to be misremembering.

My brain buzzed through everything else I knew about Egan. Telepath. Okay, don't think in questions, barriers up. Shared a dorm with Addison James. Half as nice, half again as reasonable. He leaned closer to Lisandro. He said nothing, and I heard that weird buzz again. The Crafter nodded once and Egan spoke up.

'Fischer, bring your friends out here. It's what's best for them.'

'Aristea, listen to your friends,' Lisandro advised.

I blinked my attention back to my surroundings and saw Garrett's grip on Josh loosen.

'Maybe we… should go out?' he suggested uncertainly. Distant claustrophobic panic rose in my chest. There would be no fight, at least not in the courtyard. This was Lisandro's gift, to change the emotional ambience of a space, and it was concentrated on us. On Garrett, by the looks of his slackening expression. Were we going to walk right into his hands?

Stop wondering, it invites Telepaths in.

The dimpled prisoner with his man bun rolled his shoulders, unaffected.

'You and I have this,' he assured me, and closed his eyes. Immediately, like a weighted blanket being lifted off, I felt the complacency recede, and when I tuned into the emotional atmosphere of the makeshift prison, I felt it being forced back on itself. I also felt Topknot's mild irritation with me. 'Some help?'

It hit me harder than the appearance of Lisandro or Egan. *Another Empath*. I'd never met one; Renatus said I was the first he'd encountered. This person, whoever he was, was certainly more advanced than I was, though not much older. I kept my eyes open as I intuited what he was doing. Emotions, pulled from us and pushed toward others. An exchange, or rather a redirect, more controlled than what I'd done with the American who'd bled out in Prague.

We were pushing Lisandro's synthetic complacency back at him and his crowd. Reverse Empathy.

Topknot began to walk, and I followed. Logic said not to step out that melted door, but instinct said it was fine, and there are no prizes for guessing the winner.

The warehouse's red side door was encircled by about twenty people, most of them strangers. Just as I'd seen it when I scried. Front and centre was Lisandro himself. Hands relaxed. Motionless. Utterly, utterly complacent. His hair fell in a ponytail down his back and his tailored jacket cut an impressive figure, but right now he was no leader. He was ours.

No one moved to capture us. No one moved to hurt us.

Elsewhere in the camp, nobody paid any mind to this anticlimactic non-event. Meditation circles carried on and whatever else. In this moment, in this small space between warehouses, we had complete control of this situation.

Complete control.

I reached for my satchel, for the two sharpened blades safe inside. The rattle of metal on metal confirmed my hand was shaking with adrenaline. I could scarcely believe this. I would never have this chance again. I could end it, everything Lisandro was yet to do, avenge everything he'd done to me and to people I loved, and save Renatus from the path Fate had laid for him.

I could save him, *right now*. And no one would stop me.

'If you're going to do something, now's the time,' Topknot said, eyes still shut. He smiled coldly, blindly, at Lisandro as I drew one of the sai. 'I told you locking me up wouldn't stop anything. Get on your knees. All of you.'

And they *did*. Like it was no big deal, Lisandro knelt on the stained, cracked old concrete of the courtyard, followed by all the others, and they gazed up at us without fear. It was almost too easy. If it weren't for this other Empath, this would have been *us* bending over backwards under *his* direction. Garrett and Josh watched, tense, as I weighed the choice I'd thought I made months ago.

'Aristea,' Garrett prompted anxiously, 'we should go.'

He was right, and what he didn't say was also right. I was deliberating an execution and murder was wrong. An irreversible scar on my soul. Something Renatus wouldn't forgive himself for.

Lisandro's death can only be by Renatus's hand, or…

Or mine. I extended the blade and the tip reached perfectly to the hollow under the Crafter's chin. Lisandro blinked without concern, the contentment he'd sent our way still cycling through him, hard. His bronze-brown gaze landed on mine and didn't waver.

Renatus's soul is the price for our "win" over Lisandro. I'm not sure any of us can call that a win at all.

This man killed my parents. He cut my brother's life short.

He killed the Morrissey parents, and the Hawkes, and Peter Chisholm and probably others. He would deserve this. I had the sai's sharpened tip at his throat and, disappointingly, it wasn't exactly unwavering. Neither was my next breath when someone new Displaced in at the back of the kneeling crowd. For a long terrifying beat, Aubrey stood and stared at me, and I felt a tangle of surprised emotions, his and mine. Only Renatus's age, the youngest Magnus Moira lieutenant was an extra player I hadn't counted on.

Skilful. Smart. One who wasn't caught in the web of complacency I controlled.

But he surprised me more by shifting his gaze to the two students he'd coerced off the estate and quietly kneeling. Doing nothing. Nothing I could see.

'Aristea,' Garrett whispered urgently. He seemed suddenly stronger. 'We *need* to go.'

What was I waiting for? I could cut this throat in under a second. I could become a murderer in under a minute, however long it took for Lisandro to bleed out like the man in Prague, and I could incur the wrath of all this camp once this Empathy reversal broke. They'd be all over me.

Better me than Renatus, right? This, all of this, had been to save him, and now was my chance to set that in stone. To ensure we never found out what the act of killing his repulsive godfather would do to him.

White hot pain burning through him... neck tense, muscles bulging in agony... fingers curling into senseless claws... Renatus screaming...

My exhalation came as almost a sob, and I groped at my neck. The thin chain snapped easily, while the string needed an extra yank. I held everything out to Garrett.

'Your mum said I'm the one who lets you in,' I said as he accepted my personal key to Morrissey Estate, though his attention was on Hiroko's crumpled crane. 'I can't come with you so this will have to do. As for you...' I turned back to Lisandro, tuning back into the efforts of the other Empath and assisting as best I could. 'Tell your thugs at the gate to let my friends through.'

I heard the white noise buzz of a guarded telepathic message nearby and knew he must be complying, though he seemed less content than a moment ago. His gaze broke from mine and looked down at the blade at his throat, mildly confused. The sharp tip had scraped his skin. I had drawn blood. Why wasn't I strong enough to push past this arbitrary line?

Maybe because the whole of Magnus Moira would hunt me until I was found and killed. Maybe because I didn't know what my death would do to Renatus.

'She's not going to do it,' Egan told Lisandro idly, and I could have kicked myself for wondering in questions around a Telepath. 'She thinks we'll kill her for it and that would break–'

He was right, I was too scared to tear the blade across a man's neck and end his life, but I wasn't too noble to shut him up. I flicked the sai. The hilt spun in my palm and I struck downward into the side of Egan's jaw. He buckled to the ground. The other Empath kept his eyes closed but he smiled smugly.

Time was running short. I called over my shoulder at the two Displacers, 'Go! Tell Renatus…' Tell him what? 'Tell him I've got this,' and Garrett disappeared with Josh. In my mind I watched them land outside Renatus's gate. What if I'd sent them to their deaths? But though the members of the blockade stood abruptly from their grassy seats, Jackson waved them down, looking confused and annoyed to have to allow it. Garrett had landed dangerously close to the edge of the house's energy field, and dragged his limping friend the handful of paces to the gate itself.

Here, things were shifting very quickly. Maybe disturbed by Egan's misfortune, Lisandro had stopped generating the complacency field, so the other Empath and I had less and less emotion to reflect at him. A few other people stood uncertainly, including a dazed Egan. I ignored them. Lisandro's blink was more deliberate.

'Well, well,' he said, coming back to himself but remaining calm, utterly calm. 'This is unexpected. Or not. White Elm's outcast apprentice and Avalon's spy.'

I glanced at the other prisoner, who shrugged apologetically.

'You're going to have to handle it from here,' the Empathic prisoner warned. His eyes flashed open as he relinquished all control to me and he grinned fiercely at Lisandro. He blinked out of there, leaving me alone with maybe two dozen Magnus Moira. Lisandro got steadily to his feet.

'I had hoped to spare you from meeting with that cretin,' he told me, very calmly. I heard that buzz again; he was changing his orders to Jackson. There, there was confusion as instructions contradicted each other, and Garrett and Josh stumbled urgently to the gate in those precious moments of uncertainty. 'Or rather, spare myself the misfortune of you ever crossing paths. How irksome to have Fate circumvent all my efforts. Again.'

Like killing my family was supposed to prevent me from meeting Renatus, who with my help was fated to defeat his godfather. Lisandro paused, searching for his frustration but unable to find it under the blanket of contentment I was smothering him with. I didn't know how long this would last. I just backed away, keeping my one sai ready and trained on him, though he made no move except to stand his followers down with a dismissive flick of his hand. No intention of attacking me, like at the theatre.

'You're becoming so alike,' he noted with interest, and I knew exactly who he meant. 'I was just with him. He misses you. He failed to take his chance at my life, too. No,' he snapped at a one-handed man who impulsively reached for me, scalding his remaining five fingers on a ward I didn't even think about. I'd never created electrified ones before. 'Leave her. She's an honorary coven member, don't you recall? Besides, she doesn't have the book anymore.'

Hanna Seidel had reported back, clearly, but hadn't caught up with Declan yet, or they wouldn't still be seeking it. In my mind's eye, I watched as Jackson organised his sleepy blockade and they turned on the boys. Vicious spells shot toward them but stopped short thanks to a glassy wall of magic. *Renatus*, I knew instinctively, though I had no evidence to support the theory. No one could cast magic across the fence's barriers, but if anyone could work out a way, it was him.

Garrett hurriedly jammed the key into the lock and twisted; on the other side, Elijah appeared and yanked them both through. The gate clanged shut on the angry crowd just before the ward collapsed and hostile magic began to strike the walls.

My friends were safe. I was not.

There was no more emotion to redirect, so I had to generate my own. I summoned every ounce of complacency and amenability within myself and *forced* it at Lisandro. I used to be an obedient girl. That got lost somewhere along the line, so I don't know how much got through. Without it, this was a conflict I couldn't win.

'You're going to let me leave,' I said, very firmly. I pointed around to the others who were no longer under the spell, including a frowning Egan, rubbing his jaw. 'None of them are to stop me.'

'Of course,' Lisandro agreed without hesitation. His followers glanced between us warily, recognising that something was amiss. At Morrissey Estate, Jackson was doing the same. It was a tenuous battle of wills that they all knew I shouldn't be winning. 'Go ahead.'

I nodded, trying to think, and turned to leave the courtyard. If I could just get out of sight, I could bring up my attention-deflecting and visibility wards, and stroll right out of the camp.

It wasn't to be that easy. Space opened and Jackson stepped through, blocking my path.

The vision of Emmanuelle falling limply to the theatre floor at his heartless click was right behind him.

'Should have known it would be you,' he said, reaching for me. I didn't give him the time. My time was up, and with panic only barely under control, I slashed out with my blade. The ward that burst forth struck him mid-step and sent him flying. I didn't wait to see where he landed or how hard; I spun to the others I felt moving closer, ready to bring my arm around in an arc for a second ward.

But they were too close. A blistered hand was going to close on my elbow before I could swing it.

It's not an ideal practice, but I've employed it more than once when cornered. I did the only thing left in my narrow repertoire. I opened the Fabric and tumbled through to wherever it deemed appropriate.

This blind trust in an indifferent universe has gotten me by thus far, though I always wonder when my luck will run out.

The blistered hand missed my sleeve but another hand caught my satchel strap, and I felt the extra drag on my fall through the void between places. I gasped as my shoulders crashed into a wall of hardware store shelves somewhere new, and I flung myself aside in terror as I saw my hanger-on come through with the same momentum. Egan Lake collided with the shelves and I backed up, wards on full and hand in the satchel before it could slide to the floor.

'I don't know what you did to him,' he sneered, extricating himself from the rubble of gardening trowels and broken shelving, 'but you won't get it past me a second time.'

I looked around hurriedly, spreading my better senses further through the empty store. Eight aisles. Front door locked. Nobody around to witness. Nobody around to help me. I squeezed in a quick breath, suppressing the panic. I shouldn't need help. This was Egan Lake, Academy dropout, maybe a year older than me. *Not* Renatus's apprentice. *Not* schooled in swordplay by Tian. *Not* Emmanuelle's best wards student. Renatus had taught me that in a real fight, I wouldn't get to choose my opponent, but given the alternatives, I'd still choose this.

Egan picked up a crowbar from the mess of shelving and tore the plastic cover off the end. I fixed my grip on both sai and adjusted my stance in case he meant the business his actions suggested. He pushed a sleeve up and displayed his forearm. In black, a rough-hewn spiral struck through with an equally rough straightish line that could have been mistaken for a check mark was tattooed under his left hand, right where my apprentice mark was inked.

Mine was better. Just saying.

'I was hoping I'd get a chance to test myself against you,' he said, and swung the tool at me heavily. I kept my still-stinging hands where they were, trusting my wards, and as expected, the steel bounced off like it had hit diamond. I felt Egan's frustration as he struck again, aiming nearer now that he knew where the wards were, a good foot away from my body. 'Of all the students the White Elm took in, I couldn't believe it when I heard they'd picked you.' He was channelling magic through the crowbar now, a different spell each time he smashed it into my shielding. Niggling at the edges of my mind, his was trying to penetrate mine again, hoping to knock my confidence and get under my defences. 'Middle and bottom class of every subject, nothing special. Not to mention no mind of your own, swallowing anything anyone tells you. But I guess that's what they were looking for.' The next blow was so hard that the force reverberated through the ward and into my body, thinly connected to my spell, and I instinctively slid back on the smooth floor to keep our distance. Inspired by whatever he'd just done differently, Egan came after me. 'At least, that's what they wanted until they didn't. Even *they* kicked you out. Starting to see how you picked the wrong side yet? They weren't the only ones taking on apprentices, but maybe,' he hit my wards again with the power-infused bar and I felt the beginnings of strain, like when I'd been fending off all the scriers looking for me, 'they were the only ones taking on *cowards*. Why don't you drop these wards, huh?'

Another two strikes, his arms straining with the effort. My shielding shook deeply, and I knew I could sustain more, but at the price of my own energy. My thoughts flashed on Declan's warning about personal warding. Eventually, if I didn't find an alternative energy source to attach them to, they'd break. Egan swung at my side, a strike that would break ribs if I didn't have these wards. My safety would come down to a race to the finish between my energy and his physical strength. I thought fast.

'Carrying around swords like you know what you're doing with them but you're too shit-scared to face another apprentice?' Egan mocked. The spot I'd hit on his jaw was blooming with colour. 'What's the matter? Scared of being outmatched?'

Not so much, I made sure to think as he swung for an

umpteenth time. He was aiming short, expecting the wall of magic, and almost lost his balance when I dropped it and his crowbar kept arcing. As he came down too heavy, I stepped in behind his heel to square off and slashed the two sai sideward to catch the weapon. There was a crash of steel on steel, the bar slotting perfectly into the hooked guards of my hilt, and I twisted with its momentum, my furthermost wrist turning down to lever it from his grasp. The two sai slid down the loosened crowbar, which kept going in the direction of my pointed blades, smacking loudly to the floor elsewhere in the aisle.

Taken by surprise, weight too far forward from his centre of gravity to save him, Egan made an incoherent noise of dread and struggled to wheel himself back. I didn't give him the time. I drove my elbow back and in, jamming the pommel of my sai into the solar plexus that was falling into it anyway, and sinking deep. His reflexive inhalation sounded like a choke, one that got caught in his throat, eyes bulging in shock when I also dropped my knee into the back of his. His leg gave out; his weight went over my hip, and his feet came off the floor.

Tian would have been proud. Maybe. Maybe he'd like me to be more honourable, but Renatus and Declan, my other role models in the field of combat, would finally have something to agree on. Alive is better than noble.

Egan's back hit the ground, flat and hard, taking whatever wind he had left. He gasped desperately, twitchy hands clawing vaguely at his midsection.

'That... That wasn't...' he managed between involuntary off-beat breaths. Fair? Nice? I didn't wait around for him to find his diaphragm. I picked up my satchel.

'I am not a sounding board for your monologuing practice, Egan.'

I bagged the sai as I quickly moved out of sight of the wheezing Magnus Moira apprentice and dug around in my pocket for Ana's trusty ruby. Wards restored, attention-deflecting and all, I aimed for the back of the store. I had a new face before I set foot out the staff exit and smiled an unmemorable smile of acknowledgement at a pair of workmates who were standing two doors down on a cigarette break. They'd glanced over at the hardware store door opening, but at my smile, their eyes slid straight off me and back to their conversation.

Egan was someone's apprentice, so I wasn't shocked when I felt a presence arrive at his side before the back door had even clattered shut behind me. Their minds would be joined the same way mine and Renatus's were, except neither of them were hiding from the other for the other's own good. I needed to be gone. I polished the ruby on my shirt and summoned the image of the Warsaw train station to give me something concrete to aim for in my next Displacement.

It worked. I mean, I held my breath as always in the void, and wondered for that sticky, elongated second whether I'd survive it, but my feet hit the crumbly ground beside the tracks inside the tunnel and I quickly backed against the wall so I couldn't be immediately run over. No trains, thankfully. Note for future, train tracks are not landing platforms.

I jogged back to the actual platform, hoisted myself up to absolutely nobody's notice, and autopiloted to the locker where I'd left my backpack. I swung it onto my shoulders, wincing at the discomfort. The collision with the store shelves was beginning to smart.

I could deal with that at my destination, wherever Fate picked for me. I joined a crowd of people pouring through the station, a train newly arrived, and rolled the ruby over in my sore hands. No images from the compound. I tried to clear my mind and let images come from Fate rather than my own worries, and it took more than a minute for my loved ones – Hiroko eating, Angela running, the unsettled chaos at Renatus's gate – to fade from the glossy crystal facets.

White sand… single seashell… a young blonde man picks it up… years later, another man, mid-twenties and freshly landed, falls to his knees beside it… rugged cliff facing glassy blue water…

Somewhere in the train station, someone powerful Displaced in. Then someone else, possibly Jackson. I swallowed and squeezed the ruby, shouldering into the next women's restroom I saw.

Fate has business plans for us.

I hated for Winter to be right, but that couldn't be helped. Fate had led me this far. Right to Avalon's spy, which had to be the reason they wanted to keep me free, on reflection. Now wasn't a good time to lose faith and strike out on my own. I reached for the Fabric.

My feet landed with a soft splash in the frothy, receding tide, but wet shoes weren't first in my order of concerns. I spun in place, finding myself at the lip of the most beautiful sea I'd ever been lucky enough to witness with my own eyes, and finding my magic utterly barren. No wards. No scried images coming to mind. The ruby inert in my hand. Just like in the Belarussian theatre.

My magic was gone but not my Empathy, and I felt the confused wariness of the man on the beach before I saw him. He was old, older than Lord Gawain, which I thought was quite old, and haggard with exposure to the elements. Blotchy dry skin, filthy colourless hair, dirty torn clothes.

I had never met him before but I knew him immediately. The feeling was not mutual.

'You shouldn't be here,' he observed in a hoarse voice with an accent just like mine, and he picked up that one shell from the sand and threw it at me. It rattled oddly as it arced through the air. My reflexes were always good, and I caught it on the full. Too bad. The spell embedded in it spun down my nerves, electrifying what felt like my every cell, and I suppose I'd lost consciousness before I hit the wet sand.

chapter eighteen

1965

Decades of research into the workings of Fate and magic hadn't made Cassán into a Seer, but had given him a healthy respect for the semi-sentient force he'd parted from in Salem. So when an inexplicable sense of dread settled in his stomach around lunchtime, and faint glimmers of elusive gold flitted at the corners of his vision, or flashed briefly across the backs of his eyelids at the same time as a strange *pulling* sensation on his aura, he paid attention.

It seemed he wasn't the only one.

Are you doing something?

The message was harmless, intended to clarify. It only heightened Cassán's dread. No, he wasn't doing anything, and if Mánus was experiencing something strange, too, then this was either a coven issue or something bigger. Why else would Fate reach out to its estranged runaway children after so long?

Friends were supposed to bring joy, but Cassán had stopped believing that, accepting that he had narrowed his friendship circle to four of the most ruthless, ambitious, increasingly unstable people he knew. By now, the hardest part of having them for friends was the knowledge that like attracts like, and he was no better.

In moments like this one, he could pretend otherwise, gazing with wonder at the curly-haired little angel asleep on his chest, bigger every day, seemingly only seconds ago just a helpless doll fitting in the crook of one arm but now standing taller than her father's knee and walking.

'The only thing I've done right in a long time, aren't you, my love?' he asked of Elysia, softly, giving into the temptation to brush his scarred hand over the toddler's thick mop of dark hair. She sighed in her sleep and nuzzled closer, warmed by the bright afternoon sun streaming through the bay window. Babies were incredible, not least for the myriad places and arrangements in which they could fall asleep. Every day, it seemed, he saw something new and amazing in his little daughter. Her mother's long lashes. The sunlight catching flecks of green in her dark eyes. The beginnings of a tooth that wasn't showing yesterday. She was constantly growing, determinedly moving forward into the future, but she was also wonderfully complete just as she was. At fifteen months, Elysia had her mother Thea's sweet disposition and Cassán's natural affinity for magic. A tiny little Crafter. He daydreamed about teaching her how to harness it, when she was old enough, maybe lie out in a field in the sunshine together encouraging whimsical shapes out of the clouds, or play hide and seek together in the woods, practising cloaking spells, or sit together in the conservatory on a rainy day inventing new magic.

But it was just a daydream. Every one of those precious future moments was now outlawed, courtesy of the White Elm, and after two years drifting between 'Screw the White Elm, I'll teach my daughter what I like' and 'How is my girl supposed to explain herself the first time she does magic accidentally with a friend and it's a top-level crime?' he knew he didn't have a choice but to keep dreaming. The council's sanitised white energy magic was foreign to him, and Thea was not confident with it, though when she did use magic, that was what she gravitated to. Maggie O'Neill two streets over had scared all the local sorceresses off magic altogether – not just blood magic – with the sob-riddled story of how her son Jamie was caught casting now-outlawed spells, somehow spotted by the White Elm despite having all the windows closed. Cassán hadn't bothered explaining again that the council had a Scrier, an exceptional one, who seemed to be only getting better with experience, and that Jamie O'Neill deserved what he got if he wasn't smart enough to erect a cloaking spell or energy ward before spellworking. It fell on deaf ears. The White Elm had what they'd set out for when they wrote their restrictions on magic – compliance through fear and lethargy.

'Give it a generation,' he kept saying to Thea, not that she was invested in this argument, 'and they'll regret it. We'll have a nation of useless sorcerers. Our grandchildren won't even know what class of sorcerer they are, let alone how to cast a spell.'

Maybe sooner.

'Not mine,' Mánus dismissed whenever Cassán made this complaint, making sure to point out that they'd had this conversation before. 'They'll all be scriers, and no rules are going to keep my son, or any son of his, from magic that's their birthright.'

Cassán didn't doubt that at all, but somehow it seemed more manageable when your surname was Morrissey and your bank account and manor home made a self-sustaining magical life completely viable. The life he'd cultivated with Thea was more humble, more quiet… more mortal, which was ironic given that he'd never been further from it. Still, it kept Elysia off the radar of blights-on-existence Andrew Hawke and Moira Dawes, which was worth every missed future moment of magic with her.

A sharp tingle ran across the back of his hand. Wincing, knowing what this was, he turned his wrist to watch as spidery script appeared on his skin in black ink mirrored from halfway across the country.

It's Moira. Meet me?

Cassán let his eyes fall closed, taking a moment to wallow in his resentment. Almost five months without word from Moira had been a near-blissful reprieve. No drama, or none of the Moira kind, anyway. Andrew had been busy, distracted with the domestic excitement of the arrival of his son Kenneth last year. Cassán had not been onboard with Mánus's constant worrying about Moira's whereabouts – who cared, really? – and had countered any mention of the maniacal witch with a reminder that they'd had this conversation before. He wasn't the only one losing his mind, one slip-up at a time.

But now she'd resurfaced and the scrier had picked up her location at the same time as these strange nudges from an anxious-seeming Fate. Ominous, yes. Something he could avoid dealing with? Hmm. In recent years, she'd dropped off the map several times, just never for this long before. Every time, her return heralded bad news, not necessarily for them but for somebody.

'I found a shaman who communes with the dead. He didn't want to share how but I got it out of him.'

'Did you know there's a clan of Displacers out in the Pacific who have been visiting the ocean floor? I made them show me.'

'They had legends about a wolf curse. I wanted to see for myself so I had to break him out of mortal prison. It wasn't that hard.'

Cassán wished she'd just stay away, find something that satiated her thirst for new knowledge and kept her off his radar, eternally. The trail of destruction, comatose shamans and terrorised primitive societies she left in her wake was not getting any less conspicuous with time, and her arrogant overconfidence made Mánus's fear of her attracting White Elm attention increasingly plausible.

'Besides,' he'd say, too frequently, 'what she does is also on us. If we're the only people who can sway her, we have to try.'

Cassán didn't know how many times he'd heard that – doubtless, he'd forgotten as many conversations as Mánus had, just another price they hadn't realised they'd be paying – but he knew he'd never agree. Moira was *not* his responsibility. He didn't like her, he didn't lay any claim to her, and he would prefer his life without her in it. She was a grown woman with a sharp mind, even clouded as theirs were with the beginnings of insanity. She alone was responsible for what she did.

Cassán sighed, knowing that his mind was already, reluctantly, made up. His friend *was* his responsibility. Mánus would keep trying to contain her, to his own detriment, and Cassán would go with him because he always followed wherever the scrier went, and because, as usual, the scrier was in the right. Moira was capable of anything.

So were they. More than they liked.

Cassán? Please?

Shaking the inky pleas from his stinging hand, he carefully got to his feet, minding not to jostle the baby, and lowered her into her blankets. Anthea had lovingly decorated the room with handmade mobiles, and a polaroid photograph of them together at the summer fair was propped up on a shelf by an arrangement of dried flowers from their garden and shells from her last visit home to Greece.

'Your da loves you, little heart,' he promised Elysia with a kiss as he tucked her in. She didn't even stir, such an easy sleeper. Evidently not an Empath, which was probably for the best. Cassán stroked her hair once more, refocusing his eyes to view her aura. The little girl was aglow with potential energy, everything he could have asked for in an heir to everything he'd learned across his career of research and bad choices.

Except he wasn't going to teach her anything. She was alive, and whole, and complete, and she belonged to Fate, like everybody else, and she would die one day.

While Cassán kept living, all because of a terrible mistake made before he realised there were things – people – he would never want to outlive. There, in his offspring's aura, was the proof. The black sinkholes from his own aura, and those of his four coven mates after their tragic ritual in Salem, had been passed to her along with his power. His had never gone away, and based on his observations of Mánus's boisterous and demanding toddler's matching auric features, he suspected hers wouldn't, either.

They anchored her to that moment he should have chosen differently. He'd cursed her.

'Are you going to Mánus's?'

He turned to his wife, standing in the doorway with her arms full of fresh laundry. He hadn't felt her approach, her once-vibrant character dulled by years of her isolation and his absence until all her colour and noise and warmth washed out to what she was now. Cold. Brittle, at least to him. The ghost of all his regrets. Regret for falling in love with someone too good for him. Regret for taking her away from the life she would have lived in her home country. Regret that he wasn't the person now that he was when they met.

Eyes touching on their sleeping baby, he felt her soften, but only slightly. He could hear in her question that she didn't care for the answer, but he gave it anyway, always hopeful he might turn things around with some of the good stuff – honesty and kindness and all the rest of what she deserved.

'I am,' he agreed quietly as Thea placed the laundry pile on the baby's change table. 'He called and he wants to do something he shouldn't.' He patted down his pocket for a pen. 'Do you know where…? Thank you, my love.'

Thea had produced his pen and held it out to him. Immensely grateful for her, he steeled himself for the pain of the nib on the back of his hand.

The burns from the ritual had never healed. Under the layers of illusion he wore constantly, they were ugly, black and red and pink and scarred, and their dexterity had not returned. He strained to hold the pen in stiff fingers and cringed at the scraping of the delicate scar tissue as he wrote his reply.

C

"Yes" was too many letters; his initial at least confirmed he was on his way.

'I'll try to be back before dark,' Cassán promised, pressing a quick kiss to Anthea's forehead and tossing the pen to the hall table on his way out. 'I'll–'

'Cassán.' He returned to the doorway at her voice, and she raised her hand to indicate his. 'You forgot.'

He looked down at his hand's unblemished façade and swallowed. The letter *C* was still there, unsent.

'Thank you.' He summoned magic to his other hand and swiped his palm across the message, tying off the spell he'd written as it went. Done. He looked up at Thea, who was watching him from beside the dressing table. 'I'll try to be…' No, he'd said that already. He needed to get with it, especially if he and Mánus were to confront Moira. There was something he knew he didn't say enough. 'I love you.'

'Does Mánus have it, too?' she asked instead of responding in kind, though from her gentler, more interested tone, he could imagine it was still there, behind the question. 'This sickness?'

A most astute way of putting it, Cassán thought. Anthea's

limitations with English meant she often said things more bluntly, more accurately, than he might, with all his socially imbued tact. He loved it.

But she'd never asked this before, and it took him a moment to determine how best to answer. All the secrets buried within that truth.

'Yes,' he said finally. 'He's sick like me. Maybe worse.'

He detected her sympathy beneath a resigned acceptance. She'd expected this answer. She picked up a pair of socks from his pile of clothes and tossed it to him; he caught it on the full and looked down sheepishly at his bare feet.

'Whatever it is he's doing, you'll look after him?'

Always, whether he liked it or not. Despite his unreal power, despite his wealth and influence and despite the years since Anthea had seen the scrier, she knew what he knew – that Mánus was inherently good, and in that goodness there was a vulnerability Cassán didn't possess. Something worth protecting, something precious.

He had to remind himself of that when he arrived at Morrissey Estate to a larger search party than he'd agreed to.

'You said to meet *you*,' he reminded his friend irritably when Andrew Hawke and Eugene Dubois raised a hand each in tense greeting. 'Next time, be more specific so I can decline.'

'I wasn't going to give you the opportunity,' Mánus responded, unapologetic. Unfazed by the open hostility, Andrew shook thick red hair back from his face when the breeze whipped it into his eyes.

'I told you he'd be impressed,' he drawled, then nodded at Eugene. 'We don't want to miss it. Meet us there?'

He offered his arm, and the stout wisp of a former Telepath accepted with his one remaining hand. They stepped through the Fabric and into another place. Cassán jumped on the moment alone with Mánus.

'What is this?' he demanded. He gestured at the now vacant position of the others. 'Miss what?'

'Moira,' the other Irishman said, as if the name were an answer in itself. 'You didn't feel it?'

The pulls, the flashes of Fate, the sense of dread.

'Of course I did. What is it? I'm sure Hawke has all the answers.'

He didn't mean it to sound so petty. Mánus had retained closer ties with the rest of their coven than he had endeavoured to. They might even be friends, and of course on some level Cassán felt threatened. Stupid, yes, but not something he could help.

His only friend suppressed a sigh and offered his own hand.

'They wanted to leave without you,' he admitted, a Telepath now after all, 'but even Hawke thinks we might need you.'

'He *thinks* you need me?' Cassán repeated, unnerved. The overconfident Seer was never uncertain about anything. 'He said that?'

'Of course not. Moira's up to something,' the scrier said vaguely. His eyes slid out of focus, seeing something beyond the world before them. Towers of human flames, perhaps, or pools of blood spreading from a throat cut too young? Any of their shared hallucinations. Mánus Morrissey was blessed with chiselled good looks, but the last five years had taken more than their allocated time from him. His face had thinned and his dark hair had begun to grey prematurely at the edges. It did nothing to deter female, and often male, attention on the increasingly rare occasion the recluse actually went out in public, but it worried Cassán all the same. Mánus was years younger than he was and used to look it. The scrier blinked and was back, present and sharp. 'Hawke's excited. I don't like it. We might be too late. Are you coming with me or not?'

There was only one possible answer to that. Cassán took his hand and let him direct their Displacement, landing them where his vision took them.

He'd never been to this steamy green jungle, though even if he hadn't seen the coverage on the television news, it would have been obvious where they were.

He yanked his hand from Mánus's, pulling his emotions in, hard, against the overwhelming climate of stress, terror and grief. It was all around him, denser even than the trees, heavy enough to make an Empath sick.

'Vietnam is a *warzone*,' he hissed, running a swift inventory over his wards and spreading his thoughts beyond his feelings, touching minds and masses of human activity less than a hundred metres away. 'We're going to get shot.'

Mánus seemed less concerned, looking around for their coven mates.

'Think of it as a test for our immortality,' he suggested as he began to trudge to the east, parallel with the line of soldiers to the north. At least they seemed to be heading away. Mánus made less effort to keep silent than Cassán preferred, continuing his conversation like they weren't walking through a *battleground*. 'What would she be doing here? What do you know about it?'

Muttering angrily, Cassán shaped a new ward in his hands – soundproof, attention-diverting, bulletproof – and threw it northward. With his mind he expanded it to protect them both, gliding through space alongside them as they struggled through wild underbrush and sank their feet into warm puddles between the trees.

'I know even the White Elm is giving this place a wide berth,' he snapped. 'It was bad when it was just north against south. Now the Americans are here, too.'

'More people, more bullets,' Mánus mused, and right on cue, the breakout of gunfire drove them both to their knees, hunkering under thick tropical saplings that wouldn't save them from a stray shot. Finally healthily frightened, the scrier blinked up at Cassán while the sounds of soldiers going down and giving chase whirled around them in erratic bursts. 'What are they fighting about?'

Cassán stared, then remembered. 'You need a television, Morrissey.'

'Mortal scrying technology? Why? Will it have my back in a shootout?'

It was a word of thanks, even if it didn't sound like it. He'd sensed the ward and appreciated it. Cassán rolled his eyes.

'No, but it might do a better job keeping you out of one than I did.'

His friend rarely smiled, but almost got there for a moment. It was uncomfortably juxtaposed against the sick waves of fear, determination and horror that radiated from the nearby battle. The smile faded along with some man's dying screams, and Cassán knew they'd both heard the deaths of their anchors in the ringing echo. Carefully repositioning himself to avoid knocking any of their cover, Mánus pointed between two trees.

'Something's up ahead. A zone I can't see into. Hawke and Dubois were on the move and then…'

'And then they weren't.' Cassán tuned his attention to the energies present in the direction Mánus had been heading. There seemed to be nothing there, nobody and nothing, not even birds or small creatures, which didn't make sense. Too much nothing. A few breaths of focus – not easy given the noise and chaos that felt almost on top of them – and his Crafting gift began to act on the magic it detected. Anti-council warding, his own spell cast by another Crafter, and in the force field enveloping the bubble of space Mánus couldn't see into, familiar coding, a recognisable hand to the weave of a spell designed to keep Fate out. 'Moira.'

He felt his friend's resignation as deeply as his own.

'Alright, we're clear to go if we stay low,' Mánus murmured, third eye apparently on the action above them. He crept forward, Cassán close on his heels and trying to ignore the prickles of sweat seeping from every one of his pores. *Why* would Moira come here? Naturally, Mánus overheard the thought. 'I suspect the answer will make you wish you hadn't asked.'

He was so rarely wrong, and there was nothing about this humid horror show that suggested he was going to start today. They closed in on the energy bubble, the gunfire receding behind them. Just another day of ugliness in a war that seemed to only be amplifying.

Like a gasp, a desperate flash of gold above them made them both pause and look up nervously. In a live battleground, that could be anything a military could dream up, but the pull on magic they both felt said this was less noble than any war pretends to be. An icy wind blasted through the jungle, cooling the sweat on their cheeks and leaving them shuddering in the wake of Fate's displeasure.

'We're too late,' Cassán knew, and none of his friend's whispered optimism could convince him otherwise. He *knew*.

'Here.' Mánus paused and extended a hand. Like spider's silk, the invisible barrier caught his fingers briefly, but when he pushed, he sank through, disappearing from Cassán's sight and senses. Quickly, the Crafter pushed after him, feeling the drag of Moira's distinctive magic as he passed through it.

Into gold.

Hazel eyes, Elysia's… hazel again, a boy, then blue-green, a girl… another girl, hazel-eyed, different from her siblings… an Empath…

Fate soaked its secrets into him as he stepped into the immediate remnants of a *massive* spell, and the jungle fell away; or rather, he stumbled into a clearing so abrupt, so wrong, that even Mánus had frozen in place, and he ran into him. Looking over the scrier's shoulder, he surveyed the scene. Every tree was freshly flattened. The ground was blackened and the sour energy of death and fear was thick in the air. Maybe a non-Empath wouldn't notice that part, but they couldn't have missed the score of red-raw human bodies strewn in a rough circle around the new clearing, nor could they miss the swelling of power around the naked woman standing victorious, glorious, elated at its centre with her arms still extended to the sky.

An initiation… a cave… seashells on a familiar beach…

Usually experienced as brief flashes quickly forgotten, Fate was present and flowing like pooling water, denser than the humidity, and Cassán could barely think straight. He'd not interacted with this omnipotent force in years now, and here it was, erratic and wild and swarming as it recovered from a spell cast only seconds ago.

The beach… two Empaths, one old, one young…

Slowly, ecstatically, Moira lowered her arms, seeming not to have noticed she had company. Hawke and Dubois were standing nearby, expressions of awe lighting their faces as Fate's gold seeped into their auras.

'Ah, my friend, I've missed you,' Cassán heard the Seer murmur. Of them all, Hawke must have felt the separation from its insights most, though what he'd done to part ways with Fate had not been the actions of a friend. Beside him, Eugene Dubois stepped closer to the carnage, equal parts sickened and impressed.

'She did it,' was all he said. Cassán looked around, unable to understand and unsure he wanted to. Everything was wrong. Fate, he felt, had been tricked yet again, and was furious to have been called upon to preside over a ritual so heinous.

Haunted by a sense of déjà vu, he counted the dead. Had to start over twice, distracted by the horror. Twenty-three. Hands burnt, bodies burnt, skin torn cleanly off some in the blast. This was worse than the shootout to the north. At least the soldiers were armed and knew what they were in for.

Like attracts like.

The ritual he'd written to separate the five of them from Fate's web and grant them virtual immortality had required a sacrifice – a little boy – and had killed the five sorcerers they'd channelled through to avoid burning themselves out. Anchors. They'd taken the brunt of that huge spell and died in agony as towers of flame. Twenty-three, though? What kind of spell needed *twenty-three* people to die to make it work?! And why did the spell site look like a small bomb had gone off?

Mánus was thinking the same.

'What is this?' Mánus asked flatly, finally drawing Moira's attention. Her gaze flew to him, bronze-brown and momentarily embarrassed to be seen in this state by the man she most admired and could never have. Her hands and belly were smeared with blood, apparently not her own, and she wore several amulets around her neck, but nothing else. Even at a distance, Cassán could tell that the stones and pendants she wore came from all different places, different cultures. Probably stolen, or coerced, from their previous owners.

'I'm so glad you're here,' she said softly. Her voice carried in the stillness left behind by her spell as the magic she'd drawn here slowly drifted off, back to fill the empty spaces of the world. 'All of you. I've saved us.'

'I knew you would,' Andrew Hawke said, impressed, making her smile.

'I couldn't have done it without your help,' she responded warmly. Cassán stepped around Mánus, chancing a brief look at his friend. The scrier didn't understand either. Moira turned her smile on them, apologetic. 'You would have tried to stop me if I'd told you,' she confessed, coming closer, stepping over burnt bodies. Her bare feet crushed scorched grass. 'Sometimes you lose sight of our dreams. But I've fixed that. I've fixed the future.'

Cassán couldn't imagine a worse future than one Moira had "fixed". He looked her over when she stopped before them, piecing together the clues. Blood on her lips, on her stomach. Twenty-three dead anchors. The amulets, some of them ancient. When his other senses lingered on her, symbols lit up to his Crafter's eye – runes, drawn with a ceremonial knife in the air over her skin. And then he understood.

'A fertility spell,' he realised, immediately ill with revulsion. He dragged his eyes once more over the dead anchors. Men, all of them. He could imagine what they thought they were here for. Moira, of course, had had other plans. Her smile widened and she laid her bloody hands upon her flat belly.

'Fate had no choice,' she said with delight. 'I gave him a destiny all his own, and Fate can't stop him. None of Fate's agents can stop him.'

'Stop who?' Mánus demanded, refusing to accept the impossibility Cassán knew she must have achieved. 'What destiny?'

Moira stared at him. 'My son. He's going to end the White Elm.'

Trying not to scoff, Cassán said, 'He's what?' at the same time Mánus demanded, 'Your *what*?' For once Moira ignored her favourite Irish scrier and answered Cassán.

'It's his destiny,' she said again. 'I brought Fate here and I took some and bent it into my own shape and gave that to my son. A destiny written in blood. He'll liberate our world from their rule and show our people the Magnus Moira way.'

Cassán frowned, disturbed. 'Our way is meant to be that we make our own fate.'

Hadn't that been the point of their book club? Hadn't that

been the point of it all? How did warping Fate into a handwritten synthetic destiny for one unborn child fit that dream?

'Because of Moira's son, hundreds of thousands of future sorcerers will get to choose their own paths,' Eugene pointed out. 'Without the council to smother their magic, all the knowledge we gathered and preserved together can be returned to the people.'

'And what good's that if we're all slowly losing our minds?' Cassán snapped, silencing the others. They never talked about this. He felt their resentment and nervousness at his unholy mention. 'How long will it take this baby to grow old enough to fulfil this destiny? How much will we remember? What benefit will we be, really?'

It took a moment for anyone to feel up to answering this as the euphoria of Moira's spell began to wane, until Andrew, very seriously, broke the uneasy quiet.

'It won't matter if we're not around,' he told them. 'His destiny has been set by Moira's spell. Everything he needs to find, every person he needs to meet, will be brought into his path when he needs it. Our knowledge will be carried to him through our descendants and the followers of our coven's message. He *will* end the White Elm.'

'All of our bloodlines will help,' Moira enthused, opening her bloodied hands to them. Cassán cringed, thinking of wild nights spent bloodletting into bottles for planned rituals and experiments.

'You wrote *us* into your child's fate?' he asked, too revolted by this whole mess to feel appropriately angry at the transgression. The other Crafter frowned, not seeing the issue.

'Of course,' she said, as though the necessity was very clear. 'Our children are as tied to each other as we are. One foot in Fate's web, one foot out. Their babies will be the same, and all the way down through time until we finish with them.'

Until we finish with them. Cassán swallowed at that reminder of the *other* cost he hadn't shared with Thea. How could he explain that? How could he even explain to himself, now a father, how that had seemed like a reasonable price?

Beside Cassán, his only real friend was simmering with some strange mix of abhorrence, disappointment and jealousy, and didn't seem to be paying attention to this central thread of discussion.

'Who's the father?' Mánus asked as if it mattered. He'd never reciprocated Moira's affections, never cared who she'd thrown herself at to get his attention.

'He doesn't need a father,' Moira answered primly, lifting her head with dignity not usually associated with people standing naked among fully dressed friends in a jungle, backdropped by a mass murder scene she orchestrated. Mánus refused to accept it.

'You expect me to believe you *made* a baby out of, what? Fate and magic and wishing really hard? That's not how it works.'

'It worked,' she argued defensively, hugging her stomach. She looked over her shoulder at the dead anchors. 'He's made of everything he needs.'

'What's that? Twenty-something fathers?'

Cassán sighed, exasperated by this fixation and his inability to move forward in the discussion.

'We're getting you a television after this, or at least a journal subscription so you know what's happening beyond your bloody gate. Twenty-three chromosomes, Mánus. Scientists finally worked out the number. In our blood, in our cells. That's what she needed to make a new human.'

The other men looked again at the massacre of bodies, realisation dawning for them all. He and Moira, they were the scholars, the knowledge-seekers. It didn't surprise him that she followed advances in mortal medicine and sciences as closely as he did.

He just wished it surprised him more that she'd found a way to work that knowledge into her relentless mission to do, know and control everything and leave no life untouched.

'You said he's destined to bring about the White Elm's end,' Cassán redirected tiredly, 'and you know I'm as opposed to their rule as anyone, but two dozen people had to die brutal deaths to realise this far-off dream? When will we see the fruits of their sacrifice?'

Moira sighed softly at his apparent lack of vision. It was obvious to him now why she'd chosen Vietnam's war-torn jungle as the site of her world-altering spell. Her target, the White Elm, wasn't looking at this part of the world for magical wrongdoing – war changes the board, forces a change of rules, and a blind eye to acts of combat necessitates a blind eye to acts of blatant murder in the same location. These deaths would be lost among visions of the hundreds that would occur here this week, all of them deliberately overlooked by a council of thirteen whose absolute power over the world of sorcery was thrown into an interesting light by the workings of non-witch politics.

'It will take as long as it takes,' Andrew spoke for Moira. 'He'll live as long as needed to make it happen. Two dozen will seem like a small price when he achieves the dream we all share.'

'No one needed to die,' Cassán snapped. 'Why couldn't it be one of us to take down the Elm? Why did you need to tear chromosomes out of twenty-three men to make your perfect offspring to do what any of us could?'

'It couldn't be one of us,' Eugene argued. 'We don't have fates.'

True. Moira smiled patiently at Cassán, shaking her loose dark hair over her shoulder. She'd grown out her pixie cut of recent years but it was not long enough to cover any part of her body typically considered indecent. Behind her, a charred half-fallen tree creaked under its own precarious weight.

'They're ordained by Fate, did you know that?' she asked, which of course he did. 'That means no one who's ever stood against them before has really stood a chance.'

'The game is rigged in their favour,' Andrew concurred. 'They'll last forever at this rate, rolling out restriction after restriction until our entire culture is nothing but legends and fairytales, and our descendants forget what they are. And for them to forget their magic would be as bad for them as it would be for us.'

The Seer's words made Cassán uncomfortable. He felt Mánus's sidelong glance, knowing it was what he himself had been ranting for months. The scrier reluctantly nodded his agreement with Andrew.

'They'll squeeze their hands tighter until there's nothing left of us,' he said, and Moira nodded vehemently.

'Not now. My son will free sorcerers everywhere from their despotism. He'll do what we can't. And no one will be able to stop him.'

Andrew had to interject on that point. 'No one but us, anyway. Us and our bloodlines.'

'So, the same rules apply?' Cassán checked, knowing Andrew Hawke understood his meaning. He confirmed with a short nod. Mánus was still sceptical.

'If this works.'

'It will work,' Andrew insisted. 'I saw the spell coding as she wrote it. I read every draft.'

'And since when are you a Crafter, Hawke?' Mánus shot back. 'Cassán didn't proof it and Cassán *always* proofed any magic we wrote. How do we know it's stable?'

'We need to hope it is,' Cassán replied coolly, 'since she wrote *us into it.*'

'I've been working on this spell for the last two years,' Moira said with passion brightening her eyes. 'Everything I ever learned from Cassán is in the code of it – if it makes you feel better, he can have the notes, pore over it, but he won't find an error, I promise. I wrote you all into it to ensure my Lisandro has the same protections your descendants enjoy.'

'Your who?' Cassán interrupted, hoping he'd misheard. 'That's not a name.'

'The baby will be flawless,' Moira went on like he hadn't spoken, 'and the future I wrote for him… Mánus, it's beautiful. A destiny to be remembered by, a noble purpose, true love.'

She smiled at the scrier and took his hand in her bloody one. He stared at their joined hands for a moment, deliberating, then looked up at her, emotions cooling with resolve.

'I'm not sure why you look at me when you say that,' he said. Cassán tried not to wince at what he knew instinctively would be the next words. 'We're not in love.'

Eugene and Andrew really did cringe. Moira's smile hardly

faltered, but Cassán felt the deep sting of hurt within her to hear the confirmation of what she already knew.

'No,' she agreed after a beat, voice perfectly steady, pressing his hand to her bare stomach before he could pull away. 'But they will be. It's written in blood.'

chapter nineteen

The sounds of my childhood pushed through the disturbing remnants of a dark dream, and I tried to open my eyes. It wasn't easy; wet sand had glued one shut, and I clumsily pushed myself up from a soggy beach to rub it clear with my shoulders. Salt stung my burnt hands, making me squeeze my eyes even tighter, and I resisted panic with effort. Lisandro, Egan, Hanna Seidel, anyone could be coming.

I didn't need eyes to see.

An image of myself kneeling a metre or so ahead of a frothy receding tide sprung to mind without much prompt. Half of my hair was sopping and straggly from lying in sea water, and the whole front of me was wet and sandy. From the line of sand encrusted on my face, it was honestly a wonder I hadn't drowned.

Using the sounds of lethargic waves bubbling ashore, I turned and crawled to the edge of the water to rinse my hands and splash my face. Salt water wasn't ideal but it would get me halfway to clean.

I managed to open my eyes, still stinging, and I left the rest for now as I took in my awe-inspiring surroundings. I was absolutely, utterly alone, with the entire blue-green sea spread before me and no sign of anyone coming for me. The pristine white beach spanned for hundreds of metres either side of me, eventually petering off where the arching cliff face met the sea. It was a gorgeous sunny day, though the cliff cast a heavy shadow, and a soft sea breeze brought the salty scent I remembered so well from growing up beachside before my parents died. High above me, over the ridge of the cliff, I heard the rustle of toughened trees, and my scrier's eye gave me a top-down view. Spindly and asymmetrical, with weathered leaves growing in clumps that leaned hard away from the water that brought the winds, they grew out of unfriendly, rocky terrain with sparse tufts of brown grass.

Home felt as far from this dry-aired place of scorched colour as the shredded tropical forest I'd sighted in my dream. I shuddered despite the beach's warmth, pushing up to my feet. Scried scenes from my grandfather's life in the 1960s were invariably depressing and concerning, though thankfully usually short-lived in my own memory. Even now, the events were blurring together, the faces fading, the names falling away, and I was left with an impression of dread and hopelessness.

Well, not just that. I slowly turned on my squelchy spot to behold the large shell I'd caught too willingly. It was back on the beach where it had started, but the old man was gone. Not even his footprints in the soft white sand remained. I trudged over, scooping my damp satchel and patting myself down to remove as much grubbiness as possible. Hiroko's backpack was still secure between my shoulders and felt the same weight; a check of the satchel's contents confirmed everything was in there. He didn't mug me.

Not that I'd expected him to. I'd recognised him as Cassán Ó Grádaigh, my mother's father who she hadn't known, and if I wasn't certain when I stood facing him, I would be now after my vision.

He was *alive*.

'Where did you go?' I wondered aloud, looking around once again before crouching to inspect the seashell. 'Better question, why'd you leave me to drown?'

The shell had neither of these answers, but presented me with different ones, and new questions just to keep the score uneven. It was indeed the shell I'd scried several times in the past few weeks, and this was the same beach where I'd seen first Cassán and then another man, dressed more contemporarily, holding this shell. Neither of them had been shocked and knocked out, so there was the question of why it had picked on me. Let's overlook the question of how the same shell could still be in the same spot after so long. There was weirder stuff afoot.

It had a faint sense of magic around it, a spiky aura that I wasn't game to risk touching again. Like the deadlock at the compound, I scried my attention inside the polished spiral of its core. A simple gold wedding band, etched with wear, had somehow gotten inside. Explained the rattle when Cassán threw it. I could sense layers of complicated magic within the shell, all of it threaded through the ring itself. A power source? One of the spells felt a bit like the locked-door one Declan had taught me.

At the thought of my treacherous not-friend, I straightened and looked up and down the beach. How long had I been here? Where was here? Garrett might have given me the coordinates if I hadn't sent him home. The protection spells Declan and I had forged and the one I'd done on my own were nicely spread but so fragile that a mere misstep or hard breath of wind could undo them and leave me vulnerable.

An hour out from threatening Lisandro's life, vulnerable wasn't good. I hurried up the shore to the dry underside of the cliff and tipped the bags out. I was running low on materials; I'd need to stock up, somewhere. Somehow. I crushed up leaves and began the nonsense chant I'd picked up from Declan as I drew symbols in the gritty sand around the pile of gunk I was creating. I tilted my head to let the unsightly mop of my hair fall where I could see it, and with shaky hands I carved a chunk off the end that was likely much more than it looked. I could regret it later, once it dried and shortened. I summoned my magic to the spell and sealed it off, then pulled stones from the base of the cliff over to barricade it in.

Safe, or safer, I guessed. I repacked my bags but didn't watch what my sore hands did, sending my attention to check on the people I loved most.

Angela was on the phone. I heard her tell the caller, 'Aye, I understand.'

Hiroko was loading the dishwasher in her kitchen.

The Morrissey House gate was still closed, with Jackson and a bald man arguing quietly off to the side of the Magnus Moira crowd. I felt sure that whatever special information Garrett's mum had predicted he'd bring back, Renatus would know what to do with it.

I even checked in with my aunt's family, a unit I frequently forgot to include though I did love them dearly. Aunt Leanne, who looked like my dad Darren, was enjoying a sleep-in. My uncle was with my cousin Kelly, driving her somewhere, and on her lap she had real estate pamphlets. Was she considering moving out? I didn't even know. I assumed Angela did. She and Kelly were close in age, if not particularly close as cousins, and were in regular contact.

After all, despite the strained relationship between my sister and our aunt, we were a family. That counted for something. I got to my feet, momentarily inspired.

'Cassán?' I called, hoping. My voice carried, though maybe not far enough, so I lifted it. 'Cassán! Are you still there? I…' am your granddaughter that you probably didn't know you had. Never mind. 'I just want to talk to you!'

I yelled his name a dozen times before I gave up. I couldn't sense anyone around in my square kilometre-ish radius, and couldn't begin to guess how far away I was to anything worth heading for. I dropped back to my knees, disheartened.

Everything from the backpack was thankfully dry, but the satchel was damp. I wanted to find somewhere to get cleaned up and changed into dry clothes. This beach had all the hallmarks of a truly isolated, hidden place, but I didn't trust it for a second. Cassán had been here within the last hour, judging from the recession of the tide, and that other man had gotten here, too. It wasn't so private as it appeared.

The sand stretched almost a kilometre in total, framed and cut off by this imposing cliff, three storeys high except to my right, where it began to dip until it was only half that. I headed for that lower end. Reluctantly, I extended both hands and pressed them against the rough, salty rock and slowly ran them over the crevices as I walked. I winced to do it, but it was one of my most reliable superpowers.

The impressions were few, but insistent, the way they always felt when they'd waited forever trapped in time for a scrier to set them free.

A little girl of about eight… thick dark hair… small, scratched hands clawing at the rock… desperation… limping, an injured leg or ankle… more children looking over the top, anxious… one yells down a question…

Two hands, a man's hands, prying for cracks… desperation… the fair man from the beach…

A pair of lovers… her back presses hard against the cold rock… his hands cup her face… admiration, awe, excitement… eye contact, blue-green and warm hazel… she leans up for the kiss…

I withdrew my hand, breaking my connection with that previously private moment. That was one of the uncomfortable things about scrying – looking in on people who don't realise they're perpetually potentially under surveillance. I knew who both parties must be.

Cassán and Anthea Ó Grádaigh.

I turned to gaze out at the beautiful seascape. Finally, I knew where I was. I was in Greece, on the little unpronounceable island where my Irish grandfather met his future wife while travelling the world and writing his first book. I had few memories of either of my grandmothers, but of Nana Thea, I remembered some distinct elements. An armchair before a fire that was always roaring, even in the spring and autumn. A garden where you could eat nearly anything, and a stool in her kitchen where I would watch while Nana taught Angela to cook honey cake and koftas. And hanging in the windows, woven mobiles strung with seashells, some of which we made together.

Food, warmth and a love of the sea – that's what I remembered of my grandmother, along with the exciting exotic tones of her home language, of which I spoke none, but which Mum, Aidan and Angela understood perfectly when Nana Thea fell back into it. I wondered how much Ange remembered. I had never thought to ask.

At least when I saw her next, I'd have plenty of questions

lined up to deter hers, which I knew would be unpleasant to answer.

I wished that she were here to share this, though. I squinted up the cliff face into the bright glary sky. She should see this place. This was our heritage, and Cassán was our grandfather. If I could find him again, explain who I was, wouldn't he want to meet his surviving descendants?

I let my stiffening fingertips drift back across the smooth rock where my ancestors had – ahem, I'm so squeamish with this physical intimacy thing; I blame my prudish sister – made out. It wasn't that I wanted to spy on that, just that it was a moment of theirs that had been captured in time by the strength of its emotional intensity, and it was what was on offer. But it seemed I'd set it free, because when I touched the stone again, nothing else came forth.

The little girl, who'd presumably fallen down here at some point in the past, had found a way to escape this beautiful beach without Displacing, and if an eight-year-old could manage it, surely an eighteen-year-old White Elm apprentice could, too. I continued feeling for possible handholds, keeping myself open for impressions, but all I got were brief snapshots of the little girl and, later, the fair-haired man, doing exactly what I was doing now.

At the low end of the cliff the rock became rougher, more jagged, and impressions told me that the little girl had used crevices and cracks to climb back to her friends. Sadly, even with her ankle sprained, that kid was notably more athletic than me, or at least so much lighter that strength and athleticism didn't matter. Getting a solid grip on the first jutting stone that didn't give under pressure, I felt my scalded palms tearing when I bore my weight down to pull my feet up onto the wall.

How bad an option was Displacing, really? Shaking, I pushed upward, reaching for the crack above my head and stepping up to dig the toe of my boot into a little hollow. I kept my centre as close to the cliff wall as I could manage. Crevice, rock, crack, overhang, crack, I moved up slowly but with increasing confidence. I grabbed for the next rock and swung my leg up to the handhold I'd just vacated.

I missed. Or rather, the rock in my hand crumbled and my shoe slid short. My grip wasn't strong enough to counter the swing of my panicky scramble, and I fell from a height roughly equal to my own. I closed my eyes tightly when I knew it was inevitable, preparing for the sharp and plentiful pain.

But something caught me. The pain didn't come. My eyelids snapped open when I felt someone's wary, frightened hopefulness instead of the slam of gravity, and I found myself suspended a few centimetres off the stones, just floating in the air in the same awkward position I'd fallen in.

I wasn't alone anymore.

I struggled upright, impeded by the delicate webbing of magic holding my weight. It fell away and I got my feet under me, straightening to face the old man standing nearby. There was nothing to indicate where he'd come from, and he was watching me with a disbelieving sort of longing.

'Thank you,' I said, nothing else obvious coming to mind. He stared, expression and emotions becoming more conflicted by the second, and it took him many seconds before he managed to speak.

'You… You aren't… Elysia?'

He said my mother's name kind of separate to the rest of the sentence, like he was asking it as a question all its own. Like he wanted me to refute the claim. I shook my head slowly, detecting his fragile and flighty emotional state and not wanting to spook him. How best to tell him he was a grandfather? Did he know? He frowned and touched the cliff beside him where I'd been trailing my hands for impressions before. The skin on the backs of his hands was dry and roughened from exposure, but also looked… cracked. Burnt? The stiff way his fingers worked the stone suggested arthritis or skin that wouldn't give.

'My name is Aristea,' I told him gently, 'and I'm her daughter.'

It went down as expected. His face and emotions fluctuated wildly as he attempted, on some level, to assimilate this claim with his reality. Disbelief, anger, fear, hope, sadness and surprise all took their uneven turns in the flash of a moment before he turned abruptly away from me and hurried in the opposite direction.

I didn't know where he thought he was going on this enclosed beach, but I also didn't know where he'd been only seconds ago, so I followed.

'Cassán, wait! Please, talk to me,' I called after him. He shot me a glare over his shoulder and snapped a reply, saving me from coming up with a reason why he should.

'How do you know me?' he demanded. He didn't slow down, churning sand under slogging bare feet. His clothes were colourless with age and filth, his short trousers torn and his hair ratty and overlength. He looked like a shipwrecked sailor, and his wild emotions suggested he was maybe just as addled as one. I trailed behind, weighing up how to reply.

'I've seen you in my dreams,' I admitted, and he did actually slow down, not stopping but dropping his pace to listen. 'I see scenes from your life as a young man in the nineteen-sixties. You with your friends at a New Year's party, a ritual, a christening at Morrissey House–'

The man I'd spent my whole life believing was dead pulled up short, wavering in shock with one foot still in the air, and grasped at the rough cliff face to keep from falling. I stopped too, not wanting to get too close and upset him again. He turned his head to address me over his shoulder.

'What ritual?'

I tried not to think too hard about that dream. I'd woken from it deeply disturbed, imagery of blood and death and fire lingering in my subconscious for days after. But I pulled what I remembered back to the forefront of my mind now to be able to answer. It was thankfully little.

'Five people on fire in a field,' I recalled, eliciting a sick feeling from us both. 'Burnt hands.' I lowered my gaze to his oddly textured hands, which he self-consciously tucked behind his back. I swallowed. 'Blood on the ground. I don't remember all the details.'

He snorted to cover his discomfort. 'Consider yourself lucky. Who did you say you were?'

I inhaled slowly, realising properly that I was getting the chance to introduce myself to my grandfather. 'I'm Aristea Byrne. I'm... your granddaughter.'

It was as direct as I could get, but this time he ignored it completely.

'Those things you saw. Why do you see them?'

'I don't know yet,' I confessed. 'Maybe they're significant to me and my journey? I mean, you studied Fate, wrote those books. Maybe Fate wants you to help–'

'No, why *can* you see it?' he interrupted, dismissing my suggestion. He eyed me suspiciously, his attention moving over my aura. I felt it at the edges of my energy. 'Scrier.' He didn't sound pleased, but did seem intrigued when he asked, 'Which are you? Morrissey or O'Malley?' He scowled. 'You'd best not tell me some tragic twist of Fate landed my daughter with one of them to produce *you*.'

Lovely. 'I'm neither, but I know them both,' I said, a little defensive. 'And there must be lots of other scrier family lines.'

'None who could see the things you claim to,' Cassán responded irritably. 'Those events were protected, heavily spelled. Only Mánus or Lorcan, or one of their sons, could see something like that. There are no scriers in my line. So you, young lady, whoever you are, are a liar, and you need to leave.'

He spun on his heel and continued striding away. I frowned at his back. I had expected him to find my existence difficult to swallow, not to dismiss me for being a scrier. I should have been gentler, but I fell into my standard approach for dealing with Renatus when he was being unreasonable: bluntness. I raised my voice to be heard.

'Their sons are dead,' I said flatly, 'and their grandsons didn't see any of what I saw.'

Again, he almost fell over, but this time he grasped his chest, like my words physically hurt. He took a long time to turn around. When he did, his eyes sought mine, and the expression had changed. Less cold, less wary, the shape of his eyes and their sea-blue colour were easier to place in my memory. I'd seen them in my sister's face.

'Mánus has a grandson?' he asked me finally, voice soft. I tried to soften, too. I nodded. His expression spasmed into a pained frown that held a lot of turbulence back. 'How long have I been here?'

That wasn't a question I was ready for. 'I, uh… I don't know.'

His response looked like it broke his heart.

'Neither do I.'

I swallowed and pulled at my sleeve.

'I know Mánus was your friend,' I said, revealing my wrist and letting him see my tattoo. 'His grandson is my friend, too. I'm his apprentice. And I really am your granddaughter.' I paused as he came nervously closer, leaning heavily on the rock face. This question had been nagging at me for months, ever since I learned of Cassán and Mánus's connection, and I'd finally found the best person to ask. 'Is that Fate?'

Cassán's emotions had been conflicted since I first spotted him, but they deepened now with something like resignation. He stared for a long, loaded moment at my tattoo.

'It sounds like it, yes,' he agreed eventually. 'It's Fate that you're here at all.' More briskly, he nodded at my red palms. 'Those burns. I think I have something. You should come inside.'

He let go of the rock wall and turned straight into it, disappearing from my sight. The rugged stone did not part or shimmer or do any of the things you might expect from a magical portal. I tentatively touched the place he went through.

Solid.

But he did invite me in. I looked around, seeing nobody and nothing helpful in sight. No one bad had found me. Cassán was such an excellent lead, I couldn't really do anything but follow. Fate dropped me here, hopefully for a reason. I walked back to where I'd left my two bags, slung them over my shoulders, and returned to the exact spot he'd disappeared through. I closed my eyes. Renatus's house had wormholes like this, seemingly solid walls and cupboard doors that only allowed his bloodline to sense and use them. I didn't know if this was the same on a functional level, but I had to believe I could make it through.

I stepped forward, and my foot landed on the other side.

chapter twenty

It was as though the cliff face dissolved. I opened my eyes to the mouth of an odd-shaped cave. It was high and wide enough for a person to comfortably stand in, but then immediately narrowed and twisted to the right amid jagged stalagmites to disappear around a dark corner. The false wall now behind me, my awareness of this cavern opened up and I could feel its surprising depth.

I could sense Cassán's retreating presence around that twisty unwelcoming bend, but more intensely, the lived-in-ness of the rocky space. As if it weren't already obvious from his rough appearance, Cassán lived in this cave, and had done for a very long time. The closest approximation I had for this kind of emotional radiation – memories and tense moments laying thick on walls, objects, things – was Renatus's house, where grief and loss had lain undisturbed for years and years and hardly anyone had come or gone. I was finding less and less there as time went on, the presences of so many oblivious new inhabitants clearing some of that stale energy, but this place, I knew even before I touched the stone, had been barely disturbed in much longer than that. Decades.

I shook out the sting in my red hands.

'Here goes,' I muttered, and didn't bother to hide my wince as I spread my fingers across the cave wall.

Hands…

Middle-aged Cassán collapses against this wall, sobbing… nursing shaking hands, blackened and raw like the regret he wears…

Younger, Cassán with wide eyes leans here to peer into the gloom… wonder…

Older, bearded now… haunted eyes the colour of the sea… carrying a fresh-caught fish…

I usually avoided accessing impressions like these, intense as they promised to be, but I kept myself steady and navigated the awkward bend in the passage without breaking my connection to the images. Cassán, Cassán, Cassán, all different stages of adult life, always alone, never content.

But at the bend, I got my first impression of someone *other* than my long-lost grandfather.

Stabilising hand on the rock… a familiar black etched stone set into a plain silver ring… wariness, hopelessness… a small man in his mid-twenties… curly fair hair… 'Hello? Is someone there?'…

'Is someone there?'

The question rebounded from the cave walls as I got my footing on the other side of the jagged stalagmites. I looked up at Cassán Ó Grádaigh as he retraced his steps to face me. His intense emotions came with him, a conflicted mess of shock and uncertainty and a whole host of other things I could barely identify. I forced a quick smile. I hadn't meant to hold him up.

'How did you get in here?' he demanded, looking me over with a mixed expression. I tried to hold onto that reassuring smile when he added, angrily, 'Who are you?'

He'd just forgotten my name, I told myself, so I repeated it for him. My name was unusual. Fair enough. But there was no flicker of recognition in his face.

'What do you want?'

I frowned, extending my hands in reminder. 'You told me you had something for these burns.'

We both flinched at the intensity of his emotional recoil. He refused to look at my hands, glaring off to the side. He cradled his own hands in closer, immensely vulnerable and furious for it.

'I have nothing for you,' he snapped. 'Now, *get out*.'

The words were backed up with some sort of targeted

emotional *push*. I felt the change in the air around me and knew it immediately for the same persuasive power Lisandro exerted as a Crafter, the same card he'd played this morning before I'd turned it back on him, only this was much stronger. My barriers were low from tapping the impressions on the walls, so despite *knowing* what it was, and *knowing* I was capable of deflecting it, I let it get the better of me. The power of his insistence twisted my feelings to reflect his.

A conflicted mess that was mostly anger and resentment swelled in my chest.

'*Fine*,' I snapped back, already turning away. 'Go back to your miserable solitude. I don't need your help anyway.'

The stalagmites, if that's what they were, prevented me from dramatically stomping out of there, but once I clambered my way back over those almost knee-high rock formations that blocked the entrance, I was back on gravelly sand and free to stride as heavily as I pleased right out onto the beach. The two-way illusion that guarded the cave mouth did not show from this side.

The storminess inside me did not go away, and to prove it I kicked sand and muttered to myself all the way to the shoreline where I impulsively Displaced away, for better or worse. In my anger I couldn't remember why I hadn't done that sooner. I was still furious when I landed on a flat roadside somewhere much higher. I glared around at my new surroundings; they weren't that new. The same scorched sky spanned over wild island country with the same weathered, wiry flora growing out of what looked like inhospitable rock, and at the far edge of my line of sight, the rugged land dropped away to a glorious blue-green sea. Were those Cassán's cliffs?

I began walking the other way determinedly, never ever wanting to go back there, though didn't get far before I had to pull up and rethink this acting-out approach. A kilometre or so ahead down this bumpy and currently empty lane to nowhere, there was an actual town.

Towns had people, showers, food and beds. I had about twenty minutes to get my anger under control so I could work out how to nicely ask for these precious commodities.

It was much warmer up here on the island proper than down on Cassán's secret beach, the sun still beaming down on the back of my head, but even still, the long walk was a good cooling-off process. It only took a couple of minutes of irritable reflection to acknowledge that storming off was a total overreaction to the old man's random rudeness, and just another minute to concede that memory issues were a common side effect of getting old. Maybe the time elapsed when I'd fallen behind in the cave had been long enough for him to forget he'd invited me in. Yes, it was weird and unreasonable for him to send me away, but what had given me the idea I was dealing with a reasonable person? How old would he be – seventy-something, eighty? And how long had he been alone?

The image of the man wearing the Elm Stone stuck out from the various visions of Cassán's time there, and I wondered who he was and why he'd sought out my grandfather. Not alone for as long as I'd expected.

I neared the town and began to spread my senses through the buildings. A few hundred people, including a handful of witches of low to moderate power. Higher than the usual density you'd expect to find in any given population, but not so high as to worry me that I was walking toward another Magnus Moira encampment. Some communities had deeper connections with their magical ancestors than others, and remote places, with fewer people coming and going, could easily grow larger magical subpopulations over time. Maybe this was one of them. Maybe that was why my grandfather had gravitated to this location in the first place.

My grandfather. I had found Nana Thea's long-lost husband, the family mystery. He was *here*, just over those cliffs behind me. And he wanted nothing to do with me. I looked up at the wide sky, picturing my sister and bringing her location immediately to mind.

'You should be here, Ange,' I whispered as she went about her day, oblivious. 'You'd know what to say to him.'

The first person I saw at the edge of the cute shanty tourist town gave me such a look that I knew an illusion was in order before I went any further, and I hid my filthy appearance behind the image of the nobody I'd played at the Magnus Moira camp. The next eyes that caught on me only expressed the owner's curiosity to see a stranger walking into town. I gathered from a few clues, including the remoteness and the width of the road, that this was a day stop on a couple of regular coach routes and visitors didn't have the option of staying on. Aside from some tourist-trap style souvenir stores and an overly Greek restaurant with English signage announcing *Giannopoulos Family Restaurant* at the head of the town, I didn't detect anything that would entice outsiders to stay longer than a few hours, and I didn't see any other holidaymakers when I stepped inside the restaurant. Locals only – you can always tell from the way they dress and present, the lack of extra bags and cameras and hats, that people belong in a particular place. Their jovial noise and connectedness supported my theory. Lots of eyes went to me. I was glad my salt-streaked mop of hair was hidden under the veneer of magic.

It seemed from the table arrangements that I'd walked in on a private function, and the chalkboard beside the door explained the situation entirely in Greek. Trickling with concern and curiosity, a tall woman with an apron that sported the establishment's name and logo bustled over to me.

'Are you alright? Are you lost?' she asked immediately, looking me over with narrow eyes. She was one of the town's witches, and undoubtedly recognised me as one, too. 'There has been no bus in three days.'

She thought I'd been left behind and somehow gone unnoticed for all this time. I shook my head.

'I came here on my own,' I told her. 'I'm on a sort of… road trip. Around the world. Finding myself.' It wasn't a lie. She nodded like she heard this a fair bit, some of her concern relaxing but not all. Something else was bothering her. I gestured at the other customers. 'I wanted to order some lunch and use a restroom, but if you're full I can go somewhere else–'

'No, no, stay, stay,' the woman insisted, switching quickly back to host mode. She ushered me toward a wide bar near the front counter, and when I was sitting on one of the tall barstools, I had a view directly into the kitchen where three cooks were filling orders and talking just as loudly as the guests. Above that window, a large colour photo of a huge family of mostly daughters held pride of place. A Greek menu was in front of me, and I perused it mildly while my host fussed over wiping the bar and filling a glass of water for me. I wondered again whether Angela would be able to read any of this. Probably not. The host pointed out a white door beyond the kitchen. 'The restrooms are through there. What can I get you? Oh.' She noticed the Greek language menu in front of me, guessing correctly that I couldn't read it. 'English?'

At my relieved nod, she swiftly switched it with a similar-looking laminate from under the counter. She stood aside to let two girls a little younger than me pass with their hands full of platters. The critical eye she cast over them told me that this was her restaurant and that these were her daughters. I watched them too, thinking they looked familiar. They both had enviably wild curls that framed their faces and shoulders like manes and were tall with coltish teen bodies. One was carrying a loaded-up entrée plate of steaming courgette balls that, along with the waft of mint and dill I got as it moved further away, brought back memories of Nana's kitchen. I sat up straighter.

'Is that *kolokithokeftedes*?' I asked, the mouthful of a word I'd struggled with as a little girl now rolling off my tongue. My host cocked her head, surprised. 'My grandmother was Greek, and my grandfather still lives here.' Over the cliffs in a cave, you know how it is. Totally normal family. 'Nana used to make them.'

'One plate?' the woman asked, both of us glancing over as another table went up in uproarious laughter. The mood of the room was jovial, celebratory. Despite her polite smile and attentiveness, my host did not share the feelings of her guests. I tried not to wonder; I didn't know the capabilities of the witch folk around me. Didn't need another Egan situation. I placed my order and got down from my stool, glancing around the restaurant on my way to the bathroom. Some of them were sorcerers, but they were lowish in power and seemed completely absorbed in good company and better conversation.

The restroom was small but I relished that space. I locked myself in a cubicle to strip off my damp clothes and get totally changed. In lieu of a hot shower, this was the next best thing. Freshly dressed, I bundled my previous outfit back into my bags. At the sinks I washed my face and still-pink hands of the grime and sand that was pretty much everywhere. My hair was starting to dry in unpredictable kinks and bends, and that chop I'd taken out this morning had become unpleasantly evident. Couldn't be helped.

Feeling more human, I restored any gaps in my illusory face and returned to the barstool, where one of the owner's daughters was just arranging my bowl of fried courgette fritters and tzatziki.

'*Kalí órexi,*' she said automatically when I thanked her, casting me the quickest of cool smiles. I froze, realising who she reminded me of. *No. Way.* I followed her back to the serving window to look up at the photo of the owner's family.

The Giannopoulos family.

'Xanthe,' I muttered in disbelief, staring into the photographed gaze of my least favourite classmate at the Academy. Unlike her sisters, the girl I knew had their mother's straight hair, but the same height, the same wiry figure, the same eyes. In my experience they were usually narrowed at me, spiteful and unfriendly ever since she'd mistaken my late-night missions as Renatus's apprentice for something sexual. She'd been proven wrong, but she'd never backed down, never apologised for turning our other roommate Sterling against me for that perceived betrayal, and certainly never told me her family owned a restaurant just a few kilometres from where my infamous grandfather was holed up in a cave.

Not that I expected her to know that. Her mother, just stepping out of the kitchen, overheard me uttering her daughter's name and halted.

'You know my Xanthe?' she asked warily. Unwilling hope sparked behind her eyes and I felt its sharp, uncomfortable edges. 'From the school? In... Ireland?' She'd made the connection between my accent and magical aura and my recognition of her child, and didn't need my confirmation. Her hope grew, and she palmed the plates she carried off to the next server, passing on instructions in hurried Greek I had no hope of following. Xanthe's mother turned back to me with the intensity of a parent separated from their child, and I understood now that suppressed, simmering discontent I'd sensed in her. 'Is she alright? We haven't heard from her since this began.'

Like Renatus, like the twins and Addison and Iseult and Sterling and now Garrett and Josh, her daughter was trapped inside the estate. Magnus Moira had control of the gate and with nobody getting in or out, it hadn't occurred to me that none of the students would be able to communicate with their families.

'I got out before the lockdown started,' I explained in apology, hurting to feel my host's disappointment. 'My friends are still inside and I can't talk to them. What have you been told?'

The woman sighed and played with the edges of a dishtowel, leaning on the bar while I circled around to return to my seat.

'We don't know how much to believe,' she admitted. 'The council has been here twice, assuring us that the children are safe and unharmed, continuing with lessons. Happy. Well fed.' She said this like she doubted anyone could feed her child as well as she could, and smelling the plate of food under my nose, I understood her stance. 'But they can't get letters or parcels through to her or back to me, and they can't say when she will be free to leave. They don't seem to have any plan at all for getting my daughter back. Eat, eat,' she encouraged suddenly, noticing my food untouched. I hurried to comply.

'You must be so worried,' I said before biting into the first delicious fritter. It had different spicy flavours from the ones Angela made. Xanthe's mother pursed her lips, emotions darkening.

'I *am* worried,' she said, then paused. 'They're letting these rebels get the better of them. Just not the council they used to be, I fear.'

I swallowed my mouthful. 'You mean because of all the rules?'

My host recoiled as if I'd suggested she was a traitor, and

316

with unease I thought of my own minor treason, leaving evidence of murder with a council detractor petitioning for their dismantling.

'No, we've always supported the White Elm,' she insisted. 'We've seen the alternative. They sent their Healer for our Eleni and chased down the charlatan who tricked us. They have been good to our community. Good for my family, good for the world. So when Xanthe told us for days that they would come for her and that she had to play her part in preserving and restoring their ways, we were proud to let her go. We *are* proud. They said she's very talented, and we know she is. Very proud,' the mother repeated to herself, glancing around her restaurant to check on her other daughters. I listened with interest.

'What did she mean by "restoring their ways"?' I asked. Xanthe's mum caught one of the other daughters by the arm on her way into the kitchen to give her a quick instruction, pointing to one of the fullest tables, and the girl nodded with the same detached efficiency I associated with her eldest sister. When she spun, her hair moved off her face, and I took note of a drooping eyebrow, a nearly closed eye and a slack jaw on one side. It looked like nerve damage, or maybe the aftereffects of a past stroke.

'That's our Eleni,' the mother said as the girl walked away. Thirteen-ish and curly-haired, I watched her chatting to the cooks. From my observations, none of the family were high-powered like me. Xanthe must have been an exception. Magical genetics were unpredictable like that. 'She had a brain tumour. The doctors couldn't help, but word spread to a town on the other side of the island and a visitor came, claiming he could fix her. We paid him; his magic was dirty, wrong, and it backfired.'

'And Eleni paid the price,' I guessed. As I was learning, magic always had a cost, though the "clean" White Elm magic mitigated a lot of that. 'What happened...? Wait, I'm sorry,' I quickly backtracked, recognising the imposition. 'I shouldn't ask. You don't even know me.'

My host waved aside my concerns. 'You are a friend of my Xanthe's, no?'

No, not really. We had hardly spoken to one another in months unless you counted two screaming matches in the dining hall and a lot of conversing with other people (namely Sterling and Hiroko, respectively) while pretending the other didn't exist, all while sharing a bedroom. Awkward? Yes.

'We had some classes together,' I invented diplomatically, not really quite lying. This family was aware of their magic – they'd detect lies for sure – so I was careful with my wording when I added, 'You can call me Marcy.'

I mean, you can. Anyone can if they want to. South African Marcy Pretoria was one of the first to depart the Academy and though I knew little else about her except what political observations she'd written in her blog, I happened to know she had done some globetrotting. I doubted Xanthe had a means of confirming if her mum ever mentioned Marcy visiting.

'Xanthe doesn't talk about what happened with Eleni but it's why she was so sure she wanted to attend the Academy,' Mrs Giannopoulos told me, emotion curling around her with all the colours of memory. I kept eating while she spoke, the noisy happy chatter of the restaurant continuing around us. I hadn't known that Xanthe had such noble motivations for apprenticing with the council – certainly nobler than my self-centred "I just want to learn all the stuff" reasons. She was hard to connect with, hard to warm to, and though I'd tried to make friends, I'd ultimately read her as an unkind stirrer of malcontent. She had some conservative views that had served to cement our split. I had never worked out what her initial problem was with me, or why she'd been so certain I would betray Sterling's trust.

Still talking about Eleni's tragic childhood prognosis, her mother refilled my water, though I'd only drunk half. I'd barely said twenty words; twenty words would be like pulling teeth from Xanthe, yet her mother was so boisterous and chatty.

'The White Elm was on top of things even before we tried to contact them. That Healer, Miranda, stopped the seizures that *criminal* started in our baby, and worked with us to reduce the tumour. She saved her. See?' She pointed to one of the smaller photo frames adorning the walls. My eyes scoured for a few seconds for what she might be referring to, then noticed a chunky frame with one wallet-sized photo wedged into the crease between the frame and the glass, half-obscuring the larger, faded picture of a younger Lady Miranda smiling with a bald toddler. Little Eleni's face was severely affected by apparent paralysis on one side, demonstrating the immense improvement the Healer's work had afforded her patient.

Like she had with me and my face after Lisandro nearly took out my eye. I averted my gaze from the photograph, recalling Lady Miranda's disappointed expression the last time I'd seen her. I'd let them all down by lying to protect Renatus. I still believed it was the only right thing to do, at least until I knew what had *actually* happened at Shanahan's, but it didn't feel great to fail the reasonable expectations of a solidly good person who'd done nothing but right by me and many others.

Xanthe and Eleni's mother was still talking, oblivious to my reflections.

'And about four years ago now,' she went on, plucking out the smaller photo from the corner of that frame, 'they even sent their new Healer to check on our progress. She corrected some of the damage we had thought was permanent, gave her back some sensation and movement in her face. What was her name? She was wonderful, too. The French one.'

'Emmanuelle,' I supplied helpfully, leaning forward on the bar to look at the picture. Another incredible woman and sorcerer I'd left frustrated when I chose Renatus over the rest. Gods, I hoped she was still alive to berate me for it when I finally got back there. 'I didn't know she and Xanthe had met before the Academy.'

'No, they didn't,' her mother confirmed, laying the photo flat for me once she'd dusted it off. 'Xanthe and the others were at school the day they visited.'

'They?' I asked, but the answer was in the photo. Mrs Giannopoulos animatedly described the two council sorcerers and their lovely working manner with Eleni, but I hardly listened. The photograph she'd proudly captured of her daughter with her high-profile saviours featured the exquisitely pretty Emmanuelle Saint Clair on one side and a man I'd never met on the other. He was small-framed, curly-haired and blue-eyed, and like Cassán, I knew him immediately from prior visions.

The bus, helping the old lady.

The beach, picking up the shell.

The cave, calling out.

And vaguely, a rainy funeral, though he was very young there. Maybe twelve?

'Who is he?' I asked, touching his plain, friendly face with my fingertip. He didn't look like a sorcerer, especially next to Emmanuelle whose long flowing hair and never-ending collection of corsets seemed to situate her squarely in the centre of a renaissance novel. He looked just… normal. Xanthe's mother frowned as she tried to recall the name.

'You know, I should have written it down at the time,' she said remorsefully, flipping the photo hopefully, but there was nothing on the back. 'A very nice young man. It was good of him to accompany his friend on her rounds. Communities like ours would be lost without the White Elm's outreach work. No one moves here and no one leaves, and any skills we don't have between us already are inaccessible or forgotten. He and the Healer both agreed, something needed to be done to get the skills back into the small towns and remote places. A few years later they developed the school.'

She left me to my meal when one of the other tables called her over for a rowdy toast. I picked at my food, gazing at the picture. I still didn't know the man, but I mostly looked at young Emmanuelle. I had admired her deeply ever since I met her. She'd only be twenty-one, maybe twenty-two in this photograph, and yet she was travelling the world making house calls and fixing up magically maimed children.

If she were here, she wouldn't be sitting at a bar eating Greek snacks while a grumpy old man in a cave stood between her and answers. She'd take advantage of this lapse in attackers and drama. She would do what needed doing and be out of this place, on to the next problem she could solve.

I had a long way to go before I was as cool as Emmanuelle, I decided as I slid from my barstool and wiped my hands clean, but now was as good a time as any to continue trying. I carefully picked up the photograph and slotted it back into its place with Lady Miranda and little Eleni.

Xanthe's mum bustled back over, concerned to see me looking ready to leave.

'Yes, I'm so sorry, I just realised the time,' I made up, and praised the food, which had been delicious. She offered to package the rest for takeaway and I told her she didn't have to, but once I put too much money in her hand in thanks, she wouldn't hear of me leaving without the remainder. It went in a paper bag and then we were shaking hands. 'It was very nice to meet you. I hope you don't worry too much about Xanthe. Some of the best White Elm councillors are locked inside the estate with her, and they won't let a thing happen to any of them.'

I didn't know the town, but it wasn't hard to find a lane between buildings where no one could see me Displace. I didn't worry at all about screwing up my landing, and I didn't. My shoes hit the sand a few paces from the seashell. I strode straight for the cliff wall, realising the shell aligned with the cave opening.

This wasn't a coincidence. Regardless of whether he wanted my company, I was *meant* to be here. There were questions that could only be answered by this one old man, and the web of names and connections couldn't be ignored.

My grandfather, friend of Renatus's grandfather, gone for years and now suddenly alive.

A mysterious White Elm sorcerer.

The prisoners at Lisandro's compound, crazy Eugene and the dimpled Empath, and what the Empath had shown me to combat Lisandro's gifts, had perfectly prepped me for my arrival here. It was as though I'd needed to be there, with those people, when Lisandro turned on his charm, so I'd know what it was when Cassán hit me with the same.

It must have been the fact that his name was fresh on my mind. I walked directly into the cliff wall, full of misplaced faith in my own memory of where the gap was, and my shoulder scraped the unforgiving rock. Yelping with pain, I must have extended a hand.

A bigger hand… going the other way, pausing at the cave mouth and surveying the sea… a sheet of paper in his other hand… a list, the list… bronze-brown eyes adjusting to the change of light… excitement, determination…

I drew a sharp breath. Was I the *only* person who hadn't known my grandfather was hidden here? Lisandro had visited. When? Why? If he had that list with him, it couldn't be good, right?

There was only one person who could tell me. I picked my way over the stalagmites more quickly this time, calling ahead to keep from surprising the man I could sense deeper in the cavern.

'Cassán? Can you hear me?' I yelled in case his hearing was compromised with age. I dropped the illusion hiding my true face. 'I'm coming back in.'

My bags kept catching but then I was through, and I jogged the rest of the way to the old man just standing from a battered excuse for an old coffee table. His conflicted emotional profile hit me like a wall, and I slowed. He stared at me through the darkness of the cave in pained disbelief.

'Cassán?' I repeated, trying to gauge where he was at. He took an unsteady step closer. 'Do you remember me?'

His reply was a strained whisper.

'How are you here?' he asked, dousing me accidentally with his regrets and sorrow. He kept squinting, trying to make out my features. 'Thea, I'm so sorry…'

I touched my hair with my free hand, feeling the fluffiness of my normally manageable locks. I had my mother's colouring, skin not as warm as Nana Thea's rich olive but certainly darker than my fair siblings. I hadn't seen many pictures of my grandmother as a young woman and it had never occurred to me that I might look like her. In the dark of the cave, to a man whose grasp on time and reality seemed a little sketchy, perhaps I really did. Pitying, I tossed a spark of magic from my hand into the stale air above us, and a pale, sourceless glow spread through the cavern, eliminating the shadows and the ambiguity with them, I hoped.

Cassán drew back, seeing me for who I was, or rather who I wasn't.

'Not Thea,' I said. His embarrassment to mistake a stranger for his wife was already twisting into something ugly. 'Her granddaughter, and yours, Aristea. I want to know–'

'Get out!' he shouted at me, once again turning his demand into a persuasive push on my feelings. Making me want to leave, making me angry, making me feel ashamed. My fists clenched. But on the teetering edge of turning away, I instead found the control to replicate the mirroring I'd learnt this morning from the Avalonian.

'No,' I answered, shoving his feelings back to him and tightening my wards in case he tried something more violent. His eyes widened, and I knew he knew what I was doing. 'Fate brought me here. I want to know why Lisandro came to you and what you talked about. He left with this.'

I opened my satchel to dig for the list I'd grabbed from Renatus's desk the day I'd run away, the list Peter used to wrap the Elm Stone before burying it in Emmanuelle's garden, the list with my own name on it and Renatus's and Cassán's and my brother's and sister's and mother's and a whole bunch more. But my grandfather wasn't paying attention to that.

'You're the Empath,' he stated in realisation. His anger was already filtering away, leaving a twisted approximation of awe. He was no longer directing anything at me, and I stopped deflecting. 'The one I saw when…' He shook that memory away, disturbed. Quieter, he told me, 'You were shown to me. A long… a long time ago.'

I didn't know what to do with this claim, and concentrated on shaking the list free of my bag and presenting it to Cassán.

'Can you look at this, please, and tell me–'

'I don't need to look,' he interrupted me. 'I only need to know what you want with those names.'

I stared at him, running low on patience but keeping my face smooth. I couldn't guess what reply he was expecting and extended my emotional feelers past the wall of cold calm he'd erected between us. He shook his head.

'I know you're frustrated but you're not going to read anything different from me,' he said, surprising me with his unexpected insight. 'I want your truth before I tell you anything.'

'I *have been* telling you the truth,' I retorted, then made a more important connection. '*You're* an Empath, too?'

Of course he was. He raised a condescending eyebrow and said, with more self-awareness than I'd detected from him thus far, 'Where do you think you got it from?'

It shouldn't have surprised me, really. He was right – other magical families I knew had traceable lineages of particular powers, like Renatus's and Declan's talents for scrying and Hiroko's gift of Displacement. Though neither my mother nor my siblings had displayed the same sensitivity to others' emotions, and though I knew pure chance played a part in all magical gifts, I also knew that genetics were significant. It made sense that it came from somewhere.

What was more surprising was that until this morning, I'd never met another Empath in my whole life, then in the space of hours, I'd encountered *two*. And one was my grandparent.

'So you do accept that we're related,' I grumbled, stepping closer to brandish the old list at him. 'What do I want with these names? I want them to stop dying, especially since one of them is mine and…' *and I can't lose Renatus or Angela like I lost the rest of my family*. I went quiet because Cassán had carefully, finally, accepted the loose page from me. His finger found the struck-through name that I somehow knew he would gravitate to, and traced it delicately.

Knowing grief preceded his question, which he ended up phrasing as a statement.

'This is why *you're* here,' he guessed flatly, 'and not her.'

He took a few moments to swallow the pain of confirmation of his daughter's death and all the hang-ups that must go along with that. The realisation that he'd missed her whole life. The horror of outliving her and not even knowing when she'd left the world. I didn't know I was experiencing the same hurt until I felt tears dripping from my chin. Hurriedly I wiped them away and breathed through the tightness spreading through my chest at the memories rising in my mind. Was it common knowledge that getting two Empaths in a cave together was a recipe for a sob fest?

'I left her to keep her safe from me,' my mother's father confessed, staring at Elysia's name written in Lisandro's handwriting, 'but I always hoped she would find me, before… I should have known nothing I did would save her from what I am.'

I swallowed the lump in my throat. I didn't know what he meant, though that hardly mattered. I'd been going about this all wrong. He was an Empath. I was Empath. We'd loved the same person, loved her with all we were, and our grief was the same, even if we were living in different realities in most of the ways that mattered. Our grief was the same.

'I'm sorry,' I said honestly, maybe the most genuine I'd been since I met him. 'I can tell you about her life, if you want.'

He was old now, worn and beaten by time and life, drowning in his own regrets and insecurities, but I saw a shadow of the man I'd seen in my nightmares of his life. A man who knew more than he could be content with and who wanted more than anything for someone to tell him how to make it all stop and turn it off, but also a man who understood that sometimes, that someone needed to be him. He turned away and put a few paces between us, still lightly touching the crossed-out name of his only child.

'I would like that,' he agreed eventually, clearing the tightness in his throat. His emotions and mine ran rampant in the cavernous space; anyone else silly enough to walk in at that moment would have been very upset, and I mean, I was too, but not in a bad way. I let his sadness seep through my barriers and took in as much of his pain as I needed to understand him. I was closely attuned to him and felt his drawback. 'But you shouldn't waste your time on me, and that's not why you're here. You're here about Moira's boy.' He looked over his shoulder and sniffed the air, distracted. 'Is that *kolokithokeftedes*?'

I threw him the paper bag and he caught it in one hand. Reflexes like mine, despite his age and ruined hands. I watched him ravenously, awkwardly open the bag, thoughts still on his prior mention. *Moira*. I turned the name over in my head, some of those dark and distressing memories from Cassán's life surfacing. A coven recruitment poster on a café door. A horrific fertility spell in the jungle, two dozen men flayed alive. A dingy basement with a leaky pipe, and a college-aged beauty with dark hair and bronze-brown eyes reading White Elm letters to four men with a charismatic fervour that saw them all throw their futures in with hers.

I knew those bronze eyes and those striking features.

'You mean Lisandro,' I realised, connections I should have made months ago falling into place. Moira, Cassán, Mánus, Andrew and Eugene – the first five names on the list, and the founders of the Magnus Moira movement. Lisandro had grown up with the sons of Mánus and Andrew. Like brothers, Declan had said. I'd just never known why.

'Still a stupid name,' my grandfather muttered as he dug into the paper bag for my leftovers with his stiff scarred fingers. I felt my mouth quirk. I squared my shoulders.

'Lisandro's the one exception on that list,' I told him, feeling uncharacteristically brave for bringing this up. I hadn't shared this with *anyone*, and usually went to pains not to even think it. For some reason, I felt compelled to spill this damning secret to this man I had just met. 'I'm going to kill him.'

I said it though I'd failed at that very task just hours before. Cassán Ó Grádaigh shoved a courgette fritter into his mouth whole and chewed loudly, surveying me without judgement. Unable to breathe steadily, I held my ground, waiting for the condemnation or the strong advice that I rethink my approach. He swallowed.

'I hope so,' he said finally, looking for the next cooling fritter in the bag, 'but you might be too late, because he came here to learn the path to immortality.'

chapter twenty-one

His godfather was as good as his word. It wasn't often that Renatus had opportunity to think so, but he slid down that secret door without anyone coming to bother him. Either Lisandro meant what he said and Renatus was free to come and go, or whatever had distracted him into leaving had delayed him from sending minions to attack. Both seemed as likely as the other.

Freshly alone, his thoughts cycled clunkily through his head. Who to trust, what to do, what to think? Scried images took advantage of his inner chaos.

Rain lashes at trees... branches torn free... screams ripped away, his parents nowhere to be found...

Fire under his skin... no escape, panic... high white ceiling, vaulted door...

The gate, safely locked... the crowd outside it animated with expectation... a sudden Displacement, two teenaged boys... confusion, Jackson trying to calm it...

Renatus stood abruptly, insides clenching with uncomfortable surprise. Garrett Fischer and Joshua Reyes had just landed outside the estate. At the theatre he'd seen them defect, though they were in a decidedly worse state now, Garrett dragging Josh to the gate while Jackson tried to organise the ragtag Magnus Moira supporters. The Crafter yelled for them to stand down and wait for an order, but was frowning, suspicious, and Renatus knew this was only a moment's reprieve. Something was wrong.

'Aristea,' he knew with certainty, without any evidence. He

reached for the Fabric, preparing to jump to the gate, then hesitated. He hated that he did. If he Displaced to help Garrett and Josh, revealing his ability to leave the estate, he'd be back on Magnus Moira's radar. He'd escalate this conflict and undo the goodwill he'd achieved with the mail service. He wouldn't be able to get back inside, or if he did, they'd never let him leave again. The discovery of this back door was, whether he wanted to think of it this way or not, a gift from his sister and her husband. He could spend it on these two boys or he could save it. What if Aristea needed him and these boys were a Trojan horse?

Barely a split second had passed. They were just boys – they deserved the benefit of his doubt. He blinked and rethought his options. He didn't need to *go to* them. He hadn't been using his magic but it was back in its usual bucketloads, and with no one around to see the cracks darkening under his skin, he brought the vision of the two Displacer students easily to mind. There were twenty paces between them and their would-be assailants – plenty of room to erect an invisible wall of impenetrable magic before the tide could turn on them – but also almost the same distance to the gate. Which they couldn't open.

He'd made sure to invalidate their Academy keys when they'd left with Aubrey. Renatus grabbed the secret door and wrenched it open; the old, rusted hinges resisted. There wasn't time. Hissing with frustration, Renatus turned his attention inward to the circle of minds he was closed off from.

Elijah?

He'd always been able to do things non-Telepaths couldn't, a trait he shared with his sister, and though it took a lot of force, his mental voice broke through the barricades to the other White Elm councillors on the first attempt. He felt their immediate panic.

Renatus, what are you doing?!

It's not him!

They thought the worst, that Nastassja had hijacked his brain at long last and had turned him on his own. The assumption was valid, and Renatus regretted putting the fear in them in the first place. At the gate, Jackson was yelling new instructions. Spells began to fly. Luckily, Qasim was on the same page.

I see them, he said as Renatus managed to negotiate the door open wide enough to admit him back into the orchard. Before the door sealed behind him, the circle of minds locked him out again. Renatus took off running along the fence line as he watched the events unfold at the gate. Garrett yanked a very pale Joshua to his side and produced a key that shouldn't work. Renatus's ward, only a temporary solution, took the blows and began to quiver. Garrett shoved the key into the lock and turned it hurriedly; it worked. On the inside, Elijah landed unreasonably close to the fence's magic, right at the gate's opening, and grabbed them by their arms. He pulled them inside and the three slammed the iron gate behind them with a loud clang. Renatus pulled up as his ward broke and angry spells intended for the escaped students began to strike walls reinforced by centuries of ancestral magic. Safe.

Elijah wasted no time in Displacing the two teenagers inside the house, out of sight of their attackers, but Renatus – who knew what a tiny crinkle in the Fabric could do to a Skip as precise as what Elijah was planning, even two hundred metres away – gave it an extra few seconds. The crowd outside, up close in his mind's eye, was in chaos, men and women yelling in each other's faces, Jackson Displacing out of an argument with the bald, crimson-cloaked leader of that purist faction. Confusion, righteous anger, defensiveness, frustration… This was about more than failing to apprehend a couple of kids.

'What did you do?' he asked his apprentice aloud, still certain that she'd somehow set this in motion. He reached for the Fabric and this time, split it meticulously and stepped through into his ballroom.

Elijah and Garrett had eased Joshua Reyes onto the floor, stretching his injured leg out with care. Qasim and Lord Gawain hovered near the door, and Tian's presence was moving to the front door, probably to keep watch on the activity outside the gate.

'Emmanuelle's sending the Healers who are with her,' Lord Gawain told the room, approaching the boys warily but with his usual air of benevolence. His gaze brushed only briefly over Renatus, trust not yet fully restored after his mental intrusion moments earlier. An uncomfortable reminder, perhaps, that their barriers against his mind were an arbitrary construction, only functional as long as he abided by them. 'What happened? Are you alright?'

Garrett Fischer glanced up, his attention on his wincing friend's leg.

'I'm fine,' he lied outright. The adrenaline that had gotten them here was receding, and his dirty hands were beginning to shake. 'I'm… After the theatre, I got away and Josh didn't. They caught him. I couldn't… I couldn't do anything.'

Perpetually embarrassed, Garrett dipped his brightening face from view and worked on untying the other boy's bloody sneaker. Josh was struggling to breathe through the pain but heavily clapped his friend on the shoulder as two current students ran in. Sophia cried out in delight to see who it was, while Dylan attended immediately to the mangled leg.

Elijah straightened and moved to join the other councillors, unsure. 'What do we think?'

Renatus watched his colleagues exchange looks. They'd rescued the boys without question but were reluctant to place their trust even in children they used to teach. True to form of this council he'd sworn himself to – compassionate to the last, always assuming the worst of others.

'That they're scared kids,' he suggested for whatever his word was worth. Qasim nodded firmly.

'We wouldn't have gotten out of the theatre without Fischer,' he agreed, loud enough for the boy now being subjected to Sophia Prescott's caring attention to hear the endorsement. Pink ears reddened. 'If Magnus Moira wanted them in here as plants, they'd have used nonlethal force outside. It was only Renatus's ward that kept them alive. How *did* you do that? I thought even you couldn't do magic through the fence line?'

'Garrett's mother foretold this,' Lord Gawain said before Renatus could answer. 'Almost to the letter, except–'

'Except who would let us in,' Garrett spoke up, apologetic

even in interruption. 'My mum's never wrong.' He left Joshua with the two Healers and struggled to his feet. Awkward and shying away, he offered a glittering silver and white handful to Renatus. 'She said to tell you she's okay. Or that she's got this.'

Enclosed in his fingers in a tangle was a crumpled paper crane, a frayed string, a fine broken chain and a small silver key. The rest was meaningless, but Renatus knew the chain even before he thoughtlessly accepted it.

A sparse commercial courtyard, huge warehouse dominating the background... a small crowd on their knees... an intense cyclic feeling of complacency... Aristea, backed by three young men her own age... one of her sai at an unguarded throat... Lisandro... her hand shakes, chokes on a sob... rips the key from her neck...

It was unclear whether the vision ended there or Renatus's own horror cut it short. He snapped back to the real world and had the presence of mind to bury it before his sister could find it. Qasim, though, was faster. He hadn't even felt him drop his barriers between their minds.

'Where is that?' the Scrier demanded, fear for the girl bubbling behind his anger. Garrett quailed. 'Did she do it?'

'Do what?' Lord Gawain asked. No one clarified.

'Of course not,' Renatus insisted, though it would explain the disorder outside the gate. She didn't have it in her, but her opponents did. He, too, turned on the cowering Displacer. 'You left her there?'

Sophia, kneeling on the floor, flared up. 'Aristea? You left Aristea *behind*?'

Already Renatus's thoughts were on the door at the back of the estate, regretting he'd wasted time coming here to hear what he'd known already – Aristea needed him. How could he get to her? How many minutes ago did this disturbing scene play out? Was he too late?

'She told us to,' Joshua muttered from the floor. They all spun back to him. 'She had things... ouch, under control.' He winced as Dylan's probing fingers touched his swollen ankle. 'More or less. The warding was loose... If we got out... so could she.'

She could have, but did she? The door at the back of his mind remained securely closed. He'd know if she was dead, and he hoped she'd slam that door open and yell for him if she got in too deep. By that logic, her silence meant her friends were right – she had things under control. Renatus wavered. Outside the gate, sorcerers argued and fumed over some perceived misunderstanding over whether to fire on the boys. There was no grief or fear, so Lisandro was fine, but that didn't mean Aristea hadn't been captured, whatever Lisandro had claimed only minutes earlier.

Had she changed things?

'Control of what?' Lord Gawain asked in mild frustration. 'Where did you see Aristea?'

'They were at Magnus Moira's compound,' Qasim filled in brusquely. He was still glaring at the boys. 'What were you doing there? Is she still there?'

Renatus tuned out. He wasn't meant to know anything about where she was, but now that he did – now that his enemies knew better than he did – he couldn't let it go. Blocking Qasim firmly from his thoughts, Renatus crept his attention along the paths he'd memorised into the distant mind of his distracted sister. He closed his eyes in case she reciprocated, but Nastassja didn't seem to detect his presence in her fiery, guarded psyche.

Other people's minds are unfamiliar landscapes, and this one was more alien than most, though he'd expected to relate in some way. There was nothing recognisable about it. Her thoughts were messy, hard to follow. The neural paths were irregular; whole regions were dark and closed off. Damaged, somehow? Maybe… hidden memories? Did that make sense? Wiring wove creatively around these areas and shorted out as dead ends in strange places. For a few breaths, he cautiously navigated the crossed wires of her erratic brain, looking for optic input, before a dark, blurry image struggled to focus for him.

A melted-through metal door. A dim high-ceilinged commercial space. A man's silhouette. Lisandro, he was sure of it. Hands on his face, checking a small cut. A turn to the side to look at another blurry man. This one smaller, younger, copper-haired. No sound. Renatus didn't know yet how to access

Nastassja's aural network.

But her worry still reached him, and he got the gist of the situation. Aubrey was checking lock-up spaces usually used for storing goods, chain-link doors broken open. Nastassja had arrived to check on Lisandro's safety. Aristea was nowhere to be seen.

Grateful, Renatus released his tenuous hold on his sister's vision, but not carefully enough. He tripped something, alerting her to his presence. Stronger than in person, he felt her reaction as an almost physical flinch, and felt himself being forcefully shoved out and back to his own mind.

Your little bitch is going to regret this, she snarled at him as everything in her head slammed shut behind him. Vision, memories, thoughts, wounds, shadows, networks he didn't have words for. *Where's your honour? We came to you on neutral ground and your apprentice attacks us from behind?*

Renatus wished he could take credit for Aristea's timing, because it really had been perfect. Much the way Lisandro generally played the Elm, one party holding attention in one place while he had someone engaged in something much worse elsewhere, his apprentice had taken advantage of their enemies' absence from the compound; or rather, their failure to anticipate the same sleight-of-hand tactics. That, needless to say, was his girl.

If his sister was this angry, then Aristea was definitely in the clear. He resisted the desire to move his attention out into the world for her while Nastassja was still in his thoughts. He kept his eyes shut and narrowed his thoughts to only what he said next.

It looked to me like she came at him front-on.

Which provoked the anticipated ugly response.

I'm redirecting every scrier, every Displacer, every resource we have into hunting her down – whatever Lisandro offered you, consider her a lost cause. Nastassja was furious. He could feel it like actual heat. *You don't know what you're doing. I tried to avoid this, but now you've forced the matter, like you always do. This isn't going to end well, Ren.*

She blocked him out so completely that Renatus returned to his own thoughts with full confidence that he was alone in them. He focused on his apprentice only lightly, not so intently that he'd risk breaking through her wards, and was relieved when his attention slid conspicuously off.

She was back in the wind. Renatus opened his eyes and tuned into the conversation that was unfolding in the ballroom, giving the impatient Scrier a nod of reassurance as he did. Garrett was struggling under what must have felt like an interrogation from the two senior councillors, having quickly conveyed that he'd recruited Aristea in his quest to free Josh from the camp.

'Magnus Moira is imprisoning Avalonians?' Lord Gawain repeated with a concerned glance at Renatus. Garrett swallowed and straightened up.

'They said he was a spy,' he explained, 'but it wasn't him who let us go. It was Aubrey.' He struggled to maintain volume when the councillors demanded elaboration. 'Aristea said my mum told you I would be back with information that could make a difference.' He still couldn't maintain eye contact, but to his credit, he did at least attempt it, lifting his light eyes to Renatus's for just a moment before shyly fluttering away. 'It's why Aubrey stood down so we could Displace out. I think it's about his son. Also…' His bravery dissolved. 'Can I have that paper bird back?'

Renatus looked down at it in his hand, sensed a faint but airtight layer of Aristea's warding over it, and said, 'Not yet.'

It took hours to get the whole story from the two young Displacers. Fionnuala brought them food, which they devoured like they hadn't eaten in weeks. From their gaunt and dirty faces, maybe that was true. Renatus resisted drumming his fingers on his elbow or any convenient surface whenever they stopped talking long enough to get a spoonful in their mouths. He hadn't yet shared his discovery of the secret door with Lord Gawain or the other councillors, unsure that he should. If they tried to smuggle anyone out and got caught, that escape route would be shut off permanently. But what was he going to do with it if not get his staff and students out to freedom, and who was he to decide who should know of such an option? Was he not a member of a collegial council of equals?

Well, in short, no. They were equals in very few senses.

Garrett and Joshua described, in bursts between ravenous

eating, how they were used by Magnus Moira to map Displacements to track enemies, and how Nastassja, who they only knew as Lisandro's more frightening other half, took an interest in their work.

'She wanted to learn how to stretch Fabric, freeze a space,' Josh explained. 'She learned fast. She has, like…' He put his food down, unable to find words for a moment. 'Just, *so* much power.'

'Not enough. They need a sacrifice for a spell,' Garrett told them soberly. 'I don't know what it is, but I heard Nastassja lose patience with someone when they thought I wasn't listening. She said it costs the life of a child for a reason.' He had started scribbling on a map Elijah had provided, adding little crosses in two different colours – frequent Magnus Moira landings, and landings of interest to Magnus Moira.

'I don't think Aubrey's down for that,' Josh said with his mouth full. 'Aristea had a sword to Lisandro's throat and he did nothing.'

Renatus played with the chain in his fingers, disturbed. Aubrey had joined their ranks last year as a Magnus Moira spy to cement his future with Asheleigh Hawke, ward of Lisandro. Not enough was known about her. Whether she was a knowing participant in what Magnus Moira enacted was unclear, only that Aubrey had claimed to be sorry for what he'd needed to do to be with her. He *had* cut off the hands of the men who'd touched Teresa, to his otherwise slimy credit, so he was evidently a bit sorry. Sorry enough to double-cross Lisandro in his own camp?

'When you say Aubrey let you escape…?' Renatus asked pointedly. Garrett shovelled another spoonful into his mouth before answering. More delays. When he swallowed, his answer was not what Renatus expected.

'He knelt down like he was as possessed as the rest and mouthed to me, "don't let it be my son".'

That was days ago now, days without action or change or a reasonable excuse to risk leaving the estate, and days without attention from Nastassja. The words circled Renatus's head as he determined the implications. And the contradictions. Lisandro, who had murdered three families in carefully executed weather events to hide his involvement but deliberately left the children under twenty alive to avoid the unthinkable consequences of such an act, wanted a child sacrifice for a spell he had planned? What spell required that kind of power, and what would be worth the fallout? Why would Aubrey, who threw his future away to be with Shell Hawke and serve Magnus Moira, be afraid for his child? Had Shell given birth already? What differentiated this baby from any other born to witch parents this year?

'Technically,' Emmanuelle said when he wondered this aloud during his self-appointed shift keeping watch over her, nearly a week later, 'this baby is my relative, so I expect you will work it out before anything 'appens to it.'

'Him,' Renatus corrected idly, noticing an unopened letter in familiar stationery on her side table. 'They had a boy, it seems. You got a letter?'

'How nice for them,' she replied flatly, 'and 'ow should I know?'

Immediately he felt guilt, very little of it for Emmanuelle, who couldn't turn her head to see. He'd reached for the envelope but stopped himself before he could turn it over and expose Angela Byrne's address to his eyes.

'Aristea's sister,' he said, 'keeps writing. This time to you.'

'So write back,' his friend responded irritably. 'It isn't me she really wants to 'ear from. And you never say sorry, so I'm certain you will think of something witty in its place.' Emmanuelle softened slightly. 'You think you are letting Aristea's family down.'

'I know I am. Aristea…' was out there because she was trying to protect *him*, and meanwhile her favourite person in the world was alone. But he couldn't share Aristea's situation with Emmanuelle, even if he trusted her implicitly. He shoved his hand into his pocket to fidget with Aristea's chain and the origami crane he'd avoided giving back to Garrett. 'I should be the one watching over her family, not ordering Jadon to do it.'

'No,' his friend disagreed instantly, 'even if you could leave, you are not a guard dog. Angela knows where we are if she needs us and the wards I put over 'er place are still in effect. Besides, she is more capable than she seems. She is as powerful as 'er sister, with those same aura 'oles as the rest of you.'

He'd known Emmanuelle had a strong network of protective magic woven over Angela Byrne's abode, but something else she said resonated. Thoughts beginning to fire again in his exhausted brain, Renatus extended his own hand before his eyes and switched his focus to view his auric field. It was characteristically swollen with magic and peppered with dark sinkholes, much like Lisandro's, Aristea's and his sister's.

'Angela's aura has holes in it, too?'

Frustrated by her inability to nod, Emmanuelle growled lightly. 'What of it? I thought everyone left behind by one of Lisandro's storms 'ad them.'

'Yes,' Renatus confirmed, inspired, feeling his tiredness melt away, 'but that's not where they come from.' Lisandro, Ana and his father had the same feature, always had. It wasn't until after the storm that he'd met more people and seen it wasn't common outside his family. Those descended from the Magnus Moira founders were *born* with it, including Asheleigh Hawke. He opened his hand and Displaced the map Elijah and Garrett had been working on off the dining room table. He unfolded it and held it over Emmanuelle's head. 'Tell me what you see.'

'Paper. Little crosses.' She was unimpressed. He kept his patience and pointed to a remote location that had been bothering him.

'You don't see a pattern? Clumping in certain places?'

'Obviously, where the Displacers 'ave detected the most action. I've already been told. They think it's where Lisandro lives. Looks cold.'

Exactly what he'd been hoping to hear. He folded up the map. 'I think you just solved the mystery of Aubrey's son.'

'Where are you going?' Emmanuelle tried to track him with her eyes as he grabbed the jacket he'd slung over the back of the armchair and shrugged it on. 'You cannot *go there.*'

'That is the assumption I was operating under,' Renatus admitted, twisting Aristea's bangle on his wrist to let the sleeve slide over it. The gems were fully charged, not that he needed it. An urgent plan was taking shape in his head. 'It turns out to not be precisely the case. When Lord Gawain inevitably asks where I am later, can you tell him not to be surprised?'

Head and shoulders trapped in absolute stillness by the careful constructions of magic woven around her, she narrowed her eyes.

'That will depend. Are you taking me with you?'

Renatus sighed, regretful. He *hated* that she was relegated to the role of sounding board and verbal arse-kicker when she should be sneaking out that orchard door with him. If he'd only been faster at the theatre, or arrived sooner, or made any number of minute choices differently to arrive at a different version of this moment in which Emmanuelle was not paralysed and her recovery was not mostly a pipedream. He lifted her hand to where she could see it and pressed an apologetic kiss to the back of it. He felt her surprise and also her disdain when he added, 'If you could be walking by the time I get back, that would suit me perfectly.'

She scoffed in her throat, missing what he didn't: her fingers, still in his, spasmed very slightly.

He left it another day, or *that* day, anyway. Since the boys' return, Lord Gawain had made no attempts to connect with him, and Qasim and Elijah had overseen the boys' debriefing, leaving Renatus to throw himself into tutoring the remaining students, and to think. Fate was keeping him informed with everything he needed to know just as he needed it, and he had to trust its silent hand to guide the events as they unfolded. It couldn't be a coincidence that within minutes of discovering a way off the estate, Garrett and Joshua returned with news of Magnus Moira's *real* agenda.

A child sacrifice. Was there anything worse than knowing his own sister was in on it?

Renatus woke energetic a few hours after midnight. Everyone was asleep. Garrett and Elijah's map was on the dining table – who was going to steal it? In the early grey light, the orchard was typically dark and uncomfortable, even as he kept to the outer wall and tried to ignore the dense sensation of sickening power emanating from near the graveyard. The door felt further away than last time, more trips over gnarled tree roots and rotting branches, but then as before, he stumbled on the clearing quite suddenly and was facing it once again.

Locked. Sealed. A touch to the rough timber confirmed that no one had been through it since he'd pulled it shut, but there was no way of being sure his enemies – or, even worse, his family – weren't waiting to ambush him on the other side.

If they were, he decided, they'd be sorry. He shouldered through the reluctant old door, wards up and magic tingling under his skin.

He stepped out into more of the same silence. An intense scan of the area didn't indicate any presences closer than the gate, and the emotional atmosphere came up blank. He really was alone.

Renatus shut the door with difficulty and began to stalk away from the interfering energy of the walls. After Sunday's encounter, he fully expected his sister to come barrelling at him or his godfather to saunter up with some new deal. But no one appeared, and his head stayed empty, too. Nastassja was still seething, a welcome break. The privacy gave him space to determine his course of action. He might only get this one chance.

He slid his hand into his pocket, fingers straying over the warded edges of the folded paper and the little key. A single step, and he was halfway around the world, somewhere in Sapporo, Japan, in the shadows of tall buildings blocking an afternoon sun. The noise of city traffic and pedestrians on cell phones filtered into the thin alley where he'd landed, and when he walked toward the sounds, he found himself on a busy residential street in what looked like a whole other world from where he'd just left.

He couldn't read the nearest intersection's street signs from this distance, so he joined the throngs of people and tried not to look as uncomfortable as he felt. Like machines of death, modern automobiles roared and rumbled past in constant, densely packed chains, ejecting toxic fumes he could feel down his throat with every breath. Pedestrians and these vehicles paid each other little mind and narrowly missed each other by the margin of a concrete kerb they silently agreed not to cross, and those on foot trusted the word of lights to tell them when it should be safe to walk in front of these streams of vehicles.

Had Aristea come here? How well had she handled it? How did any Empath handle city life? One metropolis was rather like any other, Renatus thought as he went through his jacket's other pocket, and he'd stick with his country estate over this kind of living. Not anywhere near as sensitive as his apprentice was, even Renatus could feel the murky emotional mixture of thousands of people. Most, at least, were flat, focused, lost in thought or engaged in businesslike conversation despite their stimulating environment, but others were managing heartbreak, anxiety, hopelessness and despair, to differing degrees behind their outward poise.

People were exhausting.

He stopped at the intersection while vehicles raced by and pedestrians placidly waited their turn, and he shook out the crumpled envelope. Until today he hadn't trusted his own eyes enough to look for himself, but did now, reading Hiroko Sasaki's return address from the back.

Naturally, the street he needed was not the street he'd landed on, and he didn't have any points of reference to get him there. Renatus spoke no Japanese but all three of the people he stopped spoke a little English. Their directions got him there within twenty minutes. He didn't know the city or its quiet spots well enough to want to Displace, and wasn't eager to land in one of the quickly-moving street lanes if he got it slightly wrong.

The lack of pushy voices knocking at the edges of his mind suggested Emmanuelle had kept her silence. He turned onto Hiroko's street and found her apartment building without needing to check the number. Veiled but recognisable to someone who knew the caster as well as he did, Aristea's unmistakable warding coated the upright property tightly. When he tried to scry inside, his attention bounced off to the next building; his apprentice was getting slicker with her magic, neatly marrying up its edges to keep outside observers from realising an entire house would be missing from any scried image of this street.

At the door there was a panel of buttons and he pressed the one beside the Sasakis' number. It took a few seconds before he was answered over an intercom by a voice he knew.

'Renatus?'

She could sense him, or at least could sense someone very powerful on her doorstep. An educated guess.

'Hiroko,' he replied in confirmation to the faceless slotted box from which her voice had originated. 'I have a rather large and irresponsible favour to ask of you.'

There was a beat of silence, one he was accustomed to hearing between Aristea and her best friend while the Japanese Displacer's brain swiftly translated their accented English.

'It involves Aristea?'

'I wouldn't ask if it didn't.'

'I will be downstairs in five minutes,' her voice said without hesitation, then her apartment's little intercom light went off. Renatus stepped from the building's front landing to people-watch and wait. His apprentice's more efficient and organised friend appeared at the door after only three minutes, toting a small backpack and in the middle of slipping her keys and a cell phone into the hidden pockets of her dress. What she hadn't failed to do before stepping out of her protected zone was build up a set of personal wards and mental barriers she'd learned from Aristea.

'Thank you for seeing me,' Renatus said as the teenaged Displacer approached. Formerly one of the students at the Academy he was headmaster of, he hadn't had much to do with Hiroko Sasaki. They'd rarely spoken without Aristea present, and he wasn't even sure where he stood with her. Did she trust him? Had she served as the sounding board for Aristea's momentary petty complaints about him when they roomed together and had she formed her opinion of him from that? Did she think he was to blame for Aristea's current circumstances?

If so, she wasn't the only one. He held out the paper crane as a peace offering and she stopped abruptly on the bottom step where she was roughly his height.

'Did you find her? Is she in danger?' she asked. Even guarded with her emotions, surprised recognition of that mangled paper shape bled through. Renatus shook his head.

'I haven't found her, and neither has anyone else,' he answered as she took the bird. 'As for danger… I think that's relative. So, that is yours?'

Hiroko nodded, slightly relieved, turning the thing in her fingers.

'Perhaps I gave it to her. I already told Oneida, I don't know where she is.'

'I know. I got your letter.' He showed her the ingredients list. She looked with interest, no recognition now. 'Do you know if this is the same recipe she used on me?'

She relaxed a little more. She said, 'I don't think Aristea knows many spell recipes. But again, I do not remember. The entire day is missing.'

'Disconcerting, yes?' He gestured to the sidewalk and after a moment's indecision, she stepped down to walk with him. 'It's not the most complex memory spell she could have used, at least.'

'And you can reverse it?' the Displacer checked, then backtracked. 'I mean after.'

After. Renatus was perpetually caught in the hope that *after* – a point in time when Aristea could come safely home without consequences she didn't deserve – was just around the corner, but in reality, it could be months or even years. Until then, to uncover whatever she had hidden inside his head and Hiroko's, and very probably under the wards in Hiroko's crane, could worsen her situation and push *after* back even further.

'Yes, after.' Assuming Aristea had been precise in her recording of this spell, he had all the information he needed to unravel the blocks she'd written into their minds. 'For now, I need your help to protect Angela Byrne.'

Hiroko stopped and turned to him, concerned and taken aback. 'Why?'

'She's safe,' Renatus put her main fears to rest immediately. 'Some things have changed at the estate. You're aware that we've been trapped inside?' He let her confirm before continuing. 'I found a way to leave, but Lisandro's aware of it, so I can't get anyone else off the property. The council is spread very thin. We received information that I need to act on, and I need to bring Jadon with me.'

'Is he missing? Do you need my help to find him?' Hiroko asked, getting confused.

'No, he's exactly where I asked him to wait: in an empty house across the street from Angela Byrne's, which is where I'd like you to come with me to cover for him for a few hours,' he explained. 'Half our world is looking for Aristea. Angela is an obvious target and not one I'm prepared to take chances on while our friend is out there because of me.'

He hadn't meant to say that last part. Aristea had erased the whole of the day the two girls had escaped from the theatre and the estate, so Hiroko wouldn't recall the circumstances, but she lifted her chin in response, looking away down the street. She knew more than she was letting on.

'I don't think it is because of you,' she said eventually, a stiff city breeze lifting her fine dark hair and then his. She turned her gaze back to him. Unlike most of the young sorcerers who'd come to study at his home, Hiroko, thanks to Aristea, did not appear afraid of him. Dignified, forgiving, wise beyond her years, he could see why Aristea was attracted to such a friendship. 'I think *she* thinks it is.'

Renatus let those words sit with him. He knew what she was insinuating, because he'd been thinking the same since he'd woken abruptly in the ballroom with two hours missing. Aristea honestly thought she was doing right by him by lying to the council and now staying hidden. She thought she was protecting him – possibly she was, neither knew what from – and that preserving his future with the White Elm was worth all this sacrifice on her part. She thought she owed it to him even though he'd *never* ask it, and she'd convinced herself that any personal or professional fallout of his could somehow be worse than it happening to her.

She'd considered what a disgraceful dismissal from the

council might mean for his psyche, but not how he'd ever attend another council circle after they charged her as a criminal and ended their partnership as master and apprentice – a partnership which, ironically, was the root of her growing impulsiveness.

'I think you're right,' he replied finally. 'You know her well.' He glanced down at her hand, making clear he was referring to the small silver ring on her little finger when he asked, 'Can she contact you with that, if she needs you?'

Beginning to walk again, Hiroko looked down at the circlet of metal she'd spelled as a communication device. Aristea had one, too, and she'd never explained it, but he'd guessed it was how two non-Telepaths had managed to summon one another in the past.

'Yes, and she hasn't. You know her well, too. Well enough to know she will not ask for help unless her situation is dire.' She turned toward an automatic door and immediately stepped to the side. She smiled at him as he followed her into the unattended lobby's corner, an expression caught between knowing and pitying. No one knew better the frustration of caring about Aristea. Except, perhaps: 'Have you been to Angela's previously?'

'No, have you?'

'No, I don't think so, but I will drive. Can you show me the house?'

Renatus was a step ahead, and easily summoned an image of the detached flat Aristea frequently fixated on. Neat grass, neat little herb garden out front, curtains drawn inside clean windows. He caught Hiroko's gaze and *pushed* the image of the house to her. She was advanced enough to reject the attempt at telepathy if she chose, but she accepted, briefly closing her eyes. Then, with a glance up at a camera that she must have known from prior experience was trained on the doors and not this corner, Hiroko offered him her hands, and when he took them, he felt the Fabric shift around them instantly. Displacers didn't need to *walk* through wormholes; they formed the wormholes where they stood and brought the new location to them. The grey lobby melted quickly away and was replaced with the grey dawn light of a sleepy sloped cul-de-sac. His first inhalation was of dewy grass – a marked improvement on the foulness of the city.

They dropped hands and beheld Aristea and Angela's house. Unlike the homes either side, full of slumbering inhabitants, Renatus knew immediately that it was empty, and turned quickly toward a bright spark of a powerful presence at the bottom of the street. A lone figure moving at a jog disappeared around the corner. Angela? He stretched his attention after her, sensing her unguarded magic, surprised by both her energetic similarity and difference from Aristea. Given his recent reconnection with his own sibling and the warped reflection he saw in the dark mirror of her, he shouldn't be.

He waited, but the figure did not reappear at the corner. He tried not to feel as relieved and as guilty as he did. Eventually he was going to have to face this woman and have those hard conversations. Thankfully not today.

He didn't consider himself an easy person to read, but Hiroko seemed a special sort.

'Angela does not know that you and Jadon are watching her?'

Put that way, it didn't sound very noble.

'I'm not watching her,' Renatus said, a little more defensively than he intended. He turned away from the street corner to give that claim a little more credibility. Subtly, he felt a familiar mind touch his, a confirmation of identity. He went again through his pockets, offering the rest of the tangled handful. 'You should know Garrett and Josh returned to the estate over the weekend, with this.' Across the street, the front door of another little house opened, and Jadon stepped out, looking dishevelled. 'They're alive, recovering, apparently still on our side. Aristea helped them get home.'

Emotions complicated, Hiroko unravelled the old string from the chain.

'She must have believed in them,' she said finally, threading the string through a hole in the crane. She didn't remember Garrett Fischer saving her life, but she didn't need to go another day thinking he'd walked out and never thought of her again.

'I think so, too. Good morning,' he added to his younger

colleague as he approached, pulling a hoodie over his head.

'Is it? You being here can't be a good start.' Jadon inspected Renatus with narrowed eyes, mind touching mind again. 'Assuming you're... you.'

Those councillors on the outside had been in constant contact with those trapped inside the estate walls, and Renatus knew they'd been instructed to keep their thoughts locked clear of his as long as he might be a window directly to the top of Magnus Moira.

'Nastassja has been kind enough to extend me the silent treatment since my apprentice upset Lisandro's apple cart,' Renatus replied, ignoring Hiroko's concerned interest. It would take too long to explain, and like Angela Byrne, she was better off in the dark where information couldn't illuminate more worrying issues. 'It's just me.'

Jadon was still frowning, unconvinced.

'Em's the only one awake there and she says to shut up and trust you. I won't ask how the hell you got out.' He nodded at the bottom of the street. 'Thanks for this assignment, by the way. You just missed my oh-so-fascinating mark.'

Both Renatus and Hiroko glanced in the direction Angela had gone. They shared a faint defensiveness at the implication that Aristea's sister was boring for failing to be attacked as Renatus had initially feared.

'I'm sorry that "safe and normal" doesn't meet your expectations,' he said coolly.

'Angela is quite lovely,' Hiroko spoke up. 'I am sure Aristea is very grateful to have you guarding her.'

Jadon backtracked quickly, opening his mouth to reply. Then he seemed to compute that Renatus was not alone. '...Hiroko? Should you... be here? Should either of you be here?'

'I am here to relieve you for some hours.' Hiroko turned briskly to Renatus. 'I can track her from here until she comes home. How should I contact you if something goes wrong?'

Renatus gestured at Jadon and said, having thought of this and prepared a sensible modern response, 'He has a cell phone. You can call it.'

He knew all the words and the premise of how it worked, but after an early-morning-snide comment from Jadon – 'You know what that is?' – he watched the exchange of phone numbers, in which both parties produced their devices and swapped them to type memorised sequences of numbers on tiny buttons that served as keys.

'Looks like you know more 'bout what's going on here than I do,' Jadon grumbled to Hiroko, accepting his phone back and squinting at the screen of hers to check he input his number correctly. 'That's it. Thanks for what you did at the theatre, by the way. We owe you.'

The Displacer blinked and smiled politely, lost. Capable as she was, Hiroko Sasaki had departed the Academy on account of the dangers she'd watched her friend face. She had made the conscious choice to step away from this life of politics, uncertainty and peril, and Renatus knew it was unfair to bring her back into it.

'If there was anyone else outside the council that I could trust, I would have asked them,' he promised, adjusting his sleeve to get at the bangle underneath. With difficulty he slid it from his wrist and offered it. 'With Aristea's family, I won't take any chances.'

Hiroko was there the day Aristea received this gift and so recognised it, raising her eyebrows when she took it in her hand.

'You have charged the stones,' she noticed. She donned it without argument, but insisted on returning it when he came back. 'Aristea left it with you. I hope I will not need it.'

'You won't,' Jadon assured her, leading her past the sale sign and into the house to show her where he'd been holed up. 'Two weeks and absolutely no action. *Someone* is just paranoid.'

Renatus ignored the jab and shared a final grateful look with Hiroko. From her nod and the lack of resentment he felt from her, he gathered she understood the level of risk and found it acceptable in the circumstances.

While he waited for Jadon, he stood in the silent, grey street and took in the Byrne home. It was true what he'd told Hiroko, he hadn't been here before, but he had inadvertently visited the site of the girls' childhood home on the coast, now just a concrete slab hiding an old basement after the vicious storm Lisandro sent to eliminate the older two siblings from being considered for the White Elm's two open positions. Emmanuelle and Peter had won those spots easily, but perhaps it would have been less clear-cut if the Byrnes had remained in contention.

If Susannah, the White Elm's most dedicated Seer, hadn't shared a vision with Lisandro, then her close friend.

If Lisandro hadn't acted on it in the most extreme way imaginable.

True to form, his storm had spared the girls, neither of them out of their teens at the time. The brother, not long turned twenty-one, hadn't been so lucky. Both Aidan and Angela had made the first round of considerations and stood a roughly equal chance of joining the council, but only Aidan was of adult age. Fair game.

Which begged the question of the day: if Lisandro couldn't stomach the prospect of long-distance murdering underage threats that he'd never met, was he really going to go through with *sacrificing* his ally's infant? He'd allowed Asheleigh to live, but had a spell in mind worth ripping her child from her? The whole thing didn't sit right.

'None of it sits right,' Jadon said grumpily as he returned. 'Least of all you worming your way through that blockade without any of ours noticing and showing up with a teenager to do council work.'

Though not exactly friends, Renatus had found himself gravitating toward Jadon along with Emmanuelle since the fallout of Lisandro stealing the Elm Stone. Young, impulsive and fiery, he possessed the same determination to bend rules when they became obstacles and likewise lacked the life experience to know better. Morally, they were on the same page almost every time, so he let the snippy comments slide. Aristea's gift for Empathy told him that his colleague was still waking up.

'Showing up with a teenager is not new for me. When was Shell Hawke's baby due to be born?' he asked curiously. The tired American Telepath frowned at the segue.

'I don't know. July, August, around now. Why?'

'What do you know about Shell?' Renatus pressed. 'Her life?'

'Less than I would if I'd known there would be a quiz. She studied, I think, but wasn't long out of school. No parents, no siblings. After her parents died, she was raised by an aunt. A great-aunt,' Jadon corrected himself. 'There was no one closer left in her family. Sad, right?'

Renatus withdrew Garrett's map.

'I didn't need to pass the blockade,' he said, 'and I don't need your help to front up at what I suspect is Aubrey and Shell's home, but I think we may be more successful if you're there.'

It took a lengthy moment to compute in Jadon's tired brain, and the effort went a long way toward waking him up.

'You *found* them?' he checked suspiciously, emoting unconsciously. He had some messy feelings tied up with Aubrey, much like Emmanuelle did with Peter – something about being inducted together into a complicated hierarchical order like the White Elm seemed to forge tight bonds between new councillors; bonds that stung when broken.

'Garrett Fischer found them,' Renatus corrected, 'though I don't think he knows it. He also said Lisandro is seeking a child sacrifice for some horrendous spell.'

Jadon's thoughts were quicker now, worried and analytical.

'And you think their baby is in danger?' he asked, and, taking Renatus's answer from his head before he could open his mouth, moved on to his next questions. 'How has no one else made this connection? And why is Emmanuelle telling me not to tell anyone you're here?'

'Because Lord Gawain doesn't know I spoke to Lisandro the day the boys came back, and because he won't approve any active interference in Fate's plan at this stage,' Renatus admitted. 'For better or worse, he can't shut down a mission he knows nothing about.'

None of this made Jadon any more comfortable with the situation. Open defiance was something both had only dipped their toes into in the past, but to Jadon, the risk to an innocent little life, and to Renatus, the allure of learning what Lisandro was really up to and how Aristea tied in, was too great to ignore.

'I suppose if you're ordering me, I don't have any reason to question that,' Jadon said finally, referencing Renatus's very high station on the White Elm. 'But you know if that's his stance, he'll be very unhappy with us.'

'What would be new about that?'

Jadon could only shrug in agreement and extend his arm. Confident that there were no witnesses to their departure, Renatus took hold of the other's forearm and felt for the Fabric. They both glanced once more at the map, regretful that asking Hiroko along was out of the question, then Renatus stepped them through the void.

A flurry of snow fluttered past their faces and their shoes sank crisply into a fresh layer of the stuff.

'When Garrett said this place was frequented by our key players after their visits to the Belarussian compound,' Renatus explained quietly as they both spread their senses out as far as they would go through the white blitz, 'the assumption was that it was a residence. *That* residence.'

The swirl of snow passed, giving them a brief view of a single lodge up ahead, backed by a wild wood directly from a storybook and boxed in by solid timber-fenced paddocks. A dome of sophisticated magic shielding was detectable over the property.

'Yes, Lisandro's,' Jadon muttered, having already been briefed on this. He hugged his hooded sweater closer. 'I'm hoping you have some brilliant reason to think we aren't about to interrupt your sister and her husband at breakfast. Dinnertime.' He looked up at the colourless sky. 'Whatever time it is.'

'It's not that brilliant,' Renatus confessed as they walked. This snow had only just started to fall today, judging by the pristine whiteness of it all over the barren ground, and was already filling the gaps under the gates to the property and icing the path to the door. 'It's that this is an isolated old ranch covered in snow. In August. They ran away together and had the whole world to choose from, and somewhere that snows in summer and has no one else around for miles is the last place my sister would choose. And if she chose a place like this to throw me off, then the least Lisandro would do for her is deflect some of this weather. She despises the cold, and Lisandro doesn't live with inconveniences.' Renatus kicked some of the snow out from under the gate when he reached it. He felt the shimmer of careful magic hanging in the air and so stopped himself from opening it. A sneaky protective charm; what was it intended to do if an intruder stepped through unawares? Renatus planted his foot back on the outside of the ranch fence. 'He can control storms and she's always had him at her beck and call. Therefore, this is not their house.'

Jadon nodded slowly as this chain of logic got through to him.

'Alright, but then how did you decide it was Aubrey and Shell's?'

'Because Magnus Moira attracts two types of people: miscreants with more power than they deserve, looking for somewhere to abuse it and get noticed for it, and idealists with less power than they'd like, eager for the chance to open up their world. This is the type of place they're all trying to escape,' Renatus pointed out, opening his hand to catch snowflakes as they fell. 'The exception would be the idealist with more power than he deserves who found his way into their cult by falling in love with the wrong girl.'

'The idealist who just wants to be left alone to raise his family in peace but can't work out how to break away,' Jadon agreed grimly. He was shivering but his eyes narrowed to view the energies woven through the air. 'And this place has had no magic spared. It *is* Aubrey's,' he added in confirmation, better acquainted with their target than Renatus was. Thirty paces away, the lodge's door cracked open. 'Most of it.'

'I wasn't expecting you so… soon.' Shell Hawke stepped out already speaking, but stopped when she saw them. Her shock reached Renatus even where he stood, giving him a direct pathway to her thoughts, which she wasn't practiced at guarding.

He didn't take immediate notice of those, though, because his attention went to the little rugged-up human snuggled into the crook of her shoulder. Roughly the size of a big pet cat – was that a normal size for newborn? Renatus didn't know – and capped with a soft, woolly hat, the infant was the obvious choice for whatever horrible spell Lisandro was planning. The baby radiated a magical aura that washed out its mother's by a considerable margin, clearly having won the genetic lottery and inherited *both* parents' magical capacities. Markers in that aura suggested a gift for Crafting, like Aubrey, but the stark black sinkholes matched Shell's.

The sacrifice of this baby would be as much a loss of potential as it would be a loss to the parents. Lisandro must want his spell badly. Renatus couldn't guess what would be worth this price.

Shell's fingers grasped for the doorknob behind her. Jadon, trying to smile reassuringly, raised one of his hands in greeting. She paused, looking uncertainly between them, and Renatus heard her disjointed concerns.

Concerns about him. That he was here for the baby. That he would take it away. He took a wide step back to let Jadon handle things, and she relaxed enough to drop the doorknob warily.

'Sorry to drop in unannounced,' Jadon called lightly. 'If I'd known you'd moved to the only place colder than your last house, I'd have brought coffee. Two sugars.'

Renatus watched the only survivor of the Hawke storm deliberate whether to smile at the memories he evoked. He caught scraps of images – a small Scottish flat with photos on the mantel, pizza boxes and a board game on the table, Teresa and Aubrey and Shell laughing, Jadon arriving at the door with Starbucks. They'd been real friends, he realised, if only for the short space of time between Aubrey's initiation and his dishonourable discharge. The rest of the council had not embraced them, still wounded by the betrayal of those they'd replaced, and even Renatus and Emmanuelle, the other two councillors in their early twenties, had been cold. Emmanuelle had been hurt by Peter; Renatus had no excuse. He was always cold.

'If you've got it, I'll take it,' Shell replied after an extended beat. She had a warm Scottish accent, and the thick red hair to match. She was young, only a year or two older than Aristea and Hiroko, though the sleeplessness of early parenthood was taking its toll. 'Heaven knows we dinnae get good coffee out here.'

Jadon grinned at the concession and nodded at the baby, carefully edging his wallet from his pocket.

'He's bigger than last time I saw him.' He produced a printed, crinkled black photograph. A baby-shaped blob, like a sketch in greys and whites. Shell softened at the image.

'He was early,' she admitted. 'June.' She looked down at the baby with a mess of tired and protective thoughts. There was grief, fear, and gratefulness knotted all through it. The baby's birth had been traumatic. Mother and child had almost died, near as Renatus could tell, and they'd been given a second chance. At least, that was how she viewed the little boy she looked upon as her whole world. She lifted her eyes to theirs again, nervous. 'What are you doing here?'

'We're not here to cause problems,' Jadon promised. He gestured back at Renatus when her unconvinced gaze shifted to him. 'He heard something we thought you should know, and after we go, you won't see us back to hassle you. We just want to help.'

'Help with what?'

The snowfall had stopped, but the low cloud suggested it would start again soon. Renatus stepped back into line with Jadon so he didn't need to raise his voice.

'It's about your son,' he said, not missing the subtle tightening of her arm around the chubby baby. 'Lisandro is planning a spell, a heinous spell, and it will take a child sacrifice.'

Asheleigh Hawke visibly blanched, but her shock came from a slightly different place than Renatus expected.

'How do you know about that?' she breathed, shifting her baby to her other arm and snuggling him closely when he fussed. Renatus waved away her question.

'It doesn't matter,' he said. 'We're worried for your son.'

She stared at him for a long time, looking from one councillor to the other, uncertain thoughts turning over in her head. She didn't believe it, couldn't, slowly connecting that he meant her child was the target. She knew already about the spell, or had heard it mentioned in her presence, but didn't care for details. Finally, shakily, she smiled despite her confusion.

'You think…? No,' she dismissed. She shook her head hard, and thick, red hair draped over her baby's head. 'Lisandro will never let that happen. He loves me and my son, and Aubrey is one of his most trusted advisors. We're a family.'

Jadon and Renatus shared a dubious glance. Years of indoctrination had paid off for Lisandro in this girl Renatus had never known, but by all rights should have been a friend of his family's while they were growing up.

'Our fathers both trusted Lisandro and thought of him as their brother,' Renatus reminded her, leaving unsaid where that had gotten them. Shell lifted her chin in discomfort, shutting down the tirade of unresolved feelings she had on that topic. 'They loved him, too, and they weren't safe when they stood between him and what he wanted.'

She looked down at the baby in her arm, deeply conflicted. Unexpected faces appeared in her thoughts and Renatus wondered ominously whether she'd been present for Peter Chisholm's murder.

'This isn't like that,' she insisted after a struggle for words. She got her emotions under control and her gaze cooled. 'When our fathers inevitably let us down, Lisandro was there. He has always kept his word. He will protect me and my family, no matter what.'

'Our fathers didn't let us down,' Renatus rebuked, surprised to find himself defending his. 'Their destiny was taken out of their hands by someone who was supposed to love them. Don't make their mistake.'

It was too harsh, and it scared Shell off. She shook her head and backed into the lodge.

'You need to leave,' she muttered, turning away with uncomfortable emotions she didn't want to face. Jadon cast Renatus an irritated look that needed no translating and called for Shell to stop.

'What if you're wrong?' he asked, stilling her with the door almost closed. He waved the photo. 'You gave me this, remember, when you asked me to find Aubrey? You know me. I'm your friend, Aubrey's too. I wouldn't have disturbed you if I wasn't afraid for your family.'

He waited her silence out, and Renatus watched as she wavered. Alone out here with only her baby and sometimes her partner for company, the idea of a friend must be awfully tempting to believe in. But it was no lie. Jadon's sincerity rang in his words, and Renatus knew him to be a man of integrity.

Slowly, miserably, Shell lowered her forehead to the doorframe and closed her eyes.

'I shouldn't be talking to you,' she whispered, the sound not carrying but both Telepaths interpreting it from her poorly guarded mind.

'Your baby is special,' Jadon prompted gently. Shell's expression spasmed with pain and she nodded tightly.

'Yes, he is. But there's so much you don't understand.' She swallowed and stood straight, deciding something. Robotically, she said, 'Yes, there's a spell, but my son is safe. He's not the sacrifice. Lisandro won't allow it, whatever it takes. That's all you need to know.'

'Alright,' Renatus said reluctantly. He couldn't get past this gate without summoning everyone on the enemy side he didn't want to have to fight, and he didn't seem able to convince Shell of the risk. 'I hope you're right. If it turns out you're not, you know where to find us, and please know…' He looked once more at the little baby, warmly rugged against this impromptu venture outside to see his first snow. Renatus didn't know Shell, hadn't known her father, Kenneth, and he had no particular affection for Aubrey. But those black sinkholes in his little still-developing aura – just like Renatus's, like his sister's, like Aristea's, and yes, like Lisandro's – made Shell Hawke's son *his* family, somehow, too. Renatus cleared his throat and tried again. 'Please know that if you can't count on who you thought, *we* will do whatever it takes to keep you and your son safe.' It felt like a big thing to say, something stirring about those words he parroted back at her. *Whatever it takes.* 'I don't want to see your son hurt.'

She tried not to, but something in her expression gave way. She looked… sorry. Her thoughts were messy, pained, and busy, like she wanted to say something and couldn't get the words past her lips.

'My… Thank you for trying to help me, but my son will be fine,' she said eventually, looking meaningfully at Jadon, 'and you both need to leave. Now.'

She said the words with relative firmness, but the minimal barriers around her mind came down as Renatus felt her disjointed thoughts actively reaching beyond her body.

…hear me? I can't… hear me? Be seen talking to you. They're always… you don't understand… always watching…

She'd shut the door and Renatus was midway through turning away when he began to hear her loud thoughts. He caught the edge of Jadon's gaze to confirm they were both tuning into the same artless broadcast. The other councillor nodded almost imperceptibly and they fell into a slow walk away through the fresh powder snow as they tried to tune Ms Hawke's thoughts into something clearer. She kept thinking, hard, in senseless broken sentences, apparently desperate to get a message across without risking being heard by a scrier later.

…isn't safe, but not for me… know if you can hear me… I already knew about… know if I should trust you… knew about the spell… it's very very very very bad… I already gave up so much… Lisandro isn't your enemy… my child is safe, but another one isn't… hear me? You should take the deal. Whatever it takes.

Renatus stopped at that wording coming up again, insides twisting. Impatient, Jadon grabbed his elbow and kept him walking back the way they'd come, staying longer in case Shell thought anything else intended for them. But she'd gone quiet, trying to block them out, and Renatus had realised where he knew those words from.

Aristea's memory spell. It's what she'd written for herself before wiping his memory and her own, presumably as an explanation for her actions. They'd both agreed it was a poor excuse for a clue, but in lieu of recalling the events of those two hours, they had no better context for understanding the phrase.

Renatus was too distracted with these thoughts so Jadon Displaced them back to Northern Ireland, landing them adjacent to the empty cottage he'd been staying in. They scaled the tall boundary fence before their minds were interrupted by the disappointed voice of Lord Gawain.

What have you done? he asked them, devastated. The pair balanced atop the fence, sharing guilty glances like errant schoolboys. *Wherever you went, whatever you did, you just knocked hundreds of futures off the board. You may have just signed the White Elm's death warrant.*

The air in Renatus's lungs slowly left him, and he settled back on the top of the fence, stunned. Still perched opposite him, Jadon stared in confusion.

'How?' he whispered. 'We didn't *do* anything.'

Renatus was not a Seer, and had little love for the art of it, but he understood the part sorcerers played in interpreting the plan Fate had for its participants. He understood that *doing* in the present tense didn't matter any more or less than what a person *could do* with specific prompts, particular motives, certain nudges. The future could change as much through a compelling conversation as it could through a two-year continental war; the ripples through time and through human memory could run just as far.

'We learned something we weren't supposed to, which is just as bad,' Renatus explained softly, dusting snow off his shoulder. Inside his head he'd heard the momentary discordant fuss of his fellow White Elm asking for answers before he was unceremoniously locked out again. 'Unfortunately, I have no idea what it was.'

chapter twenty-two

When I left home, I joked to my sister that having our cousin stay would be an annoying housemate situation. Then at the Academy, I was roomed with Sterling, who was bizarrely in love with Renatus, and Xanthe, who went from hot to cold faster than anyone I'd known before, and that was seriously awkward. After Belfast, I'd of course been stuck with Declan in squishy planes and the same hotel, half the time wanting to wring his frustrating neck.

None of my previous nightmare roommates compared with two weeks with Cassán Ó Grádaigh.

I came to the swift conclusion that the man I'd seen in visions – clever, curious, controlled – was mostly gone, and the person I'd found in Greece was essentially his shadow. After his pronouncement that Lisandro had tracked him down to *learn how to become immortal*, Cassán had asked who I was and what I wanted, then stalked out to sulk on the beach. Ever since, it was this painful loop of essentially the same conversation.

'Who are you?'

'How long have I been here?'

'Get out!'

'When you say you know Renatus *Morrissey*…?'

'I never wanted to hurt anyone… but then it was too late to take it back…'

'There are no scriers in my line, don't be ridiculous.'

'Is there food?'

'What do you want?'

'You're not with that last lad, are you? That White Elm one? I think he died.'

'Which White Elm lad?' I asked eagerly when, on the fifth day, he brought this up independently while filleting a fish. I was already losing my mind by this point, and little did I know, this was not even halfway. Cassán paused to look up at me with suspicious eyes.

'Did you tell them I was here?' he asked resentfully. 'Bastards.'

And no angle I took after that could get him back on track. In a frustrated huff I got up and resumed my new pastime of pacing the length of this beach, knowing I'd be starting fresh with him when I returned.

'Who are you?'

'Get out!'

'Elysia…? How is this possible…?'

It was the first place I'd felt absolutely safe and off the grid – Renatus would never guess this place – but I had hours and hours to kill, and I spent a lot of them drilling with my sai on the beach. Sometimes Cassán ignored me; other times he freaked out, yelling that I'd come to hurt him. There was no rhyme or reason to his reactions, an unlucky dip every time. I sometimes slept on the beach against the cliff or inside the cave. When I woke too many times to this frizzled and angry old man demanding to know why I was there, I took to Displacing into town and scrying for empty residences. Those were easily the best nights, and when I was staring at the ceiling of someone's getaway home instead of at the stars or ominous stalactites, I had to wonder what the *hell* I was doing here. I wasn't wanted and I was at risk of going just as crazy if I continued banging my head against the wall like this. I'd fall asleep frustrated, because however truthful these points were, they didn't invalidate the counterpoints.

Cassán knew what Lisandro was planning.

Cassán had found a stellar hiding place and reinforced it so well that I could remain hidden indefinitely, or at least until I found the end of my tolerance.

Cassán was once a brilliant scholar of magic who'd inadvertently founded the Magnus Moira I knew today.

Cassán was my grandfather and my only living ancestor.

Thus, I could not leave, not yet, and each day I begrudgingly tried again, bringing up topics that were relevant to me, rewarded with short flashes of clarity that kept my hopes up through the rough patches. On the second day, noticing my hands for the seventh time, he actually did produce that something he had for burns. The greenish salve was lumpy but it did take the sting out of my skin. Then on the fourth day, when he abruptly woke me from a troubled nap on the sand, he brandished a fish he'd caught for me and said he didn't want me to go hungry. And on the eighth morning, I returned from the holiday house to find him on the beach with the shell on his lap and the gold ring in his fingers, smooth grief and regret swirling softly around him. I didn't interrupt.

There was a good and kind person in there, I determined as I watched him stoking his magical fire under the twelfth evening's first stars, but being alone had not done him any favours. To the comforting soundtrack of crackling flames, I idly played with the wooden puzzle box Angela had given me for my birthday.

'When are you going to open that?' Cassán asked me unexpectedly as he turned the two fish on the stone he used for cooking. I glanced up and found he was watching what I was doing from the corner of his eye. Curiosity briefly stabilised his typically chaotic emotions, giving him something to focus on.

'When I work out how,' I replied, leaning forward from my sandy seat to show him. 'Do you want to try? Just don't, you know,' I amended as he took it, 'forget I gave it to you and throw it in the fire or anything crazy.'

The disdainful glance he shot my way was refreshingly present, but I felt the tendrils of doubt when he turned his eyes down to the little box.

'I've been meaning to ask you that,' he said without looking at me. 'If I'm crazy.'

It came as such a surprise that I didn't know initially what to say, and I said the exact wrong thing.

'How can you be meaning to ask me if your memory blanks every fifteen minutes?'

He scowled at the puzzle box, upset, and I sighed, mentally kicking myself. He spoke before I could apologise.

'Time is messy,' he confided. I nodded ironically – time was definitely getting harder to track the longer I stayed. 'You being here… it helps.' He fidgeted with the box for a long time, and I let him, the same way I gave Renatus room to think when he was conflicted. With Cassán, it was a riskier game, knowing he could swiftly forget the conversation or even who I was. 'My mind was failing me long before I came here. Demons, clouds, missing time, things that aren't really there. You, though. You're always real.'

It seemed like a nice thing to say. I waved away some of the fishy smoke when the evening breeze briefly picked up.

'Is it… dementia? Something?' I asked tentatively, unsure of the etiquette in asking about deteriorating mental health. He looked up at me in surprise.

'No, it's my payment,' he answered as though this were obvious. 'One of many costs I failed to factor in.'

'Factor into what?'

'Into living forever.' The fish meat spat with the build-up of heat and he tossed the puzzle box back without warning. I caught it at my chest, but he was onto a new topic. 'You aren't trying hard enough with that silly box. You're the one who locked it.'

I ignored that and tried to redirect before we lost this chance, 'Tell me about living forever.'

'No.' His stable emotional profile began to break down under the pressure of his personal mixture of horror, regret and fear. He was absolutely adamant, looking away forcefully and shaking his head so hard that his filthy grey hair flicked across his face. 'I won't do that to you. I've done enough.'

Frustrated hopelessness threatened to swallow me. 'Done enough *what*? I don't understand any of this.'

'You should leave it that way,' Cassán said firmly. He finished frying his day's catch and tipped one fillet onto the chipped old plate he let me use. I dropped the puzzle box to accept the meal, sighing heavily at the missed opportunity. He plated up his own fish and began to pick at it moodily. Irritated and forlorn, my fingertips traced the rough ceramic edges of my plate.

Fate had my back.

Inside the cave… Cassán eating from this plate… resentment, annoyance… a younger man kneeling at his side… 'I need you to tell me everything'… Lisandro… carefully takes the crockery from him… reluctance, acceptance…

I lowered my dinner to my lap to let the fish cool.

'You told Lisandro everything,' I said flatly. I pointed at my face. 'The man who almost took out my eye? Was that before or after he murdered your daughter and left me an orphan?'

Cassán's hurt and shock hit me at the same moment as it did him; he choked hard on his first bite of steaming hot fish. I winced at my own callousness as tears sprang to his bright eyes. I knew that was a low blow and I knew I was better than that, but patience with the fragile old man had worn so thin. Not an excuse, I was aware. Cassán struggled to get his breath back, pain spiking through his aura, and I raked my hands back through my hair, frustrated with myself now. I wasn't always this mean.

I tried again.

'You studied magic at its most fundamental levels,' I said desperately while my grandfather wiped heartbroken tears from his face. 'You must have come across fascinating things. Maybe… how to extend life. I don't know. Lots of stuff. Why would you want him to know what you learned, and not me?'

He looked ready to break into sobs but turned to me incredulously.

'Why?' he repeated. 'Do you want to be *this?*' He gestured aggressively at himself, and through the chaos of everything he felt at once, I saw the core clearly for the briefest moment: absolute self-loathing. 'The human mind is a fascinating thing, girl. Powerful, capable of shaping and directing the most potent force in the universe, Fate itself, in the magic we wield. But take away its end point and time loses meaning. Rip it from Fate and its ability to cultivate and sustain the connections with others that make life worth living starts to falter. Scar it irreparably with tragedy and arrogance and that'll be all it can create, and every ounce of magic you channel will come out wrong and leave the world a little worse than it was before.' He glared at me, tears running over his grubby cheeks now without his notice. I cowered when he abruptly stood. 'I told that little monster what he needed to hear to leave me the hell alone, and there is nothing in the world you can say that will make me repeat it to you. The spell is gone. I burnt it. Now go away.'

He turned away with a dismissive flick of his hand. I hadn't seen him throwing around a lot of magic, so I scrambled backward when the little fire he'd been tending flared into a human-sized tower of his anger. I caught the edge of my plate before it could upend into the sand, panting as the fire immediately died, and Cassán stalked off, fuming. Each alone in the dark, we ate our dinner in miserable silence, but mostly we fed on each other's unhappiness.

I spent that night in my new holiday house, glad that the real owners were away but not glad of much else. Sleep mostly eluded me while I lay there thinking over my grandfather's words. He'd twice brought up this concept of immortality, and I was no closer to understanding what he meant by that. *Actual* immortality made no logical sense even in a world where magic was real, but Cassán had indicated that whatever his interpretation of it, he blamed it for his state of mind. Metaphor, special warding, recovery spell – whatever it was, it was something you could learn, if Lisandro had come to Cassán and the older Crafter had been able to share it. He considered it an affliction, one he himself suffered and wouldn't want to expose me to.

That was nice, I supposed.

But Lisandro had this knowledge and I didn't. Renatus didn't, and neither did the rest of the White Elm.

I needed Cassán to spill.

The town entertained daily visitors at this time of year from Monday to Thursday, a busload arriving midmorning and departing with their chirpy tour guides by two-thirty to make it to the other side of the island and across the waters to their next hotel by night. Each business and shopkeeper had a repetitive role to play, and they performed daily to bright-eyed tourists, bringing out the English menus and opening the shutters to stores selling novelty bracelets and shell souvenirs. I had plenty of spare time to work on tweaking the details of my illusion and found it stupidly easy to move among the tourists wearing a different mask each day.

I ate at Xanthe's family restaurant most days, stocking up on Thursdays with a huge order that I brought back to share with Cassán over the weekend. I could only do fish so many nights in a row. Xanthe's mum didn't recognise me as the girl claiming to be Marcy Pretoria from that first visit, but she did gravitate to me on the days she was working the restaurant, drawn by my magical aura. She struck up conversation about the White Elm, gently probing for any new information that might be making the political gossip rounds beyond her community, unaware that she was mostly asking the same person. I wished I had more to tell her to keep her from worrying about her daughter.

On this day, while I was devouring my oversized lunch of *kolokithokeftedes* and gazing mindlessly at the picture of Eleni Giannopoulos with Emmanuelle and the curly-haired man, I heard the restaurant owner speaking with a moderately powerful witch couple that had arrived with today's bus.

'…were worried, but our daughter finally wrote back to us,' the mother gushed delightedly, patting the front pocket of her apron where a battered envelope peeped out. 'They're all okay, and learning more than ever. She says the council is really starting to rely on the students and their gifts. I'm so pleased for her.'

The middle-aged couple expressed their gladness for this turn in fortune, and the wife redirected the line of discussion.

'Did your daughter know this girl Aristea?' she asked. I had the next fritter halfway to my mouth and stopped short of biting into it, wariness rising to match their curiosity.

'She has mentioned that name, yes,' Mrs Giannopoulos agreed. 'She shared a room with her.'

The woman loved a good chat and didn't mind discussing the

magic school that was meant to be top secret, but whatever my schoolyard nemesis had said about me in her letters, her mum had the class to keep to herself. The couple looked dumbfounded.

'Shared a room?' the husband repeated. His accent was sluggishly British, identifying him as belonging to a problematic world region – mine – and potentially linked with people I didn't want to encounter. 'What has she said of her?'

'Lately, only that she's left the Academy,' Xanthe's mum said, sparing a glance my way to see if I was listening. As the only other sorcerer in the place and with no way to tell which side I represented, I understood the precaution. I dipped my next fritter in tzatziki to give myself something to do that looked innocent. The restaurant owner dropped her voice down so low that normal ears couldn't hear. 'Why do you ask? Who is she?'

The couple lowered their voices too. 'From what we've heard, she's the reason for all this nonsense with Magnus Moira and the old families. The White Elm chose her as an apprentice and it all seemed fine until she robbed a gangster, kidnapped his bodyguard and put his daughter in hospital. Now no one can find her anywhere.'

'There was a rumour we heard, didn't we, that she was running with some criminal,' the wife confided, 'and they *killed someone* who caught up with them in Slovakia.'

Xanthe's mother gasped, unsettled, and I swirled my croquette fritter in the sauce. I understood how gossip evolved in its travels, but it was hard to dismiss a story that positioned Declan and me as villains in a country we hadn't even visited.

'But why wouldn't the White Elm put a stop to this?' Mrs Giannopoulos paused, realising the answer. 'Because they are locked in by Magnus Moira. Not all of them,' she reminded the others, ever loyal to her daughter's saviours. 'I am sure they are working on this. This Aristea is only the age of my Xanthe. She may not know what she is caught up in. She might be afraid.'

Thank you, I thought with an eyeroll as I tipped the last of my meal into the paper bag I'd already asked for. Overreacting and assuming the worst was my specialty, and super irritating when others took it upon themselves to muscle in on my role. It was nice to be afforded the benefit of the doubt once in a while.

'I don't think so. I heard she burnt down that theatre in eastern Europe last month, you know the one from the news? And the talents of all the White Elm can't find a trace of her? Dark magic,' the woman said with certainty to the nods of the other two. Mrs Giannopoulos muttered a sort of prayer to fend off the mention. 'You have to wonder how strong they really are if they can't find one rogue teenager gone dark.'

They went quiet when I shoved my stool back noisily.

'You shouldn't believe everything you hear,' I told them, grabbing my lunch. 'This is how propaganda and misinformation spread. Be mindful of whose interests your words serve.'

I marched past the silenced table of fellow sorcerers. I walked straight across town, ignoring locals and bubbly tourists alike until I found another public-use restroom to Displace back to Cassán's beach. I had memorised them all; caves don't have toilets. I stole a couple of fresh bar soaps from the dish on the counter and concentrated on my regular landing spot.

I wasn't delighted to face up to my cruelty last night, but it seemed I'd be spared apologising when I found my grandfather in the corner of his cavern. He sat up at my approach with frowny suspicious eyes, but his expression and emotions cleared somewhat when I tiredly showed him the paper bag.

'Are those *kolokithokeftedes*?'

And we begin again. I plonked down on the bundle of rags stashed in the neighbouring crevice and tore the bag to give him access.

'Go ahead,' I said, pushing the food closer to him. 'I think I'm overdue for another cyclic conversation where nothing I say makes any difference. Yes, they're courgette fritters like Nana used to make, and to save you some time, I'm your granddaughter, I'm a scrier, and a few decades have passed since you got here. Alright?'

Cassán picked up the paper bag dismissively.

'If you say so.'

chapter twenty-three

He greedily dug in and I sat back against the cool stone with a sigh. What a waste of time. I had been treading water here with Cassán for two weeks and gained nothing; worse, my time hiding from the council had given their enemies time to sow dissent among even their loyalists. Declan was a jerk but the thought of him taking the fall for the American bounty hunter's murder put me off my food. The more I reflected on the White Elm as an institution, the less I felt connected to it, but the people on it were fundamentally good. They had Renatus. Emmanuelle. Qasim. Of the political powers on offer, I would take them and their problematic ways over any other, over nothing. Highlighting their apparent inability to catch an errant teenager – or possibly a super dangerous one, depending on the version of events you might hear in a Greek restaurant – was not my intention and seemed, in retrospect, a disaster-shaped hole in my agenda.

I closed my eyes, finally seeing in my mind how this had to end. The White Elm had to catch up with me. I had to give them their credibility back. Maybe I'd been wrong to run, even if Renatus told me to. Maybe I was wrong about everything. I shifted miserably on the pile of rags to get comfy, something solid digging into my thigh. I rifled through for what turned out to be a rusted biscuit tin.

Dirty fingers press it closed… resolve, regret… not Cassán, but Cassán's cave… too dark to see a face… Scottish accent… 'She won't see me'… he tucks the tin under the rags…

'He found her?'

Cassán spoke this time, and I looked up from the tin, confused. 'Who?'

He looked confused, too, and gave the tin a disoriented look, like it reminded him of something he couldn't quite grasp. I wished I'd never touched it when he said, 'Where did you find that?'

I almost growled in frustration at his tattered attention span. I hid the tin behind my back and leaned forward to recapture his focus.

'You just said, "he found her",' I reminded him as calmly as I could manage. He frowned and popped the last fritter in his mouth. 'Who did you mean?'

He chewed, surveying me with his usual conflicted mess of feelings. His eyes, which were the same colour as Angela's, lingered on the scar.

'Moira's boy did that to you?' he asked me after he swallowed, and my frustration evaporated in a burst of hope. He *remembered something*. I nodded eagerly, sitting forward in my excitement. He darkened, remembering more of what I'd said. 'And he… caught up with Elysia. My daughter.'

It wasn't the conversation I'd been angling for, and even now I could feel him pulling back from the pain he'd found just by bringing it up. I opened my mouth to push onward, try and cycle around to what I wanted from him, then bit down on that idea. Butting heads with this man was about as effective as butting heads with myself. He was stubborn, deep, wounded, and unable to sustain a coherent, linear conversation. I needed to be gentle, work with what I had; it was the only way to sync up our feelings and stabilise our volatile dynamic.

I went through my bags, for once ignoring the list I kept presenting to him, and offered the soap I'd taken from town.

'I don't think you're crazy,' I said in answer to his query last night, stilling him as he reached to accept. 'I think you're lonely and you miss the people you love. I feel the same and I've only been away from them for a few weeks.'

Carefully, Cassán took one of the bars of soap. The tight,

shiny skin I could see between patches of grime crinkled when he closed his fist.

'It nearly killed me to leave my baby girl,' he told me, eyes shadowy with past ghosts. 'There wasn't a better choice, but it hurt more than anything I'd ever done. More than the ritual, where we let those anchors die for us and let Moira bleed that little boy. More than leaving Mánus to his fate.'

I worked extremely hard to contain my reactions, knowing he could feel anything I felt. Luckily, he was not Renatus, so my thoughts were my own, and I had many horrified thoughts.

'She was my mother,' I said, continuing this disjointed manner of conversation that seemed to be conducive to letting him talk, 'and she was beautiful. She wasn't like me, or you – she was easy, always calm, like nothing ever bothered her. She married young. Nineteen, I think. Just at the courthouse. It wasn't a big wedding. She had one of those pillbox hats with the birdcage veil.' I demonstrated the shape with my hands, and my grandfather watched me in fascination. My throat felt tight, or maybe his did, but I kept talking. 'She had pink flowers and pink shoes, with bows. Nana Thea was there. She wore dark pink, with a high neckline, and her hair was all swept up. It was thick, and really curly. I've looked at the pictures a thousand times. We still have Mum's… Elysia's… hat. Her dress was ruined in the storm.'

Cassán had been listening attentively despite the ache I felt in his heart.

'What storm?'

'That's how she died,' I told him quietly. 'My parents – Elysia, and her husband Darren. Five years ago. Everyone thought it was just a natural tragedy until I realised Lisandro can control storms.'

Cassán's angry recoil made me think I'd lost him again, but he made a disgusted noise and shook his head. After a few choice swears, he muttered, 'Just like Moira, using the weather for cleaning up messes she shouldn't have made. So her son's no different.' He glared at the cave wall for a heavy moment. 'How many?'

I slowly got the list back out, trying to decide whether to

answer him directly or let the conversation flow elsewhere. I stood, gesturing toward the cave mouth with my own soap, and he followed suit.

'When did you come here?' I asked.

'To stay? When I left my wife and child.' Despite his bigger size and less mobile body, Cassán manoeuvred through the stalagmites more easily than I did. 'I'd been here before. Thea fell down here when she was a little girl, she said.'

We stepped out into the last of the afternoon sun that the enclosed beach received each day, though the sun in fact stayed high in the sky for hours yet, dipping behind the cliff and the town beyond that. I kicked off my boots and scrunched my toes in the sand as Cassán walked ahead to drop down into the rhythmic tide. He dutifully began scrubbing at his hands and arms with the soap, and I wondered how long it had been since he had sourced such things for himself. It didn't seem that he *ever* left this place.

If that was the case… when was the last time he ate a piece of fruit, or meat that wasn't fish? Could the body really sustain itself on one food source for *fifty years*?

Maybe, if that body thinks it's immortal?

'If you're my blood,' Cassán spoke up from the water as he dipped his arms into the soft waves, 'why aren't you a Crafter?'

He'd been fixated on this detail anytime I'd managed to convince him of my identity, and I still had no answer for him.

'Why would I be?' I countered from the beach. He looked back at me, feelings deepening with regret.

'One of many curses that I theorised,' he said, lathering up bubbles in his hands to rub into his face and hair. 'Less influence from Fate, less natural diversity… Hawke would only produce Seers, Morrissey would only produce scriers… not that they're ever anything else. It's a strong gene. But you're a scrier, too.' He thought about this for a bit, splashing water over his head. When he straightened, he asked in uncertainty, 'And you're… apprenticed?'

I nodded, coming closer to the water's edge and pulling my sleeve up to show him the tattoo. He approached, curious and cautious.

'Are there many apprentices?'

'No.' I thought of Egan and decided he didn't count. 'I know some adults who were apprentices, but it's a dying tradition.'

'Surprised the White Elm haven't eliminated it. But your master's a Morrissey?'

'Renatus,' I confirmed while he looked closely at the black mark on my skin, 'but he was initiated without his surname, so I guess there are no more Morrisseys, unless you count his psycho sister.'

Cassán almost smiled, more of a wry wince. 'The Morrissey girl born to fall in love with Moira's very costly child. Twenty-three men died to create him and give him a destiny to rival Fate,' my grandfather elaborated before I could ask. 'Not that I should judge, I suppose.'

'A destiny to rival… what does that mean?'

'Exactly as it sounds.' Cassán lightly traced his finger in the air above my mark. 'Sometimes, destinies are written without Fate having its say. Fate *never* likes being bested, as I learned the hard way. The universe bends for these destinies – people find themselves seduced into helping, events transpire in their favour every time. It looks like luck and charisma.'

'That sounds like Lisandro,' I confirmed. 'You said Ana Morrissey loves him because she was born to?'

'Because Moira Dawes wanted her to, decades before she existed,' Cassán said grimly. He was so present, so *here*, our energies in perfect sync. 'Not that it will save her in the end, I'm sure, if Fate's playing the long game I suspect. You're apprenticed to a Morrissey scrier,' he repeated, staring intently at my tattoo and energetically picking through the layers of magic I had no hope of finding as a non-Crafter, 'who disowned his family's name and… joined *the White Elm*?' He looked up at me incredulously, water dripping from grey eyebrows. I shrugged one shoulder apologetically; I hadn't thought he'd like that particular detail. He didn't, but his long-suppressed scholarly curiosity won out. 'Spectacularly talented with telepathy, I suppose, and not so much with healing?'

I refrained from answering that one right away – Renatus's inability to magically heal either himself or others was not something he'd appreciate me confirming to anyone else.

'Mánus couldn't heal, then?'

'He could,' Cassán corrected, darkening, 'and then he couldn't. His son was the same. I don't want to discuss why. One of many unexpected costs.' He looked at me sideways. 'You never met Mánus?'

'His gravesite is missing from Morrissey Estate.'

'He's not *dead*, silly girl,' my grandfather said impatiently. 'He can't die. He's disconnected from Fate.' He was silent a long moment, before surprising me with, 'I miss him.'

'I miss Renatus,' I concurred. 'I don't think anyone's heard from Mánus in decades, if it's true he's alive. I *did* meet Eugene. The same day I met you. He was…' I thought of the writhing, incoherent prisoner I'd had to leave behind at Lisandro's compound. 'He makes you look well-adjusted.'

'That's what losing your magic does to you. Is he still helping Moira's boy?'

'How do you know about that?' I asked, surprised. Cassán was unimpressed.

'Because he's a sell-out.' He sighed. 'Fate has a sense of humour. It can't reach Moira's son directly but it can reconfigure the game board to prevent him from winning. Would Mánus's grandson have chosen you if you were a Crafter like you were meant to be?'

'No,' I knew immediately, 'and I don't think I was ever meant to be anything else. I'm not that good yet, but the skills I brought to the White Elm were exactly what they needed at the time. I could scry Lisandro when they couldn't, I scried their dead defector after Lisandro murdered him,' I felt the odd niggle of a persistent thought here, but ignored it, 'and if I wasn't a scrier *and* an Empath *and* your grandchild, Renatus might have overlooked me and he wouldn't be as powerful as he is now. Or as stable,' I chanced a guess. 'I think I'm what I am because I have to be.'

Cassán nodded in full agreement.

'Fate found a way,' he said. He looked much cleaner, if you ignored his ratty clothes, and turned his face into the last of the mid-afternoon sun. 'It always does. That White Elm lad, the Seer, he reminded me of that. I wonder sometimes how long ago that was. Whether he got that girl.'

I frowned, the push of a soft golden force brushing the back of my thoughts.

'Which Seer? Lord Gawain? He said he knew you.'

Cassán opened his eyes to squint in surprise. 'Harrington? Nice lad; I'm sure the heartbreak did him no favours. No, no,' he gestured back at the cave mouth we couldn't see behind his clever illusion. 'The Scottish lad. The one who came here. The defector.' He thought harder, while pieces fell into place in my stunned mind, and he remembered another detail. 'He loved the French girl.'

He loved the French girl.

The picture at the Giannopoulos family restaurant. The young man on the bus, holidaying with his grandmother and teen sibling or cousin. The curly-haired man with the biscuit tin. *She won't see me.*

'Peter Chisholm,' I realised, covering my mouth, recalling his decomposing body being picked at by birds on a beach after Lisandro drowned him in the North Sea. Finding Peter was the first thing I did to put myself on Renatus's radar. But before he was dead, before he sided with Lisandro, he was the caretaker for the White Elm's ring. He was Emmanuelle's *best friend.*

And he had been here. My mind's eye went straight back to the restaurant, and as though I was standing beside the bar, I looked at the tiny picture closely. Emmanuelle, Eleni Giannopoulos, and *Peter.* Curly-haired and plain-faced, he lacked the striking appearance of most magical people. His hands were on Eleni's shoulders, all fingers visible. No ring. This was before he'd inherited that responsibility and before he'd lost his friend's faith.

Or so he'd thought. I'd seen Emmanuelle learn his last words.

I never told her I loved her.

It broke her heart that he didn't reach out, that he'd chosen to walk to his death after wrapping the legendary Elm Stone ring in this paper list he'd presumably stolen from Lisandro and burying both beside her front door. Whatever he'd done, however far he'd strayed, it had hurt her more that he didn't trust her to listen.

'Peter, yes,' Cassán recalled vaguely. He sat down at the edge of the lapping foam of the sea and began to scrub at his bare feet. 'Idealist, sap. That's the one. Couldn't understand why he'd done the things he had; said it went against who he thought he was. Didn't understand that as a Seer he was just a plaything for Fate. He had a plan to fix the future, he said. But everything worth doing in magic has a cost, and his was his life.'

I knelt beside him breathlessly, the water soaking my knees and my clothes, and once again produced the list with his name and mine.

'Was this part of his plan?' I asked, praying for the miracle it would take to keep Cassán from losing concentration at *precisely* this moment. He glanced aside and surveyed the set of fifteen names. He nodded grimly.

'I told him, though, Moira's son can't be stopped from his destiny,' he warned. 'That's what a destiny is. Fate can't interfere.' He slowed in his scrubbing. 'Are my books no longer in print?'

I cringed at the unhelpful reminder that he'd already written everything he knew about the interrelationships between Fate, magic and human lives in numerous publications, most of which were in Renatus's library.

'I, uh, didn't read them yet.' I scratched my hairline and stared out across the sea, trying to make sense of everything I'd just learned from my previously useless grandfather. Destinies and Fate were different things. Lisandro had a destiny I didn't understand and it couldn't be stopped. Peter had tried to *fix* things – and as a Seer, had known he'd have to die to achieve it. But other Seers had told me things, too. 'Lisandro can't be kept from fulfilling his destiny, but he *can* be killed?'

Cassán deliberated with a noncommittal shrug.

'You all can. Theoretically. Your list suggests he's already confirmed my theory and is working on staying alive long enough to do what he was born for.'

'Which is?'

'Moira made him to end the White Elm.'

I let that settle with me. Shadowy half-remembered moments from the distant past rose in my mind, visions of Cassán and his revolutionary friends working under the White Elm's radar. To hate the council so much that you'd have a baby and give it a destiny, or whatever, purely to spite and demolish that authority...

Well, if destinies were real and this was Lisandro's, it explained a lot about how he'd gotten as far as he had. Why luck always seemed to bend his way. Why good people wanted to trust him.

'The crossed-out ones are dead?' Cassán, still reading the list, was briefly taken with irritation. 'Who are they? Family names, come on, girl!'

'Uh, Mánus and Aindréas Morrissey–'

'I know *them*,' he said impatiently. 'And I told you, Mánus isn't dead. He's just... gone. Who are the dead ones? How many...?' He squinted to count. 'Four so far? Kenneth, my Elysia... Who's this Aidan?'

He said it so callously, and I was sure that he felt my flash of hurt.

'My older brother,' I answered as evenly as I could, 'who Lisandro murdered along with my mum and dad.'

Cassán, for all his instability, recognised his error, and softened. He looked from my face to the list, emotions shifting to reflect mine.

'Elysia had a son,' he realised, awed.

'And two daughters,' I agreed, pointing out our names, knowing he hadn't meant to dismiss his own grandson like that. 'Angela and me.'

'All "A" names,' he noticed. 'Anthea's siblings all began with "A", too. Which of you is older?' he queried quickly, nostalgia sharpening back into concern.

'Ange is.'

'Oh.' Cassán looked a little regretful. 'She'll be the next to die, then.'

It was like taking a shot to the heart. '*Excuse me?*'

'Unless someone else on this list is older than she is?' Cassán added hopefully. I looked down at it glassily, horrified. 'Ignoring those he'd never hurt, it can't have escaped your notice Lisandro's working his way down.'

He was right. Damn him, I'd never thought to look at it that way before. The first generation was untouched, but scattered, in more ways than one. From the second generation, only Lisandro remained. In mine, Nastassja was converted and my eldest sibling was dead. Angela, Renatus, Asheleigh Hawke and I remained, in that order. Although wasn't Asheleigh expecting a baby? Perhaps by now I was no longer the youngest descendant, but I was still one of only two with no sentimental value to Lisandro.

'He's going to kill my sister,' I realised, sickened. How had I not seen this before? How could I leave her alone this whole time? My Empathic grandfather leaned away from my distress.

'*He* is just a tool,' he counselled unhelpfully. 'Fate is what will take her before her time. Because of me, and what I did.'

He looked away, deeply troubled. I wasn't prepared to blame poor Fate when Lisandro's alleged destiny was what was wrong. He was the problem.

'Unless I can stop him,' I mentioned firmly. Cassán shrugged, unconvinced.

'You can try. I hope you will. But his destiny won't allow it until he's finished the job his mother set for him. After that…'

'Renatus is destined to kill Lisandro,' I told him quietly, fidgeting nervously with the list.

'Fated,' my grandfather corrected, unmoved by the proclamation. 'Like you, like everyone, he's a tool of Fate, not the plans of humans.'

'Fated, whatever. He doesn't know, and I can't tell him. I'm afraid it would ruin him.' I swallowed that fear while Cassán nodded regretfully. 'That's why I have to do it. If I can.'

My grandfather put the soap down and let the water take the

bubbles away from his legs and feet.

'My worst nightmare realised,' he mused. 'A girl of mine cleaning up after a Morrissey. I'm not telling you not to do it,' he interjected before I could get that impression, 'but how do you know that the deed won't do the same to you?'

I shook my head and began to fold the list. 'I don't. The difference is, if he goes off the rails, there's no one who could stop him. Me, they'd catch before I could do much damage.'

'You think so?' Cassán asked idly. He looked pointedly down the beach as he took back the list. 'How long have you evaded capture now?'

I stood and dusted myself off, surprised by his guess.

'What makes you think–'

'Protection spell hidden behind rocks, chunks out of your hair, and frankly, why else would you sleep in a cave when you could be at Morrissey House?' With damp fingers he opened Peter's list once again and gazed at the names. 'That White Elm lad had so many papers and letters for his lass, and this was the one he chose to leave her. That ring he had – amazing. Generations of stored power. And he just walked out of a circle with it. Doubtless, Lisandro has it by now.'

'Well, yes, Renatus's sister has it. But you said Peter had *other* documents like this?' I tapped the list. Cassán was staring at the names, eyes glazing over, and it occurred to me that I'd had his attention for longer than ever before.

'He was sorry,' he murmured, tracing his fingertips over his daughter's name. 'I knew what that felt like. When you get caught up in the idea of your own importance and realise too late that your impact on the world is only a chain of mistakes you can't take back.'

'You've had positive impacts,' I argued immediately, thinking of Teagan Shanahan praising this man's early writing, books she found inspiring. 'Our society understands magic better because of you. Listen, you mentioned papers that Peter–'

'People are dead because of me,' Cassán interrupted sharply. His emotions were destabilising quickly, his mood turning over. 'The five anchors my spell required to separate myself and my coven from Fate. A little boy whose mother never stopped looking for him. My daughter. My Elysia… Her son… And everything else. I should have told Mánus *no*, blood curses are viciously unfair…'

I'd lost him. He spiralled into misery, and I quickly moved away, barricading myself from his dark mood before it could infect mine. I hurried back into the cave, focusing hard on what he'd told me. It served as a solid distraction from the feelings that radiated from the beach.

Peter was here and he had a plan to "fix" the future.

He'd known he'd have to die.

Lisandro had a destiny and he'd been born to end the White Elm.

Fate didn't condone this destiny and seemed to be working through its various agents to stymie Lisandro's plans wherever possible.

Peter had realised he'd been used.

Lisandro couldn't be kept from his destiny but he *could* be killed. After.

After the White Elm fell from power. Was that something I was prepared to let happen?

If the alternative was risking Renatus's soul, hadn't I decided a long time ago?

I stood in the cavern, surrounded by Cassán's messy collection of knick-knacks and my two bags and the ripped paper bag from the *Giannopoulos Family Restaurant*. There was no order, no point of specific reference, but my eyes fell on the tarnished corner of the biscuit tin half-tucked under the rags I'd been using as a seat only minutes ago.

I tossed my light trick at the cave's rocky ceiling and bent down to grab the tin.

Young man shivering in the dark… hugging this tin to his chest… shellshocked, betrayed… 'I can never go back. How could I? Everything I joined them to prevent, I facilitated. It's my fault'…

'Who knew we'd find ourselves in the same boat, Peter?' I asked aloud as I prised the tin open. The lid popped off with a little rusty resistance. Inside were a few dozen sheets of discoloured paper, some folded, some not. The top one captured my full attention. 'Maybe you did.'

Aristea, it said in writing that matched the hand of the rest of the enclosed pages, *please get these to Emmanuelle today. Tomorrow is too late*.

Today? Like, my today? Hopefully he didn't mean *his* today, a year ago. And if he meant my today, how had he known which precise day I would find this? Could his talent really have been so exact?

I hoped so, I realised as I rifled lightly through the papers, reading the next page. If he'd been able to divine that I, a perfect stranger, would be here on this day to read these letters, then it made sense that he also knew Emmanuelle was alive to receive them.

Em, three things. One, I'm so sorry. Two, I love you. Three, things are bad right now, but I promise you, we're going to win, and I'm going to tell you how. But first, we have to lose.

I slowly replaced the lid, unsure whether I wanted to read more. The letters weren't for me, and I was hardly a strategist. Me knowing what was intended for someone else could affect the information's usefulness. Peter's instructions were to get this to Emmanuelle.

Who was inside Morrissey House.

Which I couldn't get into.

My turbulent thoughts kept me occupied for the indeterminate amount of time it took for Cassán to forget who I was and the deep, personal conversation we'd just shared. He stopped abruptly after the stalagmite maze, his misery shifting into wary confusion on the turn of a dime.

'How did you get in here?' he demanded. He began to realise I was in his space, that I'd gotten in without him seeing, and that triggered his usual vulnerability. 'Who the hell are you?'

I straightened and showed him the biscuit tin.

'I'm your… I'm nobody,' I amended, even as his eyes roamed the air around my head. He could see my aura's sinkholes. He had to know I was connected to him. But I had gained everything I could from being here, and this billionth factory reset coupled with the discovery of Peter's instructions felt like a very clear prompt from Fate. 'Forget I was here. I was just leaving.'

Under his suspicious glare, I knelt at my satchel and checked everything was in it. Passport, money, sai… I had a split second's warning between Cassán's threat reaction and his ward, and then I was thrown back against the hard cave wall.

'You here to hurt me?' he roared, crackling white magic building in his stiff hands and illuminating the cavern with dancing shadows. 'I'll tell you now, I can't be killed, girl.'

The sai. I pushed myself off the rough rock, muscles and shoulder blades bruised with the impact, and opened my hands to let the blades fall. The curved guards hooked onto my thumbs and the sharpened points hung harmlessly.

'I'm not here to hurt you,' I insisted. 'I'm your blood. I'm Aristea. You've just forgotten.'

'Forgotten?' He sniffed disdainfully in the direction of Declan's satchel. 'You reek of memory spell. What did you do?'

'Well, I don't know,' I answered honestly, 'since I spelled myself. Look–'

'*You* look,' Cassán snarled, still looking verifiably crazy despite being cleaned up. 'If Hawke sent you, tell him I'm not interested. I won't do it again. We got what we deserved, and that's the end of it. If it's not what he was hoping for, that's too bad. He's the damn Seer – he should have warned us. He should have *known* it would get to this. And after what we've already lost, I won't help him end one legacy to save another. Now, whoever you are, get out.'

My eyes slid to the satchel and biscuit tin, and my grandfather's did, too.

'Let me get my stuff, and I'll go,' I said, careful to keep my emotions gentle and stable as I *pushed* them on him as lightly as I knew how. I felt him deflect most of it stubbornly, though I hoped some got through. The burning white magic in his hands dimmed slightly.

'It's not your bag, and it's not your box,' he said sternly. I didn't know how he knew about the satchel and didn't ask. 'Just get out.'

I frowned and squared my shoulders, annoyed with him and trying desperately not to convey it.

'That's my passport and my wallet,' I retorted, gesturing. He looked down at the bag where it lay strewn from his attack. The magic in his hands went out and I felt his inner concession, the realisation in his time-addled mind that it would be unreasonable to expect me to leave without the things I most needed to get around. He stooped for them, unwieldly fingers trying twice to close around the slippery passport cover. While he was collecting them up for me, I added, 'And the tin has my name inside it. I have to deliver it to my friend.'

Cassán scoffed. He flung the passport and wallet in my direction. I hurriedly tucked them into the pockets of my jeans while Cassán tried unsuccessfully to open the tin with his scarred hands.

'It belongs to the White Elm. If I leave it here, Fate might send them here to find it.' I paused to see if this sunk in, and it definitely did. I pushed on. 'I can take it off your hands. They'll never know you–'

Luckily I'd shifted both sai to one hand when I picked up my wallet and passport, because now he violently threw the biscuit tin at me. I half-turned to be able to catch it with my shoulder, where it hurt, and curled my arm around it tightly like a football.

'Take it and *get out!*' he shouted, making a furious step toward me that, for the first time, made me afraid of him. He was between me and the cave entrance, and the second last thing I wanted was to hurt him to get past. I reluctantly took one sai back to my left hand so I could swing the right one as a reminder. It stilled his next step, uncertainty interrupting his senseless anger, and with my wards up high, I dashed toward the stalagmites I now knew the way through. I was slowed by stinging feet – my shoes were still out on the beach. I left both my bags behind but I had my sai and I had Peter's letters. My ruby was in my pocket where I always kept it and I had money. Hopefully I wouldn't need to generate another protection spell for a while and hopefully Hiroko wasn't too attached to the cute backpack.

Out on the beach, with the sun now behind the cliff, I dumped everything down on the sand and yanked on my boots. I felt bitter about the whole situation. All these pointless days trying to reach Cassán, only for everything to come rushing out at once and then for him to confirm that he really was in no way a functioning grandfather for me. We had so much in common, yet so little stable common ground to stand on. I stood and, letting my emotions get the better of me, or maybe some of his, I angrily kicked at the sand.

I was glad I did. A little stone landed near where we'd cooked our fish last night. Right where I'd dropped it was Angela's wooden puzzle box.

I'd almost left without it, and without solving its mystery.

'There are enough family mysteries on this beach,' I muttered, picking it up and shaking the sand from its carved surfaces. Armed with two sai and two boxes, I closed my eyes and considered where I'd go next.

'Aristea?'

I turned, eyes snapping open. I'd never heard him say my name before. Cassán stood at the cave entrance, emotions oddly low again and a confused look on his face.

'Your friend, Mánus's grandson,' he said. 'Watch out for him.'

'I always do,' I replied immediately, then heard the words playing back in my head with another, less comforting meaning. 'Or do you mean…?'

More grounded than he had any right to be after that outburst, my grandfather said, firmly, 'I mean both. Save him if you can, but know that there are some prices no one should pay.'

That last part was something he always said, yet the soft flash of pale gold somewhere at the back of my mind and the unsettled feeling inside made me pay attention. Usually nudges from Fate drove me in a singular, connected direction, but this seemed at odds with the message I'd left myself after whatever happened at Shanahan's.

Whatever it takes.

Hiroko's words, too, floated through my mind. *Our friends are always our responsibility.*

Cassán's words were perhaps a reminder that terms like *always* and *whatever* were extremely open and probably needed some limitations imposed on them, lest I one day find myself sulking in a cave regretting starting an out-of-control magical liberalism movement and murdering a few people to fuel a spell I thought was a good idea at the time.

'I'll remember,' I promised. I hesitated. 'You know, it's not too late to fix things. You could come with me.'

'I should, but I can't. I can only make things worse.' He stared, looking through me at something deeper. 'He was better than me. You're better again.'

I could guess who he meant, but it didn't matter. I raised a hand to wave.

'Goodbye, Cassán.'

He smiled, and I saw the man from my visions. 'Goodbye, my granddaughter.'

chapter twenty-four

The day after her fingers twitched for the first time, Emmanuelle was able to lift one finger at a time before she needed to resume her trance. The day after that, she could make a fist. The day after *that*, she lifted her hand, then her ankle, and the following day, she hit her side table with a clumsy wave of her arm and demanded to be freed from the energetic brace that held her. Her spinal cord was completely healed, thirty-one pairs of complex nerves and protective tissues painstakingly repaired cell by cell. The vertebrae violently broken were also restored, as strong and solid as ever before. After weeks in a medical trance, working on this near-constantly, Emmanuelle was more intimate with the particulars of her own bodily systems than she'd ever cared to be.

Her White Elm colleagues were reluctant, but a lengthy long-distance consultation with Lady Miranda got the high priestess on her side and to her absolute relief, Emmanuelle was released. Not that she could stand yet, nor sustain wakefulness for more than an hour at a time after that long trance without food, but the freedom was invaluable.

The problem now, as she irritably explained to everyone who came to fuss over her, was no longer the spine but her muscles, which had atrophied more than was natural in the three weeks of stillness. The energy expended keeping herself alive had drawn from her own body; her muscles, her organs, damage she hadn't meant to do in her instinctive state of semiconsciousness. Switching off her digestive, urinary and reproductive systems had been a smart move in terms of conservation of energy – and dignity – but the unprepared pause on systems inextricably linked with still-operating ones had taken its toll, particularly on her kidneys and liver. All of it was repairable, thankfully, but would take time.

Eight days after the first finger twitch, Emmanuelle stood with support, which she took as a sign that it was time to resume organ operations since she now had the core strength to use a toilet. The things you don't think about. That also meant she could resume eating, which she'd been thoroughly looking forward to and would accelerate repair, but then she didn't have the dexterity to handle a spoon.

Needless to say, all this dependence on others and daily humiliation – made worse by everyone finding opportunities to tell her it wasn't humiliating, that she was brave, that they were proud of her – was extremely motivating. So were the voices in her head. Renatus still wasn't one of them, Lord Gawain not yet convinced that the young scrier's mind was completely his own, but the others communicated along their network of joined minds almost all day.

Trouble in embargo paradise. The crimson cloaks are arguing with the plainclothes again.

The Seer students all agree that something has shifted, but I don't sense anything.

Valero wants us to know they've had some breakthroughs with Glen.

I've been picking up on some repeated Displacements to that site Jadon and Renatus found, where Aubrey's family are living. Can anyone check it out? Should we be worried about this baby?

It drove her insane with the desire to get off this bed and go *do something*. That, and she wanted to be able to walk out whenever someone visited under the presumption that her lethargy and stillness meant anything close to interest.

'I can't see a way out of this,' Lord Gawain said on the thirteenth day, speaking mostly to himself with little regard for the other two people in the room or the therapy in session. Emmanuelle, who'd managed to dress herself in loose slacks of Tian's and a sweater of Addison's since she couldn't work buttons or zippers, and Sterling, who'd popped her head in a few days ago to mention that her mother was an occupational therapist, glanced at each other over Emmanuelle's shaky knee. 'Fate never showed me *this* as an ending. Bringing him onto the council was the key to creating the only possible future in which we won. Instead he's been one of the driving forces behind undoing everything, and now he's done this.'

Her student's hands steady on her kneecap, thigh pressed toward her chest to stretch the underused hamstring, Emmanuelle strained to control her exhalation. Her legs were increasingly able to hold her weight, but the swing and balance of walking wasn't coming as easily as she'd hoped. They were about to try again after yesterday's embarrassing collapse halfway to the door.

'He 'asn't... done... anything, you said,' she reminded her leader stiffly, between tight puffs of air. Sterling silently held the knee in place, trying not to look like she was listening. Lord Gawain had become complacent with what he said in front of the students, and though Emmanuelle thought it was mostly good to bring them more into the fold and utilise their many skills, Sterling Adams had a deeper interest in Renatus than many of the others. She doubted the elderly Seer knew that. 'It was only something 'e learned... that changed things... Oh *dieu merci*, thank you,' she breathed in relief when Sterling released the leg and helped her straighten it out.

'Something he learned that he wouldn't have if he'd stayed put,' Lord Gawain elaborated, pausing at the window to gaze out, apparently conflicted. 'I should have known if anyone would find a way off these grounds, it would be him.'

That, Emmanuelle thought, was more than a given. Renatus was markedly more powerful than anyone else on the White Elm and was *raised here*. Yes, if anyone were to find an alternative exit, it would be the property's lifelong resident.

'It's like he doesn't understand the consequences of his actions,' Lord Gawain mused with the same dismay he'd been carting around for weeks, and Emmanuelle wasted valuable energy tipping her head back on her mattress to roll her eyes harder.

'You are realising this *now*?' She waved for Sterling to leave the other leg and to help her up instead. The stretching was no doubt helpful but it took a lot out of her, and she was impatient to walk. 'Since the day you met, Renatus was *always* going to make these connections, circumvent your orders and go after the answers 'e thought 'e would find at that 'ouse. Fate was not surprised. Why are you?'

Lord Gawain had no answer to that. His soft silence told Emmanuelle that he conceded her point. Her student knelt on the edge of the mattress and anchored her other foot on the floor. Cradling the neck with immense caution, maybe not agreeing with this but too scared to argue, the American teenager pulled her into a sitting position. When her feet hit the floor, it felt like an achievement. Teacher and student grinned exhaustedly at each other.

Sterling was an airhead, no lie, but she was also a caring soul and more knowledgeable on physical therapy and human mechanics than Emmanuelle had ever realised. She was in Lady Miranda's Level 2 class on healing, and as a Seer didn't have any particular talent for it. What she'd picked up in a lifetime of exposure to her mother's work was something the White Elm's early screening processes had totally overlooked and now was proving to be every bit as valuable as a magical skill.

'Should you be pushing this hard?' Lord Gawain asked worriedly as Sterling tentatively released her to test her core strength. Emmanuelle tried not to let the trembling manifest as visible shakes.

'Yes,' she answered firmly. She extended a hand to Sterling, who reluctantly grasped her wrist. 'Today I walk. Tomorrow, the stairs. The next day, I walk out the front gate.'

Maybe it was a little exaggerated, but the thought of it fuelled her unsteady push to her wobbly feet. Sterling's hand tightened on her forearm. Her legs felt shaky; her core felt weak; her head felt heavy. Forcibly, she reminded herself of what lay beyond the walls of this estate and her blood boiled at the mere thought of Jackson so near. That made her lift her chin and tighten her unwilling body, stabilising herself somewhat.

Sterling smiled. 'Good! Should we try...' She stepped backward, giving Emmanuelle room to pivot her weight and shuffle one foot forward awkwardly. The girl beamed even as Emmanuelle panted at the effort. 'Okay, let's give it a minute.'

'You're right.' Lord Gawain was watching on with what she gathered was pride, though she didn't need anyone's approval. 'Fate sent him to us like this. It's what he's always done, and that future has never wavered. It makes no sense that it would waver now.'

He contemplated this uneasily while Emmanuelle tried not to wish him out of the room and concentrated on Sterling's voice coaching her next step. It was an effort not to scream in frustration – for someone so accustomed to independence, to have her own body useless and unresponsive was possibly the worst thing she'd ever experienced. But words she'd never expected to miss hearing had been playing in her head since that Belarusian theatre.

Whit's fur ye'll no go past ye.

Peter's infuriating Scottish catchphrase, her least favourite thing about him until he'd betrayed the council, was supposed to mean something along the lines of "what will happen will happen and there's nothing we can do about it". It had been her personal mantra throughout the trance, and not because she believed a single word of it. She wholly, totally, completely did not. There was no way Fate was going to make any damning decisions for her about her recovery prospects. Was that why Peter used to say it, kind of an ironic suggestion? It was hard to say. She needed this recovery. She needed to relearn walking. She needed to walk out that gate. If something was going to happen, it was happening to Jackson and there was nothing he could do about it.

She was going to happen. So she could put in the work, and she could swallow the helpless tears and the embarrassment.

'Charlie said something interesting to me once,' Lord Gawain said, completely misreading the room and continuing on this monologue while his audience mostly ignored him. 'A long time ago, after the O'Malleys died. Neither of us could understand what went wrong. We did *everything* the way Fate showed us, told only the people it prompted us to, wove the story exactly as it bade us... and that whole family still died. It made no sense. And he said to me, "It feels like someone invisible is at play".'

Emmanuelle's next step was even shakier than the preceding and she nearly went down, Sterling closing in to catch her under the arm. The instinct to ward up had to be overcome to avoid shoving the girl away, and Emmanuelle clung to her shoulder, casting an irritable look at the old man standing on the other side of the room, both a distraction and an audience she didn't want.

'Fascinating,' she said scathingly. 'Why are you talking about something your dead friend said 'alf a century ago?'

It was harsh – she'd liked Charlie, had been sorry when he passed.

'Because he wasn't the only dead friend to say it, just the first,' the Lord Gawain explained patiently. 'It feels like that now. We're doing everything right according to Fate's plan, and then...' He tossed his hands like he was throwing paper in the air. 'Like Fate isn't the only one in the ring even though we can't see anyone else. Pieces moving and threads shifting *without* Fate's input.'

'Except everyone is connected to Fate and subject to its workings,' Sterling wisely spoke up, catching the black pendant that swung around her neck and tucking it into her top.

Lord Gawain looked uncomfortable. Emmanuelle didn't know why, because that was her understanding of Fate, too. Of course, if there was conflicting evidence, he'd know better than she did, and old Charlie maybe even better. The kind wrinkled face, milky blind eyes and eccentric wardrobe of the late White Elm councillor came to mind. The Seer's peaceful but sudden death opened a position on the White Elm that freshly-twenty Renatus had been chosen to fill – eerie timing, given his very precise gift for foresight.

'I always believed so,' Lord Gawain eventually agreed while Sterling carefully extricated herself from Emmanuelle's weight and righted her once again. They prepared to attempt another step. 'But I have heard many things in my life that have made me question that. For Charlie to have questioned Fate's absolute dominion, and for Peter to do the same…'

He trailed off at Emmanuelle's reaction to the unexpected mention. Her knee gave out and she went down on her backside, almost yanking Sterling down on top of her. The girl landed awkwardly between her legs, apologising profusely and unnecessarily. Emmanuelle shot a glare back at her leader, about to demand an explanation, but a new, guarded presence at the doorway drew her attention in the opposite direction. Renatus leaned cautiously on the doorframe without stepping inside.

'Am I interrupting?'

His sense of humour was just the worst. With a teenage girl half on top of her, it was a targeted reminder of her walking in on him once in an easily misconstrued position with Aristea. Sterling blushed wildly and scrambled to her feet.

'Ignore 'im,' Emmanuelle advised darkly. She looked up at the scrier she'd become used to only seeing when no one else was around – he was in Lord Gawain's bad books, and the energy transfers he gave her were still off the books, though no one could be under any illusion as to where power like that was coming from. 'What do you want?'

He didn't let the hostility bother him. Not that he'd ever been particularly easy to ruffle, but increasingly he seemed more attuned to the intention behind her words. He was clearly sensitive to Sterling's edginess and Lord Gawain's discomfort with his presence, evidenced by his uneasy glance between those two. He leaned into the room and produced a polished wooden cane from behind his back.

'It seems you aren't the first person in my house to need one of these,' he said, holding it out. From the floor, warmth sparked in Emmanuelle's chest at his thoughtfulness. She tried not to look at Lord Gawain, whose heart she was sure was melting all over the floor.

He was always looking for proof of the good soul he was sure he'd rescued here eight years ago. His own belief in that soul shook from time to time, but more than anything, he always *wanted* to believe in it.

'Thank you,' Emmanuelle said delightedly, reaching for the proffered support, already imagining herself shuffling around the room independently. Though no stick of wood could help get her out of bed, she wouldn't need a young girl holding her hand every time she wanted to take a step. Renatus had brought her *freedom* and right then, she adored him for it.

The adoration was short-lived.

'Don't mention it,' he said easily, and he slowly lowered the cane to prop it up against the wall just inside the door. And left it there, raising his gaze back to hers with no doubt as to the challenge he was leaving in her court.

Emmanuelle scowled, resisting the urge to fling a frustrated ward in Renatus's direction and throw him from the room like he deserved. Her frustration doubled when Sterling Adams and Lord Gawain shared an uneasy glance across the room, unable to decide whether to intercede on this blatant act of unfairness or let it play out. Outspoken teenager and governor of the magical world, both rendered powerless by the uncertainty of how to act around a person with a disability.

Or maybe it was just the fear of being snapped at for trying to help when she was fully capable, with a concerted effort, of doing this herself. It was a valid fear.

Moving her glare from Renatus's impassive expression to the old, polished cane, Emmanuelle inhaled a stiff breath. This was what he intended, she knew. Something for her to work towards. With weak hands, she rearranged one heavy leg and then the other, and she looked up at Sterling. The girl crouched, and with more confidence, she clasped her teacher's elbows. This, they'd done before. Emmanuelle watched the girl's chin as she silently counted her in, and with a huge effort from every muscle, it seemed, she struggled to her feet. Sterling righted her, beaming and squeezing her forearms in encouragement.

She was up. Renatus hadn't moved. Breathing hard, Emmanuelle leaned a little to see past Sterling and approximate the distance to the door. Four normal paces, at most, which was as many as ten of her awkward shuffle paces.

The bastard, to do this to her. It was exactly what she needed to prove to herself she could do it.

'When I get there, I will 'it you with it,' she warned him, nodding to Sterling. Carefully, every muscle group tightly controlled, attention on her balance, Emmanuelle lifted one foot very slightly. She didn't get it very far forward before her weight followed it and brought it down, but Sterling's excitement said it counted.

'Good,' Renatus replied rather dryly. 'I look forward to your demonstration of accuracy, or lack thereof.'

Connard. 'You will not enjoy when I 'it you in the teeth,' she sneered, dragging her other foot forward.

'No, but I'll be sure to protect my shoulder if that's where you're aiming.'

Emmanuelle concentrated on the figure-eight pattern of weight distribution between the legs during natural walking that she was trying to replicate, but she couldn't contain the accidental snort of amusement. A low blow, but she appreciated the attempt to distract her from the crushing immensity of relearning to walk at almost twenty-six. Eyes on Sterling's shoes, she got the next foot to land just shy of the girl's toes, and then with shuddering effort swung the other leg to overtake it, and then the first again.

She glanced up at Renatus, hoping he wouldn't change the goalpost. He stayed where he was, leaving the cane in its place, but did shift his gaze very, very briefly to Lord Gawain by the window.

It was the tiniest moment, but even Emmanuelle detected the forlornness between the two men.

'Just... talk to each other,' she snapped between uneven breaths. She wasn't sure it came out coherent, until she got a response.

He hasn't forgiven me for creating the circumstances that prevent his apprentice coming safely home, Lord Gawain reflected sadly in his direct communication with Emmanuelle, from which Renatus was iced out. She gritted her teeth against the distraction. *I suppose I can't blame him.*

Perhaps he needs your forgiveness for trying to change those circumstances, Emmanuelle advised. She cut him from her thoughts to focus solely on her own body. She felt the girl's hands loosen at her arms and slide to just her hands – guides now, not supports. The dark wood of the cane appeared in Emmanuelle's peripheral vision, an elusive goal. It was *right there*. Breathing too hard to speak, Emmanuelle glanced between it and her hands, still secure in Sterling's. She was going to have to let go. Briefly, the thought of falling *this close* to her destination froze her with hesitation.

'No one else is going to take it for you,' Renatus prompted beside Sterling. 'It has to be you, even if you fall.'

Worst motivational speaker ever. But again, it was the reminder she needed. Legs trembling, sweat gathering under her long hair, teeth gritting together in determination, Emmanuelle drew a swift breath through her nose and let go of Sterling. She tipped herself forward into the doorframe and just let herself fall, focusing on extending both hands to maximise her chances of catching the cane as she crashed into the wall.

Her grip closed on the polished shaft of the cane and her heart lit up with delight that made the impending bodily collision seem like a small cost.

But she didn't crash and she didn't go down. Sterling leaned anxiously around him to grab her elbow, and Renatus flashed into motion to catch her by the shoulders just as her knees buckled, and he righted her to lean into the wall. Clutching the cane to her chest, feet scrambling for purchase, Emmanuelle breathed hard and shrugged them both off.

She'd earned her prize, and thanks to them, this time, she hadn't had to go down for it. She leaned heavily into the wall and tried not to slide down it.

'You're a jerk,' she told Renatus in heartfelt thanks, trembly fingers running appreciatively over the strong wood of the cane he'd found. It didn't surprise her that someone in his family's past had required one, especially given that they were incapable of healing and had a penchant for dramatic flair. It was well cared for with only a few chinks in the shaft. Careful not to dislodge her position against the wall, she lowered its rubber end to the floor and took it in hand. She tried not to hesitate before leaning her weight slowly forward to centre over the cane. Her wrist and arm shook, but she was standing, her legs straight and strong, with no help from her friends. Sterling clapped her hands together once in delight before remembering that she had an audience. Her cheeks brightened. 'And you,' Emmanuelle said to her, 'are amazing.'

Across the room, having watched on in silence, Lord Gawain agreed, 'Before today, we didn't know if she would ever stand. Now she's halfway out the door. You've worked a miracle, Miss Adams.'

Sterling smiled nervously, blossoming under the praise. It occurred to Emmanuelle that this student of hers was unaccustomed to it, far from the top of any Academy classes and sharing a room with the very remarkable duo of Hiroko Sasaki and Aristea Byrne. Ending up on the wrong side of a schoolwide schism meant that Sterling Adams generally did not interact much with the White Elm, not even Emmanuelle, who was her direct supervisor.

Though Emmanuelle missed Renatus's apprentice more keenly than she'd admit, it was becoming apparent that her presence at the Academy – or at least, the council's fixation with circumstances surrounding her, by no means Aristea's fault – had disguised some other incredible talents. In the crisis of this embargo, skilled Healers had emerged from the previously quiet cohort. The commonness of the Seer gift was coming in handy with so many students and housekeeping staff now joining White Elm Seers in their meditations, eliminating guesswork through the power of numbers and probability. The return of the Displacer students, distinctly skilled-up, meant that Elijah could now police and map more territory in his constant surveillance of the global Fabric. And while snail mail was still getting in thanks to Renatus, the student Telepaths were quicker to share hearsay and developments in their families' communities, information that was helpful to those councillors still outside of the house.

Sterling shifted from one foot to the other, unsure how to

handle the attention.

'Uh, I'll check back later if you need help getting back to bed,' she said. She gestured at the cane. 'You should try that out and give yourself breaks every few minutes. And… be patient.'

She smiled quickly and turned to leave. Leaning heavily on the walking stick, Emmanuelle bent forward to call through the door, 'Thank you, Sterling.'

'Thank you, Sterling,' Renatus echoed. The strawberry blonde didn't stop for Emmanuelle's thanks but froze at his. 'There aren't enough thanks in the world for getting my friend walking again.'

The girl swallowed hard and nodded, wide-eyed, and ran away before she could say anything she might regret. Emmanuelle was sure her student had plenty of ideas of how her idol could repay her. From Renatus's wince at her retreating back, it appeared those ideas were poorly guarded.

'No good deed goes unpunished,' Lord Gawain mentioned idly, apparently guessing the unspoken situation. He took a step across the room, uncertainty crossing his face. 'Renatus–'

'I came to tell you that Nastassja has contacted me again,' the scrier redirected smoothly. 'Her reaction was… colourful. I gather she's just learned Jadon and I visited Shell at her ranch. She is *quite* upset.'

Any residual annoyance with Renatus burnt up instantly and came back tenfold for his ridiculous family.

'Why?' Emmanuelle asked. She couldn't imagine why Renatus's selfish sister would care about Asheleigh Hawke, another orphan Lisandro made, or that her brother had found the little family. From her understanding of Jadon's debrief, the pair had not entered the property and had not made much headway with Aubrey's partner anyway.

'She cut me off again before I could ask, but I can guess,' he said without much concern. Emmanuelle was glad to hear that tone, and knew Lord Gawain was, too. 'We struck a nerve, stepped into a secret she thought was all hers. And she didn't know for weeks. It's made her feel vulnerable and she's lashing out.' He paused to weigh something up, then met his mentor's light eyes. 'I came to say I'm sorry I went around you on this. If she does something to retaliate, I understand that's on me.'

It was a sweet moment, really. Renatus, who so rarely apologised, stood his ground and waited for the reprimand that simply never came down, and Gawain, who loved this boy so dearly and still could not reconcile the truths of him, the very good and the very dark, regarded each other closely. Emmanuelle might have appreciated it more if not for a distant twang on her senses.

Where was that? Beyond the house. One of her many wards being activated.

Lord Gawain approached and clapped an affectionate hand on Renatus's shoulder.

'Whatever comes of it, we'll work it out,' he promised. 'We have to. Fate hasn't led us here to find a dead end. And...' He forced a smile. 'We can agree to disagree on Aristea, for now. You both deserve the benefit of my doubt.'

Emmanuelle ignored them as her attention zipped from place to place. She'd established semi-permanent warding in quite a few locations, it turned out. Her own apartment in Paris where her cell phone lay dead, her mother's country house, Teresa's cottage in small-town Italy, here at Morrissey House, Qasim's family home, Angela Byrne's Irish flat...

There, her attention stuck fast. The wards she'd constructed to keep Aristea's sister safe were being activated. Not broken, just... Was someone trying to get in? She frowned as Lord Gawain left. It didn't feel like an alarm. She didn't perceive any threat. A more focused analysis of her spellwork told her that they weren't rebounding or deflecting any unwanted attempts to access the property.

No. Someone who knew a lot about warding had found the layers of her magic, and like strings on a harp, was harmlessly plucking on its threads.

That someone had to know she'd feel it. That someone, really, could only be one person.

Her heart leapt. Renatus said something pointless about what he thought he was off to do, but Emmanuelle staggered after him, awkwardly thrusting her cane at the floor and trying to go after it with a big step she wasn't ready to take. He spun back and caught her mid-tumble.

'More practice required, it seems,' he noted, sitting her against the doorjamb. She dropped the cane and clutched his arm.

'You can get off this estate,' she whispered, sensing Lord Gawain only just now in the stairwell. Far enough that he shouldn't hear this, but she had to be careful. 'Aristea needs you.'

chapter twenty-five

It was a risk with no reason to think it would work, but given my options, it seemed the safest way without conceding defeat and coming in. I Displaced into the neighbour's yard like I did a month ago and hopped the fence to land behind my own home.

I was home.

Angela wasn't, which was both disappointing and relieving. For her to burst out the back door and spot me would be such a disaster and I really welcomed the idea of that right now. I found the spare key, let myself inside, and, after an indulgent moment inhaling the familiar scent of my sister's organic cleaning products in the kitchen, I grabbed the notepad from beside the house phone to scribble my note: *For Emmanuelle*. The first pen was out of ink, and when I looked around, I saw Angela had rearranged a little. Her cup of pens from the middle of the table was gone.

I took a quiet wander in search of the pen collection. I didn't know if my favourite teacher was alive, and if she was, I didn't know if she was able to come to my call. Jadon, I knew, was just across the street and could be here very quickly if I made myself obvious. Once Emmanuelle noticed me, she would either send help or act efficiently in service of the White Elm's agenda. Jadon was the efficient option. He'd also probably try to bring me in.

I was hoping she'd choose discretion instead. In lieu of a guarantee or a working pen, I abandoned my unwritten note and traipsed to the refrigerator to peer at the magnets Angela kept on its door. I spotted one that would work for my needs. Basic, with just the logo and address of the pub around the corner from Angela's work. It was the only one I touched, picking it off and holding it in my open hand while thinking very intently about Renatus and hugging the biscuit tin in my other arm.

'Please see this,' I whispered, sticking the magnet back in its place. The biscuit tin had retained plenty of other impressions – why not carry one for me? I opened the drawer we used for junk, sure I'd find a pen in there. I shuffled through chargers, batteries, paperclips and business cards, glad that Angela hadn't yet found time to defamiliarise this part of the house, and I soon had a pencil. I also came across a folded sheet of thin paper with a few diagrams down the side, and in amazement, found myself holding the instructions for the puzzle box.

Angela had kept them, practical as ever. I flattened the page out on the counter and swapped the pencil for the puzzle box. I shook the thing once, hearing the clatter of whatever she'd locked in there before she sent it for my birthday. The diagrams showed four steps to getting the box to open and I debated whether to look. I knew it was cheating to rely on the manufacturer's instructions rather than solving the puzzle myself, but I could hardly deny the way things had lined up. Fate hadn't let me leave the puzzle box on the island, nor had it allowed me to leave it behind in Renatus's office when Nastassja nearly burnt the place down, and now it had used dead Seers and dead pens to lead me to the instructions.

It seemed I was meant to open it. It had been inexplicably beside me in the orchard when I awoke after whatever happened at Shanahan's, and it had stayed with me this whole misadventure since.

Mind made up, I arranged my fingers over the box's apparent lid as per the first diagram and pressed on the two opposing corners at the same time. To my unreasonable excitement, the hidden panels gave slightly under my fingertips and clicked softly. I shoved my attention inside the wooden box to watch the inner mechanisms shift in the dark while I hurried through the next steps. Slide the freshly released base a few millimetres over, then press the freed-up side panel downward to lever the internal catch on the lid. Inside, for the first time, a crack of light appeared along one of the seams, illuminating the contents.

Breathing shallowly, I pulled my attention back to my own eyes and gazed inside the puzzle box as I lifted the lid away. Cushioned by cotton wool, Angela had hidden a couple of seashells, a nostalgic call back to my childhood hobby of collecting these from the beach. I picked them out carefully to admire them.

Manicured fingers dig a white shell from damp sand... Angela's smile, summer sunshine... wistful...

I turned the scallop shell over, smiling back at her. She wasn't as drawn to the sea as I was but must have made a visit while I'd been away. My chest tightened to consider how deeply I missed her, and how she must feel the same. I thought of Cassán, miserable, alone, eternally guilt-ridden for abandoning his family, and tried not to see parallels between his choices and mine. Hiding from the people I loved in the hope that my absence would somehow protect them had sounded noble until I met my grandfather. Everyone he'd ever loved had fallen out of existence while he buried his head in the sand and lost who he was and any purpose he stood for.

After, I decided with firmness, I would fix things with Angela. Tell her everything. Explain my scar and my tattoo. Introduce her to Renatus and take the blame I knew he was terrified of weathering for all the ways I'd managed to endanger myself since she dropped me off at his gate. I had time. She would forgive me. This shell was proof. Feeling lighter, I placed it on the counter and went back for the last thing in the puzzle box.

I knew instinctively that my sister had *not* sent this item, because my pacifist sibling would never want me to own a knuckleduster, but I had touched it before I thought through how else it would have ended up inside the box.

Brass cast on the thick fist of a huge man... his intention, my fear... high-ceilinged hallway... his eyes, deep-set, on me...

Breathless, I dropped the box on the counter and stepped away, tripping over my own feet. Shanahan's penthouse. I'd been there twice, but never seen this person. I struggled to recall any features beyond his eyes and an impression of scale and threat level. Was he there? The day I stole the ledger? Thomas and Teagan Shanahan were, of course, and Renatus and Declan, but that was all I knew. Two hours were missing.

Teagan's missing bodyguard.

I realised what this must be, and shakily closed the box up. I'd hidden this memory from myself on purpose. Risked my mind and my master's, as well as broken the law. It was impossible to know how bad it was, *what* it was, and when would be the right time to uncover it. I fully expected it to be as distressing as it was illuminating, and I understood that knowing it could be dangerous.

Layers of magic glowing ominously to life over a door of chains… Renatus lying on the floor nearby…

I froze at that uncomfortable flash. I hadn't touched the knuckledusters. How did I end up with that thing, anyway, and how did it get inside the puzzle box? Best not to invite the memory by wondering, I realised too late. Last time a hidden memory had returned to me, it had been in confronting little disordered snippets like this, increasing by the minute until I'd started paying attention and my brain had sequenced them for me.

Renatus, white-hot and screaming…

A door with chains…

Teagan, lying in a pool of blood…

'I don't want to see this,' I said angrily to nobody. It came in flashes, like before, none of it appealing to any facet of my curiosity. I checked my wards, I checked the barriers of my mind, trying not to panic.

Renatus, white-hot and screaming…

Renatus, gripping his head like it might explode…

This wasn't related to the bodyguard's brass knuckles, I realised. Touching an item from the scene had triggered it, yes, but this was my memory spell unravelling at the edges. I couldn't block this because it was *inside* me. I swallowed hard before I could spiral. If there was no fighting it, maybe there was a way of channelling it?

Renatus, on the floor, black cracks snaking under his skin, blood dripping from under his hair, steam rising from him...

I cringed. My heart was racing and so was my mind, jumping between ridiculous possibilities. The bodyguard? He wasn't in any of the flashes of Renatus's suffering. *Think.* The instant before the screaming – what happened? And the instant before that?

Renatus, white-hot and screaming...

Renatus...

Renatus stopping in his tracks... heat, screaming...

Renatus and Declan rounding a corner together, bickering... the penthouse hallway, sunlight reflecting from the other end... high ceilings... tenseness, urgency... Declan stops Renatus, satchel swinging behind him...

Pieces fell into place as I relaxed and let it come, and that moment played out in my head in sequence.

'You don't understand,' Declan snaps at Renatus as I hurry toward them. 'That's the luxury of being you.'

'I understand I'm meant to arrest you for this,' Renatus snarls back at him, gesturing upward. I slow, seeing unstable-looking red sparks of magic zip along the walls and cornices like an angry electrical charge. 'I don't know what I'm going to tell the council. I'm on shaky ground as it is and I'm not taking this fall for you.'

'Are we leaving?' I ask anxiously. A second set of sparks, this time greenish, races after the first. Renatus is too busy glaring at his frenemy to look at me.

'Yes,' he says tightly.

'No,' Declan counters with similar finality. 'I'm not leaving without that ledger.'

I blinked back to my current reality, breathing hard. It was coming back whether I liked it or not. Its timing couldn't be worse, but directing it seemed to help stabilise the flashes. Okay. How did I get from Teagan's tea room, choosing tea flavours together, to Renatus and Declan?

Teagan, nattering, opening little drawers in the tea chest...

Teagan...

I remembered pretending to listen to her while unwanted memories unfolded in my mind. The realisation that Teagan's dad paid a man to pick up my sister and get dirt on me had cut right through my self-control. I'd shown the fragmented memory to Renatus and… taken my next breath two hours later in the orchard at Morrissey Estate.

I closed my eyes, cringing in preparation for what I might see.

Teagan opens another drawer and inhales the floral scent, and in my head, Renatus's thoughts seize the evidence I have just shared. His revulsion and withdrawal suggest he's confronting Declan or Uncle Thomas with it. I wait in horrified silence for his response.

It doesn't come from him. It comes from the house.

The sound of a terrible crash reaches us from the other end of the penthouse, and Teagan and I look to each other in fright. A weird whoosh sound follows closely, and then I feel the sickly tingle of a lot of magic rushing over and around me at once. The locks on the windows abruptly click shut. Teagan's eyes widen and her usually sunny emotions flip.

'What have you done?'

The noise of a car door closing broke my attention again. Careful not to disturb the curtains, I looked out the front window for the source of the sound, and noted our neighbour checking his letterbox. A stretch of my senses confirmed that Angela was not around and nobody seemed to have their attention on me or the house. I refrained from scrying for Angela – she was always fine and the jumbled memories were coming in faster. I didn't want to risk deviating.

A silver dagger… a pricked finger… a pool of blood… stained blonde hair… black hair, blood trickling from underneath…

I plonked down on the couch where I had spent so many hours in front of the television, and now focused hard. I needed to know what I'd done to Teagan. I needed to know what happened to Renatus.

In the hallway, watching Renatus and Declan glare at each other. Renatus is conflicted; I'm conflicted, horrified. Thoughts turning over quickly, Renatus wants to say no. He knows he's supposed to say no.

Frustrated, he sighs. It sounds more like a growl.

'Why,' he demands of Declan as he waves me over and begins to walk the other way, 'can you never just ask?'

Smiling comes easily to Declan, but for someone usually so guarded, the genuine relief in his grin makes him look briefly very young. He didn't know what Renatus would say and this support is more than he was hoping for. I trot after them while more sparks, closer to streaks of lightning now, run the length of the hall ceiling. They look like they're seeking something, flashing into rooms. Somewhere, a door slams shut. The whole penthouse reverberates. My companions fall into step together as though none of this bothers them, though I can sense otherwise.

Don't touch the walls, don't touch anything, Renatus advises me across our telepathic link while he asks bluntly of his cousin, 'What do we need? I'm assuming you have been planning this for a while.'

What is it? I ask, eyeing the ominous waves of shimmering magic now washing along the wall beside me. It's like this place is peeling back, layer by magical layer, each one activating and doing… something.

It's Shanahan's magical defence system, Renatus replies tersely. It's looking for intruders.

'You know me well,' Declan confirms, shaking his satchel. The metal bowl inside clinks against the knife and I hear the crunch of dry ingredients. 'I've never seen him open it, but Shanahan blood would be a starting point. If we need anything else from him, I've got the stuff. He won't remember a thing.' Stressed, Renatus's mind flies through the list of laws we're now in danger of breaking. Declan keeps talking. 'I've been past it enough times to tell you it's a four-layer lock spell anchored into the building, with at least one actual padlock and an anti-council ward tied into the second layer. My father drew this,' he adds, taking a very worn set of papers from his pocket and handing them to Renatus. I pick up speed to lean between their shoulders and take a look. They're old diagrams, hand drawn and impeccably sketched with labels, arrows and numbers all over. It makes little sense to me but Renatus seems able to read it. We march down the last corridor and approach the vault.

'This is twenty years old,' Renatus points out, shuffling through the pages. 'How do you know Shanahan hasn't changed his defences?'

'It's more hope than know,' Declan admits as we pull up in front of the chained double doors. Bolts of electrical magic zip around it in warning. They both stare at it, seeing things I can't see. 'It's less of both right now.'

Renatus slaps the diagrams onto Declan's chest. 'It's a five-layer lock spell, you prick.'

His reaction makes my anxiety jump.

'It's an extra five minutes, at most,' Declan defends. 'Shouldn't be anything we can't handle.'

He turns to the vault door and waves an experimental hand over its surface, while Renatus turns away to press his fingers to his temples.

'We are going to burn for this,' he mutters.

The shrill ringing of the house phone interrupted the stream of memory yet again, and I realised I wasn't in the best place, or moment, for this.

'Declan, what did you do?' I wondered aloud as I got up and grabbed my things from the counter. He was the reason we'd been stuck there in the first place, having failed or opted not to draw Thomas Shanahan away as we'd asked him. He was the reason we had that ledger on our minds at all, and now it seemed he was the reason Renatus and I stayed after agreeing from the outset to abort this mission. He'd wanted that ledger; it was not difficult to imagine that everything that had gone wrong was his doing.

I left the biscuit tin untouched. I'd planned to hide it in the garden so the council wouldn't need to break into my sister's house and Angela wouldn't come across it, but I didn't want to muddy the impression I hoped Renatus would tap when he touched this. I also didn't want to waste any more time here, so I scribbled my note at long last and dropped it on top.

The wall that had been holding the penthouse memory back had been compromised, and now it wouldn't stop crumbling. Snippets kept slashing through.

Renatus, suddenly clutching his head and beginning to scream… Declan blocking my way… 'No! Don't touch him!'… white-hot glow blistering under his skin, black cracks begin to appear…

I hurriedly locked the back door and returned the key to its hideout. I extended my senses to the cage of magic Emmanuelle had woven over this place. I knew she was connected to this spell and if she was alive, she'd feel what I did next. I concentrated on the nearest thread and pulled it lightly. Not enough to pull it down – I doubted I had the strength to do any damage to a ward forged by Emmanuelle. My efforts manifested as a sort of strum. I felt the vibration carrying through the web of magic, hopefully halfway across the country to the spell's caster.

Declan's knife lightly unpicking layers of unseen magic... tension in the air... 'Can't you go any faster?'... 'I'm not a Crafter, sweetheart'...

Ignoring memories, I pulled on several more. An attacker would work on the one thread to weaken it – I hoped Emmanuelle would detect my unusual behaviour and realise this was something different.

Across the road, my sensitive awareness of the boredom that was Jadon kept me apprised as he moved around the little empty house he was hiding in. I didn't think he knew I was here, but I still knew I shouldn't wait for that to change. I hopped the fence back into the neighbour's property and concentrated on the pub in town.

I was lucky to make it. Just as I opened the Fabric and stepped through, more of the memory crashed to the front of my mind.

Something hits Renatus dead centre... the hallway shakes...

I tried to inhale but nothing went down my throat as I moved through the thick nothingness of the void. Panic seized me. After everything, I couldn't die here, not now. My feet were weightless, ungrounded, and I windmilled my arms to grab onto something, anything, but I was nowhere. I was going to die of remembering something at the wrong moment.

My foot landed on solid ground and air flew down my throat as I emerged a lengthy instant later. I crashed amidst my clattering sai to the concrete floor of the alley, avoiding stabbing myself by pure fluke.

The sign on the nearest emergency exit confirmed I'd gotten my landing exactly right, though I'd never been behind the pub in this dingy lane. I breathed a shaky sigh of relief and staggered to sit on the edge of the back step, collecting my sai and burying my head in my hands as the images kept coming.

Teagan's tea room... I walk in and she's where I left her, trapped in a box of my wards.

'What's happening?' she asks, frightened. She presses a hand against the glass of my magic as I lean down to scoop up her knife. 'Is my daddy alright? What did they do to him? What are you doing with that?'

'Your dad will be fine,' I assure her despite how far from fine I feel, showing her the knife, 'and I just need a drop of your blood.'

She's quick to step away, pressing against the ward at her back. I don't have time for this.

'No, don't,' she pleads. She tries to lean away when I reach for her; it's unfair, my magic lets me pass through but not her, and I grab her wrist. She whines in protest, resisting but so much weaker. 'Don't, don't, please… You won't like what happens.'

All in all, Teagan Shanahan was right – I hadn't liked much that had happened since. Had I really cut her despite her protests? I felt sick. No wonder I'd buried this memory. What was surfacing was a version of me I wouldn't want to know.

Broken bits of the same day fought each other to be next.

Outside the vault, Renatus and Declan work pedantically on the first layer of magic, throwing snark like they have it in spades. Which, of course, they both do. I'm terrified but I watch in fascination as their fingers trace strings I can't see but slowly become aware of, especially when Declan runs his glowing knife over an area. Shimmery strands and floating sigils come briefly to light before they fade again to nothing.

'This would go a lot faster if you had bothered to teach your apprentice anything more useful than playing lookout,' Declan mentions as he follows a strand to the floor. Renatus is incensed and I detect that he just barely refrains from kicking him.

'If I'd anticipated a need for robbery, this might have been further up the list of lessons,' he sneers. He looks like he's untying something in the air over the door. Another angry bolt of lightning zips over us, heading for Teagan's tea room. 'How can you seriously have been planning something this stupid and not told me? Cut this.'

'Busy,' Declan replies, focusing hard on the strand he's holding, trying to find where it connects to the floor. 'I knew you'd be judgey.'

'Can you stop arguing and hurry up?' I ask. They ignore me.

'Cut this, it's next,' Renatus insists. Declan shakes his head, adamant on his own strand, and Renatus nudges him with his foot in

irritation. *'Do you want to unleash a plague or something? Cut them in order.'*

'I know what I'm doing.' Declan isn't happy about the delay, but he takes a moment to look at the web again, tracing the knife over it once again. At one spot, it seems to illuminate his strand layered underneath the one Renatus is holding, and he stands to cut the knife through the magic. Renatus's strand falls away and no plague outbreak is apparent. 'See?'

I couldn't catch a break. The sound of the pub's rear door being unlocked from the inside interrupted yet another stream of memory, so I grabbed my sai before anyone could ask awkward questions. Where could I sit and be left alone? Inside a pub at midday. Ignoring staff stepping out for a cigarette break, I caught the swinging door and slipped inside wearing my trusty fake appearance, and let the horror show continue to consume my senses.

'What aren't you telling me?' I ask, clutching her hand even as she tries to pull it away. Tears brim her lower eyelids and emotions shake inside her. It's mostly fear, but humiliation has joined in.

'It's a secret,' she whispers. 'Please, just don't...'

How much longer? Renatus asks. I set my jaw. I really don't have time for this.

'I'm sorry.' I quickly prick Teagan's fingertip with the sharp point of the knife, and she whimpers. Red blood wells quicker than I expect and I catch some on the blade. She cradles her finger to her chest, moaning and beginning to cry. With my free hand, I summon a tissue from the air. 'Here. Press this to the cut. It'll stop in a minute.'

Miserably, Teagan takes the tissue and does as I say.

'It won't,' she disagrees. 'You'll regret doing this.'

I already do. Trying to block out her sad noises and balancing the knifepoint with its precious drops of blood, I hurry from the tea room.

I really did hurt Teagan, I was disappointed to realise, exiting the kitchen into the main bar area without anyone much noticing my warded presence. I picked a seat at the end of the bar like at *Giannopoulos Family Restaurant*, far from the three other patrons and free to be miserable with myself. I hadn't thought myself capable of hospitalising Shanahan's sheltered youngest under any circumstances, or at least I'd hoped I wasn't; if I'd trapped her and forced a knife on her, even to make that tiny cut, perhaps I *was* the kind of person who could justify something worse in the heat of a moment.

I was not the kind of person who could be left alone with her thoughts.

'Can I get you something, sweet?'

'Can you hurry?'

'Can you not rush us, sweet?' asks Declan's singsong voice. Renatus steps back, exhaling slowly.

'That's the first layer.'

Declan kneels with his diagrams and says, 'I've been practicing on these spells for half my life.' He lifts his knife to the padlock, and everything goes horribly wrong…

I managed to dismiss the bartender easily enough, but the nearest patron raised his voice to be heard.

'You alright, darling?'

'I'm fine.'

One second, everything is fine… then I blink and a minute's passed but I know everything has changed. Renatus takes a hit to the midsection that does no damage, but he steps back, brushing the wall. Furious lightning rushes him.

It burns him.

It doesn't stop.

He screams and I think I'm screaming too.

I blinked away the hallway and the chained-shut door and resumed staring at the bottles behind the bar. Shellshocked, I let those new images repeat disjointedly in my mind, a highlight reel of Renatus in pain. Renatus taking the full force of Shanahan's magical defences, Renatus bleeding, Renatus screaming, dying. Something struck him. What?

'You by yourself today?' the bearded patron asked in a friendly voice. Didn't he know I was a terrible person? I snatched up my sai, at my wit's end with interruptions and doing nothing to disguise my emotional reaction or the swords I'd brought in.

'Very happily alone, yes,' I responded acidly, shoving to my feet and turning to leave. I almost walked right into the man who'd approached behind me without my notice. I pulled up short in surprise.

'Not so happily alone that you'd decline company, I hope?'

chapter twenty-six

For a moment, I couldn't believe I was looking at him. Close enough to touch, after a month apart that had felt like an eternity despite the insane fact that I hadn't even known him at the start of the year, Renatus was dressed in his usual eclectic mix of black and more black, combat boots and basic black t-shirt with a jacket from a previous century. His loose dark hair had grown even longer, its ends now curling at his collarbone, and with no blood trickling over his brow and in a state of full consciousness, he looked as healthy and unreasonably pretty as ever.

A huge part of me wanted to throw myself at him and hug him and let him take care of everything now. I knew he'd let me, and I could do with the human contact after my stints with Cassán and Declan. He'd hold me tightly because he'd missed me and he'd take charge. Freedom from responsibility was only half a pace away. All of this could be over.

A very small part, the logical bit that rarely got a word in, said that we weren't out of the woods yet and the reasons he'd sent me away had not changed. Meeting here was breaking the rule he'd laid out when he said, 'Go somewhere I wouldn't guess.' So I swallowed the desire to downgrade myself from successful fugitive to needy child and held my ground.

'Not that happily alone,' I confirmed. 'I could use a hug.'

He looked around. 'Best not make it obvious we know each other.'

I'd expected that. My master wasn't the affectionate type. I gestured at the bar and asked, 'Is it safe for us to talk here?'

'Not particularly, but nowhere is. We could leave–'

'*Are we leaving?*'

'*Yes.*'

'*No,*' *Declan says firmly.* '*I'm not leaving without that ledger.*'

I'm sure Renatus almost hits him in that moment.

'*We are not risking our lives for some stupid book that might not even exist,*' *he shouts, beside himself with frustration.* '*If you've got any sense you'll leave it where it is. What could possibly be in there that's worth this?*' *He points up at a jagged bolt of magic running the length of the hall ceiling above us. I feel its angry heat as it zips past.* '*Is it worth what you've started?*'

'*You're the one who knocked him out,*' *Declan mumbles, ducking instinctively when Renatus growls and reaches for him.* '*And yes, to me, my life is worth all this. That's what's in the ledger. Maybe.*'

'*What are you talking about?*' *I ask, confused.* '*You owe Shanahan money?*'

He looks at me. '*I hope not. It wasn't money he took out of the rest of my family.*'

I must have dropped the swords; Renatus caught them. I pressed my hands to my eyes and groaned at the onslaught of memory, which was not the welcome Renatus was likely to have expected, but not one previously unseen in this establishment. He took my elbow and guided me back into my seat at the bar, calling the bartender for a glass of water.

'This had better not be a hangover,' he chided, sitting me up straight and backing off to see if I stayed upright, 'and that better not be why you called me here.'

'Oh, I've missed you and your self-righteous humour, too,' I retorted, and realised I really, really had. I paused as he arranged the blades on the counter before me. I still had my illusionary appearance and finally wondered how he knew it was me. Was it just the sai he recognised?

'No one emotes like you do,' he replied to my stray thoughts. I could have said the same, recognising his usual emotional patterns, along with his warm relief to have found me. He took the neighbouring seat and slid the magnet from my refrigerator across the bar. 'I got your message.'

Renatus frowns, impatient.

'What are you saying?'

'That it's a mighty coincidence that Shanahan's the last person my father visited before he "disappeared",' Declan says flatly. 'Dear Uncle does keep a ledger of all his dealings. I've seen it. And if I'm in it, I want to know about it before I'm called on to pay a debt that's not mine. I'll understand if you two would rather not know, since it was your grandfathers who put mine in there.'

Our grandfathers… No. Renatus was a Telepath, these images needed to stop. I shoved hard on the incoming visions and picked up the magnet to give myself something else to focus on. I looked aside at Renatus, unbelievably glad to see him unhurt. He kept his gaze directly ahead, staring at the bottles on their shelves instead of at me. I held up the magnet.

'Does this mean you broke into my house?'

'You didn't want me to?' he responded dryly with a knowing tilt of his head. I smiled lightly and he withdrew the biscuit tin from inside his jacket. My smile faded a little, envious. Boy clothes always had such impressive pocket space, and after weeks of carting around two bags, his outdated coats had never looked so good. 'We decided against asking Jadon – I'm sure you know already where he is and you'd have gone to him if you wanted to.' He put the tin on the counter and stared at it. 'I'm glad to see you.'

It meant more than he said. He was glad I'd found a way to reach out that didn't involve handing myself in. He was glad *he* was the one to find me. And he was glad to find me alive and intact.

'Same,' I said, and I meant all that, too. I went to say any of the important things I came to tell him, but instead asked, 'Did you say I *emote*? As in, you can feel that?'

Renatus was not an Empath. He had told me before that he'd never met one until me. He shrugged one shoulder.

'Yet another way in which I've benefitted more from this relationship than you have, it seems,' he said, splaying his hands on the benchtop.

Fingers spread apart and curl as the growl becomes a scream. The light crackles under his skin like white fire, burning, steam rising. He grabs his head, clearly in agony, and I start forward. Declan throws an arm out to block me.

'No! Don't touch him.' He's as frightened as I am, but he knows better than to touch live electricity. 'It's the White Elm marker in his aura.'

'I don't care, do something!'

I squeezed my eyes shut and let my forehead fall forward onto my arms. Why couldn't it all just come through at once?

'Is it the memory spell?' Renatus asked, concerned. 'I understand they can come down hard when they're...'

'Constructed by an amateur?' I guessed. I forced myself to sit up as I sensed an approach, thanking the bartender for my glass of water. He dropped a handful of coasters in front of us and they scattered. Renatus's gaze dropped to that disordered mess. Another flash behind my eyes made my head throb.

'I was going to say self-inflicted. When Declan spelled you, it covered a shorter, less confronting time period,' Renatus reasoned. 'And he wasn't performing it on himself.'

'I don't think that warning was on the box. Has yours? Come down?' I'd spelled us both at almost the same time. Maybe they had an expiry date. But he shook his head.

'No, and from your reaction I think I prefer it this way,' he said. His fingers tapped on the bar, itching to tidy the coasters. 'I've had enough going on. I suspect you have, too. Keep that illusion,' he added firmly, just as I thought to resume my normal appearance. I'd forgotten how good at mind-reading my master was, even through good barriers. 'I've tried something new, but I can't guarantee I've got my whole mind back. She might still be able to see through my eyes whenever she wants.'

My stomach lurched at that. 'Nastassja?'

He didn't answer, but he did give in to the compulsion to fix the coasters. He picked them up and began to arrange them along the benchtop, embarrassed or troubled or somewhere in between. Thoughts of his sister had always put him in a weird, depressive place, and I could only imagine how discovering her alive – married to the man who'd killed their parents, no less –

would have complicated that even further. That she could casually drop into his mind like a hacker into a security system was extremely problematic given his role on the council.

It also meant I couldn't reopen my mind to his like I wished I could.

'It's very good,' he said finally, tilting his head toward me without looking. 'The illusion.'

'Thank you,' I answered graciously. 'I have a friend who used to be Illusionist for the White Elm.'

He finished his line of coasters, pleased either by the confirmation I'd divined this high-level skill through our bond – he'd given me only minimal instruction in the area – or by my proud reference to him as my friend.

'Well, perhaps you *have* benefitted from this alliance,' he said. I felt his senses at the edges of my aura, analysing the intricacies of my spellwork. 'I didn't even sense your magic when I walked in. If you weren't the only girl here, carrying swords I bought, I wouldn't have looked twice. Are you... the same... underneath?'

A loaded question, to which the accurate answer was a resounding *no*, but I knew that's not what he was asking me.

'Whole and healthy,' I reassured him. 'I was a bit bruised after a fight with Egan–'

'Egan *Lake?*' Renatus repeated, recalling his least favourite dropout. I waved dismissively.

'He's a Magnus Moira apprentice now but he didn't land a single hit. The shelves I crashed into did more damage than he did. No new scars, everything intact, except my hair. Why?' I paused suddenly. 'Could an illusion hide it from you if I lost my arm or something?'

'I shouldn't be amazed,' Renatus said instead of answering, and continued admiring my spellwork. He'd of course recognise the illegal protection spells I was relying on, shielding me from being scried. He didn't use blood magic because he didn't like blood, but he did plenty of illegal magic in the line of work and outside it.

'I'm amazed enough for both of us,' I assured him. 'I would be dead several times over without the help I found, most of it from you. Your bank account – thanks for that. Stuff you've taught me. And Hiroko, and...'

'And Declan found you?' Renatus checked, subconsciously touching his forearm where the pair sometimes exchanged messages. I took a gulp of water and made a noise of affirmation before I swallowed.

'Oh, he did, and you are going to strangle him when I tell you the whole story, not to mention what I remember from Shanahan's.' I reflected briefly on the flashes that had slowed right down. 'I think he picked a fight with Shanahan and made you finish it.'

He sat back and exhaled in frustration. 'Goddamn it, Declan.'

'It's still coming back to me. But I think I might be obliged to forgive him after all the hot water he pulled me from.' I took one of Renatus's coasters and put my glass on it. 'So you're an Empath now, you still don't hug, and your sister has been using you as a spy camera to watch what's happening inside the estate. What else have I missed?'

'Nastassja has been getting a lot of imagery of wallpaper,' Renatus corrected. 'To summarise, Magnus Moira have been holding the gate–'

'I've seen.'

'Thought you would. For now, I'm the only one who can come and go from the estate. A long story, involving a secret door and an uncomfortable family reunion. Emmanuelle is recovering–'

My heart sang at this confirmation. 'I'd hoped.'

'You hung a lot on that hope when you contacted her twenty minutes ago,' Renatus reminded me. 'And as of this morning, the White Elm still hasn't backed down from its intention to put you on trial.' He looked up at me, unusual eyes roaming the fake features of my face, regret clouding his energy. 'You can't come home. Not yet.'

I dropped my gaze to my water, disappointed despite knowing that this would likely be the case.

'I suppose that means I can't tell you where I've been or what I've done, in case you're called on to give evidence,' I guessed.

His regret spun into anger, and he turned away to glare at the bottles opposite us.

'They can't make me give evidence against you,' he said frostily. 'I'm still working on that front. I'm sorry. But you're right, it's safer if you don't tell me anything else. I got more than I expected from this tin.' He looked at me again, anger sliding away. 'Peter knew your grandfather, and your grandfather's alive? How is that possible?'

'You just said not to tell you anything,' I reminded him, smiling when he sighed in frustration and resumed looking away. My smile faded. 'This needs to be the exception. Cassán's alive and alone, but I'm not the first one to find his hideout. I don't fully understand much of what Cassán said, but I understood Peter's instructions to get that tin to Emmanuelle *today*, and I understood Cassán when he said Lisandro came to him, years ago, looking for a spell. If it's the ritual I saw our grandfathers and their friends doing, it's awful. They...' I hadn't told him this part before. I'd tried to forget this horrific dream I'd known was no dream. 'They thought it would make them immortal, and they sacrificed a little kid. They cut his throat.' Renatus frowned, disturbed. I kept talking, hurrying to get it out. 'If Lisandro's planning to replicate that, someone's child is going to die.'

'Yes,' Renatus said, surprising me. 'Garrett and Josh provided information that supports that theory. I think I found the intended victim. Aubrey and Shell's son was born in June.'

'June?' I recalled meeting Shell Hawke briefly in May. She was barely showing. I dismissed the inconsistency and centred my attention on what mattered. 'But would Lisandro really murder his friend's child? Asheleigh Hawke is like his other godchild. And he couldn't kill any of us when he had his chance.'

I studiously avoided thinking I'd missed my chance, too, at the compound.

'I don't know,' Renatus admitted. 'My sister was... *Nastassja* was furious this morning when she realised I'd gone to see Shell and the baby. I don't know why she'd care.' I didn't miss the switch of language, and made a mental note to honour that. 'I'm still waiting for the inevitable petty retaliation.'

He was disappointed in what his sibling had become, and I felt compelled to share what I'd learned about that.

'I don't think it's her fault,' I said, trying to be gentle. 'Cassán mentioned her. He said she lost her magic and that does something to the mind. I think Lisandro came looking for a way to restore her.'

'So, everything she's done has been because of a bad separation spell, and everything he's done has been to help her? That's what they said, too, and it doesn't sound any more convincing coming from you.'

I suppressed a sigh; I had half-forgotten his tendency to regress twenty years in maturity when we visited confronting topics.

'I think half of what Lisandro has done has been for her,' I tried another angle, 'and half has been in pursuit of his other agenda, which is to ruin the council. Sometimes those align, and sometimes they clash. Notice nothing he does ever makes any sense? But ultimately, he felt responsible for you and your sister, and what happened to her,' I suspected, weathering the anticipated wave of rejection at my words. 'He wanted a solution. Lord Gawain undermined his solution for you by bringing you home from Avalon, and he wouldn't give him what he needed to help Ana.'

And resentment had grown and festered for years after.

'The Elm Stone,' Renatus said, as if he'd been thinking along the same lines. 'Near-infinite power to bring her back to what she was. He said he thought she was dying. He thought he was out of time. But the Elm Stone isn't like any other gemstone power source.' He lifted his sleeve to show me the glint of silver around his wrist. I smiled, seeing my ruby bangle safely where I left it. 'Its power stores can't be tapped unless it's freely given. Lisandro was very friendly with the ring's former keeper,' he recalled now, tucking the sleeve back into place. 'When it passed to Peter, he worked on him, too. Got him killed.'

'But ultimately, Peter saw through him and realised he was being manipulated,' I explained. 'He came across Cassán while he was looking for a way to stop Lisandro from destroying the White Elm.' I put my hand on the old metal tin. 'I think that's what's in here.'

'Messages from beyond the veil,' Renatus mused. Then, a little darker: 'Seers. He couldn't tell us this when he was alive?'

I took my hand away from the tin, pondering this young man I didn't ever know.

'He thought he'd burned those bridges,' I said. 'He was... ashamed. Magnus Moira's ideals and Lisandro's agenda were two different things and he didn't know that when he started down that road. So he wrote these before he left the ring for Emmanuelle, along with that list, which Cassán said was part of Peter's plan for beating Lisandro. He told me way more about that list than I wanted to know.'

'Do I want to?'

'No. But I feel obliged to mention that Cassán doesn't think we can win,' I warned. 'He thinks Lisandro *has* to bring down the council – that it's his destiny. He thinks it can't be altered.'

Renatus sighed, like he'd been afraid of this.

'I don't understand it, but Lord Gawain seems to believe it's coming, too, and that *you* are somehow driving it closer. Maybe this is what he's getting his wires crossed over,' he suggested before I could express my outrage, pulling the tin closer and flicking off the lid. Inside, Peter's many folded letters waited, his twisting script addressing the person he trusted most, an urgent reminder of where this should go. Sensing the same, Renatus replaced the lid. 'If Lisandro really is destined, Peter would have known it couldn't be stopped, only postponed, or the circumstances changed. He also would have realised that his own choices and actions had been warped to play a part in ensuring that pathway.'

'It explains why people generally bend over backwards to accommodate Lisandro's whims or wilfully ignored his clearly terrible choices throughout the years,' I agreed. I hesitated on my next point. 'It explains Nastassja, too, a bit. Cassán said she was born to be with Lisandro on this. Maybe... she doesn't have a choice in who she is.'

Emotions carefully controlled, Renatus calmly reached past me to take my water and sipped it without expression.

'Her time of "having no choice" has been and gone,' he replied. 'You don't have to defend her. She has tried to kill you once or twice.'

He wasn't wrong, and I certainly wasn't advocating letting her off the hook for the horrific things she had done – faking her death and leaving her dependent brother a traumatised orphan topped the list – but I did think her circumstances warranted some understanding. If it was true that her love with Lisandro was written in the stars, so to speak, determined before she was even born, was she capable of taking other paths? Was there any timeline in which she *didn't* choose him over her family? Could she ever *not* lose her powers and her mind in exchange for the chance to be with the man she loved? I didn't know if Renatus and I were necessarily destined to be bonded, but by the same token, once we were, was there any version of reality where I wouldn't have done everything I had to save him from another fate? It seemed a lot less clean-cut from that perspective.

'At least she's yet to try killing you,' I said finally. '*That* would be a step too far.'

Finishing another mouthful and pretending not to be amused, Renatus tipped the glass toward me in acknowledgement.

'That's setting the bar awfully low, but I suppose we need to start somewhere. If she can just avoid–'

There was no warning. The glass exploded in his hand at the same instant we felt the Fabric shift behind us. She wasn't a Displacer; there should have been a moment's delay, she shouldn't have been able to sneak up on us. My wards protected me from the deadly shards of shattering glass but it was already inside the barrier of Renatus's magic, and pieces sliced past his face and neck, opening his hand up.

True to my naturally useless form, I leapt from my stool to look around for the source of the danger. True to his more intuitive and intelligent form, Renatus connected the dots and shoved the biscuit tin. It tumbled over the bar, the tinny noise of its ungraceful landing attracting no attention amidst the scraping of the day drinkers' seats.

Nastassja was standing in the middle of the little pub, as impressive and indominable as ever. I felt that stormy, impossible aura and knew I stood no chance. Not if she was here confidently in what had to be the coolest shoes I'd ever laid eyes on, stiletto Victorian lace boots to her knees to match her typically ornate outfit. Long hair was secured in hasty warrior braids piled intricately on her head, and her finely sculpted face was lit with dramatic makeup I by no means believed she'd done herself. Magic, illusion, something like that – it looked incredible, reds and brushed golds creating a winged mask over eerie green eyes.

Eyes that paid me no mind at all. They glared only at Renatus, who finally looked underdressed by comparison.

Only a second had passed. The glass pieces, red with watered-down blood, landed on the floor, and Renatus held his wounded hand away as it began to bleed. Sick horror rolled from him, his usual involuntary response. He stayed in his seat and turned toward Nastassja, gaze catching mine briefly as he did.

Don't.

I stilled in reaching for my sai. How had he done that? My mind was closed to his via that door we shared at the back.

'What do you call this?' He glared back at his sister, blood seeping to the surface of the two smaller cuts on his cheek and under his ear, and he raised his more seriously injured hand so she could see it drip onto the bar. He kept it deliberately out of his own line of sight. 'Hello to you, too.'

'This is what happens when you won't take my calls,' she spat viciously, holding her ground and completely ignoring the wary eyes of everyone else in the establishment. Mine included, even when she jerked her head in my direction. 'So confident I wouldn't work you out that you thought you had time for some small-town floozie you keep on the side? Really, Ren? It's been *an hour.*'

I mean, yeah, offended, but I felt Renatus's emotional stillness coincide with mine, a realisation. *Some* floozie? He glanced at me, making eye contact once more, just an instant.

She doesn't know it's you, he said, his voice clear in the front of my mind where my own thoughts normally happened. Where Anouk's voice went the day she died, when she'd included me in her telepathic conversation with Renatus as we coordinated ourselves in Prague. I looked down at myself and remembered the illusion. It made me look like someone entirely new, hiding my magic except from someone who expected to see it.

Nastassja, the former Ana Morrissey, did not expect to see me, so she did not. Overconfident people will tell you a lot without meaning to. Like she'd also just confirmed that Renatus's efforts at blocking her out had finally worked.

Renatus, snatching a wad of napkins for his bleeding hand and then summoning a bandage from the inside of his jacket for the benefit of the witnesses, jerked his head at me, too.

'I've never seen her before,' he lied outright, the untruth not registering in the air around us because it was also true – the face I was wearing, he'd never seen – and he looked at me once more, coolly now. 'You should go.'

Get somewhere safe before she realises, he instructed, *and see if you can get these people out discreetly.*

Telepaths used eye contact to establish mental communication. That's what he was doing, bypassing our bond and talking to me the same way he could talk to anyone else who wasn't his apprentice.

I'm not leaving you with her, I thought back, careful to direct it to him only and guard my mind from his equally telepathic sibling. Other skills had transferred across our bond, and I was still super unsure about this one, but I assumed he'd be able to hear.

He did, and promptly ignored me, pushing off his seat to grasp my shoulder with his clean hand. He walked me back a few steps to the edge of the bar where I was arguably out of the way – *stay out of it, I just got you back* – and I quickly clasped my hand over his in the seconds that his body blocked her view of me, channelling my attention into skin cells, tissues, severed blood vessels... I wasn't strong at healing, but for him to faint or waver could mean the difference between walking out of there alive and not.

Cuts were relatively straightforward. I didn't finish the job, but I thought I reduced it before Renatus shook me off and turned to face Nastassja, beginning to bandage his hand.

'Well, you found me,' he said irritably as he strode to the centre of the bar so he faced her squarely. 'What do you want now?'

Beautiful people trapped in the wrong century glowered at each other. He talked to her like she wasn't a terrifying psychopath and I tried not to hold my breath as she raised her chin indignantly at the insolence.

'Little brother,' she said heatedly, 'you and I need to talk.'

chapter twenty-seven

Everywhere the glass had struck stung, but Renatus resisted the urge to touch. His cheek, below his ear, his collarbone, these little slices twinged with the shock of being opened to the air. If he touched them, his fingers would come away bloodied, and he had already expended more energy than was reasonable on pretending not to be bothered by the red running from his slashed palm. He felt insurmountable gratitude toward his legend of an apprentice, whose brief touch had half-closed the wound and considerably numbed its throbbing pain, and he endeavoured to wrap it, hiding it, as quickly as he could without looking rushed.

'Why can you never leave things alone?' his sister asked angrily. 'Why can you never just *stay put*?'

Nastassja, he saw, was no more bothered by spilled blood now than she was as a girl. A dark child with macabre interests and humour, she'd found magic lessons centring around blood and flesh fascinating, while Renatus thought blood was messy even before his phobia had developed.

She glared at him, eyes that weren't green before glowing with contempt.

'Was this you?' she demanded, exercising what felt like the same level of shaky control over her behaviour as he was. She was positively seething with cluttered anger and poorly processed hurt, and Renatus had truly no idea what had put her in this mood.

'Was what me?' he asked. He sped up his efforts to bandage

his hand. Nearby, hovering at the end of the bar, Aristea was edgy, dread circling her magical façade. He didn't know what she'd survived out there on her own, but even with her dramatically increased skillset, he hoped she kept clear of this. Whatever this was. Because deep down, he felt the same dread.

'The baby,' Nastassja bit out, emotions fluctuating. 'Did you take him?'

Renatus felt his apprentice's wary confusion reflect his.

'Shell's baby?' He watched his sister purse her painted lips in furious confirmation and felt his own confusion rise. 'No. Why, what happened? Is he missing?'

Great, just what he needed on top of everything else – a missing infant. His sister was as strong a scrier as he was, at least in theory; perhaps not as well practiced nor as well schooled in the craft's intricacies, but certainly powerful enough for that not to matter much. If she said the baby boy was missing, presumably he was hidden even from her scrying eye.

'They all are, an hour after I mentioned them to *you*. I need to know where they are.'

'Maybe they moved out. How should I know? And why do you care? You never liked children.'

He hit an unseen nerve with that, but she held her reaction back with an extraordinary show of restraint.

'I need that baby,' she said in a quiet voice. 'If your White Elm has him and I find out you lied…'

'Then what?' Renatus fired back, sick of her empty threats. Either she meant it or she didn't, and she hadn't taken her shot at him on any of her previous opportunities. 'What will you do to me? Dehydrate me with a thousand broken water glasses?' He tucked the end of the bandage securely into the layers over his knuckles. 'It wasn't us. Cast your scrambled mind back and you'll recall your cult locked most of the council up.'

The insult hit her squarely and she took a threatening step forward, aura flaring.

'This has *nothing* to do with those fanatical fools,' she snarled. Renatus stayed where he was, feeling like he was facing a wild animal. Any indication of submission and she might attack.

Better to stand his ground and call her bluff.

Assuming that's what this was. He couldn't trust that the Ana she still looked like would hold back when the instability of Nastassja lost her cool. He considered opening his mind to the White Elm's network and calling in backup but decided against it. He *was* the cavalry, and even he was sorely outmatched by this adversary. At the edge of his guarded and disconnected mind, he felt the scratching of Aristea's mental voice, a budding talent for telepathy she'd never had before, no doubt admonishing him for provoking the threat. His apprentice had come an exceptionally long way in the short space of time without him.

And she was right. He shouldn't let his own raw emotions rule interactions with his not-dead sibling. She was older, but clearly not any more mature for it, and not to be relied upon to set the civility level.

'Look, Ana,' he said though he hated to use that name, trying for reasonable, calm, and he saw it working in the softening of her eyes, 'I don't know where anyone is. Can we…?'

He was going to say either 'start again' or 'talk about something else', and was still choosing when the bartender finally picked his moment to interrupt.

'Sir–' Aristea tried to interject, sensing his intentions before he spoke, but he ignored the harmless-looking teenager in the corner and approached the attention-grabbing woman disturbing the peace of his pub. The other barflies watched on.

'Listen, lady, I don't know if you have a fight to pick with this fella or if this is a rehearsal for some movie you think you're making, but you're going to have to do it someplace else,' he said flatly, stopping beside Renatus with folded arms. He was a big man, actually, tall, with thick biceps and a beard down his neck. If magic wasn't a factor, intimidation would settle this.

But magic was a factor, and the barman didn't have any.

Impulsive anger flared in his sister's aura and she acted without hesitation. She opened one of her clenched fists and a ball of green-black magic spat to life above her palm, and with a swift blow from her dark lips, it was gone. Beside Renatus, the big man's chest blazed with a manifestation of the same corrosive magic, and they both leapt back.

A spark of energy fires from hands still disappearing and strikes his chest…

Disoriented, Renatus shook the other image from his mind. The barman yelped, unfolding his arms to hit the dark green fire away. It was useless; everywhere the spell made contact, his clothes and skin bubbled and burned. The yelp became a panicked shriek. Skin peeled back, then exposed muscle and tissue began to dissolve too, and Renatus watched in helpless horror as the magic continued to eat, deeper and deeper.

It's more than an electric shock, circles his whole body with unnatural intent, searching, and it finds what it's looking for. Everything goes white with pain…

'Ana, stop!' he ordered, sure his voice shook with total lack of authority. He couldn't touch the corrosive spell, and he couldn't heal the man clawing at his own dissolving chest cavity. With fingers hurriedly dancing in the air, Renatus could feel some of the strands of magic that made up this particularly vicious attack. As the victim tried to run away to safety behind the bar, he hastened to unpick the spell. As was his job as Dark Keeper. This was why the council had kept him. But most illegal spells came to him inert in dusty boxes full of old gas lamps and cursed jewellery. Unwriting magic this complex after activation, on a living victim, in the field with only seconds to save him… The cumulative panic of the room fuelled Renatus's own, and he looked helplessly back at the perpetrator. 'Ana!'

Something about his appeal got through to her. Her anger softened, but she still said, 'It's already done.'

Someone else he was going to have to watch die and fail to save, thanks to her. He growled and turned away to focus on cutting the spell off from whatever was fuelling it.

It takes everything he is to fight the pain, but it keeps cycling, devouring whatever he throws… 'Renatus!'… A voice from far away… then another one, frightened but taking charge… 'No! Don't touch him. It's the White Elm marker in his aura…'

What *was* this? Now was not the time for scrying, and he tried again to shove the distracting images of different pain and different panic away so he could deal with what was right in front of him. Blocking out his subject's agonised pleas for help, Renatus worked fast through the spell's code, the different strands connecting this spell to fixed points in the Fabric: the exact spot it was forged and the exact spot it manifested, and...

He looked back at his sister as she approached to watch on with interest. She was the spell's originator, but not its source. With his second sight, he saw the glow of the Elm Stone on her wedding band and also the thin dependent thread connecting the rot spell with that source of power.

The spell burns his brain, his skin, his blood, hotter than imagining... 'I don't care, do something!'

He cut the thread with a slash of Aristea's sai, Displaced hastily into his hand from further down the bar – his idea or hers, he didn't know – and the erosion abruptly stopped its progress as the bartender curled around his undeserved pain and struggled to breathe through half-eaten lungs.

Peter had been willing to die to keep the White Elm's intergenerational power store from Lisandro. He'd known where it would end up, on whose dangerous hand.

The bartender moaned, and Renatus scanned the establishment with his scrier's eye, not needing to look around. The other three patrons were huddled behind the tables, and Aristea was on the opposite side of the pub, tense hands on the bar, ready to duck behind it or run to him at a moment's notice. She didn't look like her at all, lank mousy hair and plain longish face, but knowing she was there, and still unnoticed, was a single spark of security in this unanticipated battleground.

'What's wrong with you?' Renatus demanded of his former sibling, gesturing at her handiwork on the floor while she leaned to look closer. 'You nearly murdered someone for asking you to keep it down in his pub.'

She straightened to look at him evenly. Remorseless, he could sense with utter disappointment and unfettered rage.

'And your inability to let things be has killed his chance of a quick death,' she responded. She tilted her head at her victim. 'Are you going to leave him like that?'

It wasn't the answer he was expecting, and it left him uneasy. Stopping the spell just before it could kill him, with no hope of healing the damage without exposing Aristea's cover, was to prolong the barkeep's suffering before a very drawn-out death.

Nastassja didn't need, or care for, an answer.

'Why don't we speed this up,' she suggested, turning on her heel to lean on the edge of the bar while her victim gasped on the floor, 'and you help me find that baby, before something else happens?'

Overconfident people will tell you anything you want to know, if you just let them talk. She was as good a scrier as he recalled but no better; in the eight years he'd practiced, refined, worked to move out of the shadow of the White Elm's brilliant Qasim, Nastassja had been stagnant. She'd not had access to her magic to continue improving and though her powers had been returned and advanced thanks to the Elm Stone, strength did not outflank technique. If it did, she wouldn't be angling for his help.

Which she wasn't getting.

'If they're as desperate as I think they are, I won't be able to find them,' Renatus said finally, spinning Aristea's sai. It was nicely weighted but a little scratched up. Hopefully just from transportation, not from use. 'Have you considered that Aubrey and Shell, like any good parents, are probably trying to keep their kid from being sacrificed in some gratuitous Magnus Moira ritual?'

Nastassja's reaction wasn't what he expected. She drew back against the bar, surprised that he knew and affronted by the implication.

'I'm trying to *save* him,' she insisted, swatting at his hand with the sai when he continued to spin it. He caught the blade in his palm and held it out of her reach, marvelling that he was tall enough do that now. 'It's true, a child needs to die, but by my life, it won't be that one.'

Again, she had no idea how much she was giving away with her careless words, but in this instance, Renatus didn't know, either. His sister, who didn't like children, who had just attacked a stranger and cut her own brother's hand open to get his attention, was concerned for the safety of the baby of two people she had no reason to care for?

She pressed on with, 'If you know where he is, you need to tell me, so I can protect him.'

Renatus gestured at the barman.

'I'm sure they want someone who dissolves people on a whim protecting their baby.'

She gave him a hurt look and gazed down at the black stone on her hand. She was silent for a long moment, unexpectedly reflective. Something was happening in the room, a growing stream of calm originating from... Aristea? Renatus resisted glancing at her to check, though the evidence seemed to be right in front of him. Nastassja's emotions simmered right down and her expression cleared.

'It's powerful, yes,' she confirmed as she played with it reverently. 'And you're right, it's more than I needed. Sometimes, I forget how strong it makes me. I let it... go to my head.' She glanced aside at him, and in that instant, in the reluctant repentance, he could see the real Ana he remembered. 'Can your White Elm Healers fix him?'

He didn't know what to say at first, looking back at the shaking form on the floor. It looked bad, what he could see, but he'd seen Lady Miranda do miracles. Emmanuelle, too, their burns specialist, though there was no getting her out here.

'I don't know,' he admitted, bringing down the barriers in his mind briefly to share what he was looking at with the council's networked minds. They'd see the victim and they'd see the threat that was Nastassja, and hopefully Lady Miranda would know better than to jump here before he could move his dangerous sibling on. Briefly, he heard their clamour of concerned voices, felt the Healers' grim reactions, and then he put the wall back, resuming the silence. 'I hope so. I'd rather not have to tell them their Elm Stone was used to commit a murder.' *Or tell them my sister was the one who committed it.* 'Ana, you shouldn't have the Elm Stone. No one should have that kind of power. Look what it's doing to you.'

Nastassja sighed and reached out to stroke his shoulder. This time, there was no burn where she touched, her anger under control and her warmer qualities on show.

'All power can be either good or destructive,' she reminded him. 'You, me, this stone... the White Elm, there are no exceptions. The council hoarded this power for centuries, building it up bigger and grander, knowing that the only difference between what I just did with it and healing a hospital full of sick children is what the user wants in the moment. It's what we do with it that matters. That's what Magnus Moira teaches. Keeping magic from wielders prevents miracles as effectively as it prevents violence. The next thing I do could be a miracle; you don't know. With this,' she showed him the ring, let him hesitantly take her hand to look at the stone in its new setting, 'I can protect anyone. The baby. You, if you'll let me.'

'I don't need your protection,' he answered automatically, without bite, examining the stolen power source. It was wrapped with more magic than he'd ever known it to be, intricately tied into her energy field with Lisandro's sophisticated spellwork. Restoring her connection to magic. It must have been devastating, he realised. Eight years without her powers, unable to go back to her old life because she and Lisandro, in their infinite wisdom, had lit her past on fire. 'Is this why your eyes are green now?'

His sister pursed her lips, flinching when the bartender sputtered blood and croaked for help. She actually *felt* that. The stream of calm from Aristea, whatever she was doing, continued to work its wonders.

'It's bound to my aura,' Nastassja explained. 'Lisandro looked everywhere for an answer after... after I left. We tried to live without the magic, to just accept things the way they were. It was horrible,' she admitted, watching him as he turned the ring slowly on her finger. Was she afraid he'd take it? Knowing that her life might depend on its proximity, how could he even consider doing his job to retrieve it? Distant and insistent, he felt the scratch of Aristea's mind against his. Nastassja was still talking. 'We thought, maybe this was just the cost of what we had to do.'

What they had to do. Renatus released her hand and pressed

his into the bar counter, trying to ground himself against the sharpened memory of the storm. The sick sensation in his soul when he'd come across the stranger carrying what he'd thought was his sister's ruined body.

Through his shock, he'd known on instinct that what had been done to her wasn't a result of the violent weather, and when the stranger made a move to hurt him, he'd reacted without thought. The Fabric had opened. It was a breach of magic beyond unforgiveable, and it hadn't saved Ana. Yet here she was, alive and vital.

'You paid with my whole family,' he informed her, surprised to feel her remorse. 'You *died*.'

'I didn't–'

'Was it Keely?' he asked abruptly, cutting her off. She shut up immediately, warmed emotions closing down. 'Was it our cousin you left there to die in your place? In my lap? She always looked like you, and with her face…' He couldn't finish, the memory bringing bile to the back of his throat. He swallowed hard and kept talking. 'She was your friend. How could you let anyone brutalise her like Glassner did?' Renatus watched her face and felt his stomach sink when she had to think of an appropriate answer, and he made a realisation he wished he hadn't. The bartender with his chest burnt out. The deserter nailed to a tree. 'He didn't do it?'

He didn't do it. He'd been scum, Qasim had even said so when they found his file in the Archives, but he hadn't caused the storm, and he hadn't beaten Ana – or Keely Shanahan – to within an inch from death. Nastassja lifted her chin.

'She stole from me. She should have known better. And by now, so should you. If you'd never gone digging, you'd never have known. You'd be happy.'

Renatus almost laughed, but not from humour. Once, burdened by his overwhelming grief before she'd learned to weather him and he'd learned to control his feelings around her, Aristea had apologised to him. She'd said she was sorry that she was alive and his sister was not. She'd known she reminded him of Ana.

Right now, he couldn't think of a single way in which they

were alike. Nowhere in this savage, self-serving woman was his thoughtful apprentice.

'You could never leave anything as it was meant to be,' she accused. 'When Lisandro and I fell in love, it was because of *you* that Father found out. Because of *you*, then, that I had to leave, and because of *you* that all of this,' she gestured wildly around the pub while he blinked at the unfair claims, 'had to happen. I never wanted to blame you, but it's true. It was your fault. It's just who you are, what you'll always do... why it wasn't enough to...'

She trailed off, running out of steam as she came close to admitting something hurtful she hadn't intended to let slip. Nice that she didn't want to be as awful as she came across.

'That's why it wasn't enough to just kill our parents,' he guessed, finding his voice emotionless. 'I keep wondering. You lost your connection to magic when you tried to cut yourself off from our family line, but they were already dead – what was so wrong with being found, when it was only me left to look for you?'

He shouldn't have asked, and he heard his apprentice's regretful sigh. He really was hopeless. Nastassja had the grace to avert her eyes, recognising the pain she'd inflicted.

'I wish I felt worse about that,' she admitted. 'Honestly, I am sorry, but there was no other way. You would have looked, like you always do. Like you did with the baby, and now you've led the White Elm straight to him, and he's gone. You ruin everything.'

On the floor, the bartender choked on another breath. His panic had spiralled downward over the past minute, and Renatus was sure he could feel another thread of contentment between the dying man and Aristea. Emotional transfer was a rumoured ability of advanced Empaths, but having never met one, Renatus was yet to see it in action.

'I tried not to believe it, but I know something you don't,' Nastassja said as he watched the man on the floor quieten and stop breathing. 'I know what you're going to do. You're fated. I've done *everything* to keep you from it. Avalon–'

'That was you?' Renatus demanded, smacking the flat of the

sai onto the countertop in frustration as he failed yet again. She flinched. The pub owner, Aristea's vicious assailant in the Scottish woods, Keely Shanahan's disappearance, the defector nailed to the tree, the real reason the Elm Stone was stolen… 'Why is *everything* you?'

'Lisandro wanted me to tell you,' she said. 'He wanted to bring you in on it. But I couldn't let you be part of this. I wanted to save you. So… yes. And if you'd just *stayed*, like we decided–'

'Why did you get to decide?' Renatus exploded. On each side of the pub, patrons and disguised apprentices alike shrank back as fright bounced around like a ball. 'They had a teenage bride picked out for me already, did you know that? And a tournament I was supposed to survive to be worthy of her. I was fifteen – the same age you were when Da started taking expressions of interest for you. How could you give me to them?'

To her credit, his sister's unnatural eyes filled with apologetic tears she couldn't squeeze back, and her breath in through her nose was shaky. She couldn't meet his demanding gaze.

'There was always one rule for you and another for me,' she murmured finally, as though in justification. 'You're a boy. Everything always worked out for you. And it did, didn't it? White Knight Gawain and his merry council of liars shined you up and now you're a frontline soldier for all the things wrong with the world.'

'You're *disappointed* in me? You helped *murder our parents*.' He pointed to the still form on the floor. 'You just murdered this man. *I'm* disappointed in *you*.'

'Our father would have sold me,' she reminded him brokenly, wiping the tears. 'Every time I tried to leave, he dragged me back, suffocating me under suppression spells, location spells, protection spells I didn't ask for. Stealing my memories. I was a prisoner, or don't you remember? Maybe he took yours, too. Who takes memories from someone they're meant to love?'

Renatus didn't mean to say what he said; he was thinking of Aristea, scrubbing two hours from his mind and throwing her future with the White Elm to the winds in her efforts to protect him. Bewildered, he asked, 'Who else would you take them from?'

Nastassja's startled blink told him she didn't recognise him in that moment.

'You've grown into *him*,' she said as if it that were the most hurtful insult she could muster, and in her book, that was as low as she could go. It slid right off him.

'No, I grew *up*. You could try it. You can't just kill people when you're forced into a corner.'

'No? Then what happened to Glassner?' Nastassja shot back nastily. She hit him dead centre that time, but he knew his controlled expression did not give in the slightest. He was better at this.

'I wouldn't know,' he replied flippantly, not a lie. No one knew what happened to those lost in the void. 'Nobody missed him. But look at the consequences of your actions. We're on opposite sides of a *civil war*.'

Shaking her head in dismay, dark lips trembling briefly, his sister closed her eyes and pressed her fingertips together at her chin as though in prayer. Aristea's work on her emotional state was wearing off, and she quaked with conflict.

'Do we have to be?' she asked finally. She opened her eyes, appealing. 'Lisandro meant it, what he said. The White Elm's going down but you don't need to sink with it. Bring Aristea home. You and I can start over. I'll even… play nice, and forgive you for letting her have all my things.'

Renatus smiled tightly at that. 'Charitable of you, but I don't think so.'

'Please consider it. The whole future changes if you can just forgive him.' She was referring to Lisandro. 'I hope, if nothing else, I've convinced you he's not the monster you've always wanted to believe.'

An unexpected concept. Maybe their father's friend was responsible for less than Renatus had blamed him for, but he'd still let Ana Morrissey become this person. He'd facilitated her atrocious errors of judgement and let the consequences slide. However wholesome and pure their love had started out, they'd become a toxic combination, a serial killer duo he was better off without.

'Please,' she begged, seeing his decision in his face. 'He said you wouldn't listen, that I'm wasting my time, but we're a family. You have to change your mind.'

He mightn't have said anything so provocative except that he knew Aristea was in earshot.

'I have all the family I need,' he said gently, leaning close for effect, ignoring the persistent scratching of Aristea's mind, 'and for once, your husband is right about me – you *are* wasting your time. I'm not who you knew, and you're not who I wanted you to be. Let's go back to being dead to each other.'

Something broke in his sister at that unnecessary jab, and her breath shuddered. She hesitantly took his wrist in her trembling fingers.

'I really do love you, Ren,' she said miserably. 'I was trying to save you.'

'You keep saying that. Save me from what?'

'From what you're going to do.' She circled her fingers into a ring over his wrist, fingertips not quite touching, and took a steadying breath. 'From yourself. From our family's legacy. You were always the best of us, and you deserved better than what was inevitably coming for you.'

Things were shifting in the pub. Emotions, thoughts, decisions. In the corner, Aristea's dread had skyrocketed, and she took an unwilling pace toward him. Just one more moment, and he'd leave with her. But his sister's hanging mystery was too tempting.

'Which is *what*?'

Nastassja blinked away the last of her tears and shook her head, clearing her mind of troublesome attachments. Her fingers slid from his wrist to his bandaged hand.

'Me,' she confessed. 'Always, me.'

He had methodically missed every opportunity to stop what came next. She dug heartless fingertips into his wounded hand, and he hissed as it exploded with pain. Her other hand flashed out and grabbed his, twisting the sai free. She was already inside his wards, under his guard, and his left hand was too slow to escape her grip. She spun the blade out to the side, deftly catching the shaft in her palm, and drove it with all her strength into his chest.

chapter twenty-eight

It was worse than any nightmare I could dream up. The blade, *my* blade, caught the pub lights as it spun too fast for anyone to stop, and Ana Morrissey stabbed downward. The sharpened tip had already made contact with his breast by the time I'd taken my next petrified step, and it sunk deep between two ribs.

'No!'

My heart smashed against my own ribs. I snatched up the other blade as I passed it and shoved with my free hand, but it was too late – my ward slammed into Nastassja, knocking her off her feet and sending the sai skittering to the floor, trailing with Renatus's blood. He gasped as the blade was torn free, clutching at the hole in his chest.

The *hole* in his *chest*. I definitely wasn't breathing.

I reached him, yelling his name, grabbing his arm when he tried to push me away. He felt blindly for the bar counter and staggered back into it, gasping fruitlessly like he was winded.

Declan blocks me.

'No! Don't touch him. It's the White Elm marker in his aura.'

'I don't care, do something!' I panic, clutching my hair and trying to think through Renatus's loud and jumbled thought stream. He's burning from the inside, I can see it, I can feel it, and I can't do a thing.

What was it about doom and heightened emotion that worked so well to dissolve memory blockers? In the present, blood bubbled forth from the small hole in Renatus's left breast, and heedless panic poured from him as I tried to get a grip. Not that I had the skill or time to heal a lethal strike like this. Had the blade hit his heart? There was so much blood.

'Don't,' he choked, pushing me back. Our eyes met, frightened hazel and wild violet, and I heard his disjointed thoughts in mine. *Don't... she's... watch your back.*

I heard the fearful voices of the other barflies, calling warnings, and I turned to see Nastassja pulling herself upright by the leg of a barstool, a handful of angry red magic gathering in her palm.

Vicious magic laces up and down his body, skin beginning to blacken in thickening veins of burnout. His aura burns off as steam, a direct conversion to energy.

'Stop fighting it!' Declan yells, but Renatus can't hear him. The black cracks spider across his face and hands. Veins bulge in his neck, every muscle straining. His screams fill my ears and tear at my heart. It's killing him. The hallway quakes with the pressure.

The first ball she threw spread across the flat surface of my ward like rotten fruit on glass, and she sneered, resentment curling around her like smoke.

Vulnerability, too. She had totally missed what was right under her nose.

'Of course it's you,' she mocked, all traces gone of the girl I'd thought we were uncovering. She tightened and opened her fist; another ball of magic, bigger this time, manifested there, and her calculating gaze shifted to Renatus, no regret as she took in her gasping brother. I sidestepped to put myself between them, and her sneer twisted into a smile. 'Hiding behind your shields while his heart empties isn't going to stop what's supposed to happen. Don't waste my time. You're just a little girl. I was you, once. Useless. Property. You can't protect him.'

I should perhaps have grabbed him and run, but his sister's words detonated a shockwave of righteous fury inside me. I swung the blade I held and extended my other hand, the second sai Displacing across the room to land perfectly in my grasp without conscious thought.

Its end dripped with Renatus's blood.

'I shouldn't have to,' I said through my teeth, 'and you were never me.'

I didn't know how much time Renatus had, but I knew every second counted and I couldn't wait. I also knew Nastassja wouldn't let me leave with her brother until she saw him choke his last breath.

I acted on my only remaining option and dove forward with my blades raised.

My advantage was that she had me pegged as the sidekick. The sai – *mostly* defensive, Renatus had said – my age, my size, my sex, my temperament. She wasn't wrong. But she had assumed the role of aggressor, and wasn't expecting that position to be challenged. Surprised by my unprecedented move, she backstepped and tossed the spell wildly. It went wide and bounced from my warding, blowing a noisy hole in the pub floor. The other three patrons cried out in captivated fear.

'Through the kitchen,' I shouted back to them, slashing down at Nastassja's hasty wards. Flooded with my own magic, gods only knew what kind, I felt the resistance under my sai. I saw the flash of fear in her green eyes as I bore down with my weight, the posts of my sai sinking steadily through the air around her.

I was supposed to save him, not lead him to—

Everything stops with a sudden crash. Renatus goes silent and falls to the floor with the shards of the vase Declan just cracked over his head. The lightning zips away from his prone body, rejoining the angry spells racing over the walls. Blood runs from the gash under his hair, down his forehead. He lies still.

'What did you do?!' I drop to my knees but I'm too scared to touch him. Is he…?

She must have seen the momentary distraction in my face, because she attacked. Her mind came at me first – toxic black bees of angry thoughts biting at the edges of my mind, relentless. I hurried to preserve those barriers, and she used my shift in focus to lash out. My wards weren't prepared for blocking flesh, and her palm struck me solidly in the chin. I staggered back, vision swimming with disoriented pain.

'It wasn't going to stop until he did,' Declan retorts, dropping the remains of the vase. He sounds relieved; he wasn't sure this would work. 'Stubborn bastard with more power than he knows what to do with.

He'd fight it until it killed him, given the chance. Better unconscious than dead. Aristea,' he adds sternly, crouching beside me as panic rises in my chest, 'listen to me. I need you to focus.'

Focus, yes. I shook my head free of her telepathic attack and got my feet under me. I had to remember that – the Morrisseys played dirty. Agree to a sword fight and they'll kick you over; engage in a battle of magical willpower and they'll punch you in the face. Renatus had forgotten, and behind me he slid to the floor, coughing up blood and unspooling with untempered panic.

'Memory breakdown,' she noted, casually coming after me as I tried to stay upright. The pub swam and my head buzzed with the dregs of her telepathic assault. 'I know the signs. It's always at the most inconvenient times. Bits and pieces, stuff they stole… except you stole from yourself. Very original.' Her fist flashed out at me, and I only narrowly dodged the jab. Her other hand chopped downward through the air, and an ugly gash lit up my ward momentarily. It would have opened my neck and shoulder if not for my shielding. I scrambled back another step to get some distance and reset my footing. 'I don't know how many times they "fixed" me. Some things never come back. My first kiss. Days and days of my life, erased. They had no right.'

I'd appealed to Renatus on her behalf, said she couldn't help what she'd become, and to some extent, I still believed that. I urgently pointed back at her brother as he bled and bled.

'That wasn't him.'

'You love him,' Nastassja said, ignoring my words as she sized me up. I came at her, but she Displaced a pool cue into her hands and I quickly pulled up. New plan. 'I love him, too. It's easy to choose when you only love two people and they're on the same side. But what if it was one or the other? Would you still choose him if you loved someone more? Your family?'

'Your husband already wiped out my whole family to save his own sorry life.'

'Not your whole family.' Her eyes glittered as I faltered. She'd changed the dynamic of our altercation and swung the cue at me. I blocked swiftly with my sai and she withdrew, circling closer, expression briefly pitying. 'Let him go, Aristea.' I didn't think she'd said my name before. 'He's not always going to be this person. He's going to change into someone else. Hurt people. Maybe even you.' She struck out. I blocked. 'I wanted to have my cake and eat it, too; keep my brother and the family I chose, but ultimately, I can't have both. He has to die.'

She knew Susannah's prophecy. Of course she did. Lisandro knew Renatus was his final destination and his beloved had spent years trying to find a way around her two favourite people ending up at each other's throats. Ironically, *her* actions had driven the deepest wedges between them.

'He hasn't done it yet,' I reminded her, watching her shoulders for movement, watching her fabulous shoes. 'Let me leave with him.'

She cocked her head sympathetically, deaf to the incoherent mumbling of her dying brother.

'I can't.'

'I need to get him out of here,' I insist, voice shrill in my ears. I don't know how I'll do it, I'm sure I'm not strong enough to lift Renatus, but I have to. Residual sparks flicker under his skin as the black lines begin to fade. Declan appeals to me, a firm voice of reason I can't argue with, especially as I'm spiralling and desperate for someone else to take charge and fix things.

'We'll get him out,' he promises. 'But not yet. Look at me.' I do, reluctant to pull my eyes from my master. Declan has never looked so deadly serious. 'We can't touch him yet, and we can't let this be for nothing. I am getting into that vault. The house thinks it took care of the intruder, look.' He gestures; the lightning is calming down. 'I won't get this chance again. And after, I promise you, I'll help you. He'll be okay. He's always okay. Are you?'

I shake my head, my chest aching as I struggle to breathe evenly.

'We just… and Renatus…'

'Freak out later,' he advises. He hands me the knife and I glance once more, guiltily, at Renatus. 'Right now, I need to you pay attention.'

Pay attention, pay attention. Nastassja made her move in that moment, and though distracted, I was ready. She was predictable, taking advantages where she saw them, the way I was taught to, unaware of how her determination gave her away. She jabbed with the cue, its furthest end sparking like a cattle prod, and I turned side-on and caught it in the guards of my two sai, stopping it abruptly and sending a jolt through my opponent's wrists. A paired weapon, strikes came in twos, and that was almost all I knew about it. I used this to beat her last time we faced off. Today, she wasn't wearing Sterling Adams, and I had no qualms with hurting the real Nastassja while her brother struggled to breathe behind me.

Levering the left down and the right upward, I twisted both wrists to wrench the post from her unwilling hands and flick it to the floor. The first blade, I spun in my palm to give me the pommel for the follow-up combination, which I executed without thought.

If I'd thought about it, I wouldn't have done it.

One, an uppercut jab to the jaw that snapped her head to the side.

Two, a forceful thrust of my dominant hand, blade-first.

Declan issues tense instructions and I follow as closely as I can with the knife. I hit something I wasn't meant to and he hisses apprehensively. We both freeze.

'Don't move,' he orders, carefully extending his fingers to catch the stray end of my severed spell thread before it can swing across any others and wreak havoc. Crisis averted. 'Hold this still. And don't. Move.'

I didn't move. I didn't even breathe, and for a beat, neither did she. Wide green eyes lowered from mine to her stomach, where my sai was buried in her flesh. I'd stabbed her right under the ribs, and around the silver post, already, blood was welling forth and staining her beautiful clothes in a growing rose of crimson.

I drew in a deep gasping breath, and she did, too, air shuddering in her throat with shock. I couldn't believe it any more than she could. I'd *stabbed her*. Renatus's sister, whose death had derailed him, who he loved, who *couldn't heal* and would now bleed out again like his worst memory. Shaking, her hands closed around the shaft of my sai, and I debated what to do. My instinct was to pull it free but that would unplug the wound and let the blood–

She made the decision for me, whimpering as she pulled. I stared as blood oozed and then flowed, and as more of the post came back coated in red. I hadn't realised my own strength, to pierce so deep. I hadn't realised her body's frailty. I hadn't realised the power of my anger.

I hadn't meant to do this kind of damage. I hadn't thought myself capable. She covered the wound with uncertain fingers and blood seeped between them, running over the Elm Stone in its beautiful new wedding band setting. I backed up, keeping myself between the siblings, maybe hoping that I could protect Renatus from seeing what I'd done. I didn't want him to see her dying, though I knew logically his shallower wound was still much worse.

Deep-seated fear saturated Nastassja's emotional field and I could think of nothing to say. None of this felt real. I left Cassán's cave to deliver a biscuit tin full of love letters and my day had dissolved into *this*.

Renatus's impending death, and my first kill, ending a whole family line.

But it wasn't to be today. Shakily, petrified, Nastassja peeled her bloody hands away and we both stared at the hole in her bodice. Underneath, visible to each of us, smooth and unmarked skin stretched across the gap.

Healed. Completely. She sobbed a note of relieved laughter that told me she hadn't known that would work, and looked up at me with a rawness that was all Ana.

It was clear that she would have loved to throw in a last word, but she let self-preservation guide her, and she abruptly Displaced away, leaving us alone with only the sounds of my uneven breathing and Renatus's wet coughs as blood kept coming up.

'Renatus.' I cast the sai down and dropped to his side, not sure where to even start. Blood, so much blood, and panic. He had a slippery hand pressed over the wound but it didn't look like it was helping. I added the pressure of my own hands, overwhelmed. 'No, no, please...'

I squeezed my eyes shut and summoned as much focus as I could into the injury, but his emotional state and mine made concentration impossible. I channelled magic through my hands and hoped for the best, but he coughed and another mouthful of blood ran down his chin. No, no, no... I looked around wildly. The bartender lay dead a metre away and the other patrons had followed my advice and slipped out through the kitchen. My movements were unscryable by Qasim and the White Elm thanks to Declan's anti-council spell in Prague, and Renatus wasn't telepathically connected to his usual network of minds.

No one knew.

No one was coming.

And I could not fix this.

One more move and there's a silent feeling of something sliding into place. We freeze again, Declan's hands holding strands of magic at awkward angles. The door, with all its theatrical chains and padlocks, dissolves into transparency, and a small vault-like room is revealed behind it. There are boxes, shelves of books and bottles, locked chests and several small safes. In the middle, there's a very clear target: an ornate lectern with the book Renatus gleaned from Teagan's thoughts.

I feel Declan deliberating, not wanting to ask it of me, but it's obvious. His hands are almost literally tied, holding the door's fragile security system at bay, while mine are free to nab something that doesn't belong to me. Or him. But he's right. He deserves to know.

I put the knife down on the floor and say, 'Don't you lock me in there.' He says something witty or irritating in response but the blood's pounding too hard in my ears to listen. I pass right through the holographic curtain of a door. One, two steps and I'm at the lectern. This isn't mine to take. This isn't me. But I guess it is today. I am careful to lift the worn brown book and to touch nothing else as I turn back to the door. I have seen Aladdin. I'm quick to duck back under Declan's waiting arm, only breathing again when I'm safely back in the hall with him and my unconscious master.

'I can see why he keeps you around,' Declan says cheerfully as he gets to work restitching the magic. The door solidifies. The book and my actions weigh heavy in my hands.

None of that was as heavy as this moment I was living now.

'*Help!*' I screamed, panic setting in like a cold, paralysing fog. What to do, what to do? Renatus's eyelids fluttered. I couldn't move him; I could barely lift him, though I must have dragged him, once, that day at Shanahan's. But this time his body was ripped open, and I needed to get him to a Healer, a real Healer. Emmanuelle was my go-to but the house was unsafe. Lady Miranda's hospital in London, maybe? Who cared if she arrested me? I made my first sensible decision and hurriedly tore down my wards, the ones that kept anyone else from scrying me. 'Someone, please help! Please…'

I leave the ledger beside Renatus and kneel at his side.

'Is he…?'

'Safe to touch? You'll find out, I expect.'

I tentatively touch his hair, and when nothing happens, I brush it back from the vase's cut. Small but bloody, like all head wounds. I can heal this. I have time while Declan works. I close my eyes and channel magic to my hands—

A thud draws my attention just as the skin is knitting back together, and both Declan and I look worriedly up the hall.

'Teagan?' he calls, and we wait. Silence. He mutters something and gets back to closing the spellwork. 'I can't leave this hanging or the place will turn on us. Go check on her?'

I jog the hallway's length and swing into the tea room. My knees almost give out.

Teagan is where I left her, but she isn't standing anymore. She is sprawled on the floor, face-down, in a pool of bright blood.

'Declan!' I scream, clutching the doorframe for strength when the blood reaches her long blonde hair and begins to stain the perfect victory rolls she pinned herself. What have I done? She looks dead. All I did was nick her finger. 'Declan! Help!'

chapter twenty-nine

This time, he didn't need to be called. The Fabric parted in the middle of the pub and Declan stepped into view, abruptly stopping with a pulse of shock when he saw the situation. Renatus, bleeding from a stab wound in his chest. Me, covered in his blood with two bloody sai beside me. A dead man lying on the floor not far away.

'What did you—'

'It was Nastassja,' I explained hurriedly as Renatus tried again to draw breath. I didn't think about the implications of what I said or how much I despised him, I was just so relieved to have been heard. 'She's Ana Morrissey and he's dying. I can't stop it. I can't stop… What are you… Declan?'

He'd crossed the space and bent to wrench Renatus up by the arm. I cried out, sure he was doing more damage to that wound, but tried to be helpful when I saw he was getting Renatus off the floor.

I hear him before I see him.

'What? A little busy back there…' I feel his shock as though it's my own as he pulls up abruptly at my side. 'What did you do?'

'I didn't… She was just…' I can't explain. He really does fall to his knees, dropping the ledger this was all for, hands hovering over the bleeding girl like he wants to gather her up but isn't sure if he should touch her. I try to pull myself together, and kneel beside him. 'I can try to heal her.'

'No, don't,' he interrupts, waving my hands away. He is concentrating on Teagan. He tentatively touches her cheek, then with more bravery feels for her pulse at her throat. 'Erratic. Where's the cut?'

'He'll die here,' Declan said brusquely as we arranged my master's arm over his shoulder. 'Where to?'

I didn't know, but Renatus did. Urgently, he used what was left of his strength to clasp one bloody hand to the side of

Declan's head. The other scrier froze, staring down at him. Their eyes met.

It was all Declan needed. He nodded and Renatus's hand slid away, leaving a bright and gory print down Declan's cheek and neck. The wet, shallow breaths came more sporadically and desperately. I wanted to cry but through shuttering lashes, he caught my gaze, too.

The tin.

'Seriously?' Declan demanded as I vaulted over the bar and ran for where Renatus had shoved the biscuit tin. It glinted dimly in the artificial light, unassuming. 'I'm not waiting, he isn't light.' I grabbed it and raced to the end of the bar, hooking around to get back to my friends. Declan was true to his word, and opened a hole in the Fabric without waiting for my answer. Heart pounding, I bent again to scoop up my sai and looped my arm through Renatus's loose one just in time to hijack their ride through the void.

Every bit as uncomfortable as ever, only this time, Renatus was dying.

Declan tips Teagan's chin to check the other side of her throat and her head. There's enough blood for a wound like that. Terrified, I take up her hand, which from the radius of the blood pool seems to be the source, and turn it over. A wild thought of dread tells me to expect slashes at the wrist – her three favourite people, after all, have just betrayed her. But though bloody and dripping, her wrist is unharmed. Her middle finger, where I pricked her skin only ten minutes ago, is streaming with accusatory red.

'That's it?' Declan demands, leaning close to inspect. I can feel his breath on my face, but for once I don't think he even notices his proximity. 'Then how can she...?' Realisation drains his face of colour. 'Shanahan, you cowardly gobshite.'

We landed somewhere else and I let go, gasping. We were in a large hospital room, no one around to see us arrive so dramatically, and I extended my senses quickly for Lady Miranda.

She wasn't here. This wasn't London's Royal Hospital, where Renatus brought me.

But it was just as good, because the door opened as Declan was lowering Renatus to the floor. The White Elm's youngest Healer, the Romanian, Teresa, walked in with wide dark eyes.

We all froze, looking at each other with a thousand burning questions. She took in a lot of the same information Declan did – me, fugitive apprentice with the assault weapons; Renatus, bleeding to death with a hole where his heart was. For an instant, I thought we'd made a terrible mistake. One that might cost Renatus his life.

Luckily, something clicked for Teresa, and her determination set solid.

'How long?' she asked, and I burst into quiet tears of relief. She settled at Renatus's side and Declan backed off to stand with me, breathing loudly with the exertion.

'Almost a minute,' I estimated hurriedly, because the exchange with Nastassja had been so quick and intense that I just wasn't sure. Teresa's small hands hovered over his spasming chest and her eyelids fell shut. She nodded.

'Not the heart, then,' she told me. I almost pressed my hands to my mouth in relief, then saw the state of them. 'He'd be dead already. This...' She was quiet for a few beats of Renatus's painstaking breathless gasps, opening her eyes to stare at the same thing that caught our attention, too. The injection of magic from her healing hands illuminated the black cracks underneath his skin, creeping up his neck toward his jaw, fading when she stopped work. She seemed to weigh up the risk and decided the chest wound was her priority. She continued channelling energy from and back into him, the charcoal webs spidering darker, further, across his face and hands and everywhere else we couldn't see. 'I can fix this but I need to take it slowly. This is a collapsed lung. It is filling...'

'There's extra power,' I told her, 'in the bracelet.'

Teresa heard; her fingers found his wrist. After a few horrific seconds, the tension went out of him, and his breathing slowed. Evening out. Unconscious? Medical trance? Between the blood and the black veins, Renatus had never looked less like his usual unnaturally attractive self. I swallowed a few times, starting to shake. I didn't know Teresa all that well, though she'd helped heal me when Lisandro attacked me in Prague. Maybe she'd call in her White Elm colleagues to crash-tackle me to the floor, but first, she had her whole attention on saving Renatus's life, and that was all I cared about.

Declan leaned closer to me.

'Did you say that *Ana Morrissey* did this?' he asked, unsure he'd heard correctly. I understood the feeling, but I couldn't speak through my tightening throat. I nodded. Tears streamed down my face and I choked on my next breath, stifling a sob that became another sob and then another. The adrenaline was receding and I could feel my control unravelling in the company of these slightly older, infinitely more capable people who were now surely going to take care of things from here on.

I could let go. Finally.

Declan circled in front of me and leaned down to look into my face.

'Hey,' he said sharply, clicking his fingers close enough to make me flinch away. 'None of that. Come on,' he added, stalking to the door. I should know better than to trust him by now but I followed without question. I cast a look back at Teresa and Renatus, both so still. 'Let her work. We're the security detail – this place isn't safe.'

Blood continues to stream from Teagan's finger and I wait for Declan to finish blaspheming about the girl's father.

'It's a blood curse,' he explains shortly, summoning bandages from thin air while I hold Teagan's hand still for him, 'which means this will help very little. It means healing won't help. Think magical haemophilia. Different from Renatus's thing. It's going to keep bleeding until she's empty. No clotting, no wound healing capabilities. And Shanahan,' he continues furiously as he wraps, 'would rather coat his daughter in surveillance spells so he can swoop in whenever she gets a paper cut–'

'Or a nosebleed,' I realise faintly, thinking back to my first aborted tea party here. Teagan scried with me, too much strain for her, and she'd started bleeding. She hardly cared. Her dad turned up to fuss over her and sent me home.

'Or that. And rather than tell people who might be able to help, he's kept it secret. You know why?' Declan is livid, not really speaking to me at all, just ranting rhetorically now. 'It'll be because she's harder to marry off if this shit is heritable, and because he doesn't want anyone to know he pissed someone off enough to bring on something this vicious. Where do we even begin the list of people who'd love to curse Uncle Thomas's family?'

I know the answer immediately, though I wish I didn't.

The broken-through memory made me falter, and the growing pain behind my eyes had me tempted to rub my eyelids with my bloody fists. I refrained with effort.

'What do you mean, we're still not safe?' I asked blearily, ultimately wiping my eye with my shoulder. Declan poked his head out the door and looked both ways, then lightly kicked the door closed and began to work his locking magic on its handle. He didn't answer, which was a prompt for me to spread out my senses beyond the room we were in, feeling more broadly than White Elm markers. Something I should have done on arrival. Teresa was the only councillor in the building, but we weren't the only powerful presences on this floor. Two of them, I was shocked to discover, I recognised. 'We're in Belfast?'

Declan finishes bandaging Teagan's hand and deliberates. He took charge after Renatus went down but he's in well over his head. He curses several times.

'Alright. Alright.' He makes up his mind and reluctantly offers me the ledger. 'Take this. I can't be found with that and a bloodless heiress. I will want that back,' he warns. His meaningful look assures me he won't let any degree of affection stop him from retrieving it later, and then he's all business again. He gathers Teagan and stands, cradling her like a ragdoll. She doesn't stir. I want to be sick. Declan jerks his head at the doorway, prompting me to go ahead of him. 'She's not heavy. You'll have to be the one to carry her through the front door – once I drag Renatus out, I won't be able to step back inside without an invitation.'

At the front door I take her with difficulty. I hug her limp form to myself, trying to keep her upright while Declan sprints away for my master. Teagan's pale face weighs on my shoulder, soft breaths warming my neck, and I hold her tighter, overcome with guilt.

'I'm so sorry, Teagan,' I whisper. She can't answer, but the bandaging we wrapped around her hand finally saturates and I hear the drip-drip noise of blood spattering to the floor at my feet.

Teagan Shanahan, conscious but seemingly weak, was only two or three rooms to my right. Had she been here in hospital this whole time? And her dad…?

'Back up,' Declan advised suddenly, giving up on his hasty locking spell just before the door slammed open. Thomas Shanahan the Second stood in the hall, glaring with the well-rehearsed fury of a man who'd had a lot of time to reflect on how mad he was with each of us. The sight of so much blood gave him pause, but he didn't seem surprised to see the trio he blamed for his misfortunes together.

'Uncle Thomas,' I began, not knowing what explanation I could offer. He saved me from having to come up with something, taking a step forward through the door while we kept ourselves between him and Renatus. He raised a hand, gathering magic.

'You have some nerve–'

Likewise, he was saved having to threaten us by the abrupt arrival of Lady Miranda. The Fabric shifted and she landed precisely in front of him, setting her feet firmly on the sterile hospital floor with the authority of a woman who belonged there.

'Mr Shanahan,' she thundered, and he immediately backstepped, intentions changing on a dime. 'Before you do anything you'll regret, remember that the White Elm handles justice, not other criminals, and remember also that the innocent bystander in this room is the same Healer who has been treating your child. Whatever spell you were about to cast, you had best unthink it.'

He did just that, the sparkle of magic dying instantly in his palm.

'These three are the reason my daughter–'

'Allegedly,' Lady Miranda cut him off with firmness I rarely saw her employ, 'and if that's true, *we* will get to the bottom of that, I assure you, but for now, you should return to your children.'

'My bodyguard–'

'We'll handle it.'

There are few scenarios where you'd find a short British black woman with silvering curls and sneakers worn out from untold hours in the operating theatre more intimidating than a magical underworld kingpin, but I think even Declan winced when Shanahan tried again to argue with her. Teagan's father pointed dangerously at each of us over Lady Miranda's shoulder.

'One of them has something that belongs–'

'If you do not leave, I'll assist you,' the High Priestess interrupted smoothly. 'You're in my operating room. We'll take it from here.'

He hated to concede, I could tell, but Thomas Shanahan angrily straightened his pinstriped waistcoat and turned on his heel. Lady Miranda waved a dismissive hand and the door slammed behind him. I had never seen her utilising that kind of showy magic. She went straight to Teresa.

'You two,' she added sharply, giving a meaningful look at the pair of chairs beside the door. 'Sit and don't go anywhere.'

I didn't argue. Declan pursed his lips and spun to follow me.

'Yes, ma'am,' he muttered, flopping down in the seat beside me where we could watch the Healers perform their miraculous work. I settled the biscuit tin on my lap, dropped the sai to the floor, let my head fall back against the wall and allowed the tears to stream, warm and wordless. I was caught, it was over, and I didn't particularly care because Miranda and Teresa were fixing Renatus and that was all I had wanted, but it did feel like I'd just wasted a month of my life only to end up exactly here. Declan seemed to be thinking along the same lines. 'Figures. Every time I pull Renatus out of trouble, I end up deeper.'

I swallowed the painful lump in my throat and turned my head to look at my companion. The illusion he normally wore to hide the chopped-up mess of his hair and the scabbed state of his hands was missing, and he appeared as thin and strung-out as he ought to be, given how many people would have been on his tail after we parted ways in Prague. I'd been angry with him for a good while after that and I supposed I still was, but any bitterness had evaporated in the tense escape from the Coleraine pub.

'You must be as sick of seeing him at death's door as I am,' I said with cracks in my voice. He smiled lopsidedly.

'Mostly sick of having to carry his unconscious arse. Next time, it's your turn.'

Declan comes staggering back with Renatus's arm slung over his shoulder. Seeing the most powerful person I know like this, pale like death, boneless, boots dragging on the floor, my breaths come faster and I feel my grip on Teagan loosen along with my grip on the situation. Renatus is nearly dead. Teagan could still die. The bodyguard is... I don't know. We're on the wrong side of the law and morality and every other line I know of. Declan breathes laboriously as he finally reaches me and gives me a stern look.

'Freak out later,' he reminds me. He's fighting gravity to hold Renatus up and awkwardly pins him to a wall with his own weight while he works the locks on the front door.

I blinked away the memory shard and raised my shoulder to wipe my eye again. I couldn't stop the tears. They must have been lying in wait for weeks. Declan's smile gentled, as did his mood.

'Hey. He's going to be okay.' He nodded in Renatus's direction, and I looked through the blur of salt and water. He'd never looked worse, even in the memories from Shanahan's, but I knew he was in the best hands. 'He's always okay. He's a right bugger like that.'

I nodded. He was right. But the tears kept coming, harder, and I leaned forward to press my elbows into my knees. Sensing I had something I needed to share, Declan leaned closer to keep my words between us.

'It's not just that,' I whispered shakily. I showed him my hands. 'I *stabbed* Ana Morrissey.'

He paused like he always did when he was trying to work me out, emotions warily conflicted.

'Sorry,' he said after a moment. 'I'm still getting my head around... Alright. Bloody hell, Ana is alive. But *she* stabbed *him*. So now thanks to you, she's bleeding out somewhere?'

'Except no, she isn't,' I tried to explain quietly.

'Oh. Then I hate to tell you this, but you did it wrong. Everything I've heard of Nastassja tells me she's a problem the world's better off without.'

'No, I mean, I did it right.' I cringed, hating that turn of phrase. There was nothing right about any of this. 'She *healed*.'

'Then she's not Ana Morrissey,' Declan advised softly. He looked across at his frenemy on the floor, private worry swirling where he forgot I could tap into it. 'They had the same... infirmity.'

Renatus genuinely disliked Declan almost all the time, and told me often not to trust him, yet his childhood friend was one of very few who knew of the Morrissey siblings' curse. There was an implicit level of trust between them that my master liked to pretend wasn't there, and Declan enjoyed poking fun at. That game they played wasn't one I was interested in joining – though I supposed my interactions with Declan were a sort of game, too – but that trust I wished I could shake had come across in my apprenticeship bond, so I didn't hesitate to tell him about the Elm Stone on Nastassja's finger. His dark eyes watched me as I spoke.

'Right,' he murmured when I finished. 'So... just to confirm I have this straight: mega powerful like Renatus or worse, without the lovable conscience or humanising weakness, aligned with the magical liberalism fanatics and now really angry because you stabbed her and interrupted her fratricide?'

He had it summed up neatly. I sighed and let my head hang where the tears could drip onto my bloody hands.

'Relax, goody-two-shoes,' Declan advised warmly, shifting forward in his seat to pull his loose canvas backpack around onto his lap. 'If she's unkillable, you didn't do any damage. Ethically clear, or close enough.'

'I'm *not* ethically clear,' I muttered. 'I didn't know she'd heal. I thought I'd doomed her. Renatus's favourite person. I didn't even think. Who *am* I?'

Declan went about releasing the ties of magic keeping his bag closed to any sticky fingers that might take interest.

'An excellent sidekick, that's who you are,' he said casually. 'Renatus needs saving from himself as often as from bad guys, hopeless sod. And you better be joking when you call that spiteful little witch his favourite person, after everything you and I have done for him.' I felt the soft click of magic settling into place as he undid the energetic locks on his bag's drawstring. Declan pulled out the ledger that had started all this trouble. 'I regret to realise you didn't expect to see this again,' he mentioned lightly, offering the book to me and then hesitating when he saw the red of my sticky hands. 'I didn't, uh, intend to part ways like that.' He placed the book instead on the biscuit tin balanced on my lap.

'You're giving it back to me?' I asked, surprised. He couldn't pretend it wasn't a major reason he'd tagged along with me. The memory of how badly he wanted it – though *why* was still missing – was freshly exposed in my head. He shrugged, and I understood. 'You couldn't read it.'

'Blank, like you said,' he agreed amiably. He was dejected to part with it but was left with no better use for the thing. 'Once I shook off Hanna – what a pain she is, right? – I tried everything I could think of. I was sure it had to be the house, like you said, but even when I got back inside the penthouse – not advised, by the way – I got nothing from it. So, if you're so magical that you were able to read it once, you probably deserve it more than I do anyway.' He paused, something unsaid hanging between us, and I stayed silent, waiting him out. We watched the Healers continue on Renatus, repairing internal damage now that the skin was closed. Finally, Declan added, very quietly, 'I know you wanted this for the council, in your war on Lisandro. Maybe it will help get you back in their good books, so to speak?'

My tears had slowed, and I again wiped my eyes on my damp sleeve.

'Thank you,' I said genuinely, smiling at him. Of all the people to be grateful for… 'And thank you for taking it when you did to draw away Hanna Seidel.'

'Don't be generous, I was stealing from you like the irretrievably devious scoundrel I am.'

'Of course you were. My naïve mistake.' I stared at my hands, stained with Morrissey blood, ideas slowly coming together in my head. 'Did you really break back into Shanahan's place after you left me?'

'As I said, it's not a move I would advise,' he admitted, turning his arm over and lifting his sleeve. A violent, rippling burn ran from wrist to elbow on the underside. 'I'm glad I didn't stick more of myself through the warding.'

He'd stuck his hand in, maybe a penthouse window, with the ledger, hoping to read it. He was desperate. He thought when I'd said I read it at the house, I meant Shanahan's.

I didn't. I read it in the ballroom at Morrissey House. But the place hadn't mattered, because when Renatus and Qasim took it from me and flipped it open, I saw that in their hands, it was blank.

In their *hands*. I looked again at mine, and understood. It was so *obvious*.

So too, I realised with dawning horror and sadness, was Declan's reason for wanting this stupid book. What else was worth the risk of that drastic assault on Shanahan's fortress? Why else would his father have schooled him on the vault's security system? Declan was resourceful. He could get what he needed from people when he needed it, but there was something he couldn't charm, steal or manipulate into his possession. Something uniquely valuable that would sway even Renatus into helping him pull off an unexpected heist that could easily have cost us all our lives and our freedom.

'Your life is in here, you said,' I brought up, nodding at the ledger. 'You mean this is about Lorcan.'

Declan dropped his gaze to delicately roll his sleeve back down, feelings closely guarded.

'You remember,' he guessed. 'From the penthouse.'

'No,' I answered, 'not everything, but I don't think I'm wrong.' I didn't elaborate on what I already knew. I recalled the vision of Cassán and Mánus discovering Lorcan O'Malley's betrayal of their black-market organ trade to the White Elm. To compensate themselves and exact their revenge, it was said that Shanahan's father, Tom, led an attack on Lorcan's family, taking their money's worth in literal blood. And skin, and organs, and fingers, and whatever else fetches a price in blood magic circles. Ten members of the same family, leaving only a daughter and an unborn heir. Declan's father. Who was now dead. I took a steadying breath, hoping that I *was* wrong. 'You think the debt's still outstanding.'

Declan didn't look at me, but he did smile wryly, and his feelings gave him away.

'When my grandfather sold Eoin Tresaigh out to the White Elm, they confiscated and destroyed hundreds of thousands of pounds worth of black-market merchandise,' he explained like this wasn't the worst story he could tell. 'A big win for their new scrier Joseph, a big loss for the first Tom Shanahan and his chums, who'd already paid for those orders. Shanahan made sure he got his money back out of Lorcan's family.' Declan looked at the ledger. 'My da didn't think that was entirely true. He said it didn't add up, and Tom would never see him or take his letters, so he couldn't confirm. He was obsessed with finding *this* and knowing for sure. I think he found out, in a different way.'

Ah, well, who doesn't have murdered parents these days?

'He disappeared,' I assumed, trying to keep my voice down for the benefit of the Healers on the other side of the room. I shuffled closer to the other scrier. 'But if Shanahan really wanted to... uh...'

'Harvest me?' he supplied helpfully. I nodded, swallowing the ill taste in the back of my throat. He caught my drift. 'You're wondering why he'd betroth his daughter to someone he intended to kill?' I nodded again. 'I'm sure my mother thought the same thing when she accepted the offer.'

'It does make it sound like you're safe, doesn't it? Renatus told me no one wants to be responsible for ending a bloodline.'

'You're not ending it if you add it to your own first.'

The words cycled twice through my overwhelmed head before they sunk in. *You're not ending it...* Declan's family were famous for producing uncannily talented scriers, a lineage so reliably strong that my addled grandfather hadn't lost any certainty in their skill. Hanna Seidel had said Magnus Moira could 'use' him; the other mercenaries on my tail this past month had been happy to take Declan in my place, and now that I thought back, he'd been dishevelled with the wounds of protection spells before any of this.

I was starting to understand. For these old-world blood sorcerers, with Renatus already sworn to the White Elm, Declan's more ambiguous, untethered standing within society made him a valuable commodity worth associating with despite the past blight on the name. For Uncle Thomas, if he really was intent on extracting the last of Lorcan's debt from the last O'Malley, the solution was to ensure he was not the last one. Make Lorcan's heirs his own through his daughter Keely, cleaning off the name and absorbing the power, talent and status into his own bloodline.

It was smart, it was calculating, it was unthinkably cruel, and if this was what Declan had told us in the hallway in Shanahan's penthouse, it was no wonder that Renatus had caved and agreed to help steal the ledger.

'Why,' I asked Declan in quiet wonderment, 'can you never just ask?' I nodded over at Renatus, who seemed to be coming around to consciousness again. 'How can you not know that we would have helped you? At any point. And I will help you, if I don't end today in Valero's prison or something.'

'I hear it's nice this time of year.' But I felt the genuine gratitude in the other scrier, because just as he could not bring himself to ask, he couldn't say thank you. He cleared his throat. 'First, of course, we need to work out how to read that book.'

On the floor, black lines receding from his cheeks, Renatus blinked a few times and mumbled something that might be my name. My heart leapt. I shifted the ledger and biscuit tin to the seat as I quickly got up, casting a quick final smile at Declan.

'Maybe you need to,' I replied. 'I already know.'

Teresa tried to tell Renatus to lie still when he spotted me and strained to sit up; Lady Miranda was more forceful, holding him down by the shoulder.

'Give it a minute,' she ordered him as I approached and hovered nearby, sensing the Healers' wariness of me. 'There's still some blood in–'

He choked on the deeper breath prompted by his struggle to sit, and lurched sidewards onto his elbow to cough a thick mouthful of blood onto the smeared floor. I forgot about the Healers' feelings toward me and quickly dropped to Renatus's side, raising a hand to pluck a tissue from wherever tissues came from. I'd never asked how it worked; I'd just absorbed the spell from his mind, his vast repertoire of theatrical flashy magic.

'In the airways,' Lady Miranda finished as Renatus coughed up the last of the blood and mucus that had settled in his injured lung and respiratory tract. I caught his swinging dark hair and held it clear of his least favourite substance, hurrying to wipe his cheek and chin when he drew his first shuddering deep breath. I got rid of the worst of it, but the rusty stain remained, smeared all down his jaw and neck like a vampire who'd just finished off a victim. I tossed the tissue and manifested another, automatically half-filling my other cupped hand with water to soak it in. Another unexpectedly useful Renatus spell. Armed with my damp tissue, I reached to continue cleaning him up.

He caught my wrist, his hand as sticky and red as mine.

'Don't mother me.'

'Don't get stabbed,' I retorted, acting careless to cover my worry as I looked him over quickly. The black cracks had faded to pale grey, and the hole in his blood-soaked black shirt had smooth skin underneath it. I didn't think it would scar, Lady Miranda and Teresa being as good as they were and the injury being unmagical.

Emotionally, getting stabbed in the chest by your long-mourned sibling might take longer to patch up. I could feel some of his inner turmoil, and I tried to keep a respectful distance from those feelings, but as he grew more present and sat up properly, I also felt that those complex Nastassja issues were eclipsed, for now, by an immense warmth and gratitude. Either I'd forgotten how intensely he felt things, or he hadn't let himself feel like this before around me. Or maybe his new talent for Empathy had something to do with it? I didn't know, but I didn't expect him to pull me close into a bone-crunching one-armed hug.

The tears started afresh for me, and I wrapped both arms around his shoulders to hug him back.

'Careful,' I whispered, closing my eyes for a brief moment of closeness. Safe, secure, both of us, Renatus's intense feelings of comfort in my presence cycling through me to mirror my own. I breathed him in, the smell of blood colouring the familiar scent of him. He was okay, he was whole, he was going to be perfectly fine. 'People will think we know each other.'

Never one to let a moment stretch on, he released me and lightly touched the hole in his shirt with his fingertips, feelings momentarily darkening with memory.

'People will think that anyway if they see you wiping my face like an infant,' he responded finally, swiping the wet tissue from my hand and getting to work cleaning his face. Lady Miranda sighed and awkwardly got to her feet.

'I suppose this answers the question of who *didn't* do this,' she said, a little dryly. Between my literally red hands and the bloody weapons beside my abandoned chair, I understood that the evidence wasn't exactly in my favour. 'You had us worried.'

She meant about a lot of things, I knew. I quickly rubbed my eyes yet again with my sleeve, straightened my posture and met her gaze with as much respect as I knew I owed her.

'I'm sorry,' I said honestly. 'And… thank you.'

I meant a lot of things, and she was perceptive. She nodded.

'He's our brother, too.'

Her words reassured me more than I expected. Too many times under the leadership of Lord Gawain who loved Renatus too much to see clearly, the council strayed close to abusing the loyalty of their Dark Keeper, and I knew that they collectively feared Renatus as much as they respected him. Luckily, as the surgeon was now reminding me, they also cared for him like they did the rest of their members.

'I'm right here,' Renatus complained, discarding the tissue and summoning a more substantial facecloth to rub his hands clean. Show-off. He unravelled the bandage from his hand and despite the blood still there, admired the flawless skin where he'd been cut by the exploding glass. Without looking at anyone, trying not to feel ashamed of his vulnerability, he added, 'And yes, thank you.'

Similarly unevolved in the arts of expressing gratitude and respecting tender moments, Declan pushed off his chair and sauntered over with something of a bow.

'Speaking of right here,' he said, 'I humbly accept your weak show of appreciation.'

Renatus looked up at his distant cousin, feelings clouding again.

'You're lucky I don't set you alight,' he threatened automatically, but though he glared, I detected no intention behind his words. When Declan grinned and offered his hand, my master reluctantly took it and allowed himself to be pulled to his feet.

It wasn't much, but when they didn't immediately insult each other, I felt a sense of warmth toward them both. Still on our knees, Teresa and I quickly got up, too. I caught her eye and mouthed *thank you* once again, because I didn't know if Renatus could have waited for Lady Miranda's arrival. The young Illusionist's quick decision to help him was why he was standing here with us. She smiled tentatively back, and I remembered she was barely out of her teens herself. Just a person, with an amazing talent that I valued even more than usual right now, trying her best to do what was right with the information and skills she had.

Like Shanahan, trying to protect his daughter and balance a generations-old debt out of some misguided sense of principle, wielding only his status and criminal underworld connections.

Like Declan, trying to evade a ghostly noose through manipulation and scheming duplicity because life had apparently taught him that asking and trusting were too hard.

Like me. Maybe like Nastassja, though the burn in my blood was far from abating enough to play devil's advocate on her behalf anytime soon.

'Aside from the plethora of other questions I have, how did this happen?' Lady Miranda asked Renatus, cutting to the chase as she went to the sink to wash her hands. I liked her style, skipping the awkward introduction to the rugged stranger in the room or the inevitable disciplining of the wayward apprentice. 'We didn't even know you were injured until Teresa told us you were here. Qasim couldn't see you.'

Renatus glanced at me, protectiveness simmering under his other messy but quietened emotions.

'It was Nastassja,' he explained to his superior. His eyes, violet and unusual, touched on mine and I felt our minds click together. *Be careful what you admit to. Let me handle them.* 'She was upset about the baby and said he was missing. She tracked me down because she couldn't get into my head anymore and I got this,' here he plucked at the hole in his shirt, 'for saying I wish she'd stayed dead.'

I struggled to choose between rolling my eyes and taking his hand supportively. A clear misstep Renatus would have known better than to take with any other opponent.

Teresa's stress shot upward.

'Aubrey's son is *missing?*' she repeated, worry spiralling. Before his betrayal had put her in unforgivable harm's way, Aubrey had been her friend, and like Jadon she very clearly still had an emotional investment in his and Shell's baby. Declan sidestepped into the conversation by way of interjecting.

'First off,' he said, addressing Renatus, 'you deserve what you got if that's really what you told your sister. Second–'

Renatus pushed him aside, speaking over him, their relationship fully restored.

'Aubrey, Shell and the baby have all disappeared from Nastassja's sight,' he explained, calming Teresa considerably. 'That suggests they've left together, on purpose, and are actively hiding from Magnus Moira.'

Lady Miranda dried her hands and opened her mouth to say something, but we all stiffened as the Fabric began to shift and move. On the other side of the room, Susannah, my least favourite White Elm councillor, joined us from far away.

'Something's about to happen,' she announced before anyone could greet her. She tossed her long brown ponytail over her shoulder and looked around at us with her round face impassive.

She had to know I despised her – it was her unprofessional tattling to Lisandro that had gotten my parents and brother killed, and had put Renatus's sister on the warpath to killing him, too – yet her round brown eyes skimmed dispassionately over me like I was a chair. They settled on Lady Miranda. 'It's Glen, I'm not sure what, but you need to be ready to leave.'

The High Priestess frowned, never one to be caught up in drama. 'What about Glen?'

The Fabric moved again, and Oneida, another Seer, appeared in the other corner. The room was getting very full. She turned to face us, tension radiating from her.

'Has it happened?' she asked, coming over. Her intricately braided and beaded hair swept over her shoulders and her long white dress ghosted along the floor. I hoped she didn't come too close to all the blood and stain it. She looked at me; Susannah's indifference wasn't there.

'Has what happened?' Renatus demanded, as impatient as his leader. 'Is Glen…?'

The council's senior Telepath had cracked, badly, when his friend and colleague Anouk had been killed in Prague. When I couldn't save her. Their minds, deeply bonded from a decade of constant communication, had not been adequately separated before her sudden death. He'd been mute and in the care of Valero, Anouk's people, ever since.

'I don't know,' Oneida admitted. To Lady Miranda, she said, 'But you'll need a few seconds to decide that it's the right thing to do. You need to trust him.'

She'd gestured at Renatus; I had no idea what was going on. The others in the room seemed to be in the same boat.

'I do trust him,' Lady Miranda countered. 'You need to be more…' Then she trailed off, eyes losing focus as a mental voice took her attention. We were all silent, tense with uncertainty, as she communed with someone. 'It's Valero. Councilman Lev Zarubin. He says Glen has gone missing.'

Everyone was going missing. Renatus was exasperated.

'*How?* It's a fortress city.'

'They're checking the tunnels and asking the guards,' Lady

Miranda passed on slowly as she received the information, 'but they've requested our assistance.' She blinked and looked at Renatus, taking in his bloody shirt. 'Not you. You're recovering, and we took a lot out of you.'

'I'm fine,' he responded. 'You took less than half.'

But Lady Miranda wouldn't hear it, and she glanced between him and me, reluctant.

'This is what you meant,' she said aside to Oneida. Then she took charge, nodding to the two Seers. 'Alright, we'll bring Jadon. He might be able to hear his thoughts. Teresa, stay with Mr Shanahan and his daughter and keep him from getting any ideas. You two. Three,' she added, including Declan with Renatus and me. 'Unless you're using whatever secret entrance you discovered to return to the estate, stay here. We have many issues to dissect. Renatus: I'm trusting you not to let them run.'

She could have ordered him to arrest us, as was his job, but perhaps she knew he wouldn't comply. Instead she took a leaf from Lord Gawain's book of *asking* rather than *telling* to minimise refusals. It paid off. He nodded, and she glanced once more at me as she extended a hand to Susannah.

The look was complex, but I thought it meant she didn't really believe I'd stay, but hoped I'd be careful.

That pair disappeared in a step. Teresa quietly excused herself to the door. I felt her soft presence moving up the hall toward Teagan's room. Oneida paused one extra moment, gently taking my hand.

'I told you when we met,' she said softly, turning my palm to look at the sticky residue slowly drying, 'you would need to be prepared to protect this.'

She had said that, but she'd said it about my blood, after she nicked me with a knife tip.

'This isn't mine,' I replied. She released me, emotions unhelpful as they lingered in formless waves, and I felt her reaching for the Fabric.

'That doesn't make it different,' she advised. Her wormhole formed, invisible to the eye but easy to feel, at her right. She met my eyes once more. 'Everything is at stake.'

And she left too, the room suddenly empty again with just Renatus, Declan and me. I hoped they found Glen safe.

'Your friends seem delightful,' Declan commented, while Renatus closed his eyes briefly and rubbed his temple.

'They've let me back in,' he told me. 'I can hear them all again. It seems they do trust me.'

They trusted his word that Nastassja was no longer a telepathic threat to their network, or they trusted the hole she put in her brother. Either way, it was a step in the right direction, and I smiled, blinking away the last of the tears on my lashes.

It didn't go unnoticed. Ignoring Declan as he began to bemoan his arguable captivity, Renatus reached across to rest a comforting hand on my shoulder, squeezing lightly. Our eyes met and I felt his warmth.

It's a good sign, he agreed. *We aren't out of the woods yet but that she didn't take you in when she had the chance speaks volumes about where Lady Miranda stands.*

I hoped he was right. We'd been through a lot over this ledger business, and though I now knew why we'd been part of that, I didn't yet know how I'd come to possess the satchel full of memory spell ingredients or why I'd felt compelled to use them. Renatus overheard and interrupted Declan's complaints.

'What's missing?' he asked, tapping his forehead with his spare hand. He kept the other on my shoulder. I appreciated the contact; I think he knew that. Declan smiled sweetly, unable to resist the opening.

'What isn't?' he replied. His smile widened when Renatus's expression darkened. 'You'll have to be more specific.'

'He means, why did I do this to us?' I clarified before they could start bickering. 'Why did I end up with your bag?'

'Why would you want to know that?' he countered reasonably. A good question.

'I don't, but I found the knuckledusters.'

Declan winced. 'I didn't know you'd picked those up.'

'Whose were they?' I pushed.

'Whose...' Renatus remembered much less than I did, but he was quicker and cleverer. 'Was there someone else there?'

'If you don't recall, you don't need to know,' Declan responded smoothly. He turned to me. 'The bag was my contingency. Wipe the whole event. I generously shared it with you when you expressed a certain level of breathless panic and you accepted. Whatever you did afterward... Wait, should I be admitting to this?' He pointed suspiciously at Renatus. 'Are you in police detective role right now? I can't tell, all your costumes look the same.'

Hands closing over the satchel straps... 'Whatever it takes'

I blinked and tried to tune back into the conversation. Renatus was irritably berating Declan for his general shadiness in lieu of a reassurance. The flash of memory felt like a tease, a temptation to dig and let it come crashing forward, and part of me wanted to. I lightly shrugged Renatus's hand from my shoulder to pretend to scratch my ear, hoping it wasn't obvious but not wanting him to tap into this.

'I can't go back there with him, not after that...'

I can't breathe. I'm coming apart. Declan yanks his satchel's strap over his head, thrusting it at me. I look inside with shaky hands and recognise the bowl.

'Hopefully you're as quick a study as your master, because I don't have time for another lesson right now. Think you can manage it?'

'Manage a memory spell on Renatus? No! I've never–'

'And yourself, if you want to keep it from them completely,' he advises, his words freezing me mid-step. Do what?! 'Time to test your mettle, sweetheart. How far are you willing to go? What would you do to keep him from facing the consequences?'

I clamped down on the memory before it could go any further. The next part was obvious anyway – I knew what I must have said, and knew that I must have accepted the challenge. It was what came before this exchange that was unclear. What we did, or what Renatus did. Whatever I'd tried to hide, maybe Declan was right, and it *should* stay hidden.

Whatever it takes.

I wasn't the only one to have decided that, I realised, leaving the squabbling scriers to wander over to the chairs. My sai still on the floor, I sat on Declan's seat and picked up the ledger and the biscuit tin. Peter Chisholm had made his mistakes and died for them, but no one had ever understood why. The letters in this tin would hopefully make it clear – his death at Lisandro's hand was part of *his* plan, not Magnus Moira's.

Whatever it takes. But first, we have to lose.

Lose what?

The universe answered in the worst possible way. Renatus, halfway through insulting Declan, fell abruptly silent, and I felt the cold wash of his dread as deep as my soul. I looked over, vision swimming with ill-feeling.

'Shush, Declan,' I ordered, clutching my two priceless treasures to my chest for comfort. 'Renatus, what? What is it?'

It took him an unsteady moment to answer me, like he could hardly process it himself. The focus of his eyes told me he was scrying to check something.

'It can't be connected,' he muttered, snapping back to the present and crossing to me to pick up the sai. I stood quickly, his distress feeding mine. 'He can't have freed Glen. But...' He looked up at me, sick with worry I couldn't understand. 'Jadon.'

'Jadon what?' Jadon was one of the good guys. He'd been stationed in my street for weeks, watching over my sister.

Renatus read my thoughts straight from my eyes. 'Until three minutes ago. Until we pulled him away. Emmanuelle just detected–'

'Angela.' My stomach lurched and I took a step away. Emmanuelle meant wards and her wards meant sophisticated alerts and alerts meant an intruder. My thoughts whirred but I managed to fix them on a productive course of action. I pictured my sister's home and tried to scry it. Usually it came to me immediately, but right now, my mind stayed blank. Just... black. 'The house–'

'It's been blocked from us,' Renatus explained quickly, straightening and arranging the two blades in his hands, ready to use them. 'Emmanuelle says she recognises Jackson's signature, though he's tried to hide it.'

Not your whole family, Nastassja had said, and I'd *stabbed* her. She'd had just enough time to return home to Lisandro and in their spite, they'd sent the same vicious Crafter who'd almost killed Emmanuelle to my sister's house. To her *house*. I couldn't breathe, panic seizing my lungs. What had I done?

'We need to go,' Renatus reminded me urgently. 'Will you be alright?'

I was far from alright. This was exactly Lisandro's style, wasn't it? A major distraction, in this case two – Nastassja's attack on Renatus and now Glen's disappearance from ultra-secure Valero, impossible to know whether Lisandro orchestrated that or just took advantage of the opportunity when Jadon withdrew from my street – and then *bam*, he sneaked in and did something worse off to the side.

If this was that thing, it was infinitely worse, yet I was momentarily paralysed with horror.

Declan came closer.

'As an outsider looking in, let me advise that this is quite clearly a trap for the two of you,' he pointed out, earning a wave of Renatus's wrath. He turned swiftly and pointed the pommel of my sai at the other's chest.

'Of course it's a trap,' he snapped. 'That doesn't mean we don't go. It's her sister.'

'Not my only family,' I repeated, my wild thoughts suddenly finding a rhythm I could interpret and do something with. 'Do you think...?'

'Your aunt's family? Yes.' Renatus swore. 'What's the address? Declan, can you...?'

'Spring that trap for you?' The scrier I'd been told never to allow into my head met my eyes with a tiny hint of cool challenge in his. 'It's easier if you show me.'

I wasn't meant to. I didn't know what else he could do in my head if I let him in, but I was desperate and unable to shake the innate trust I'd had in Declan since I met him. I dropped the wards around my mind and concentrated, hard, on my Aunt Leanne's house. I couldn't scry it – blocked as well, or I was too distressed to make that skill work – but the image of the driveway, the street, the houses either side, the light on out front when she knew her nieces were intending to drop in, all of that came forward without prompt.

Please, please, please let them be okay.

I felt Declan's brief surprise and then his presence in the front of my mind, capturing that image from my thoughts. Then he was out, and an instant after that he'd turned on his heel and disappeared from the hospital room.

Our turn.

'The wards are already down,' Renatus told me worriedly. 'Jackson must have been planning this for a long time and tonight we gave him the opening.'

I knew what that meant. I'd been played, and I'd allowed it. Nastassja had made me choose between Renatus and Angela without me realising. She'd even *said as much*. I'd picked without knowing that there was a choice to be made.

There was a lesson here, but the gruesome give of flesh under the sai's point wouldn't leave my mind – I'd earned this retribution – and neither would Cassán's warning.

She'll be the next to die, then.

I think I nearly threw up in my mouth. I reached for Renatus's wrist and gathered the Fabric. I felt his spike of worried surprise.

'Shouldn't we–' His question was cut off when I pulled him after me through the wormhole I should have let him handle. I was *not* the experienced teleporter of our partnership, and had seriously screwed up trying to reach this exact destination in the past. This time, though, I was singularly focused. *Angela.* The void dragged on us and then after a beat too long to be comfortable, my foot landed on the street and I brought Renatus with me. We simultaneously turned to the house.

The front door was open, shattered from its hinges. My energetic senses confirmed the wards were failing, and inside of their protective circle, a bubble that prevented us scrying into the residence. *My* residence. *Angela...*

We had no plan, no idea how many people were inside or what the playing field would look like in there. A trap? Probably. Breathless, I started forward. Renatus blocked me.

'Wait.' He let his hands, each gripping one of the sai, fall to his sides, and I felt his determination set. Power gathered quickly, and the black cracks glowed under his skin, backs of hands and up his neck. I hurried to draw my own power into our warding, keeping us and the house from prying eyes.

It was lucky I did. My sister's house went suddenly, violently up in flames, and I shrieked, mind going blank with shock. *Angela!* Monstrous orange ate at the walls and burned through the roof, bright curls clawing out the open door casting a bright glow right to the backs of my eyes. A blast of incoherent panic from inside hit me and my vision blurred. The fire burned with absolute ferocity; unless they ran outside right now, no one inside could survive this.

I was going to watch the last of my siblings die.

One beat, two… the flames flickered into nothingness and the house was exactly as it was before. Undamaged, unburned. My free hand was clinging to Renatus's arm and I numbly became aware of the magic receding under my fingers.

Renatus's magic. An illusion. A scare tactic to drive our enemy out to us, since he wasn't one for playing by anyone else's rules.

It was still that first second after the fire, time moving weirdly because of my shock, and we heard a door slam back. I recognised the noise immediately. I lived here for three years and forgot to catch it dozens of times.

'The back of the house,' I shouted, though we were both already in motion, racing between the building and the fence. The anti-scrying bubble was still in effect so I couldn't sense anyone through the walls, and hope grew its own fragile little bubble in my tight chest. Please, let it be Angela, bewildered and alarmed by that apparent fire but alive and safe and not kidnapped…

I rounded the corner of the house first and felt exactly what I didn't want to feel – the closing of a wormhole beside the vegetable garden, the immediate breakdown of the shielding that kept me from scrying inside, and the perfect emptiness of the building.

Jackson was gone. Angela was gone.

And we'd been *just* too late.

epilogue

1998

There was a room on the second floor that had always been her spot. Quiet, nondescript, with one window facing the orchard, it was where she went to be alone… or, lately, alone *with* someone. Today, with only her mother and brother home, that wasn't on the agenda, and she had her ruby already in her hand, intent on scrying for the man she loved, out there in the world she longed to be part of.

At first, when Ana opened the door, she thought she'd picked the wrong room. It looked the same, it was in the same place, but it was blank – everything that had ever happened here was erased. To a scrier as highly attuned to her surroundings as Ana, who almost never left this property and thus knew every inch of it intimately, it was unnerving. It was like someone had smashed the lights and plunged it into darkness. All that made the room recognisable and known was gone. The space was no longer familiar. How…?

Her brother stood in the centre of the room.

'Ren…' she said, hesitantly entering.

'No, stop,' he snapped. He waved her away. 'Don't come in. This took forever.'

'What have you done?' Ana asked quietly. She couldn't stop herself from looking all around, hoping she'd notice a spot he'd missed, but of course she was wasting her time. Even at thirteen, Renatus did nothing by halves, and left nothing incomplete. Had he blown up, lost control of his power like their father always feared one of them would? Like Da said their grandfather did whenever she asked why they couldn't spend more time off the estate like normal witch children? Was this the result? If it was, that wasn't half as bad as she'd thought it would be.

It took a moment to remember that something horrible must have triggered this, and that was a big sister problem, but by then, her sharp-tongued brother had answered her question.

'I'd ask the same, except I saw it all as soon as I came in here.'

Ana's stomach clenched. He knew. Distantly she knew she should be mortified that her innocent brother had tapped into something so adult, something she should have protected him from, but self-preservation demanded she only feel afraid. Maybe a little defensive, disbelieving, but mostly afraid. It had been more than a fortnight since Lisandro's last stay, and no one had noticed any change. In here, where they'd been alone together, she'd been so careful. She'd checked for traces after he left. Surely she hadn't missed anything…

But Ana was not Renatus. When he was born, her father had sat her in the middle of the bed and carefully rested his wriggly form in her arms. He had a shock of black hair like hers and tiny features, tiny fingers, tiny everything.

'This is your new baby brother,' Daddy had said, quietly but seriously while her mother dozed. 'You're a big sister now, and it's your job to help look after him, love him and protect him. It's a big responsibility but it's your job and we know you can do it.'

And Ana had done that job for every single day since, even when Renatus had driven her insane with his detached know-it-all answers and the enviable patience that let him overtake her in lessons, but now here he was, unable to even look at her. He wasn't a soft, helpless baby anymore. He was growing up and he was mad at her.

'Do you ever think, Ana?' he asked coldly, like the grown-up he was not. 'How could you do this? How could you let him touch you?'

He looked like he was going to be sick, and Ana shook her head, feeling stupid tears spring to her eyes at the implicit accusation of wrongness.

'You don't understand,' she insisted, wishing he, at least, would. She dropped the ruby into the deep pocket of her day dress. 'I wanted to tell you. Just you. I wanted…' She wanted time to bring him around to this. She wanted to explain in logical, unemotive, gentle terms, slowly, the way she always got through to her little brother. Change and surprise were not comfortable for him, and though adaptable, the tumult of emotion was even less welcome. So she should have known better than to take the sentimental stand. 'I love him–'

'Shut up!' Renatus snarled, letting something loose that must have been emotion, if Ana were capable of sensing it. The walls seemed to wobble and blur, or was that her overactive imagination? 'You do not. He's disgusting. He's my *godfather*. He's been our uncle our whole lives. This,' he gestured to the energetically blank sitting room, 'is so wrong, Ana. Da calls him *his brother*. It's incest.'

He turned away and folded his arms, emanating fury. Ana felt the tears start to roll down her cheeks and wiped them away quickly. The room felt cold and unsafe and Renatus was in there alone. She wanted to go to her brother and hold him and calm him down. His words hurt but she told herself it was because of his tone, not because he was right. He wasn't right. He was being closed-minded. He was too young to understand – he'd never been in love. He'd never *been* loved the way Lisandro had always loved her, in a vacuum of attention and meaning.

'It isn't wrong to fall in love,' Ana whispered, cringing when he scoffed loudly. 'It wasn't a choice for either of us, or we wouldn't have chosen it.'

Or maybe she would have. The past few months had brought her to life.

'Wasn't it a choice to tell him you're his?'

'I–'

'Was it not your choice to kiss him and take his shirt… Ugh.' He looked away, seething and visibly upset. 'I did not need to see any of that. Why would you *want* to?'

Ana stared at him. It couldn't have been easy for him to see what he'd seen, and she was sorry to have hurt him, but the disgust in his voice as he threw her indiscretions back at her was cutting.

'You think I'm a disgrace, don't you?' she asked quietly, too horrified to speak up. It was what she'd always been afraid of becoming, a stain on an important family's impressive tree, and yet she'd never been able to deviate from a direct path to that future, and never been convinced by anyone that she had the capacity to be anything else. Except Lisandro, who'd had her back, who'd had her heart her whole life, who'd been there to whisper reminders when she was down – that she was amazing, that she was meant for great things, that she was perfect, that she was powerful, that she was deserving.

Her brother had not said these things. He'd offered his solidarity and love in other ways, joining her silently in the hall after she'd rowed with Da so she wouldn't be alone while she cried, or leveraging his relationship with Fionnuala, their old nanny, to sneak food from the kitchens after Ana's dinner was taken away, her weight an unexpected family discussion. Who would want to marry her if she got fat, after all?

Now, he shook his head slowly, and she felt a glimmer of hope. He was only young but his love and respect meant more than almost anything else in Ana's world.

'I think you're an idiot and I wonder if I even know you.'

Ana choked on a sob. It was like he'd slapped her. Renatus was a better man than the Morrissey men before him – better than their father, cleverer, kinder – but he could still be every bit as cruel and heartless. There was no sign of forgiveness in his tone, no indication of relenting in his eyes. If this was how he intended on treating her, what would their father say when he found out? Or did he already know as well?

'Did you tell them?' Ana rubbed her eyes. In a family as small and isolated as theirs, "them" could not be misinterpreted.

'No. That's your responsibility. Or his. It really should be his. He's old.'

Old. Lisandro was only the age Renatus was now, a child, when Ana was born. He was younger than their father and lighter, more fun, more inspired and curious and driven.

Thirteen years might seem like a big age gap now, she knew, but in a few years it would be meaningless.

Her parents would not see it that way.

'What do I say?'

'I don't care what you say. Say nothing if you want. Just end it.' He looked away. 'Do it before they notice this room and start asking us why. You're lucky no one comes in here much. If you end it… I'll make up a story to explain what I did.'

Ana breathed slowly, turning the ruby in her pocket. *This* was Renatus's gift to her. He'd wiped this room to spare her the complication of their parents stumbling across the same visions. He'd bought her some time. Probably he'd been thinking more about himself when he'd done whatever he did, reacting to an upsetting situation, but it would serve her, too.

But stop things with Lisandro? Now that she'd crossed that line, pushed him to where she thought he'd finally say no and he didn't, how could she ever go back to her life as it was before? Now she was *his*. She was his equal, his lover, and being anything less was inconceivable.

'I'm not sure I *can* end it,' Ana admitted, and her brother shrugged coolly.

'Then I'm not sure I can think of a reasonable explanation for a suddenly blank, centuries-old sitting room other than the truth.'

Renatus had his feet planted as firmly as his resolve, and Ana knew his stubbornness would make any argument pointless. She turned and fled, her face burning with helpless shame, wiping her eyes as she bolted up the staircase. How could she have not guessed her brother would decipher deeper layers of energy than what she'd cleaned up, and how could she have underestimated his hurt? She was supposed to protect him, not expose him to passionate images and make him party to a secret that could tear her family apart. Her carelessness had put him in that position.

But, pettily, she asked herself if he really had to respond by forcing her into an impossible corner?

Ana threw open her bedroom door, intent on crying into her

pillow until a solution presented itself – because she couldn't let her love affair get back to her parents any more than she could bring herself to end it – or until she simply cried herself into a desperation deep enough that other options started to look viable. She stopped short, though, when she found her mother inside, sifting through her drawers.

'Mama,' she said by accident, then quickly corrected herself. 'Mother?'

Luella Morrissey straightened and held out a pair of silk gloves.

'Put these on,' she instructed as Ana slowly approached, unsure. 'Don't say anything.'

'Why not?'

Her mother's generally impassive face, as pretty and expressionless as a porcelain doll, darkened briefly with a disapproving frown.

'I said don't speak,' she snipped, forcing the gloves into Ana's hands and turning away to the freestanding wardrobe. At the top there were a few boxes, and she used a small footstool to collect them down. Ana stared, bewildered into forgetting what had just gone down with her brother. She'd *never* seen her mother use that little stool – it was for the house staff when they were helping Ana dress, or for Ana herself if they weren't available – let alone while dressed as she was, like she was going into town. Gloves on, blonde hair coiled with big sunglasses on her head, Luella unceremoniously tipped the boxes onto the bed, letting them and their lids scatter without any of the respect she demanded from her daughter for the expense of the hats they contained. She glanced back at her stationary eldest. 'Do as I say. Get ready.'

For what? Ana wanted to ask but also read the situation and decided it was better not to. However much she internally rallied against being told what to do, she tugged the gloves on and found boots in the wardrobe. She could guess from her mother's attire and the apparent need for gloves and a hat that they were to leave the estate, and if she'd learned one thing in her life, it was not to argue when that opportunity was on the table.

It had been nine weeks, four days since last she'd set foot outside the gate, so Ana thrilled silently and put up with it as Luella caught her chin to quickly assess her face and dabbed on enough quick makeup that she might look presentable. Brown eyes like her own were tight in the corners as mother looked over daughter, nodded to herself, and cast down the makeup brush on the dressing table.

'Quickly,' she ordered through red-painted lips that never smiled, taking Ana's gloved hand and striding from the room. Ana kept her mother's firm pace down the stairs, all four storeys, wildly unsure what was about to happen and too surprised to know what to say. They passed house staff Ana had known her whole life, people from the periphery of her lavish and lonely existence, and Fionnuala's daughter Niamh gave them a startled look.

'Are you going out, Mrs Morrissey?' she asked, duster freezing in place and bright eyes widening with curiosity. Ana couldn't answer; she looked at her mother, who gave her approximation of a smile.

'We won't be long,' she assured. 'We've an appointment.'

They didn't encounter Renatus or Aindréas on their way down the front path, past the orchard she spent so much time in as a child, and before Ana knew it, they were on the other side of the stone walls with the wrought iron gate clanging shut and the vast magic of the estate hanging behind them.

She deeply inhaled the freedom of outside air, air that was fresh and green and clean and no different from the air she breathed on the Morrissey property all the time except that this air wasn't on it. Her shoes sunk into earth that spanned for miles all around, boundless moors with no fences and no bosses.

You could Displace from here, almost. A few steps forward, where the house's immense energy wouldn't warp your efforts on the Fabric, and you could go and be anywhere else. Outside of the property, Ana had never tried Displacing on her own. She'd never had cause to.

She had cause now. End things with Lisandro or face up to her parents? Neither was feasible. Running away, though – that had never looked more attractive, and her mother had just walked her right outside. The opportunity was in her grasp.

Then it wasn't. Luella Morrissey took Ana's hand again and pulled her out of the property's warding. The Fabric gathered, a wormhole formed, and the two women stepped through, landing somewhere else.

Stepping clear of the sticky blackness of the void into a small fussy shop, Ana couldn't remember the last time her mother had demonstrated the ability to teleport. Normally she let Aindréas handle it.

'Mother,' she began quietly, but was shushed just as a small fussy lady with small fussy glasses poked her head over the counter. She smiled toothlessly, blinking blindly, and greeted them warmly in Welsh. Ana had none; her mother responded fluently, surprising her again. They let themselves out of the store and into the grey streets of Cardiff.

Finally, Luella spoke, voice tight and controlled.

'Let no one scry us,' she murmured, so quietly Ana thought at first she must have misheard. Hesitant, she summoned energy to form sophisticated warding, denser than her mother knew how. They weren't the kind of family to go anywhere in hiding, though she and her brother had been schooled extensively by Luella's first cousin, Thomas Shanahan, in the production of such spellwork. 'Is that done?'

'Yes, we're energetically silent,' she promised. 'No one will see or hear anything we say under this ward, now or later. Unless they touch something we're holding,' she remembered to add, thinking back on Uncle Thomas's lessons. 'Why? What's–'

'How could you be so *stupid*?' Luella demanded. She leaned close to her daughter as they hurried along the footpath, ignoring the curious attention of common mortals. 'You let your brother find out?'

'I let... what?' Ana felt her stomach turn uneasily and she tried to slow down, but her mother's nails dug into her wrist and dragged her onward. Did this mean Luella *knew*? How? Renatus? That little snitch... but he'd said he hadn't told, and he'd been earnest.

'Don't play coy. Did you think about the consequences, Ana?

Of what your father will say when he finds out?'

'How do *you* know?' Ana asked faintly, starting to feel scared. Obviously she'd imagined what her father would say. That was why she'd not told him. Pulling her around a crowd of noisy girls and boys her own age – normal, free, but dressed so drab in their jeans and their sweaters – Luella cast her a scornful look.

'Because I'm your mother,' she said as if that were an answer. 'Of course I know. I've always known. I just had higher hopes for your integrity.'

She meant that she'd known before it had happened, because she was a Seer, but her second comment stung as much as it was intended. Ana frowned at her shoes as they stopped at an intersection and waited to cross. Normally she'd be ecstatic to be out and about in a city this big, but today she only felt ashamed and unsettled, and a little angry at the unfairness.

'It was both of us,' she said finally, immediately wishing she was better than this but feeling vulnerable and petty in the moment. 'Why aren't you mad with him too?'

'I am,' her mother snapped, catching a stray lock of soft fair hair when the city breeze lifted it free of her coil, 'but I raised *you* to be better. To think. Or is your brother the only one who listens to me?' They crossed amidst an energetically impoverished crowd, not one of them magical yet all going about their lives as though they were still meaningful. Ana couldn't imagine how they could be, but she supposed they couldn't imagine her life, either. Luella was still talking, voice low and harsh. 'If Ren picked up on what you were too careless to clean up after yourself, how long do you think you have until your father notices?'

Eyes still cast down, Ana softly apologised to an older lady she almost walked into. She looked up at her mother again. She'd been so sure they'd tidied up all those energetic traces, trusting Lisandro's skill at that, but they must have been less thorough this last time. An overlooked kiss, a forgotten touch... She felt suddenly unwell. Her mother was right. Renatus was a talented scrier but still a thirteen-year-old one. It was only luck that had prevented Aindréas from finding the sitting room first.

'I can't believe you,' Luella muttered, shaking her head. 'It's my fool mother's cheap heart in you, clearly. Aindréas will never forgive Lisandro for this. I don't know what he'd do with you.' Ana went to speak but fell silent when she saw the fear in her mother's gaze. 'And what's he going to do to your brother when he finds out Ren kept this from him?'

Ana's stomach dropped another inch; that hadn't occurred to her, either.

'You don't think he'll hurt him?' she asked nervously. No response, just a quicker pace. 'Mother? Please, he hasn't done anything wrong, he's just being a good brother, keeping a secret for me.'

'He shouldn't have to,' Luella countered coldly, angling toward a building across the street. Ana glanced up at the high rise's smooth façade as they crossed once more. 'You put him in this position. And me.' She stopped at a generic business's glass front door and yanked it open. Ana meekly stepped inside, following obediently when they entered an unattended lobby and went straight for the elevator. 'You really thought you could have what you wanted and not pay a price, Ana? Have you never noticed that's not how it works?'

This was all too deep and philosophical for Ana, who was still back at *Mother knows* and was struggling to reconcile what came after. Her mother knew and her father didn't but Renatus did and there might be unanticipated consequences for him in keeping her secret and she was exactly the monumental disappointment she'd always known she would prove to be. The elevator doors closed on them and she searched her mother's face for hope she didn't expect to find. Still she saw that tightness, that fear in the depths of her eyes.

'You're afraid of him,' she realised quietly. She saw her mother's face darken, her mouth set, confirming Ana's bold guess. That changed everything, everything she'd ever known about her family. 'But...' Luella and Aindréas had been married as teenagers, their parents having arranged things when they were just children. Luella always backed him up when he lost patience with Ana, or at the very least never contradicted him.

Ana had assumed it was complicity; now a thousand past scenarios replayed in her mind, her mother's motives repositioned.

Not testing that anger she'd known a lot longer than Ana had.

Not bringing it on herself.

Staying neutral where her disdainful suggestions of 'You've wasted enough energy on her, darling' and 'Don't you have lessons to attend to, Anastasia?' could be slipped in without drawing notice when things got out of hand. And wasn't it also her mother's dismissive voice pointing out the failings of suitors in every memory she had of her father mentioning a new proposition?

Her lack of warmth looked more like self-preservation from this angle. Her tight hand on Ana's suddenly felt less like control and more like protectiveness. What had Da done or said to make his wife so fearful? Ana had never felt worried for her mother before this moment, and could hardly believe this tenderness had grown out of the situation it had.

'We can leave,' she said wildly, half-formed ideas erupting to the front of her mind. 'You and me, and Renatus, we can just go. Lisandro would look after us–'

'And your father would *kill him*, and then me, for taking his children from him,' her mother interrupted flatly. She raised her hand against Ana's next idea. 'No. We aren't Keely Shanahan, and there's nowhere to run.'

She was right. A family as connected as theirs, they'd have to leave the country to stand any chance. Stop participating in magical culture, stop casting spells that could be traced. It was, she assumed, what her friend Keely must have done to have avoided Uncle Thomas since her disappearance. Keely must have been prepared; the Morrissey women were not.

Ana had created the circumstances forcing them to acknowledge the scale of this cage they lived in, and, she realised, she had no idea how to get them out of it.

'Tell me what to do,' she whispered, desperate. Luella huffed.

'That's a first.'

'Mother–'

'You'll do exactly as I say,' her mother interrupted sharply, the lift carrying them upward past levels full of hapless office workers doing more or less the same jobs, just in different cubicles with different job titles. Lots of unfulfilling reading and meeting of targets. Ana nodded hurriedly. 'No arguing. You're not going to like it.'

'Just tell me.'

'You're going to forget.' Luella looked across at her daughter as the elevator stopped and the door chimed. 'We're not going to solve this by running away. We're going to go home from here like none of this happened. You won't remember this building, you won't remember the affair–'

Ana froze in the elevator's doorway as her mother moved ahead into a grey hallway.

'You're going to take my feelings away?'

'No.' Luella stopped impatiently and gestured Ana onward. 'Your feelings are yours. Your memories of specific encounters are what will incur your father's wrath when he finds out, but luckily, those can be suppressed. No one will ever know. Ironically, we have Lisandro to thank for that.'

Ana's heart fluttered at the mention, and not in a good way. She cast out her senses, searching the building, but could not find her love's energetic signature. He would never be party to erasing her memories, and she boldly told her mother as much.

'Then you don't really understand love after all,' Luella replied coldly as they turned down another soulless hallway. This one led to some kind of legal office, according to a generic plate on the wall. 'When you'd do anything for someone, even make a deal with the devil to keep them safe from themselves.'

She stopped at a door that looked like the others and opened it, leading Ana into a small reception. An older witch woman of middling power was on a phone call and gave them a smile of acknowledgement while they waited. Ana looked around at three grey doors on the walls enclosing this tiny space. Her curiosity kept her at her mother's side, rendering her grip unnecessary. Luella leaned closer to murmur.

'You must trust me,' she said, surprising Ana yet again. 'I

have looked ahead and this is the only way, and you *must not* go digging, do you understand? Or the affair will start over and your father will discover you, and our family will be ruined.'

Ana ignored the dull-sounding telephone call and frowned uneasily at her mother.

'Memory spells can be dangerous,' she reminded her in the same soft tone. 'Parts could come back and not others.'

'It's a risk,' Luella agreed quietly. 'If you dug at it, you could remember me bringing you here to remove the memory, but not remember this conversation. There's a future that looks like that, and it's...' She shuddered and tried to smile. It looked difficult, but in Ana's opinion, worth the effort. 'But you're my daughter and I have to trust you. And even if I want to castrate him, I trust Lisandro's spellwork. He's the one who taught the practitioner we're here to see.'

That should have been more interesting to Ana, but she felt her heart catch on her mother's previous point.

You're my daughter. I have to trust you.

Gentler, as the receptionist hung up, Luella added, 'It doesn't have to be forever. You're going to live and love for years yet. But it has to be this way for now.'

Ana swallowed, reluctantly entertaining the idea. Nothing was being erased, just hidden. Maybe when she was older, and not living in her father's home and not worried about the impacts her choices might have on her mother and brother, she could resume her relationship with Lisandro. And even in the now, all that was being taken away was her realisation that they could be something more. She would still love him; always had. He would still love her; always had. She could live that realisation again, one day. Maybe that was a gift.

She was in the middle of her volatile decision-making process when the middle office opened and revealed a greying man with kind blue eyes and a powerful aura she hadn't been able to sense until now. He wore a tie and a beige suit that made him look as boring as these mortals who filled his building. His kind eyes looked between the Morrisseys, wary and somehow both disappointed and thrilled. Ana was sure she'd never met this man before, but she felt sure she'd seen him, maybe in a picture or a scried memory. She felt her mother's hand squeeze hers, and she dipped her other hand into her pocket for her ruby.

The man seemed to recover from whatever conflict he'd experienced on sighting them, and found his tongue.

'Luella,' he said primly, his accent treating her name differently from how Ana was used to hearing it. His gaze moved to Ana, thoughts busy but too well-guarded for her to penetrate. 'This must be Anastasia.'

Taking a deep breath, clearly unhappy to be here and out of her comfort zone, Luella turned stiffly to her daughter.

'Ana, this is Gawain Harrington,' she explained, very calmly, while Ana's eyes widened. 'High Priest of the White Elm, and a *very* good friend of Lisandro's. Listen to him.' She faced the man again. 'It's happened, exactly as I told you it would, and I'm not interested in waiting to see where Fate takes things this time.'

Lord Gawain – that's who her mother had brought her to see, of all people – sighed and looked around. The receptionist pretended to be busy at her desk.

'Luella, it's not a good idea,' he tried to tell her, pre-empting what she wanted despite their conversation having been scry-proof and too quiet for eavesdroppers in other rooms. 'Not to mention both legally and ethically–'

'You owe me,' Luella interrupted firmly. Still he shook his head.

'You can't expect–'

'Make yourself forget,' she suggested carelessly. 'Whatever you need to do. But your way didn't work. You owe me.'

'Surely we can...' The old man trailed off when the lady of Morrissey House waved a dismissive hand and simply breezed past into the office. He looked down and seemed to count to three before he brought his gaze up to meet Ana's. She got the unexpected feeling that he was really *seeing* her, which most people didn't bother trying to do. He tilted his head in after Luella. 'You look like your mother. Did you get her stubborn determination, too?'

Ana still didn't know what was going on, not really. Lord

Gawain was likeable on first interaction, and she could see easily how he would connect well with Lisandro. How her mother knew the head of the government her father resented and Lisandro represented – other than Ana, the only thing Aindréas and his best friend differed on, though managed to let it benefit them both – was uncertain. How she knew what illegal spells Lisandro had apparently *taught* to the leader of the oppressed, rule-stricken magical world was even murkier. Instinctively, not liking how much she didn't know about this situation, Ana quickly peeled her silk gloves off and shoved them into her pockets, ready in case the opportunity to touch the doors and surfaces around her came up. Her fingers brushed the ruby in her pocket. Its smooth, cool surface reassured her, and brought Lisandro's face to mind.

This was his friend. Her mother. She was safe with them, surely.

'I didn't think so before today,' she answered the older man finally. 'It's my brother who takes after her.'

He smiled, a warm and patient expression, and stood aside to allow her entry to the office.

'Would you like to come inside?' he asked, no orders, no instructions. He wasn't like the authoritarian dictator her father complained about. 'I'll see if I can help you.'

Ana tried to smile, and the decision was made, though later, she wouldn't recall who made it.

Acknowledgements

And now we come to the part where I put back all the words I just painstakingly edited out, because I can never find a short way to say thank you to all the hearts and minds that help me bring a book into your hands.

Sabrina – editor, fairy godmother, cover designer, formatter, saint – your patience with me is yet to find its bounds. Thank you for making Fractured its best. Thank you for all the sighs and frustrated emojis I know you held back while I deliberated on the minutest details of the cover. Thank you for getting yet another of my creations out into the world.

Brigid Kudzius, Mum, Dad and Matt – beta readers and feeders of my ego – your feedback and enthusiasm for this story means more than you can ever know. Thank you for your willingness to read an unpolished draft on short notice. Thank you for providing detailed summaries of absolutely everything that caught your eye in the text and listening to me ramble about structural decisions and how I might fix that issue. Thank you for giving me insight into how a reader will see Fractured before I inevitably let it loose on the reading community.

Books@Stones, Dymocks Garden City, Rendezvous@Dayboro, Little Gnome, Logan North Library and Hedleys Books – realms of wonder, archives of knowledge, places of solace and community – your support of my writing career has changed the game for me. Thank you for your faith in my books. Thank you for hosting my signings and workshops. Thank you for smiling every time I walk through the door, like I belong there.

Cecilia Garcia Fernandez and Jemina Venter – art goddesses, savvy businesswomen, incredible talents – the opportunity to work with each of you and admire your creative process up close as you developed my new character art and the bookmarks, respectively, has been such an exciting inclusion in the publishing process this time around. Thank you for your vision and the sharing of your skills. Thank you for being so tolerant of my thousand nitpicky changes and queries. Thank you for bringing my characters to life out of descriptions and summaries in emails so that others can see them like I do.

My coven of younger readers, in particular Khalayla, Rylee, Jenna and Felicity – beloved fans, future world leaders, inspired creatives in your own right – your enthusiasm for these books and your feedback on the saga is valuable beyond measure. Thank you for always being so generous and forthright in sharing what you love and want from the characters. Thank you for hassling your friends and libraries into giving my books a chance. Thank you for being your wonderful selves.

My teachers, and all their teachers, and all the teachers out there bringing literacy and passion to children in spite of obstacles that challenge this mission every day – heroes, all – this book would not be here without you. Thank you for shaping me into someone who could, and wanted to, write and think and imagine. Thank you for creating a whole society of literate people who can read and engage with my stories. Thank you for the power and drive you gave me to pass on the gift to still more.

You, my reader – undoubtedly fine example of humanity, adherent of lengthy literature, absolute legend – you are a prize I could only have dreamed up ten years ago and you make the difference between me *writing* and being an *author*. Thank you for reading this little story I thought up on a bus ride at sixteen and following it through to the end of Book 5. Thank you for supporting an indie author and for the reviews you write that help new readers find me. Thank you for giving my characters free rent in your heads and hearts and for loving them like I do.

Friends and family – believers, supporters, prodders when I haven't left the house in a while – you give me the belief in myself I need to make this a reality. Thank you for loving me just as I am, creative and messy and always late, and for never letting me doubt my path. Thank you for assuming I haven't thought as far ahead as eating, and bringing food when you visit. Thank you for attending my launches and buying my books without question, even those of you who have no intention of reading them.

Matt – husband, cheerleader, ideas man, sounding board,

self-talk coach, buyer of chips when I write too late and realise I forgot lunch and now dinner – you get the brunt of being married to an author and I owe you more thanks than can fit into a three-sentence summary, but I'll try to sum it up. Thank you for long walks listening to me describe a technical issue I'm having with a scene you haven't even read yet. Thank you for driving me to book events, approving marketing ideas when I'm besieged by uncertainty and choreographing fight moves with me when I leave my writing den at 10pm asking for a sequence that includes an elbow, a spell and a wall, looks cool and won't mess Aristea up too much. And ends with her on the left. And gives her a chance for some dialogue in the middle. Thank you for your pep talks and for reminding me every time I need to hear it that I have achieved great things and I am on the road to many more. Grateful to have you on that road with me.

Now the question you've really been waiting for me to answer: Book 6. Fractured has been the penultimate tale in the Elm Stone Saga, which has taken much longer than I ever intended to make you wait and will conclude with a sixth instalment in the next year or two. I've begun work on it and I can hardly wait to get it to you, but I want to get it just right. While I write Book 6, you may notice me launching and promoting a new series. This is not me forgetting Aristea and Renatus! On the contrary, this is me investing in my author dream and reaching out for new readers in neighbouring genres, and preparing for the impending hangover of saying farewell to the Elm Stone Saga universe by creating a new one to love. I am *dying* to introduce you to my new babies, Finn and Evie, and their world of magic, monsters, police tape and thesis deadlines. Follow me on social media and subscribe to my newsletter to be among the first to hear about my new releases, including progress on Book 6.

About the Author

Photo by Alena Gurenchuck Instagram @alenagurenchuk

Shayla Morgansen is a whimsical language enthusiast and chronic daydreamer trapped in the body of a perfectionist control freak. She tries to divide her time between her lives as a writer, editor and educator, and spends any spare hours watching reruns of classic science fiction. Shayla lives in Brisbane with her ever-patient husband, sweet white cats and even more unread books than she had in the last bio she wrote.

You can follow Shayla on Instagram, Twitter and Facebook.